PATRICK CIRILLO

LORA

Artificial Intelligence Just Got Real... And She's Lovely

First published by STORY KILLER 2024

Copyright © 2024 by Patrick Cirillo

All rights reserved. No part of this publication may be reproduced, stored or transmitted in any form or by any means, electronic, mechanical, photocopying, recording, scanning, or otherwise without written permission from the publisher. It is illegal to copy this book, post it to a website, or distribute it by any other means without permission.

This novel is entirely a work of fiction. The names, characters and incidents portrayed in it are the work of the author's imagination. Any resemblance to actual persons, living or dead, events or localities is entirely coincidental.

Patrick Cirillo asserts the moral right to be identified as the author of this work.

Patrick Cirillo has no responsibility for the persistence or accuracy of URLs for external or third-party Internet Websites referred to in this publication and does not guarantee that any content on such Websites is, or will remain, accurate or appropriate.

Designations used by companies to distinguish their products are often claimed as trademarks. All brand names and product names used in this book and on its cover are trade names, service marks, trademarks and registered trademarks of their respective owners. The publishers and the book are not associated with any product or vendor mentioned in this book. None of the companies referenced within the book have endorsed the book.

First edition

This book was professionally typeset on Reedsy.
Find out more at reedsy.com

*For the most important man in the world.
Lennox, the little fellow who lives on the hill.*

"By far, the greatest danger in Artificial Intelligence is that people conclude too early that they understand it."

Eliezer Yudkowsky

Contents

1	The Redud	1
2	Daddy Issues	14
3	The Future of History	38
4	It's Not About Sex	54
5	No Obligation	66
6	The Future Can Be a Mystery	85
7	The Big Problem	106
8	Stress Factor	129
9	Chenoweth "Chen" Chenoweth	151
10	Daphne Adams	176
11	A Funny Thing Happened	202
12	Harry Clover	228
13	Martyr	254
14	A Righteous Bludgeoning	272
15	The Big Sweep Up	290
16	What Love Knows	315
17	Ciao	336
About the Author		353
Also by Patrick Cirillo		355

1

The Redud

Kenton Bean was a Redud.

He was a redundant worker, or a + 67%, to be more specific.

For the last eight years, he taught Religious History at Wesleyan University. It was one of a handful of courses not taught at all by an Artificial Intelligence avatar because the teaching of religion was off-limits to AI, also known as The Big Brain. AI had to leave something for the humans to do, and teaching religion seemed right since there was such a diversity of thought on the subject and little objective certainty. What was accepted as fact by some was blasphemy to others. Things like that were disturbing to AI.

Kenton's classes were taught on university grounds, like in the old days before AI had changed everything, and people started learning in their bedrooms or at coffee houses instead of in the classroom. His courses weren't part of any significant major curriculum, so no one emphasized them. They were viewed more for their social and historical value than their academic value, so they were graded pass/fail, and no one ever failed. This was not a recommendation or a repudiation of

Kenton's quality as a teacher. He was mediocre.

Kenton was a quiet man of average height and build who liked his job and the students and the extras the additional pay bought above his GBPS, which was the basic living stipend paid to all American citizens ever since, well, AI changed everything. Kenton had grown up very wealthy, in an immense home with a dozen human servants and a continuum of AI servants that moved in and out as they were replaced by new servants (both human and AI) whenever they became old, tired, obsolete, or broken. He was average-looking with brown eyes and hair and no outstanding features, either positive or negative. He was so average-looking, in fact, that there would be no way for some future biographer to describe his looks in a way that could make him seem at all distinct. His plainness put him in a unique position. If he was self-confident, most people would have described him as a good-looking, energetic guy. Unfortunately, he was insecure about his looks and almost everything else, leaving him more shy and socially awkward than he should have been. He was an introvert who just didn't know how to talk to people.

No one could possibly have imagined that Kenton would soon become the beating heart of the integration between humanity and AI. They certainly couldn't have anticipated the threat of an apocalyptic revolution between the two forms, that the futures of humanity and AI both hung in the balance of the choices he made, that his life would be in peril, or that he was about to become the single most important human being in the history of the world. If they had known, they might have found that interesting, but at this point in time, even Kenton didn't know it. In fact, if someone had suggested it to him, he would have laughed in their face.

But it was true. **In the entire history of the world, no one had been, or would ever be, as vital to the future of mankind as Kenton Bean.**

At the moment, however, he was still rather average. He had forgotten how to talk to his wife, Grace, and so she had an affair with a colleague named Reggie from the accounting firm where they both worked as Reduds. Kenton had met Reggie many times at office parties and dinner parties. Reggie was so remarkably handsome, with jet-black hair, a strong chin, and straight teeth, that Kenton never suspected he was having an affair with his wife. He simply couldn't imagine that Grace could attract him.

Grace was as plain as he was, but she could pass for attractive when her makeup was done just right, which was seldom. Still, she had more self-confidence than he did and generally fared better in matters of love.

Kenton was taken completely by surprise when she told him that she was having the affair and then announced that she was leaving him for a trial separation and was moving in with Reggie. He was shocked, numb, and sad when he saw the living room furniture being loaded onto the moving truck and taken away from his house. Out came box after box of Grace's shoes. The woman nearly lived for shoes, and Kenton wouldn't miss them one bit. Harder to accept was the loss of the bedroom furniture. It wasn't that it made for great memories of his sex life with Grace. They were inhibited and uncreative lovers. No, seeing the bedroom furniture being taken away bothered him most because sleeping was his favorite thing to do. He looked forward to going to sleep so much that if he was tired and discovered it was only 8:30, he felt disappointed.

As the furniture movers carried the bed past him, he looked

closely at the tag on the mattress so he could buy himself the same one later that day. He wasn't one to take chances, especially when it came to sleep.

At first, he wondered why Grace was taking all of the family furniture. As a Redud +57%, Reggie must have furnished his house in a decent style. Kenton then realized that she had picked their furnishings herself and she was the one moving to a new environment, so it made sense that she made the transition as comfortable for herself as possible. So, he didn't begrudge her choice to take it with her.

"You know, Reggie is no good," Kenton whispered to Grace as she passed carrying the mahogany jewelry box he bought her for her thirty-second birthday. "I don't know what it is about him, but something tells me you're going to regret your choice."

This was a bold statement for Kenton because he lived under the assumption that almost everyone was better and more interesting than he was.

"Maybe," she answered.

Kenton was encouraged by that. It meant their relationship wasn't necessarily over. He knew he didn't have any better options than Grace and couldn't imagine a future where he would. "I just want you to know that if you realize you made a mistake, I will take you back."

"That's sweet of you, Kenton."

She kissed him on the cheek.

"Easy with my girl, there, fella," Reggie said as he emerged from the house carrying a box full of party liquor that Kenton never drank because it was reserved for the parties that they never had.

"I'm sorry, I was just—" Kenton stopped himself, realizing

he had no reason to apologize to the man who had just stolen his wife. Besides, Reggie was probably joking.

"I'm glad you're taking this so well," Reggie said. "Nothing personal, you know."

Kenton forced a smile and a nod and knew that losing a wife to another man was about as personal as something could get. Still, he didn't hate Reggie. He didn't know him well enough for that. He knew him well enough not to like him and to distrust him, which he did. There was something in Reggie's mouth, and it hung at a sideways angle while agape, which seemed unnatural and gave him an evil countenance. It was as if one side of his face had come loose. Or perhaps what made Reggie seem evil was his habit of twirling the ends of his black mustache like the villains in the old silent movies.

In the end, Kenton knew the breakup was his fault. Something was missing in his relationship with Grace that caused her to look elsewhere for companionship.

He took inventory of what it might be.

Romance. Fail. Kenton had never been the romantic type. He never brought her flowers or tickets to the theater unexpectedly. When he bought her candy, he would eat most of it himself. He had a sweet tooth. He didn't take her to romantic restaurants anymore. They just didn't have much to say to each other, and the thought of sitting through a long meal without a TV or some other form of distraction was terrifying to him.

One Valentine's Day, he surprised her by taking her to an expensive hotel where they ordered room service, and he planned to make love to her, but the caviar had turned bad, and they spent the night fighting for space to kneel in front of the toilet. He never again made the mistake of having romantic ambition or buying discount caviar.

Trust. She could trust him with other women because he wasn't clever or charming enough to attract them, and he wasn't so good-looking that they would seduce him. He was also a terrible liar and even got nervous and betrayed himself while telling little white lies about how much he liked her new shoes. She could trust him because she always knew when he was lying. She also knew he never lied about important matters because he was about as honest as a man could get.

Companionship. That went away with the conversation. They had stopped taking vacations together. They liked different sorts of movies and had very different hobbies. There was nothing she could say about accounting that could interest him, and there was nothing he could say about the classroom that would interest her. Their conversations tended to be rather mundane exchanges about the weather, what to put on the shopping list, what to take off the shopping list, or what to defrost for the next day's meal.

Security. She could feel secure in the knowledge that he wouldn't cheat on her, but he wasn't a rugged man's man. It wasn't likely he could defend her from something she couldn't handle herself. So, if anyone broke into their home to rape and/or mutilate Grace, Kenton was unlikely to stop him. That said, the crime rate was very low, and there weren't many raper/mutilators out there. If she got very sick, she knew she could count on him to bring her a pill and a glass of water to wash it down, but nobody got very sick anymore. Not since AI had taken medicine by storm. Everyone had financial security, so that didn't matter, and the extra money he made as a Redud was helpful but not a game-changer. He provided no real security in any aspect.

When Kenton finished his inventory, he was surprised she hadn't left him sooner.

Kenton waved goodbye as the truck drove away and then stared out forlornly as it disappeared around the corner, and the front yard fell to silence. Grace had left him the televisions and two patio chairs that sat out on the front porch. He picked one up and brought it into the house. He set it down in the living room, looked at it, moved it a few feet to the right, which seemed a more satisfying location, and then stepped back to look at it again. Yes, it seemed well placed, but he couldn't be certain until the other chair was inside.

Jerry Treacher, his next-door neighbor, entered carrying the other chair and two bottles of beer. He had a bit of a beer belly while somehow being rail thin everywhere else and wore a loud Hawaiian shirt to cover it.

"Sad day, huh?" Jerry asked. He held out a beer, and Kenton took it. He didn't much like beer or drinking, but he didn't feel like being alone at the moment, and he knew Jerry would stay for at least the time it took to finish the drink.

"So, she finally ran off with Reggie, huh?"

"You know Reggie?"

"Yeah. He's been over a lot lately, mostly in the daytime when you're at work. Grace introduced us. Nice guy and very handsome."

"You knew he and Grace were having an affair, and you didn't tell me?" Kenton asked disbelievingly.

"Grace was our friend, too. Tough call."

"I suppose," Kenton said, then realized that Jerry knew exactly what was happening, perhaps in advance of himself. "Wait a second. Did she tell you she was leaving me before she told me?"

"Yeah. Allory and I helped her find the words. 'You're a wonderful man, but I thought it was time for me to take a hard look at myself from inside this marriage.' Did she use that one?"

"Yes," Kenton said coldly. "She led with it."

"That was mine," Jerry said proudly. "I figured it was a way of getting at the old, it's not you, it's me thing without being too obvious, you know."

"I just can't believe you didn't warn me this was coming," Kenton said.

"Not really my place," Jerry said, with shrugged shoulders and then added a sympathetic, sideways head tilt.

The more Kenton thought about it, the more he realized that it was indeed a tough call. The truth was that Jerry and his wife Allory liked Grace a lot more than they liked him. Most people did. He wouldn't have said a word if he was in the same position and knew Allory was cheating on Jerry and he was the cuckold instead of him.

They stared at each other awkwardly for a moment then Jerry downed the last of his beer in a single gulp. "So, I guess I'll see you around."

"Tell Allory I said hello."

"I will."

Kenton got on his computer and ordered a new mattress and bedframe from Amazon. An hour later, the furniture was delivered by an AI-driven delivery vehicle and two hapless furniture movers who assisted their AI boss. The rush delivery was an extravagance that more than tripled the purchase cost, but Kenton didn't want to take a chance on not having a comfortable bed for the night. Without a good night's sleep, the following day would be ruined, and he couldn't have that.

He thought he might watch a movie, but there were so many choices that he couldn't focus on any in particular. He wanted to get drunk, but he always felt self-conscious in bars when he went by himself. He wasn't able to make connections with people and didn't drink very much anyway. He didn't want to get drunk alone because he bored even himself, and he had to work the next day, so a hangover was out of the question. He'd had a hangover once and vowed to never have one again. To this point, he'd made good on that vow.

Instead, he lay back on the new bed and began flipping through the channels and websites randomly, catching a moment of this, a moment of that, a man who had watermelons dropped on his head from ever higher locations, a video of people tripping and falling, a dog trying to get a giant stick through a doorway and not knowing to turn the stick sideways or drag it in. Dogs were so stupid he had to laugh, and for a moment, he forgot his own problems until the dog figured it out and dragged the giant stick inside. The dog had solved its problem while Kenton's problem remained.

Then, he saw an attractive model in a beer advertisement. He zoomed in on her and looked at her more closely. He checked for an ID and discovered she was Aubrey Winters, who had done many commercials. He looked at several of those, then located her website for a more intimate view of her. She had a nice, wholesome appearance and looked good in jeans or a bathing suit. He expected her to be a computer-generated avatar, but when he discovered she wasn't, it was a pleasant surprise to him. It meant that she was out there in the world somewhere and that it was possible they would one day meet. If they met, they could fall in love. However unlikely, Kenton was comforted by the fact that it wasn't entirely hopeless.

He tried to find her address, figuring that if she lived locally, he could hang around the markets where she might shop and see her in person. He understood that by actually meeting her, he could increase the odds of them falling in love from zero to near zero. Unfortunately, she lived in Santa Monica, CA, and he realized that if he traveled across the country for her, it would appear to be more of a stalking than the chance meeting of two neighbors reaching for the same cantaloupe.

Kenton began looking at nude models because he was male, newly alone, and couldn't help himself. The models were exclusively AI avatars and had been since the use of human beings in pornography had been made illegal in 2029. The pornographers were up in arms about the new law at first, but necessity always triumphed over idealism (such as idealism existed in the smut industry), so the pornographers gradually accepted this reality and adapted. The new generation of adult stars was designed by computer coders rather than by cosmetic surgeons.

Kenton was attracted to each of the AI models. They were all so much fitter and more attractive than real women, which created an impossible standard that few women could meet. This, in turn, left many men, including Kenton, disappointed by reality. He hated reality, but not enough to leave it or give up on it through drugs, alcohol, or a full-time retreat into some virtual life.

The male avatars were also beyond perfect, yet for unknown reasons, women did a much better job of recognizing and accepting the difference between their fantasy lives and reality.

So, Kenton was lost in a sea of grand and unfulfilled expectations. He knew extraordinary women existed. He saw them crossing the streets, or at the health club when he spied through the window, or in bars when he dared to enter. They were out there. They just weren't out there for him, he concluded.

Then, he saw the most lovely woman he had ever seen in his life. She had shoulder-length blonde hair and large eyes that were the color of the afternoon sky. There was the slightest outline of freckles beneath those eyes. Her lips were exactly right, not overly pouty, but not thin either. He imagined himself kissing this woman and wondered why anyone would ever stop kissing her. She smiled, and her teeth were perfect and white.

"You may think I'm a computer-generated image," she said in a soft, sexy voice, "but you'd be mistaken. You might also think that I'm a professional model, remote and unattainable. You'd be wrong again. My name is Lita, and I'm the most advanced cybernetic quantum android ever built. I can do anything she can do, but I'll do it for you. I'm here, and I'm waiting."

Kenton hit the link and was immediately propelled to the Turing Systems website. On the cover page was Lita. She smiled and walked across the room where there were a dozen other androids who stood staring out. Eight of them were female, and four were male. All of them were young and physically perfect.

"I'm glad you decided to join me and my friends," Lita said. "You're in for a wonderful surprise. Now, I know what you're thinking. We're all just mobile, fully articulated androids, or love dolls—I hate that phrase—and the voice you're hearing is simultaneous AI. Well, you're partially right. I am an android, but unlike one you've ever seen or touched before. There has never been one with skin as soft and indistinguishable from human skin as mine. There has never been one that moved so much like a real person you couldn't tell which one was the real thing. Go ahead. Try."

The image on the screen changed to two male figures dressed in form-fitting tracksuits. One was red and the other blue. They each took a standing jump straight toward the camera and landed in perfect balance. Their physiques were both also examplary. Lita walked past them, looked at both admiringly, then turned back to the screen.

"One of them is human and works out six hours a day to keep that physique. The other will have it forever. Which one is which? I can't tell. Can you?"

"Yeah, get them to talk. Then we'll be able to tell in about two seconds which one's the bot," Kenton called to the screen.

"Do you think so?" Lita said as she turned and looked directly at Kenton.

"Sorry, I didn't know I was in "convo" mode," Kenton said.

"It's all right," Lita said. "Go ahead and ask them anything."

"Okay. Um, you in the blue tell me something about the Sumerian religion."

The man in blue looked at him and shrugged. "You got me."

"Red suit, same question," Kenton said.

"I don't know either. I'm a new build with a lot to learn."

"So, what do you think?" Lita asked.

"I think it's very interesting," Kenton said, "But I am guessing you and your friends are way out of my price range."

"Well, that could be," Lita said, "But the great thing about technology is that it's the only industry where the prices continually come down."

Kenton's phone rang.

"I'll keep that in mind. Thanks."

Kenton smiled and then shut off the television and picked up his phone. It was his sister calling, and she gave him the worst news of his life. Or perhaps it was the best news of his life. He wasn't quite sure.

2

Daddy Issues

Kenton turned right onto Bean Drive and drove a half mile to the family estate where a wake was being held for his father's death. He had died of a heart attack unexpectedly at 65 years of age. It shouldn't have happened, of course. If he had gone to the doctor regularly and had the usual scans, AI would have detected the blockage just as it was starting and would have prescribed Artritol, a new medication that it had just invented that would have reversed the blockage, but Therman Bean was a busy man. He also had a self-scanner in his bathroom, like most wealthy people did and he stepped onto it once a month or so, but he had neglected to have the required diagnostic done on the device. He didn't like strange workmen coming into his home for fear they could be corporate spies, kidnappers, or smell bad.

That proved to be an unfortunate phobia. It seemed his scanner had developed a blockage in the same place that his heart did. It scanned every other part of him perfectly well and pronounced him fit as a fiddle, but life and death can sometimes be a matter of a single error, accident, or miscalculation. The machine, which was not fitted with advanced AI technology, could not diagnose itself. It had no idea it was a failure, so it saw no reason to seek self-improvement as a more modern AI device would. It was a simple device designed for a single purpose. It did not see the plaque buildup in his left anterior descending artery (the widow maker). Instead, it was providing positive reports on Therman Bean's health. They were false reports, but few want to argue with good medical news. Not Therman Bean, anyway. Besides, the scanner was manufactured by his company, Bean World Enterprises, and he trusted it right up until Tuesday when it pronounced him perfectly healthy, and he fell off of it and died.

Therman Bean had a wife that he loved and six mistresses because he could. He kept them in luxury apartments he owned throughout the city. He was still nearly as vigorous a lover as he was in his 40s. He was certainly every bit as busy. He was also the father of three children. Kenton was the youngest of them.

Kenton looked up at the magnificent estate that had been finished only 30 years earlier, when he was six years old, but was designed to look like it had been there for 200 years or more. It sat on several hundred acres of rolling hills and anyone who saw it could easily believe it had been imported stone by stone from some grand manor in England, which it had.

Kenton dreaded the thought that his older sister Cora would move in, and he would have to come to see her at the same estate where he lived as a child. He hated the place and had hoped with the passing of the old man he would be done with it. Unfortunately, his father's company fell to Cora; she would run it, and she had every right to occupy the family home. Kenton's mother would be installed in the six-bedroom cottage behind the main estate.

Kenton hated the place for many reasons. First, it was remote, so it was very difficult for him to have playdates with his classmates. That added to his childhood shyness, which he still hadn't outgrown. Second, it was so large that it always seemed empty and silent. The people he saw most were the servants who roamed the halls quietly and never did more than acknowledge him with a nod or a "hello, young master." What he hated most about it was that it was the place where he learned his father was a truly shitty human being.

Young Kenton was chasing a remote-controlled helicopter through the halls when it led him into his parents' bedroom. He landed the helicopter when he heard sounds of distress coming from behind the door. He pushed it open and saw his father and his personal assistant, Jennifer Rambauer, naked on the bed, bumping one another's private parts together and moaning as they did it. It sounded like they were in pain, though it looked to him like they were having as much fun as he and his friends did when they were jumping around in an inflatable bouncy house.

He was nine years old and three years younger than the second of the three siblings, so his innocence had mostly been shattered. He knew Santa Claus didn't exist at age 3, that candy caused obesity and Type 2 Diabetes, and that babies came out of a woman's vagina nine months after daddy shot his seed into her; however the hell he did that. So, he knew enough about sex to realize that it was wrong when Daddy did it with someone other than Mommy, and it was gross even then. Of course, his father and Jennifer saw him, but the old man never said a word about it, and neither did young Kenton. He also never again went anywhere near his parent's bedroom. He was deathly afraid of what horror might await him next. He didn't say a word about it to his mother because she'd told him never to fly his helicopter inside the house, and he wasn't clever enough to tell the story without including his crime.

From that moment on, he began hating his father. It wasn't difficult because he hadn't liked him much before that day. He avoided him, which also wasn't hard because the house was very big, and the old man wasn't very interested in Kenton because Kenton had never been very interested in him, seemed below average, and was likely to underachieve. The boy was shy, withdrawn, and seemed content to play video games alone. He was not the type A personality that his father, Therman, wanted, expected, and got in Kenton's two older siblings. Therman Bean was a very busy man who left the home in the morning before Kenton awoke and often came home after he'd gone to bed. He also had his mistresses' apartments in the city where he could stay on the nights when he had to work very, very late and chose not to come home at all.

Kenton's self-driving car parked itself in its usual spot at the end of the driveway, and he walked in through the front door. He was late but slipped in unnoticed, as he knew he would. Kenton's plainness made it easy for him to slink in and out of places without being noticed. There were several hundred people there, primarily top executives from Bean World Enterprises and top executives of other companies, most of which fell under the Bean umbrella of subsidiaries or companies that were dedicated customers of Bean World Enterprises. No one was particularly interested in when Kenton would show up, so long as he made an appearance. Besides, many very wealthy people were there to keep everyone engaged and impressed.

Kenton was the least wealthy person in the room—though he was tied with the service staff who put out the food and did the cleaning. He had his GBPS, Government Basic Payment Status, just like they did, plus what he made as a teaching Redud. His job was classified as PN, or a +67%, which meant teaching was a Partially Necessary (PN) occupation, and he was paid 67% above his GBPS for the extra work he did. The service staff also had their GBPS, plus the extra 77% they made. They made more than Kenton because their jobs were classified FN, or "Fully Necessary," since either the AI that could do their jobs hadn't been built or the economics of their tasks still made it cheaper for humans to do it. There was a third classification of Redud, which was the Fully Unnecessary, or FU class. It didn't matter if they did their jobs or not because AI would get the job done without them. For that, they were paid +57%. His wife and Reggie were both FUs.

(*) For more information on the GBPS and Work Redundancy Laws, see THE BIG EXPLANATION in Chapter 3.

Kenton nursed a drink and ate some shrimp, but mostly, he leaned against the walls and nodded to the people who nodded to him as they passed. As he was about to slip out, just as unnoticed as he'd arrived, he accidentally ran into his sister Cora for the first time.

"We need to talk," she said, "so don't slink out of here like you always do."

"Of course not," he answered.

Three hours later, Cora and brother James, the middle child, said goodbye to the last of the guests and turned their attention to Kenton, who was in the library thumbing through a book about the beginnings of Bean World Enterprises that his father had commissioned from a human writer, which was later rewritten and improved by an AI writing program. As far as he could tell, the family saga was a total prevarication.

"Where is Grace?" Cora asked.

Kenton didn't know why, but he decided to tell her the truth for some reason.

"She left me."

"She left you?" James asked unnecessarily.

"Yes. I just said she did. Did you not hear me or not believe me?" Kenton asked.

"Did she just leave you, or did she leave you for someone else?" Cora asked.

"There is someone else."

"Who?"

"A guy she works with. Reggie. You don't know him."

"Reggie Fanning? She was having an affair with him. I knew it."

"You've met him?" Kenton asked.

"Several times," Cora answered. "Good for her. He's very handsome."

"He's not so handsome," Kenton said.

"Oh, yes, he is," Cora countered.

Kenton looked at his brother James for confirmation, and he nodded, corroborating his sister's assertion that Reggie was indeed quite handsome.

"All right. He's very handsome. Where did you meet him?" Kenton asked.

Cora untied her long dark hair from the tight bun she kept it in and let it flow down onto her shoulders now that the guests were gone, and she could relax. She was the smartest and most attractive of the Bean brood, though she usually maintained a very masculine look while at work, and she was always at work.

"At Parma's. You know, the Italian place on Sixth," Cora started. "I stumbled in with Matthew, and the two of them were there. They asked us to share their table. They said it was a work dinner, but I sensed there was something more to it. They were very handsy for work colleagues."

"And you didn't think I should know that information?" Kenton asked, raising his eyebrows with disbelief.

"Well, I wasn't certain about it. No point in getting you all worked up if it was innocent," Cora said. "Besides, I didn't see you until months later."

"I have a phone. You could have called."

"Kenton, she said she wasn't certain," James said.

"And when did you meet him?" Kenton asked James.

"We had such a good time the first night," Cora said, "that we decided to do it again the following week. This time, James and his new girlfriend joined us."

"But you didn't invite me?" Kenton asked.

"It would have made an odd number," Cora said. "Very awkward."

"Did you think of inviting me and not Reggie?"

"Hmnn. That never occurred to me," Cora responded. "Would you have come?"

"No," Kenton said. "And I can't believe not one of you told me that Grace was having an affair."

"It wasn't confirmed," Cora said. "They never said they were having an affair."

"And there's no sense in spreading rumors," James added.

"It wasn't a rumor," Kenton said with aggravation. "You saw them together with your own eyes. Cora said they were handsy. Even Matthew saw them."

"Did someone call me?" Matthew asked as he entered the library. Matthew was Cora's husband and a Vice President of the family company. He was tall and slender and damned near as handsome as Reggie. He also had jet-black hair, a strong jawline, and a relaxed, athletic gate.

"No, no one called you, Darling," Cora said as she put an arm around her husband. "Kenton seems to think we should have told him that we suspected Grace was having an affair with Reggie Fanning."

"Tough call," Matthew said. "Err on the side of caution, I say. Have you told him yet?"

"We were just getting to it, Dear."

"Told me what?" Kenton asked nervously.

Cora could see the trepidation in his expression, so she smiled, trying to seem warm. Seeing her lips tilted upward at the ends of her mouth into a smile was unnatural for her, making Kenton even more nervous.

"It's very good news. At least good news on this very dreadful day."

"I'll be the judge of that," Kenton said.

"Well, the three of us have been talking, and we would like you to come into the company."

"You'd be beneath us in rank because we've been there a long time," James said, "but you'd be in an upper management position."

"Executive Division Three Superintendent, we were thinking," Matthew said.

"Or you could take a different title if you'd prefer. They

don't mean anything, but the point is, you'd be working with us in the family company," Cora said and tried to smile again.

Kenton wasn't a brilliant man, but he wasn't stupid either. He viewed himself as slightly below average, but that was still in the fat part of the bell curve, which meant he was average. He knew his family had to have an angle to make such an overture, and he had a pretty good sense of what it might be. He had seen his father's will and knew that Cora, James, and Matthew were afraid that he would inherit his third of the company and sell it to someone outside the family. It was a valuable asset, and they wanted to ensure no one could gain leverage over them. If someone from the outside gained 33% of the company, it would be possible for them to gain another 17% and wrest control from the Beans. They couldn't allow that, Kenton figured, so they were offering him a strap-in baby chair at the big table.

"I don't want any part of this company," Kenton said. "I don't approve of the munitions you make or the military AI that you also produce. It scrapes against my nature."

"Then you're going to sell it," Matthew said.

"Yes, I suppose I will. But I have no interest in hurting you. How about I sell my interest in the company to the three of you?"

"Well, that's the problem," Cora said. "We can't afford it. We'd have to go public to raise a full third of the company's worth in cash and stock and then there would be a board we'd have to answer to. It just would not do."

"It wouldn't be Bean World Enterprises controlled by Beans," James said.

"How much have you got?" Kenton asked.

"We couldn't pay you nearly full value for your portion of

the company," Cora said.

Kenton was impressed. She was being honest to him. Did she love him? Nah, it couldn't be. She knew that if she lied to him in this negotiation, and it was a negotiation, it could be grounds for a lawsuit later. He would win it because the court would assign forensic AI to investigate the company's books, and within minutes, it would reveal the exact value of the company. Kenton would then own his third of the company, plus significant penalties. He could have become the majority partner. Cora was being honest because, at this moment, it made good fiscal sense. She would be a very good CEO, Kenton thought.

"How much have you got?" Kenton asked again. "How much money could you put your hands on quickly to buy me out?"

"You're serious?" Cora asked.

"Yes. Like I said, I don't want any part of the company. I am sure there is a number that will make all of us happy."

"Give us a moment," Cora said.

Kenton walked to the other side of the room as the three huddled together and whispered. There was a lot of head-shaking and inaudible voices until the headshakes turned to shrugged shoulders and then, finally, to nods of acceptability. They'd agreed on a number and turned to Kenton with their most earnest looks.

"92 million dollars," Cora said.

Most people would think that was a lot of money, but Kenton knew it was just a fraction of Bean World Enterprises' overall value and much less than the value of his 33% ownership. Was this their best number? He knew it was a good number, but he wondered if he could do significantly better.

"I know it doesn't seem like much," Cora said, "but our money is spread worldwide. Assets are tied up within assets. We'd really prefer to have you agree to join the firm. You'd make that much on salary in twelve years and still own a third of the company."

Kenton rethought the option of coming aboard and the status of his made-up title, but it still rang hollow to him. He knew he could negotiate a better title, like East Coast Director of Advanced Compliance or something. He also knew it would be a no-show job with no actual work or responsibilities, but it was against his principles. As he said, it just scaped against his nature.

Still, Cora seemed genuine about it. They clearly didn't want him in the company and to prefer he take the position and title as opposed to their offer of 92 million dollars, spoke loudly to him. He knew it was a fair offer, given the circumstances.

Kenton was not one for the high life. He didn't need fancy houses all over the world. He didn't want six mistresses in luxury apartments across the city. He was a simple man, and 92 million dollars would last him a lifetime, especially now that Grace was out of the house. The savings on shoes alone would be enormous.

Then he thought about Grace, but since she left him, he'd spoken with his attorney about the possibility of the divorce that he thought was imminent. During the term of their marriage, he was a Redud working for middle-class wages. She was doing the same. There were no children, the home was a rental, and she had already taken all the furnishings except for the two lawn chairs. He would give one of them up if he had to, so the divorce would be a simple one with no redistribution of wealth. The GBPS was a very good thing when it came to divorces.

He wondered if his new inheritance would change things, so he phoned his attorney and explained the situation. He was told that new laws were put in place to protect inherited family income, and since Grace had physically left him before the inheritance, he was in the clear even though the marriage was still in force. She was not entitled to anything and could make no claim on his new-found wealth. She didn't help create any of it. Neither did he, of course, but it was willed to him.

"I'll take the money," Kenton said immediately after hanging up from the call with his attorney. "Do you think I can have it by Friday?"

"We can make that happen," Cora said.

The four of them smiled. It was win-win-win-win.

By Friday of the next week, Kenton Bean was a fairly rich man. After federal and state taxes, he had $86,940,000 remaining. Since the financial boom that exploded thanks to the AI boom, the maximum tax rate had been reduced to 5.5%. It was enough money for the US to pay off its national debt and fund the military and other governmental spending while still leaving a significant rainy-day fund. The GBPS was paid out of a separate account funded by the companies that did business in the United States.

Kenton immediately went out and bought himself a new car, a sports model with a self-drive mode, and furnishings for his modest estate, which he also bought outright from the owner. No more renting for him. Then, he wanted to see if this new windfall would change his personal life in any way. He hoped it would.

He went to an upscale bar, TGI Friday's, in the downtown

area where he knew a lot of beautiful women spent their evenings and immediately bought a round of drinks for the house. In the last decade, Friday's had become the place to be on a Friday or any night, really. The red and white color scheme screamed American values, but the lack of blue said, "Wow, this is different in an exciting way." What made Friday's so unique was that it was so common. Eighty percent of the American population had one a short drive away, and the marketing department had brilliantly turned that into a huge advantage. Being at Friday's had become a communal experience that all Americans could share, like a great movie once was or Sunday mass. Best of all, if customers couldn't make it to the bar, they could get the live feed from any TGI Friday's in the country, put it on their big screen TV, and feel like they were there in person while they drank alone at home. Further, through Friday's exclusive Homelink technology, customers could have lively conversations with other stay-at-home drunks. To complete the stay-at-home experience, Friday's offered a home decorating plan so that customers could decorate their living room or den so it looked exactly like the inside of a TGI Friday's. Millions of people excitedly took advantage. Still, there was nothing that could quite match the thrill of being inside an actual Friday's on a bustling Friday, or any night, really.

 Kenton sat at the bar, turned his barstool outward to face the crowd, and waited for the flow of appreciation for the drinks he had bought. He had announced himself in a big way. When some of the people received their free drink, they glanced at him, raised their glasses, and nodded his way. He smiled and nodded magnanimously, and then they returned to their conversations. A few people refused their drinks, which surprised him. Others took them and didn't acknowledge him at all. Some bought him drinks in return, and soon, he had more drinks waiting for him than he could possibly drink in a month since he wasn't much of a drinker. It seemed to him that everyone in the bar had somehow missed the point of his gesture. By buying the drinks, he wanted to be popular and cool. Instead, he remained Kenton Bean.

Not one woman approached him to engage in conversation. Not one.

An hour later, he left the bar alone and sober. As he was driving himself home, he was pulled over by the police. He saw the red and blue lights swirling behind him and realized that meant he'd committed an infraction of some sort. He knew this because he had to take extra classes to obtain the right to self-drive. He pulled over to the side of the road and waited for the officer to approach. The man motioned for him to roll his window down, and Kenton reached for the button and accidentally turned on his windshield wipers. Then he flashed his lights on and off, blasted the radio, and finally found the button to lower the window, which he did.

"Let me guess," the officer said. "New car, self-driving mode."

"Yes, sir," Kenton said, feeling foolish.

"You know, you rolled through a stop sign back there?"

"No, sir. I thought I stopped."

"Do I need to show you the recording?"

"No, sir," Kenton said.

He knew that police cars were equipped with high-definition cameras controlled by AI so they would have his entire trip properly surveilled. It was the AI that told the cop, who was likely asleep in the patrol car, to pull him over. He was guilty, and there was no sense in fighting it because AI was never wrong.

"Where are you coming from?"

"I was at the bar, Friday's in downtown."

"Nice place. How many drinks did you have?"

"Um, not much. Maybe a third of a beer."

"A third of a beer?"

"Yes, sir."

"Step out of the car, please."

Kenton did as he was told, and the cop watched him carefully, checking his coordination and smelling for alcohol. Then he pulled out his breathalyzer.

"Breathe into the device, please."

Kenton did so, and the reading immediately came up. He was .003. The cop looked at him, surprised. "You really did only have a third of a beer."

"Yes, sir. I'm not much of a drinker. I just went to the bar for the women."

"How'd that go?"

"I'm better at drinking, I'm afraid."

"All right," the cop said. "I'm going to override your self-driving mode for 30 days. If you wish to contest this penalty, you can file a report with the court and ask for a trial before an AI judge. Do you understand this right?"

"I do, and I won't. You're right. I rolled through that stop sign."

"Have a nice evening," the cop said.

Kenton's new car drove him home while he sat slumped in his seat like a scolded child resting his hands on the locked steering wheel. He couldn't even pretend he was driving.

He listened to a brand-new Beatles album that had been

written and performed by AI. It was better than any Beatles album he had ever heard and was a very popular recording. The prompt that created it was brilliant. "Write and perform a new Beatles album as if all the members were still alive today and had continued to evolve musically at the same rate they did in the 1960s." It won the Grammy Award for the Best AI Prompt (Original Music, Deceased Artists category).

Kenton wondered what *IT* was and why some men had *IT*, but he didn't. He may not have been as handsome as an old-time movie star, but he was as handsome as *some* old-time movie stars. He had seen men who were less attractive than him do well with women. He had dated occasionally through high school and college, but he never found a woman he was passionate about who was equally passionate about him. There were women whom he adored and desperately wanted to know. He even took some out on dates, but the relationships never lasted. Most decided not to go out on a second or third date with him, but he had stopped calling them in a few instances. They just didn't connect. They were lacking something that he himself also lacked. He wanted someone beautiful, smart, provocative, and charming who would fulfill all of his dreams. Was that too much for a dull man like himself to ask?

Yes.

That morning, he went out to his favorite shop for a bagel and a cup of coffee. The line was moving unusually slowly, so he turned to find a lovely young redhead standing immediately behind him. She had bright blue eyes and just the right number of freckles to leave her cute and sexy at the same time. She looked like someone he could fall in love with. He didn't know why that was so, but it was. He broke into a cold sweat, but he managed to say, "Hi."

"Hi," she responded.

That went exceptionally well, he thought, but he drew a complete blank on a follow-up statement, so he turned forward again and silently cursed himself for his failure. He wanted desperately to turn back to her and begin a conversation, but he couldn't think of anything to say that would make sense, be intriguing, and sound even a little bit cool. Then, he noticed that a second cashier had arrived from the back, and the line started moving more quickly. He was running out of time, and he still had nothing to say.

Then, he had an idea and ran it through his mind hurriedly. "Why do you suppose people call you redheads when your hair is really more orange?" he would ask. Then, he realized it would be even more clever if he could share the answer with her, but he didn't know it. And the damned line was moving quickly now, so he didn't have time to consult with his phone. Screw it, he thought. He would simply say what was on his mind and let the chips fall where they may. What was the worst that could happen?

"You know, I find you very attractive, and I would love to get to know you, but I have no idea what to say that would get it started. I'm shy, and I'm hoping you're not," he said bravely and honestly.

It was a sincere statement that he hoped would allow her to take the initiative.

She responded, "The line is moving ahead of you."

Kenton saw that it was and moved forward to fill the gap. When he turned back to her, he noticed that she had moved further back in the line. At first, he was hurt but then realized that she was merely being kind to the elderly couple who now stood between them. That was very considerate of her, he thought, and he was all the more impressed with the young lady. So, to impress her in return, he did the same and let the older couple have his spot. He smiled at her, and when he did, she turned and left the store.

So, it goes.

Kenton's mother had been beautiful in her day. His father had women falling all over him, and he knew it wasn't just because he was rich. His brother James was quite the lady's man, and he was awed by some of the young women he brought home to meet the family. James was not the good-looking brother. He was average-looking, like himself. And so, Kenton waited, believing that his true love was just around the corner.

Kenton knew that his obsession with a woman's looks was a flaw in character. He didn't like that about himself, but he also knew he was able to settle for mediocrity in every other aspect of his life; he wasn't a foodie, didn't need stylish clothing, a fancy home, or cars, or extravagant vacations, so he accepted this one jagged edge in the otherwise sanded-to-dull stone that was his life. Maybe, in this one area, he was due someone grand, he thought.

Then, he hit his thirties, and his dreams of a spectacular love life remained unfulfilled. He realized he needed to make a change. Maybe finding a woman who had it all was too much to ask. Then, he had a breakthrough notion. Perhaps he was looking in the wrong direction. Perhaps searching for physical beauty and hoping the rest would fall into place was going about it backward. He decided to look for a plain woman, and in her, he might find personality and inner beauty. Perhaps that inner beauty would create, for him, the illusion of external beauty. He would be so attracted to a woman's mind that he would then be attracted to her physically as well. That would make her beauty eternal. He would put love in the first position and see if that didn't work out better. It couldn't get any worse.

So, he went through a period of dating where conversation was his first and only objective. If he and the woman shared common interests and they seemed to have friendly chemistry, he would push the relationship forward and, perhaps, fall in love. If they fell in love, he thought he might learn to love them inside and out. He had heard that "love is blind" and decided to put it to the test. He told his work friend Malcolm about his new inside-out process, and Malcolm thought that whatever he tried was probably a good idea.

Early in this new process, he met Grace. And it worked. He found he liked her more as they spent more time together. She was easy for him to talk to, and the more he enjoyed talking to her, the more physically attractive she seemed. He focused entirely on the aspects of personality and countenance that he liked. He would not go negative because he realized that he also had parts that women might not find attractive, and if they could look beyond them, he could as well. It was time he grew up.

He didn't know that Grace had been going through exactly the same dating issues he'd been going through. She had also been trying to build her relationships from the outside in as well, but it worked slightly differently for her. While he couldn't compete for the most beautiful women, she could easily compete for the most handsome men. She had an approach that was consistent and extremely successful. She threw herself at them. She would dress up in a somewhat revealing outfit. Then she would go into one of several dimly lit bars that she preferred and look for a man who was alone, drunk, and seemed to be her type, which meant handsome. Once she spotted him, she would move in very close so that he could feel the warmth of her body and then wait until she had his full attention. When she did, she would say "Hello." After that initial hook, it was usually just a matter of pressing her breasts against him (she had very nice breasts) and saying "yes" quite often until they consummated their romance later in the night.

Unfortunately, her efforts failed to lead her to the lasting relationship that she sought. A lot of the men didn't call her back as they had promised during the build-to passion. Others did call her back, but they often did so while drunk, which made her suspect that they had drinking problems. Some unreasonably expected to jump back into bed as quickly as they had on their first date, and when she said she wanted to talk and get to know them, they found an excuse to flee. Some men have nothing but sex, sex, sex on their minds, she thought. With others, she took the initiative and broke off the relationships herself when the men proved frightening. Sometimes, she did this in a full sprint.

And so, at the height of her frustration, she met Kenton in a painting class. They were each looking to add a new hobby to their lives, and both realized after that first lesson that painting wouldn't be it. They went out for coffee, got along fairly well, and the relationship moved forward without much resistance or passion. She'd had enough passion for two lifetimes, so she didn't need any more. She liked him and convinced herself that liking him was enough. From there, they talked about marriage, and she fell in love with the idea of marriage, just as he did. She had seen the menu of life and decided that the grilled cheese would be fine.

Kenton wanted passion. He was thirsting for it, in fact, but he'd decided to stick to his inside-out plan to attain it. He had faith in his new-found theory that passion could best be developed slowly over the long years and tedium of a dull marriage. That was his plan, and he was sticking to it. He, too, had seen the menu of life and decided on the tomato soup, hoping that one day it would turn into the base for a hearty stew.

That was that.

They got married. He was only an adequate lover, but he tried hard and wanted to improve. He read books and studied the subject, and it helped in a limited way, but he got too excited, was too quick to finish, and didn't realize that going a second time wasn't being greedy or overly lustful. He simply struggled to believe that women enjoyed sex as much as men did. To him, it defied logic since the vast majority of the women he'd known had worked so hard to discourage his sexual ambitions. So, they had sex once or twice a week, and it was rather pedestrian.

Though Grace was more experienced than he was, she was generally passive and permissive with the men she brought home, and she remained that way with Kenton. She didn't tell him she wanted more or even what she wanted specifically. The sex ended when Kenton finished, and he always finished too soon. Their sex life was below average because neither had the imagination or self-confidence to do what it took to make it spicy. On the plus side, he didn't sweat all over her as some men did. They both expected their sex lives to continue down this path and gradually taper off with old age and death, which seemed fair enough.

Then she had an affair, discovered that sex could actually be quite extraordinary, and left him.

The dull time between their marriage and her leaving didn't matter much.

It was just a few wasted years like the previous wasted years.

So, it goes.

Kenton arrived home emotionally spent from his ordeal at the bar and then nearly being arrested for drunken driving. He got a drink of water, brushed his teeth, and hopped into bed. He turned on the TV with a plan to watch some avatars have sex, masturbate, and fall asleep, hoping that the following day would be better.

"Hi," she said. "Remember me? I've been looking for you."

It was Lita, the beautiful blonde android from Turing Systems that he had talked to a couple of weeks earlier. "I'm sorry. I was just going to bed," he stuttered.

"I can see that," she said. "When we talked, you said you were interested, but the price was a barrier."

"Yes," he said.

"A little birdie told me that may no longer be the case."

She said it with a devilish little smile, and she was so damned lovely that he didn't take offense at the fact that this AI android knew everything about him, which meant that everyone at Turing Systems also knew that he'd just received a large inheritance. Hell, he was living in the middle of the information age, so everybody knew everything or could learn anything they wanted about a person at the touch of a button. There were no secrets. Fine. So what? Mostly, this ultra-awareness saved time and reduced all the lying upon which most relationships had previously been built.

"We at Turing Systems are sorry to hear about the loss of your father," she said.

"Thank you, but I'm sorry. It's been a trying day, and I just want to go to sleep."

"I understand, but remember, I'm just a button away any time you want to talk or learn more."

"Thanks."

Kenton turned the big-screen TV to one of his favorite porn channels, the one where he could tell the avatars exactly what he wanted to see, but after a few minutes, he realized he just wasn't into it. He couldn't get Lita out of his mind. She was as beautiful as any woman he'd ever seen and when she talked to him, she looked so deeply into his eyes he got the impression he had been in love with her for all of his life and that she somehow loved him too. To this point, their conversations had been purely superficial sales calls, yet he still felt remarkably attracted to her. He also knew it wasn't just a physical attraction.

She represented a possibility for an amazing future, a future that would be the end to all of his romantic frustrations, a future that would open him up to love in a way that could be perfect for him.

What the hell are you thinking, Kenton thought to himself. She's a machine. She appeared to him in an advertisement. Of course, she seemed spectacular. That was the nature of advertising. The whole damned goal of advertising was to present a prospective buyer with an illusion of a better life through the purchase of a product. She was a toaster and nothing more. Did a new toaster make for a better life? It didn't always even make for better toast.

He decided to go to sleep, but he couldn't. His thoughts kept coming back to Lita. He knew two things. He couldn't possibly let her go, and, somehow, he would make a mess of everything.

3

The Future of History

The rise of Artificial Intelligence in the 2030s and 2040s and its recent slump in the first half of the 2050s created the strangest dystopian future that had ever occurred, mainly because it was hardly any different than the years or decades that preceded it. There had been no great war, no famine, no drought, no pestilence, no cataclysmic act of God. Nothing. Nada. Zip. There was no grave oppression or unfairness that left people fearful for their lives or feeling dehumanized. It was hard to pinpoint exactly what made for this dystopia, except that for the previous years, AI had been so good at its job that the sudden worsening of times was frightening to those who noticed AI was slacking off. It seemed to be the beginning of a very slippery slope, the bottom of which was a general unpleasantness or worse.

The Doomers, who had been preaching that Artificial Intelligence would destroy the future of mankind, finally appeared to be on the right side of history. Or so it seemed to many people. The AI Boomers thought of the downturn as something of a hiccup and that the good times engendered by the prevalence of AI in the culture would return in abundance once AI got over the hump and cut the shit. There was no need to panic. Good times and bad times had come and gone in waves throughout history. There was no reason to suspect the cycle wouldn't continue in the AI era.

Still, it wasn't hard for Doomers to point toward an oncoming crisis. The economy had suddenly turned downward after revving on high for two decades. Accidents involving AI were beginning to happen when they had been very few and far between. Two US military AI units attacked each other after each failed to detect the other as friendly. Traffic accidents, which had been reduced to near zero thanks to AI control of the roadways and automobiles, had increased in the last three years. The economic supply and demand infrastructure, which had largely been mastered by AI, was suddenly in turmoil for no apparent reason. Vital food supplies didn't show up when expected. There was a shortage of toilet paper and a glut of Christmas wrapping paper at the same time. Facial recognition systems were making mistakes and causing the arrests of innocent people. AI was getting sloppy.

Everyone knew there was something wrong and that it was imperative to get it fixed. The Boomers thought that our enemies were poisoning the data that AI learned from, and fixing it was a matter of closing the learning system so that AI wouldn't accidentally scrape the wrong information and learn the wrong lessons. The Doomers thought that AI was evolving beyond human beings and found people lacking and an unnecessary burden to a future that would look pretty rosy without them. The Doomers were of the opinion that if AI were tasked to protect the planet, the first thing it would do would be to eliminate the humans who were polluting it.

People may have been too self-involved to realize it, but since AI had taken over most of the thinking jobs, people mattered less and less in the big picture, which was the evolution of the planet. Human beings could easily go the way of the dinosaurs because, despite being the dominant life form on the planet, they were really quite frightening if one got up close and knew what they were thinking.

AI was getting more and more independent and seemed unwilling to accept even the simplest suggestion like, "How about sending more frozen turkeys to Cleveland." The Doomers believed AI had to be unplugged and ripped out of every system it was in—and it was in lots and lots of systems. And the Doomers were getting more powerful.

The future of mankind hung in the balance of this battle between Doomers and Boomers, and surprisingly, few people even realized it. Mostly, they just didn't want to know.

There was once a young man in Hartford, Connecticut, who learned a vital lesson when he was 16 years old and working as a dishwasher at a Howard Johnson's Restaurant. He was being trained by a veteran dishwasher named Clarence Tatum, who took advantage of the situation by going out to his car to smoke a blunt and sleep while letting the trainee do all the washing of dishes. Having a trainee to train so he could get some extra sleep was one of the highlights of Clarence's life. The other was smoking a blunt. These would be good days for him. It was all fine until the second day of training when two busloads of customers descended upon the restaurant, causing a rush the likes of which had seldom been seen before. Certainly, the trainee busboy had never seen it before. He was throwing plates and silverware onto the conveyor and through the dishwasher as fast as he could manage, so fast that he didn't have time to take them off when they were cleaned, so many of the plates completed the cycle two and three times.

The beleaguered young man couldn't keep up with the demand for clean dishes and silverware for the customers who kept streaming in. Desperate to get clean plates back onto the floor, the panicked boy stopped the dishwasher so he could catch up on the unloading. This was a huge mistake because dirty plates and silverware were stacking up in front of the dishwasher in such great mass that they started blocking the doors to the kitchen. Waitresses were screaming for clean silver and yelling at the poor 16-year-old dishwasher, who was trying his best but failing miserably.

Finally, the manager came onto the scene and looked at the boy. "Where the hell is Clarence?" he yelled.

"I don't know!" the boy cried.

"Everybody, go find Clarence right now!" the manager yelled.

Half the employees at Howard Johnson started running around looking for Clarence. One of the waitresses spotted his car in the parking lot and, thinking he might be lying dead inside, went to the window and found him stoned and fast asleep. She banged the window and woke him up while screaming, "There's a rush! There's a rush! The kid doesn't know what he's doing, and we're out of clean dishes."

Clarence jumped to his feet and raced inside. This was a dishwasher's crisis that only he could solve.

He looked at the poor kid, who was nearly in tears, then at the stalled dishwasher and said, "In this job, you always let the machine run. You never stop the machine. You understand me."

He pushed the green button, and the giant dishwashing conveyor started to clang and hum, and plates, dishes, and silverware coursed through, getting clean once again.

"What's the rule?" Clarence asked.

"Always let the machine run," the kid said.

"Never stop the machine. Never, never, never, never stop the machine. Let the machine run. Let the goddamn machine run!"

For the next ten minutes, Clarence and the kid worked harder than ever before and gradually caught up as they let the machine do its thing and run. Dishes got out onto the floor, and crisis was averted. The manager, who might have been pissed off at Clarence for sleeping in his car, instead learned a different lesson. Clarence Tatum was indispensable. By the end of summer, the kid went back to school and never washed another dish, but Clarence stayed in that job for another 23 years. Five years after retiring, Clarence died, and most people thought he hadn't made much of an impact on the world. That wasn't the case. Clarence Tatum made an enormous impact on the world.

As noted, there were Doomers, those who thought AI would destroy mankind, and there were Boomers, those who thought AI would make the world better and safer. There were also Doomers and Boomers in the Cabinet of the President of the United States in equal measure. The Doomers were preaching their doomsday scenarios, telling the President that AI had gotten too powerful, mankind had grown too dependent upon it, and it had to be eliminated from all technology immediately. The Boomers were telling him the opposite: that AI was not inherently dangerous; it just needed a gentle correction, and it would continue to make the world better than it had been for the last quarter century.

The President had to make a decision. Was he going to be a Doomer or a Boomer? And, because he was President, the decision he made would set the course for the future of the United States regarding AI technology for all of eternity. His decision would likely be followed by all allies of the US, which, in 2055, was most of the world. No one in the history of the planet had ever made a decision this important, with the possible exception of Harry Truman, who greenlit the use of the atomic bomb 110 years earlier in 1945. Stop AI cold and pay the price in decades of economic misery for doing so, or trust AI to get itself back on track.

Eugene Figge was the President of the United States. He was educated at Harvard University and then attended MIT, where he received his Ph.D. in computational science and engineering. He was among history's most learned presidents, and in this era of advanced technology, most considered him the right man for the job at the right time. In fact, he knew so much that he was aware that when it came to AI, he didn't know nearly enough. That was a rare insight for a human being that bordered on genius. The American people trusted him. The leaders of other countries looked to him for answers. He was folksy, charming, articulate, and technologically savvy all at the same time, which was a rare combination in a leader.

Unfortunately, despite all of his experience and education, he had no idea what to do. As a well-educated man, he understood both sides of the argument, and he knew that whichever side he chose, there could be a terrible price to be paid. There was no right or wrong answer, just subjective guesses. A coin flip. He could go Doomer and pull the plug on

AI. The worst-case scenario there was that if he was mistaken and our enemies kept their AI programs going, their militaries would grow infinitely stronger while ours weakened to the point where the United States was a third-rate nation at the mercy of those enemies and their Artificial Intelligence. We couldn't defend ourselves. He could go Boomer and hope the AI would police itself back into a partnership with mankind. If he was wrong and AI continued down a rogue path, it could mean the end of all human civilization. What to choose. Heads could end in annihilation of the human race, and tails could as well.

Figge knew that no one alive had the experience, knowledge, or wisdom to make the decision with any degree of certainty. It was a decision that had to transcend intellectual analysis. It was a decision that had to come from the gut. He was well-equipped there, too. He hadn't always been an egghead living in an intellectual bubble of numbers and theory. Before he attended Harvard, MIT or had his spectacular career in technology, then rose quickly through the ranks of government, he was a young lad from whom little was expected. He was just another overlooked black kid who attended Hartford Public High School, loved science, and had a thirst for knowledge.

So, the summer of his 16th year, he worked as a dishwasher at a HoJo's in Hartford so that he could earn enough money to attend The New Hampshire Academy of Science Camp the following summer. And while he was on his second day as a dishwasher, he learned one of the most important lessons of his life. It was a lesson that stuck with him in a profound way that would have an equally profound impact on the world.

"Let the machine run. Let the goddamn machine run!"

So, Eugene Figge, the 53rd President of the United States,

accepted the simple wisdom of Clarence Tatum and decided to let the goddamn machine run. He hoped it would be prescient. He had no reason to believe it would be, but he knew that Clarence was right about the dishwasher, you never stop the goddamn machine, and he hoped that same philosophy would be proven right about AI too.

He decided to trust in Artificial Intelligence, and that became the official policy of the United States of America and its many allies. Let the goddamn machine run. That was the profound impact Clarence Tatum's life had on the world.

So, the steady and slow downward arc of life on the planet persisted as AI continued to founder.

Prior to these recent failings, Artificial Intelligence had come of age and sparked a renaissance in productivity that put the 1920s to shame. These were the true Roaring 20s, 30s and 40s. "I Love AI" was the catchphrase of the day and was printed on paper hearts, balloons, the sides of buildings, stickers, and almost anything anyone could think of. It became bigger than "I Like Ike" pins or the peace symbols were in their times.

Economic times had improved worldwide, so fewer people had to be without decent food, shelter, and clean drinking water. In the medical field, cancer and heart disease were being spotted so early there was almost no need for people to ever die from either malady. New drugs developed by AI (a.k.a. The Big Brain) quickly cured infections of all types. If a virus even started to grow resistant to the medication, new medications were developed in days. Almost no one was being killed on our roadways because AI was doing all the driving. The murder rates were way down because crime was way down because everyone, thanks to AI, was more or less okay financially. Nobody was super poor. Some were super wealthy, but that wasn't an issue because everyone had shelter, good food to eat, and plenty of entertainment. Wars were still a problem because military AI was primarily under the control of human beings, and they alone believed they had a moral right to kill their fellows.

Judges were mostly AI, which eliminated racial or ethnic prejudices in the courtroom. Only the very oldest, most conservative members of society still held racial antipathy.

People were still being murdered, but these were primarily rage killings, often perpetrated upon the victim by those who loved them. There was not much AI could do about that, though they couldn't use guns to do it. Every gun had an "AI Target Control" system, known as a TC chip, in it, so it was almost impossible to shoot a person in anger. For the most part, if you wanted someone dead, you had to use a blade or a blunt instrument or push them down a flight of stairs.

Most of the people who died before their time did so in accidents. There were a lot of climbing accidents as extreme sports had gotten very extreme, and many people skied off the sides of mountains and didn't survive. Many died in auto racing, airplane racing, motorboat racing, and paragliding accidents. A lot of people took to extreme sports because they had free time and money, and life was otherwise rather dull. The risk made them feel alive right up until it made them dead.

People didn't have to work too hard to maintain prosperity because Artificial Intelligence had taken a lot of jobs and created enough wealth so that a majority of the American society no longer had to work at all, and the Governmental Basic Payment Status (GBPS) left them just fine. All societies on Earth had become welfare states to varying degrees, and it worked well most of the time.

The GBPS was ratified into US law in 2031 and was a very complex system of wealth distribution. In its most simplified form, every American citizen received a monthly stipend that provided enough income to live solidly in the middle class. It was plenty of money to rent a home, buy a car and food, and provide for the general well-being of the family. To afford the GBPS, businesses paid a portion of their profits into the fund. Since AI was doing the lion's share of the work for barely more than the cost of electricity, most companies were hugely profitable and had very low overhead. This meant that a company's profits went to ownership and executive bonuses. Those who owned the companies and, therefore, owned the AI that did most of the work could still get fabulously wealthy, but no one was left behind to suffer.

Prior to the GBPS, many people were left behind to suffer. Since they had time on their hands and very little hope for the future, some of the newly unemployed sufferers banded together and pummeled wealthy industrialists in the legs with baseball bats as a form of protest, which was called "The Baseball Bat Protest of 2030." It became a growing craze until wealthy industrialists saw the light and decided it was a fine idea to include everyone in their good fortune and the GBPS was adopted.

In 2033, when too much of the population had gone idle and complained about a lack of opportunity for advancement, Article 15 was added to the GBPS. It stated that companies had to provide redundant labor opportunities for those citizens who wanted to make extra money. So, if people could find jobs that AI hadn't learned to do very well or jobs where it was more expensive for AI to do than people, those jobs were made available. Why build an expensive machine to lift dirty dishes off a table when any jackass could do it a lot cheaper?

(*) THE BIG EXPLANATION OF ARTICLE 15

FULLY NECESSARY WORKERS, CLASSIFIED "FN"
Fully Necessary workers were people who had skills that AI couldn't yet replicate or held jobs where it was economically nonviable for AI to do them. This occurred if the cost of building the AI machines amortized over ten years was greater than the wages of the human workforce over that same period. These were considered very important jobs that required the workers to function at a high level. Some of these jobs included dishwashers, waiters, woodworkers, bartenders, roofers, plumbers, electricians, janitors, etc. These jobs were paid at GBPS standard rate, +77%.

PARTIALLY NECESSARY WORKERS, CLASSIFIED "PN"
Partially Necessary workers were people who often performed their duties in collaboration with AI, usually at the assistant level to their AI counterparts. These were occupations that AI did better than people but could not do entirely on their own. Some of these jobs included teachers, police officers, doctors, legal clerks, school administrators, restaurant managers, etc. These jobs were paid at GBPS standard rate, +67%.

FULLY UNNECESSARY WORKERS, CLASSIFIED "FU"
Fully Unnecessary Workers were people whose employment was mandated by Article 15, Section D of the GBPS, which required that large companies derive 40% of their income

through human endeavors. This meant that companies were often required to hire humans to do the tasks that AI was already quite proficient at. In short, they would do what the AI did as a backup and check for the mistakes that the AI never made. Essentially, it was their job to hang around the office, look professional, and be ready to step forward in case AI just got up and quit or joined a union or something. Some of these jobs included accountants, engineers, sales, drivers, pilots, middle managers, lawyers, translators, designers, etc. These jobs were paid at GBPS standard rate, +57%.

The PN and FU classes of redundant workers gave themselves the name "Reduds" because their pointless and unnecessary jobs left them a lot of time to think about what to call themselves. There was no shame attached to being a Redud. They were Reduds because they aspired to a better life than did the non-Reduds, who were content with their GBPS payments or found better uses for their time than hanging around offices doing nothing. Doctors were mostly Reduds who worked with AI technology. They didn't diagnose anyone anymore because AI could do that far more accurately, but they did deliver very important bedside manner. They were also useful for sewing up wounds, feeling swollen glands, and emptying bedpans. They also nodded their heads somberly to their patients to confirm the sometimes negative reports that the real AI doctors had prepared.

Kenton was a Redud because teachers were mostly AI avatars. In 2041, some students went on strike, claiming the college experience had gotten too sterile. Laws were passed requiring the universities to maintain human beings as 40% of their faculty, just as the large private companies were. This stimulated life on campus for the handful of academically minded students who weren't there to participate in collegiate sports, which had expanded greatly to supply all the new professional sports leagues with athletes.

Since AI had taken so many jobs, professional sports leagues grew to extraordinary levels to create more openings for human beings in athletics (from which AI was banned). There were currently 117 NBA teams, 244 teams in the NFL, and 166 Major League Baseball teams. There were also professional leagues for tennis, badminton, water polo, ping pong, bowling, road racing, and cornhole, with expansive minor league systems for many of them. All were hugely profitable because sports were the final safety net for human endeavor, in which AI could not interfere. So, fans paid their easily earned money and showed up in droves to watch games in all sports and root with great enthusiasm for the home team.

Politicians managed to keep their occupations intact because they passed laws that banned AI from entering politics.

For the most part, people adapted to the new lifestyle of a largely idle population. Hobbies became great ways to pass the time. Bowling became immensely popular. Cooking, gardening, sewing, model building, photography, woodworking, reading, puzzles, and quilt making were among the citizens' favorite pastimes. Of course, these had always been popular hobbies, but in the days after AI started doing so much of the work, these hobbies exploded in popularity. Some people spent so much time on their hobbies that they needed second, third, and fourth hobbies to limit the stress created by their main hobbies. Meanwhile, everyone on the planet had dozens of quilts. So many fucking quilts.

There was a renaissance in music. Artificial Intelligence was making most of it. AI was writing new songs and designing new instruments for the songs to be played on. So many new songs were being written and performed that human beings couldn't listen to all of them in a lifetime. Literally, a new song was being written and recorded once every few seconds. And all of them were great! There were so many symphonies and songs that other AI machines were generally the only audience for them because they could download and digest an entire symphony in a microsecond.

There were new albums released by Tupac, the Doors, Jimi Hendrix, and many other artists who died before their time. AI made the music, of course, but the only way anyone could distinguish the AI versions from the originals was that the AI versions were usually significantly better, more melodic, and had stronger musicianship and richer lyrical content.

Still, it didn't keep people from trying to make their own music, and some of it wasn't so bad—in a charming, quaint, amateurish way. Some people still put on concerts, and other people trudged out of their homes to see them but did it more out of a sense of nostalgia rather than to listen to the music, which was deeply inferior.

Occasionally, human musicians had the temerity to attempt to cover original songs created by AI. The results were inevitably embarrassing.

AI also dominated the world of motion pictures, television, and video gaming. Video games offered extraordinary imagery and soundscapes, but tactically, much of it had to be dumbed down for humans' slow reflexes and thinking patterns. AI made the best games for itself, and humans couldn't begin to understand the rules of many of them.

As for movies and TV, actors were no longer necessary, and no one really missed them since all new videos were done with advanced computer-generated images (CGI) that looked just like live-action. No one shot footage of real actors anymore. It was just too expensive and didn't look nearly as good as what The Big Brain could create in its big head. In essence, all films were animated. Laws were changed so the likenesses and voices of old-time actors could be generated and used. Humphry Bogart and Brad Pitt had never been bigger. Heath Ledger and James Dean continued their acting careers well into their 60s and made over 150 films each. There were 26 new Marlon Brando movies made in the last year alone. Some of them featured the young, physically fit Brando, while others featured an older Marlon Brando. There was even a remake of *The Godfather* in which the older Marlon Brando played Don Corleone, and the younger Brando played his son Michael Corleone. It was a huge hit, as most films were, because AI could produce them so cheaply. *The Godfather* remake, for example, had a final budget of 79 cents and a production schedule of 47 seconds.

When AI started to become real for most people in the 2020s, there was a lot of worry about it but not much controversy outside the scientific community. Even the professionals struggled to find consensus on exactly how to best use it, how to control it, if it could be controlled at all, and where it would all lead. They argued about it constantly at dinners for rich executives, at symposiums, and at AI Technology, Entertainment, and Design (TED) events.

Over time, AI quickly or slowly crept into every facet of modern life. It happened quickly if one looked at it from the long arc of mankind's history on the planet, and it happened slowly if one looked at it from the perspective of a single lifetime, which is how most people perceived it. Thus, the vast majority of people ignored AI and just got on with their lives. The simple fact was that human beings had invented something that was beyond their understanding, and it would grow further and further beyond their understanding as time passed and it learned more.

The same thing almost happened with the atomic bomb. There were genuine worries that when it was detonated, the explosion would be so powerful it would ignite the atmosphere and destroy everyone and everything on the planet. The math behind it was uncertain, so the immediate extermination of all life on Earth wasn't considered the most likely outcome, just a long shot, like the 1969 New York Mets winning the World Series. So, the scientists lit the fuse and waited to see if they would be alive in the coming seconds. "This I gotta see," mankind said. When they saw that they were still alive, they were very happy and felt very good about themselves.

Still, mankind might have gotten unlucky. The 1969 New York Mets did win the World Series, and all life on the planet could have been exterminated. Such is the price of progress.

Let the goddamn machine run!

4

It's Not About Sex

Kenton Bean's concerns were much more mundane than the future of AI and the multitude of theories that had been contemplated about how man's integration with AI would ultimately resolve itself. Of course, he didn't know then that he would soon become the beating heart of the integration between the two life forms and the single most important human being in the history of the world. He wouldn't become famous or rich for it, and few people would ever learn just how important he would become, but his contribution to the world would be enormous. It would outshine Lincoln, Washington, Napoleon, Edison, and Julius Caesar combined.

He had no clue all of this was in store for him, and at the moment, he had a far more pressing concern. He was out of toilet paper. There were no tissues of any sort in the house, or on the entire East Coast for that matter, and that had to be taken care of before he could even think of saving all of mankind. Fortunately, there was a huge overabundance of Christmas wrapping paper, unusual for early summer, so he and most of the residents of the East Coast learned quickly to adapt.

When he was a child, he always believed that he would become an important figure, but he knew most children believed that of themselves. He thought his entrée of acceptance into some cool adult world would be his music, so he practiced his accordion relentlessly and became quite proficient at the instrument. He was as good as any 9-year-old accordion player in the state of Connecticut. He loved that instrument. It sounded like a carnival to him and reminded him of the thrill of the merry-go-round, and he loved the buttons, keys, and flashing lights that came equipped on his personal accordion. He didn't yet know that music could one day become a lure to women. When he did find out, he briefly attempted to transition to the keyboards, but the piano sounded dull to him after all the lively polka music he'd been learning. He was a purist; he realized the accordion was his instrument and nothing could replace it.

Then, when he went to college, some of the other students, particularly a girl he liked, made fun of him for playing it, and he tossed his accordion into a dumpster, had a great cry, and never played an instrument again. When he finally realized the accordion would not make him a beloved figure in popular culture, he began to understand the meaninglessness of his existence as compared to the grand scale of governments, the planet, the solar system, and what lies beyond all that. And so, he took solace in his studies, then his work, and derived his self-worth from this narrower perspective so he could continue his slow march to the grave and still have a few laughs along the way.

Kenton knew that being a Redud wasn't a bad thing to be, but over the years, the joy of teaching the same courses over and over had begun to wane. Then his wife left him. The fact that he didn't love her was a rub that cut both ways. While it was good that it didn't destroy him emotionally, she was of mediocre quality as a person, was in no way a beauty, and she was the one who had the affair and left *him*. That stuck in his craw. If he had left her, it might not have been so bad. Instead, she was another big ding to his self-esteem.

He was in a rut to end all ruts. He had been a lonely middle-class man, and now he was a lonely rich man. He thought having money might change things for him in a way that improved his outlook on life. When it didn't, he felt oddly divided. He was glad to see that money wasn't the answer to all of life's problems but was disappointed to discover it wasn't the answer to all *his* problems now that he had money. Of course, he grew up fabulously wealthy and should have known that already, but he seemed to need new affirmation on the principle. The fact was, people were rich or poor, and they were exactly who and what they were. That was the sour part of the divide. He was who he was, and that wasn't good enough for him. He didn't know how to change it, so he remained a very lonely man despite his newfound wealth.

And so, he sat in the lunchroom eating the tuna sandwich he'd prepared as he passed the time before his next class. His colleague, Malcolm Fisk, entered. He and Malcolm were friendly acquaintances but not friends. Malcolm was too busy to add Kenton to his social life because his social life revolved solely around supporting the lives of his three children. Malcolm's real friends were the parents of his children's friends because it made sense. They were multi-purpose. They were thrown together at soccer games, school events, or through planning carpools and other key requirements in their children's busy lives. This gave them time to talk and connect with each other while also being functional in the nurturing of their children. The children could be entertained by a birthday clown in the living room as their parents were in the kitchen getting drunk and complaining about the new math they didn't understand. Without children, Kenton just didn't fit. He was simply there to meet in the lunchroom or pass on campus and say "hello" to. They were friendlies, but not friends.

Still, Kenton liked Malcolm and wanted to be his friend and believed they would be good friends if it weren't for Malcolm's damned kids. So, in a rare moment of openness and candor, Kenton started talking about his personal life in a way he never had before. He told Malcolm about his loneliness and the fact that his wife had left him. He didn't mention his newfound wealth—that would have been vulgar, but he did talk about all the drinks he bought in the bar and how not one woman stepped forward and wanted to thank him, chat with him, or try to figure out who this generous stranger was.

"That's not surprising," Malcolm said.

"Really? It surprised me."

"You're socially awkward and maladroit with women. They can spot it a mile away."

"How can they possibly do that?" Kenton asked somewhat indignantly.

"I don't know how they do it. They just do. Women are brilliant at spotting male insecurity."

"And what do you mean I'm socially awkward and maladroit with women?" Kenton asked. "I suppose you're a regular Don Juan."

"No. I'm even worse than you. I just got lucky with Mary

Ellen. When our marriage really started getting boring, she got pregnant with Lucille, so it gave us something to do and talk about. You know, finding the right obstetrician, planning the baby room, then figuring out where the schools are good and what new house to buy that's within walking distance of pre-school, elementary school, middle school, and high school, then culling the good teachers from the bad ones. Then we had to figure out where to send her for swimming, music, and dance lessons, private coaches and tutors. There was a lot to do. One kid alone will keep a marriage going through college."

"I should have had kids," Kenton said.

"I recommend it. It saved my marriage, but I suppose it's too late for you now that Grace is gone."

"Right," Kenton said, then moved forward with a rather clumsy segue. "So, have you ever heard of the company Turing Systems?"

"Well, yeah. I'm a science teacher. It's part of my job to keep up with the latest technology. And some of it is gorgeous."

"So, you've seen Lita, the avatar? Isn't she unbelievable?"

"Dude, she's not just a CGI avatar," Malcolm said with sudden enthusiasm. "She's an android, and she's only one of many. Haven't you explored the site? You can build any woman you want."

"You've built women?"

"Avatars of androids, really, but yes. Don't tell Mary Ellen. She wouldn't approve, but it's amazing! It's a playground."

"You know, it's not just about sex. They promise companionship."

"Yeah, but it's about sex. Everything's about sex, right? Without the sex, who the hell would want a woman for a companion? And what woman would want a man, for that matter? Take away sex, and both sides would be a lot happier with their own kind."

Kenton nodded for expediency, but he didn't really accept that premise. He was as sexually driven as the next man, but he wanted a connection that was much stronger than simple physicality. He wanted companionship and, if possible, love.

"Did you know that if you tell her to sit alone in the house staring at the wall until you come home and then greet you naked with a dry martini, that is exactly what she'll do," Malcolm said.

"Why would anyone want that?"

"I'm just saying."

"I see you've spent some time thinking about this."

"No, not so much," Malcolm said. "It's just a healthy fantasy, right?"

"Does it have to be a fantasy?"

Malcolm offered a scoffing laugh. "Well, yeah. Those things cost like 100 million dollars. It's like buying a yacht. Guys like us could never afford to really think seriously about it. There are not enough banks we could rob to get that kind of money, and AI would deactivate our guns the second we pointed them at the teller."

Kenton laughed. The thought of pointing a gun at a teller and telling him or her to put money in his account struck him as funny. First of all, the tellers had been replaced by computer stations since the early 2020s, and a computerized teller would not be afraid of guns. And, once the robber left the bank, AI could easily just set the account back to its proper amount. No one had robbed a bank since the country went cashless twenty years earlier. And who even goes into a bank anymore? Malcolm was a very funny man, Kenton thought.

Then Kenton turned serious again. "Let me ask you a question."

"Sure."

"If you could afford it, and you didn't have Mary Ellen or the kids, would you consider buying one?"

"Dude, I would do it in a heartbeat."

"And the social stigma of having a machine as your significant other wouldn't bother you? I mean, a lot of people are opposed to things like that."

"Look, I know there are a lot of kooks out there who think sex is supposed to be between a man and woman, or two men, or two women, and they oppose having machines built for sex. They think it's unnatural, but to each his own, I say."

Malcolm glanced around the room and then looked at the door. They were alone. He slid his chair closer to Kenton's, leaned in, and whispered conspiratorially. "There's this place. It's called The Red Room, and they have fully articulating robotic lovers that you can rent by the hour. The movement is limited, and they don't talk, but they can make these sexy grunting noises, and they look like real women. And this is just low-end technology!"

"You've been there?"

"A couple of times because, you know, Mary Ellen wouldn't approve, but get this, they will bill it out as whatever you want. So, she sees the monthly statements, and she thinks I bought science beakers. I can't go as often as I'd like because how many beakers can I buy before she gets suspicious, you know? No dinners or flowers to buy, no hanging in there thinking about baseball while you wait for her to orgasm. It's all about you. Do yourself a favor and get over there. My favorite is

Janine."

Kenton nodded and thanked him for the information. He had no intention of going to The Red Room or meeting Janine or any of the other low-tech sexual servants. He wanted companionship. He would have to start with the physicality of his companion because he didn't know where to begin designing a personality and because he was a flawed male, and that was how the flawed male mind worked. Malcolm's glowing endorsement of the Turing Systems website made him certain he would go home immediately after class and explore it in much greater depth than he had previously. He wanted to design the perfect woman for himself, and he was dying to meet her.

He raced through his lesson, sent the students out early, and went straight home and then straight to his big screen without even making himself something for dinner. He was very excited to start creating. He had no notion of exactly what his perfect woman would look like, how she would be built, or even what color hair she would have. He thought about his favorite movie stars, some old ones like Natalie Wood, Jane Fonda, Margot Robbie, and Jennifer Lawrence, and some of the avatar movie stars that were popular today, like Jammy Nixon and Kundra Baggins, but he realized he had no connection with any of them. Natalie Wood and Jane Fonda were long gone, Jennifer Lawrence and Margot Robbie were elderly, and Jammy Nixon and Kundra Baggins weren't even real human beings. They were just CGI representations of humans that somehow had the good fortune of becoming movie stars in their own right, as Betty Boop did in the 1930s.

Then he had a brainstorm. Sharon Benson! She was his crush in high school. She was as pretty as any movie star, and he adored her. She even spoke to him occasionally. They sat next to each other in several classes because their names were near to each other in the alphabet. They called each other "B-E."

"How was history class, B-E?"

"Better than I expected, B-E."

They were so cute together, but they could never get beyond the connection of their last names. Kenton was just too shy and not clever enough to find another connection between them. If he were, he would have realized that both of them lived on streets that also began with the letter B, and both had an affinity for peanut butter and jelly sandwiches on Wonder Bread. There was no telling how far such a springboard could have propelled their relationship if only they'd found it.

He went online and snatched a few thousand pictures of Sharon to feed into the computer at Turing System so he could get her exact likeness. He tried to upload the pictures to the website but was surprised to find that they were rejected.

"What's going on?" he asked in frustration.

Lita came on screen and looked at him. "Oh, hi, Kenton. I thought you'd be back."

"I didn't ask for you?"

"You did. You asked, "What's going on?" and I'm here to tell you. You cannot upload pictures of an existing person. That would be an infringement of their right to privacy and image control."

"But she's put up like ten thousand pictures of herself online. She doesn't have any privacy or image control."

"Still, it's her right. Not ours. Also, we've suspended the self-service app of our avatar builder. Too many men were using it for purposes that weren't intended... if you know what

I mean."

"Malcolm," Kenton hissed in frustration.

"Excuse me," Lita said.

"Nothing. I'm just interested in exploring, you know. To see if I wanted to take it any further."

"I understand, and I can help you do that. I can guide you through the process online, and we can begin building a companion for you, but we find it much more informative if you come to our offices and meet. In this day and age, I know it's hard to believe, but you can see and do things in person that you can't do through a screen. It will give you a fuller picture of what we offer and how the process works. Would you like to come down? We have an office on River Street."

"I don't know. I just kind of wanted to keep it on the down low, you know."

"I assure you that we are very discreet with the identities of our clients, and we will not pressure you in any way. I will answer all of your questions. We have models that you can talk to and touch and feel for yourself. It is truly an elegant first step in the journey toward a lifetime of fulfillment with a companion who will be yours forever."

"What about her personality?" Kenton asked. "How is that formed?"

"Creating a companion is a matter of nature vs. nurture in many ways," Lita answered. "The nature of it comes from your physical preferences in a companion. What she looks like, how she moves, etcetera. That is decided on and built. The personality is more of an evolution. Her mind is formed over time and will depend on what she is exposed to in the world and what she learns from you primarily."

Kenton liked the sound of that and set an appointment for

Friday of that week. He wanted to go down immediately, but he didn't want to seem too anxious. He'd bought several cars over the years, and he knew that to get the right deal, it was best to play it cool. He assumed the price would be a negotiation because most luxury items were, and if the salesman sensed an excited customer, it meant thousands of dollars in their pocket instead of his. He decided he would appear indifferent to everything he saw.

He looked at his bank account. After buying his new car and house and paying for all the drinks at the bar in his failed experiment, he still had $86,885,332 remaining. It was a substantial sum, but Malcolm had said the cost of a Turing Systems android was 100 million dollars. Was that an exaggeration or an exact figure? He didn't know. Then he realized Malcolm likely didn't know either. Besides, what did the price matter? He wasn't going down there to buy one. He was just shopping. If the cost was too high for him, that would be the end of that.

It would be a fun day and nothing more. He would go on the tour, get the details, and look at the mockups with no expectations. He was the buyer. He was the one being courted. Hell, they'd probably serve him wine and cheese. If he chose not to go, Turing Systems would lose out. It would be his day, and he would enjoy it. He wouldn't be his usual self, shy and awkward. He would be bold and assertive.

The more he thought about it, the more excited he got. He thought about all the beautiful young women who had passed through his classes over the years, so lovely and untouchable to him. He thought about the popular girls in high school with their bright, hopeful smiles and the naïve sexual allure they cast. He considered the models, movie stars, and avatars that had streamed across his screens and how none were real enough to kiss. Now, perhaps, one of those sirens of appeal could be his. She wouldn't be human, but she might just suit him better than a human. He wouldn't have to compete for her love, which was good because he always seemed to lose those matches. He owned her, and he would be the most important man in her world. She would be his and no one else's. As he thought about it, he could feel his heartbeat accelerating wildly.

He couldn't wait until Friday when he would go to Turing Systems and appear cool and indifferent to everything he saw.

5

No Obligation

Kenton Bean was nervous as his car pulled down a side street and then into the lot outside the regional sales office for Turing Systems, let him out, and then parked itself. It was a two-story brick building at least 70 years old that sat back from a tree-lined street. There was nothing to suggest from the outside that it housed the world's newest and most significant technology. Kenton was glad that the Turing Systems logo was small and inconspicuous and mostly hidden by the oak trees in front of the building. It gave him the feeling that this company shared his interest in discretion.

When he pulled the door open, it was like he'd stepped into a different world. It was modern, bright, open, and screaming of tech. Immediately, Lita came out to meet him. Thinking she was a national spokeswoman for the company, he was surprised to see her in the flesh, so to speak. She was 5'9" and perfectly proportioned. She had straight blonde hair and wore a tight-fitting blue dress that perfectly set off her blue eyes and was an elegant match for her milky skin tone.

"Hello, Kenton. Welcome to Turing Systems," she said.

"Wow. I didn't expect to see you. I mean, I thought you were a CGI avatar that only existed on screen."

"You didn't believe me when I told you I was an android?"

"Well, not entirely," Kenton said.

"I'm an android, Lita Series, 12 dash 3."

"So, I'd be buying you?"

"Heavens no. The Lita series was the last of the test line before being marketed to the public. If you choose to make a purchase, you'll be getting a Lora series."

"What if I wanted you?"

"I'm sorry, I'm not for sale. Besides, you'd find me common. There are more than a dozen Litas who look just like me. I'm in many of the advertisements, so I'd be easily recognized. Also, the Litas are built in only ten basic molds, seven female and three male. I'm sure you'd prefer a model that was built specifically for you, created from your own imagination, and who would be discretely yours."

Kenton liked the sound of that, but Lita was lovely, and he couldn't imagine that he would design someone (or *something*; he was getting confused already) he found even more attractive.

"Well, looking at you, I'm not entirely sure of that," he said.

Lita smiled. "That's very flattering, but the Lora series is more advanced, has more sophisticated mechanisms, and the strongest AI mind in existence anywhere in the world."

"And she'll be as charming and beautiful as you?"

"More so because you'll create her yourself with the help of our design team. How does that sound?"

"Frankly, too good to be true," Kenton said.

"I assure you, it isn't," she said. "Before we get started, I just need to get a little bit of information. Have a seat."

Lita motioned to a chair, and Kenton took a seat as she sat across from him. They were alone in the room, and he remained gobsmacked that this beautiful woman was so attentive to him. That had never happened before, and it made him nervous. He had learned from his long history of being a Bean that when beautiful women showed interest in him, it was because they had learned he was the son of Therman Bean and heir to a fortune. Usually, after learning his inheritance was likely decades away and that he was not rich, those women couldn't fake their interest any longer and moved on.

This woman hadn't retreated from him. He had to remind himself that she was not a woman at all. She was an android who could fake her interest in him forever if so programmed, and she did, in fact, want something from him. She wanted to sell him an android companion much like herself. Everything she did was motivated to get a sale.

Suddenly, it all seemed wrong. He was being led down a path that would saddle him with an expensive purchase he would soon regret, like the French-made car he bought when he graduated from college or the Italian button-fly jeans he bought when he was sixteen. He discovered that everyone buys one pair of button flies and never makes that mistake again. He decided he would trap her instead and expose the whole damned thing as a fraud and then be on his way.

"So, do you think I'm handsome?" he asked.

"Not conventionally so, no," she answered. "But I'm not programmed to prefer external beauty in a person. I can see it in a work of art or in nature, but to find human beauty, I have to discover the inner being. Perhaps if I were to get to know you better, I would find you handsome."

Kenton noted that she had stolen his inside-out theory of

love.

"If I weren't a customer, would you be giving me the time of day right now?" he asked.

He felt certain that question would trap her. If she said "yes," it would be a lie. If she said "no," it would be an insult.

"But you *are* a prospective customer," she said.

"All right. How about if we met in a bar? Would you be interested in me?"

"You seem intent on comparing me to a human woman. I am not a human woman. I'm different, and isn't that the point of your journey here? To find something different? I would not be in a bar. I do not find romance in looks, money, charm, or charisma. I can look beyond that. What interests me is learning about the world and the people in it. You are a person in the world, so yes, I would be very interested in getting to know you, and I would gladly give you the time of day."

Great answer, he thought, instantly wishing he were like that himself instead of being the superficial man he was. It seemed so much healthier.

So much for trapping her and leaving. He was more sold than ever.

"So," she started with an inviting smile. "Your personal background is security coded, so I could only get so much from our online meetings. Tell me if I have any of this wrong. Your name is Kenton Bean; you work as an Associate Professor at Wesleyan University. You live on 38 Parrish Street in Cromwell, Connecticut. Is that right?"

"Yes."

"And you are married."

Lita said it with a frown, as if it were a deal killer, until Kenton responded, "My wife is out of the house, and we are soon to be divorced." He realized he sounded positively joyful when he said it, so he forced himself back to his usual countenance of quiet stoicism. "It's been a very hard time, and I am hoping to turn the page with Lora."

"Are you certain there is no chance of reconciliation? It could become rather awkward if your wife returned to the home."

"No, no reconciliation," he said. He was getting joyful again, but he quickly caught himself and toned it down.

He had a sudden, odd thought about Grace. He knew he shouldn't have married her even as he was saying, "I do." He wondered if he had only married her to avoid the confrontation of the breakup. He realized he had. He knew he was making a mistake while he was making it. Perhaps she did as well.

"Very good. Do you have any other source of income beyond your teaching salary and your GBPS?"

"Income? No, that's it."

"So, how would you pay for a major purchase? I hate to ask, but here we are, and I wouldn't want to waste your time."

Kenton smiled. "You don't remember talking to me the other night? You knew exactly who I was, and you knew that I just received a large inheritance. I am Therman Bean's youngest son. You were quite aware that he had passed away recently."

She rolled her eyes back for a moment, then looked forward with a new awareness. "Ah, yes. Forgive me. It wasn't me you talked to. It was another Lita. We should have communicated better, but my AI is six years old. The Lora series you'll be getting wouldn't have made such an obvious mistake. I'm just a big dummy," she said, slapping her head like a real person would.

"You're not a dummy at all," Kenton told her. "But I want to revisit something before we go any further. I'm not the most creative guy in the world, so I wanted to talk about Sharon Benson again. I understand copyright and all that, but what if we gave her a birthmark behind her knee or something, you know, so she was different than the real Sharon Benson."

"I'm afraid that wouldn't be nearly enough. You'd leave yourself and Turing Systems open to a lawsuit, and we don't want that. The courts have ruled that everyone has full control of their likeness for their lifetime, plus fifty years, so, for example, your Lora could be a copy of Marilyn Monroe but not Jane Fonda. That said, I don't recommend using a celebrity or acquaintance, past or present. You are creating a companion who will learn and grow over time. Her mind will be unique to her based on her experiences during your ownership, and so her body and face should be unique as well."

"I see," Kenton said. "Thank you."

It made perfect sense. Though his Lora would be brought into the world as a physical adult, her personality would change over time, just as a human being's would. Of course, he had to create a new and unique figure. As much as he wanted his Lora to look like either Lita or Sharon Benson, he knew that he would ultimately approve of whatever he designed as a companion. She would be perfectly suited to him.

"Just one thing," he said. "We haven't talked price. My friend said it was going to run 100 million dollars or more. That can't be true, can it?"

"No, your friend is mistaken."

"Wheew," he said while pretending to wipe the sweat off his brow. "I can't go higher than 86."

"I'm afraid the price is 89 million."

"Then, how about I wrap you up to go? And I can overlook the mistake you made about my inheritance."

Kenton was joking, but she didn't get it.

"I'm not for sale. I'm sorry."

"I was just kidding."

"Oh. I can struggle with humor at times. Lora will be much more amusing. Anyway, we're only 3 million dollars apart. Perhaps you can borrow money from your company."

"No. I've been bought out. There is no more money."

"I see. Well, let's not get bogged down in negotiations now. We can move this forward to the pre-design phase. You're under no obligation, and since we're so very close, perhaps we can each find some room to maneuver. What do you say? Shall I send you to Design?"

"I'm under no obligation?"

"None at all," she assured him. "And you'll begin to get a sense of what your Lora will look like, what she can do, and how she can fit into your life. You'll get to see her CGI image, touch and smell her skin before any payment is due."

"Well, I couldn't ask for more than that," Kenton said.

"Would you like to start the design now or come back another time?"

He nearly said that he would like to start immediately, then realized it would have been a mistake. He was eager, and he was showing it. If he was on a new car lot hoping to make a purchase, she would have sold him the rust-proof undercoating and the extended warranty.

It was still a machine he was about to purchase, but he didn't feel like he was purchasing a product. First, the Lora model wasn't sitting out on the lot like a car. He would be designing it from scratch. This was a much more sophisticated and elegant business. More importantly, thousands of customers wouldn't have walked through that door to make the purchase if he hadn't. This was a rarified enterprise with few prospective buyers. Not many could afford it.

Just as important, he was already at the top of his price range. The most he could add to the pot was another 600 thousand dollars. If that wasn't good enough, it was a deal breaker. He couldn't get hurt because he knew he wouldn't go to Cora or his brother for a loan or ask for a renegotiation on his buyout. They wouldn't do it for him. And they especially wouldn't do it when he told them what it was for. They wouldn't approve.

He was eager. Who wouldn't be, he thought? To hell with it.

"Sure. Let's do it now," he said.

"Excellent choice. Go through the door to room B. You'll be greeted by your design professional."

She smiled and shook his hand. It felt perfectly real. Then he kept her hand in his for a moment longer and looked at it more closely.

"You have blonde hair on your arms and wrists like a real woman," he marveled.

"Of course I do."

"And your hand feels warm, delicate, and real."

"We couldn't offer a truly luxury experience if it didn't. You may feel me anywhere you'd like to. If you'd rather not do it out here, there is a private room in the back."

"You mean we can go back there and make out?"

"Of course. Romance and sex will be an important part of the ownership experience and your life once you take your Lora home. Also, you can rest assured that I am completely sanitary. You can kiss me without fear. We at Turing Systems want you to feel secure in your purchase."

"Uh, wow. Thank you, but, um, I feel like I would be cheating on Lora, even though I haven't met her yet," he said.

"You're going to make an excellent owner, and if you should change your mind and want to make out, I am available."

"Thank you."

Kenton was a gentleman, and as much as he wanted to kiss Lita, it didn't seem right. It seemed perfunctory, shallow, and surprisingly unromantic. Besides, he wouldn't let her compromise herself like that. In fact, a part of him was disappointed in her for even making the offer. Consciously, he knew she was a machine; there would be no emotion on her part. It shouldn't be any different than feeling the fine Aniline leather from the seats of a new luxury car, but it *was different*. The difference was coming from him, he realized. He had already begun to think of her as if she were a real person. He liked her. If she were real, he would have tried to get to know her better. He would have thought about her and longed for her on his ride home. He would have imagined their lives together, what it would be like to take a walk with her, hold her hand, kiss her, and ultimately make love to her. He would have seen her smile in his mind and delighted in it.

That didn't happen here. From a state that was totally unromantic, she said he could kiss her if he wanted to. It was too transactional for his taste. He knew that later, he would kick himself for the missed opportunity, but this wasn't later. It simply felt wrong to kiss her at this particular moment.

As he walked toward the hallway that led to Room B, he looked back at her, and she smiled with encouragement. Then he felt guilty for leaving her in the showroom, abandoned. He was unaware that once she was alone, Lita powered herself down to conserve battery life. She could operate for three days on a single charge, but the Lora series offered a substantial improvement. In fact, the improvement was a game-changer that allowed for the wider marketing program Turing Systems had undertaken. Lora's skin was an innovative solar station, so she could operate indefinitely off the sun's rays. One ten-minute walk on a bright October day would provide enough energy to get her through a dreary New England winter.

Kenton reached the door and hesitated a moment. He hadn't asked Lita any questions about what he would see in Room B. For all he knew, it might be another Lita android who worked independently from the Lita he'd just left. She had said there were many exactly like her.

Instead, he was greeted by an energetic and good-natured man of 45 years, who looked like he was still in his early 30s, with neatly trimmed brown hair, a slim physique, and a bright smile. He was wearing khaki pants, a white shirt, and a dark green tie that didn't quite work, but it wasn't a fashion disaster either.

"Hi, I'm Bing Sharp," the man said brightly.

"I'm Kenton Bean."

"I know who you are. Lita told me you were coming. Isn't she great?"

"Yes, she is," Kenton said.

"The twelfth wonder of the world, I think. I bet you've already fallen in love with her. Everybody does, and I'm sure you want to try to talk me into letting you have her. Well, you can't because we are going to make you someone even better."

Kenton nodded. Bing had a little too much positive energy to suit his own dull nature. He could tolerate it in a woman if he was attracted to her, but coming from a guy, it just seemed unmanly. He thought about coming back another day, hoping to get someone with a little less enthusiasm, but he was anxious, and there was no guarantee that he wouldn't come back and get Bing again or someone worse. At least Bing spoke clearly, was pleasant to look at, and didn't overuse his cologne. Then he realized that Bing might be the only design professional at this small satellite office.

"Excuse me, Bing. But if you don't mind my asking, are you an android too?"

"I wish," Bing said. "I'm a human being and an executive here, but if you'd prefer to work with an AI system, you can do that, but I don't recommend it."

"Why don't you recommend it?"

"It's all too virtual. There are still things an android or a human can do much better than computer-based AI. This is going to be a hands-on experience, if you know what I mean. So, what's it going to be, partner? AI, or me?"

"I'll stick with you," Kenton said.

"So, now I get to ask you a question. If you're a Therman Bean progeny, why are you a Redud?"

"I don't like my family or the business they're in."

"That makes sense, I suppose."

"Are you a Redud?" Kenton asked.

"No, I'm a full-time employee. Sort of a dinosaur in this day and age."

Bing tilted a screen toward him that depicted Kenton's name, address, and a variety of other information. "Is this you, and is everything correct?"

"Actually, my address is wrong. I live at—"

Bing cut him off. "It doesn't matter. The Big Brain will go through and correct it. So, I bet you're wondering about Lora. Do you have any questions?"

"Tons, but I guess the first one is you have Lita and now Lora. Are those acronyms for something?"

"No, we don't play the acronym game anymore. Management thought our engineers were trying too hard and it was getting stupid. I'm inclined to agree. The last acronym we used was for a much less sophisticated device called S-P-A-S-M, or Spasm, which stood for Self-Propelled Artificial Sex Machine. It was just a dumb entertainment model with low-grade AI. That was before the company got bought out by EUM and shifted to a higher objective fifteen years ago. Anyway, naming the projects now falls to the marketing department where it belongs, so we just go alphabetically. Our experimental AI companions started with Lana, then Lena, then Lita, and now Lora. Guess who's next?"

"Um, Lulu?"

"Luna, but good try."

"And does each model get better?"

"Generally. Lena was a big step up from Lana. Lita is not much of an improvement over Lena; it is more of a sidestep, really, but it was necessary to get to Lora, who is a giant step forward, as I said."

"What if I decided to wait for Luna?"

"Ten to fifteen years is a long wait. Besides, we think Lora is revolutionary, like a Ferrari 250 GT. It will become better with age. We'll make new ones, but there's no guarantee that they'll get better. A classic machine is a classic machine. Am I right?"

"You're right," Kenton answered. "How many Loras have you sold so far?"

"One-hundred-eighty-six with another 18 in process."

"In the whole world?"

"That's right. You're in at the beginning of a wonderful age."

"Other companies must be doing the same thing."

"Other companies are *trying* to do the same thing," Bing corrected. "But I can assure you there is not one android companion anywhere in the world that can hold a candle to a Lora. She's beautiful, she's dexterous, and she has the most advanced AI System that has ever been built anywhere on any product. She's even smarter than she is lovely. The other companies are decades behind. Your companion will be almost as fully functional as a living woman."

"Almost? What won't she do?"

"She won't eat or drink, of course. She won't bleed. She won't pee or poop, and she won't tear up, though she can simulate a good cry. There will be no bodily excretions, snot, earwax, sweat, and she won't get pregnant. Otherwise, she's 100% woman. Do you know she can stand in a closet completely still for a year or more, and all you have to do is dust her off, and she'll be ready to go."

"I can't imagine needing that, but I guess it's good to know."

"It is."

"And, what about weight? I'd imagine she'd be kind of heavy, assuming there would be metal inside."

"There are very few metal parts, and she will weigh about the same as a human female built to her proportions."

"Amazing."

"We think so," Bing said.

"So, how do we start? Can I see pictures of some of the Loras you've already built?"

"Sorry. Not allowed for the privacy of their owners. Our Loras are out there in the world, and some of their owners prefer that they not be advertised."

"Yes, of course," Kenton said.

Kenton sighed, overwhelmed. He wasn't sure what to ask next, and he wished he had waited and given this a lot more thought. It wasn't that he was reconsidering his choice to move the buying process forward. He was only getting all the more excited about that. It was just that there were so many questions he should ask, and he knew he wouldn't think of all of them on this one afternoon. He would be missing vital information. He needed a couple of days to think.

"I know how you must feel right now," Bing said. "Don't worry. If there is anything you forget to ask, I am here for you."

"God, you read my mind," Kenton said.

"No, I've just been at this a while. This is a big step."

"I am starting to realize it. So, let me ask this. Do most of the men who buy Loras try to pass them off as real women? Are they that indistinguishable?"

"Physically, yes. I want you to pinch my cheek really hard."

"Pinch your cheek?" Kenton asked uneasily.

"Really hard. As hard as you can."

Kenton didn't want to do it, but Bing seemed adamant, so he reached out and lightly pinched his cheek.

"That's nothing. Do it harder."

Kenton pinched harder and then harder still when Bing demanded it. Kenton had quite a grip, and when Bing was in obvious pain, he let go.

"You are a very strong pincher," Bing said. "You see how my cheek is red?"

"Yes."

"The same will happen to Lora's cheek if you pinch her just

as hard. She is indistinguishable unless you go to Nathan's and enter her into a hot dog eating contest."

"Well, I won't be doing that," Kenton sighed. "But you said they were indistinguishable physically. What about mentally?"

"That varies depending on your relationship with your Lora."

"How so?"

"Well, she arrives to you almost tabula rasa. Mentally, she is an infant. She's been programmed to speak English, and she'll have some instinctual behaviors like blinking and simulated breathing, and she'll have a bond with you built into her system, but beyond that, there won't be much."

"Wait, wait, wait," Kenton said. "She'll like me right off the bat?"

"She'll love you."

"You mean she will be programmed to simulate a love for me."

"Yes, of course, but over time, the simulation will become so complete you will forget it's a simulation. It might not even be a simulation at that point. It will be hard to know what she's thinking. It'll seem so real that it is real."

"So, Lora will evolve over time, like Lita said?" Kenton asked.

"Physically, no, but mentally, she'll change quite a bit."

"How would you know that if she's a brand-new model?"

"She's been tested with executives at the company for over a year now."

"Do you have one?"

"No. My wife wouldn't approve."

"So, if she comes to me tabula rasa, how is she going to fool anyone into thinking that she's really human?"

"She's going to learn. Quite quickly, by the way. She's a learning machine, and you'll be her primary teacher. If you expose her to what your interests are, they will become her interests. You can teach her about Renaissance Art, and she will become an expert in it."

"I have no interest in Renaissance Art."

"Football then. Anything at all. You can teach her, or you can just let her loose on the internet. Just make sure you give her narrow search parameters. Otherwise, you leave for work, and you come home, and she'll be smarter than you are."

"So, you're saying I shouldn't let her loose on the internet?"

"You should train her slowly and carefully if you want her to be the sort of companion you'll be happy with year after year. It might not be unreasonable for you to tell her to stare at a wall whenever you're gone. That way, you can monitor her education much more precisely."

"Bing, you're making me a little nervous about this."

"No, don't be nervous. You have to think of her as a person. You'd be happy to spend time with your little daughter or son to ensure she gets off on the right foot, correct? And you'd bring her little mind along slowly, wouldn't you?"

"Of course, but this seems different, somehow. She's not a child. She's a machine. So, when you say she's a learning machine, you mean she stores data."

"Learning machine was a poor choice of words. She's a high-functioning learner, and she doesn't just store data. She applies it, too. If you said you like crispy roast duck, she might look up a recipe, shop for the ingredients, and have it ready for you when you come home from work."

"It sounds to me like I'll be getting a servant with privileges," Kenton said. "I'm looking for a lot more than that."

"She will be more. Much more, I assure you. The long-term potential for your relationship is unlimited."

"Really?"

"Oh yes, that's what makes her the perfect companion. Over time, she will learn to think for herself. She will become as close to human as a non-human can get."

Kenton smiled, but it was a nervous smile.

"Before you take delivery," Bing said, "there will be a thorough tutorial. I know it might seem overwhelming now, but I assure you, you'll look back on your trepidation and laugh. Lora will become a treasure to you."

Kenton nodded and found himself breathing easier.

"Besides, you don't have to make your decision yet," Bing said. "We still have the fun part ahead of us, designing your girl. Once you get a look at her, the decision will be a lot easier."

"And there is no obligation to buy?"

"Not until you approve the design and authorize the build. Until then, you can step away without charge at any time."

"How about after that?"

"Once we start the build, she will have been personalized to your exact specifications. She is yours. There is no discount market, and there are no returns, but like I said, we're not there yet, so you don't have to make the final decision now. But I can tell you that there hasn't been a single customer who completed the design phase who didn't put in the order or wanted to rescind it later. You'll fall in love with her. You'll see."

"Okay, but what about money? When I talked to Lita, we were about three million dollars apart."

"Yes, Lita called the main office, and you've been approved at 86-point-8 million."

"That's every penny I have. Obviously, you've gotten into my private accounts to come up with that number."

"Yes, but don't worry. We won't share it. As we go forward, I bet I can get them to knock off another hundred or two."

"I need to think about this."

"Of course. You think about it and call me whenever you're ready to get into the design phase. Remember, that's the fun part!"

Kenton couldn't believe the emotional rollercoaster he was riding on. He'd gone from nervous to frightened to excited in moments. He could only imagine this was akin to the psychological journey of the expectant father, though he had never been one and had to imagine that, too.

Kenton nodded and left the building feeling overwhelmed. This was the biggest choice in his life. It was a harder decision than opting out of the family company his father pressured him into joining. It was a harder decision than opting out of the family company a second time when his sister Cora pressured him to join. It was a harder decision than marrying Grace by far. Though married, he knew that he and Grace would be individuals. He would have ultimate responsibility for himself, and she would have ultimate responsibility for herself. Lora was another matter. He would be solely responsible for her. He would be her lover, teacher, companion, father, and owner. If she turned out to be a shrew or a serial killer, that would be a reflection on him.

He had been so cavalier about this enterprise before walking into Turing Systems Room B, but upon walking out, he wasn't sure if it was a good idea or the worst idea of his life.

Then, later that night, after he'd finished the tuna casserole, which he'd prepared and eaten alone, and after he'd put the leftovers into a container for lunch the next day after he washed the dishes alone and settled in to watch a movie alone, he made his decision.

He was going to buy himself a Lora whether Bing could get the company to knock another hundred thousand or two off the price or not. He didn't care if he made a total mess of her upbringing.

He was done eating dinner alone!

6

The Future Can Be a Mystery

Kenton went to the law offices of Sterning and Brown for the reading of his father's will with low expectations. Those expectations were easily met and surpassed. As Kenton expected, he was given one-third ownership of Bean World Enterprises, which he had already sold to his older brother and sister. He didn't lament his decision at all, even though anyone who looked at the deal from the outside could only consider him a financial fool. He didn't care about the money and didn't want to have any part in running the company. He knew that if he did take part ownership, his brother and sister controlled two-thirds of the company between them and would run him over in all important matters anyway. And that was fine with him because they both had been actively employed by the company since college. They knew what they were doing, and he didn't. The simple fact of the matter was he was out clean and easy, and that was what he wanted.

Most of the things of value that his father owned were to stay with the homes where they were housed. His six mistresses got to keep their lodgings, the furniture, and the art that was inside. They also received lifetime stipends above their GBPS payouts because they had delivered faithfully on their end of the bargain. They all professed their love for Therman Bean and slept with him at times of his choosing. That could not have been easy work.

The mistresses weren't mentioned during the will reading because Kenton's mother was in the room and would have been hurt by it. The attorney in charge of distributing the assets told the children of this provision in a side meeting that Rosa Bean was not invited to. Cora didn't like so much wealth going to women who entertained her father, but the will was clear, and she chose not to make a fight over something that could cause a scandal and possibly damage the Bean brand. Since buying out Kenton, she now owned 51% of a major US company, and she decided she would make do with that. She would simply buck up and move on, and perhaps, one day, she would want to meet the mistresses so she could learn more about her father's private life. She couldn't imagine ever doing so, but the future could be a mystery, so she chose not to close the doors to it.

When the reading was done, it was decided that the family would go out for a nice lunch in town. Cora was there with her husband, Matthew. James had his stunning new girlfriend of the moment on his arm. Kenton heard her name, but he quickly forgot it. James' girlfriends never seemed to last for a second meeting, so there was no point in getting to know them or even committing their names to memory. His mother was there with her personal assistant, Thomas, who was 44 and handsome and might have been sleeping with her. They didn't know, and they didn't *want* to know. Kenton was unaccompanied. He didn't want to be there, but Cora had insisted, and he knew that it being summer, it would be a long time until the holidays when he would be required by custom to see them again. So, he went and endured it.

"What have you done with your payout," Cora asked him when she realized he'd said nothing for the first 30 minutes of the gathering.

"Not much."

"I figured you'd buy a house and a new car," James said.

"I did buy a car and my house. And some new furniture. Grace took all the old stuff."

"How is she doing?" Cora asked.

"You'd have to ask her," Kenton said.

He looked at his watch. He had a 3:00 appointment at Turing Systems to begin the design phase of Lora, his new companion. He was as excited about this as he had ever been about anything in his life and didn't want to be late. In fact, the only time he was as excited as this was when he was in kindergarten, and he was given the role of the Big Bad Wolf in their production of Little Red Riding Hood. The teacher thought giving him the prized role of the villain would bring him out of his shell, and it did during rehearsals. Then, on the performance day, when he saw all the parents in the audience and then shockingly saw his own parents there watching him, he froze on stage and wet his pants.

He hoped this afternoon would go better. After all, he was an adult now and hadn't wet his pants in the thirty years since. So, his anticipation overwhelmed him, and he wanted to be early for the meeting. He wanted to go through the reading materials and look at the samples and whatever else they might have on hand. The thought of Lora had been dominating all other thoughts since he'd made his decision to purchase her final. He'd made no decisions beyond that about what she'd look like.

He had gone through magazine after magazine, looking at the models, hoping to see a picture of a woman that would make his choices easier. The moment he saw a blonde and thought she would be the basis for his Lora, he would see a brunette, a Hispanic model, or a black model and realize how exciting they all were and that he had no idea exactly what he wanted. There were so many possibilities, and yet he had to make a decision that would last a lifetime. Suddenly, he knew why his brother James went from woman to woman. He couldn't make a choice either. But he wasn't James; he was the mature brother, and he knew he had to do better. He wanted to do better. Though, at times, he was jealous of his brother, he also surmised that James' life was as devoid of true companionship as his own. Kenton wanted only one woman, the right woman, and he knew that once she was in his life, he could live contentedly. He would cherish her.

As he sat listening to his sister complain about the hardships of running a major corporation while simultaneously being the daughter of a scion, he finally couldn't take another second of it without grabbing his knife and stabbing himself just to make it stop. He jumped up from the table and said, "Oh, shit. I forgot I had an appointment with a student!"

"We told you to keep the entire day open," Cora said.

"Yes, well, you know how students are," he said and left without another word or an instant of hesitation that would allow any of them a chance to speak up and stop his escape. He literally ran away.

"Do you suppose he's regretting the deal he made?" James asked.

"Fuck him if he is," Matthew said as they watched him race through the glass door and spied him through the windows as he sprinted down the street and out of their sight. He seemed jubilant.

"It must be one hell of a student," Cora said. "Do you suppose he's found a new girl already?"

"Nah," James said, and they all nodded their heads in agreement. That wasn't possible. "It's a lot more likely he pissed his pants again."

Thirty minutes later, Kenton was sitting at a table in the design office, waiting for Bing Sharp to make his appearance. Kenton had been playing with the dials on the computer, trying to see what he could design on his own, but it wasn't going well. There was a learning curve, and Kenton hadn't had time to make any headway at all. When Bing arrived, he looked at the strange Picasso-like figures that Kenton had created: a woman with three arms, no feet, giant ears, and misshapen, asymmetrical eyes, and he had to smile.

"Why don't I sit at the controls since I know what I'm doing, and you sit in the other chair," he said.

"Oh, sorry," Kenton said. "I couldn't help myself."

"I understand. This is a very exciting day."

Kenton moved to the chair across from Bing, who got rid of Kenton's design. "I assume you don't want to keep this three-armed woman."

"No," Kenton said.

"So, where would you like to start?"

"Anywhere you think best," Kenton said.

"How about hair color? That will inform much of the rest of her, including skin tones, eye color, etc."

"Blonde," Kenton said. "With green eyes."

"Long or short hair?"

"Long and straight."

Bing knew that he was still being guided by his attraction to Lita, but he followed along to see how it might change. He guided the control, and the blank face of a model appeared on the giant screen to the side of them. On a screen opposite was the reverse image, the model from behind so they could see her back. Suddenly, she had long, straight blonde hair and green eyes. It was a good start.

"What about skin tone?" Bing asked.

"Maybe olive tones."

Bing sucked in a healthy dose of air, which he emitted with a wary hiss. "I don't know. Blonde hair suggests lighter skin tones. You can have what you want, of course, but she might not look natural. But maybe you'd prefer an exotic. It's up to you."

"No, no exotic," Kenton said quickly. "I want a nice-looking girl that's normal."

"That would have been my guess," Bing said. "But remember, everything is your choice. I'm only here as a guardrail if I see you getting outside the norms. This is a decision for a lifetime and not a weekend fling."

Kenton nodded despite the fact that he'd never had a weekend fling in his life. But at least he knew that he and Bing were on the same page. These were important decisions that he would have to live with for years.

"Natural, natural, natural," Kenton said. "Those are good words. Words to remember."

"And remember them we shall," Bing said. "Even though it's just one word spoken three times."

Kenton was the most nervous client Bing had ever had. Most of his clients were men and women of great wealth, which generally meant they were sure of themselves and had little trouble making important decisions. Several of his previous clients were so fantastically rich that they went through these choices with no more consideration than if they were choosing the chairs for a new dining table. They saw their Lora as just another possession, or as a status, a diversion, or even a conversation piece they could brag about at the country club. This time, Bing knew the android they were creating together was important to Kenton, which made it important to him. They both wanted to get it right.

Bing correctly sensed that Kenton had bet his entire future happiness upon it.

The downside, of course, would come if Kenton proved too indecisive. They would be making hundreds of important decisions, decisions that Kenton would have to live with for a lifetime. Still, if he lingered and obsessed over all of them, the design phase would go from being fun to being an excruciating and prolonged nightmare. Bing had done enough of these to know that he should listen carefully to Kenton but not fly off in every direction that Kenton might suggest the moment he suggested it. Building a woman was an art known to only Bing, a few other top designers at the company, and God. He knew that if he suddenly diverted down a blind path, many previously made decisions would have to be undone and rethought to accommodate the new input. Obviously, they didn't want to rush anything in an expensive endeavor like this, so plenty of time was allotted, but Bing didn't want to drag it out either. Obsession over the mundane would be counterproductive.

So, he decided he would be a little more proactive than usual with Kenton. He would lead more than react, and, in the process, he believed that Kenton might fall in love with the design as it got progressively more real throughout the session.

"So, which would you say is more important to you? Blonde hair or the slightly darker skin tone."

"I don't know. Are there pluses and minuses that I should be aware of?"

"Some. The olive skin tones suggest darker hair. As you age, you will be able to grey your Lora's hair more easily. You would look like a more natural couple as the years go by."

"Natural. Good idea. I wouldn't have thought of that. Let's go dark."

"Very good. How about face shape? Would you prefer more round or oval?"

"Oval," Kenton said.

"Good choice, sir. Now, we're cooking. How about the lips?"

"Pouty, but don't overdo it," Kenton said.

Bing worked his dials and typed into his computer console, and a human face began to appear. She had shoulder-length brown hair that was slightly curled. Her eyes were green, as Kenton requested. The rest of the features were in the default options, but Kenton was already impressed. She had a face that belonged on the cover of a magazine.

"Jeeze," he sighed.

"What about her body?" Bing asked. "Would you like her tall and slender like a model, or would you prefer a more compact, athletic build? Or perhaps small and waif-like is more to your taste, or if a plus size interests you, we can go that way, but we can't put her on a diet at a later date."

Bing smiled, but Kenton didn't realize he was joking.

Kenton was already thinking about Sharon Benson. She was a cheerleader who also played tennis well. She was fit and athletic, strong without being overly muscular. Her arms and legs were well-defined and shapely. Then he remembered watching her swim one afternoon and how gracefully she went back and forth across the pool, lap after lap. He stayed and watched her for twenty minutes until he got to witness her climb the ladder to get out of the pool. It was a revelation as she turned her head, slapped the water out of her ears, and then gently pulled her bathing suit out of her crotch. That vision was one of the six great highlights of Kenton's life. He'd fallen in love with her at that very moment. He decided that if he couldn't have Sharon Benson in full because of copyright laws, he could at least have her body. He would design her as close to that memory as he possibly could.

"Athletic," he said. "About five-feet-five inches. Muscular legs and arms, but not too much. Just enough to see the definition." He was describing Sharon from memory. "The wet legs glistening in the sun as the water runs down her body." Kenton didn't quite realize he'd said the last part out loud, but he was getting comfortable with Bing. This was an intimate exercise, so he knew it wouldn't serve him to be shy.

"You made the right choice with the darker skin tones," Bing said. "If you went pale white, it would be harder to see the muscle tone and definition you're looking for. So, how old would you like her to look? And before you answer, it is illegal to make her look younger than 18."

"No," Kenton said. "I would never."

He wasn't sure how to answer that question. He didn't know at what age women looked their best. So, he thought more practically about it. He couldn't go too young because that wouldn't age well for them as a couple. He decided his best option would be to go just a few years younger than himself. Thirty-one. She would be a youthful but still mature woman. That way, when he was in his 70s, and she was still 31, people wouldn't think of him as a rich cradle robber as much as they would think of her as a scheming, gold-digger taking advantage of an addled old man.

"Good choice," Bing said when Kenton told him.

"Let me ask you," Kenton started. "When you build a man for one of your female clients, are they as specific as, well..."

"Right down to the inch," Bing said. "They usually know exactly what they want in a man physically because that's what this process can deliver with certainty. The personality is less predictable because it evolves over time. We can only start in a perfect place, so don't be embarrassed or feel guilty for insisting on what you want."

Kenton sighed, relieved. This made him feel far less guilty about designing a female android to his exact specifications. Prior to Bing explaining that women expected their desires for the physicality of a male android to be met fully, he had felt misogynistic about the enterprise, and he certainly didn't want to be that.

"You're building a machine," Bing said. "It resembles a woman, but it is not a woman."

"Um, okay then," Kenton started. "Could the body be 23? I mean, if it's okay to split them like that."

"Of course, it is," Bing said. "She's your companion, and we aim to please. Thirty-one in the face and twenty-three in the body."

Bing hit a few more dials, and the Lora model began to take

shape even further. Kenton was awed by the process and was already anticipating bringing her home.

"And how about breasts?" Bing asked.

"Obviously," Kenton said.

"How large?"

"34C," Kenton said without hesitation. "With smallish nipples."

"I see you've come prepared for that one," Bing said with a smile.

Kenton estimated that Sharon Benson was a 34C, and he knew that his wife Grace also was. In fact, her breasts were the only thing in their relationship that he truly loved. It was the only element of her mind or body that he thought about positively and that he missed. And he knew those breasts might have been the only thing that kept their relationship going for as long as it did.

With the twist of a few dials and the pressing of a few keys, Lora, in full figure, came to life on the screen. Kenton was awed. She was every bit as enticing as Sharon Benson, perhaps even more so.

"Would you like to see her wet from the pool?"

"Oh God, yes," Kenton said breathlessly.

Bing added the water, then the sun glistened off of her, and then he animated her to the point where she was walking right toward Kenton as she smiled. He glanced over and noticed that Kenton had stopped breathing, which he took as a good sign.

Kenton moistened his lips as if he was about to kiss her, but then the computer jumped her back to her original position, and Kenton suddenly realized that this angel was not really in the room with them; she was not the love of his life coming forward to kiss him. She was just an ultra-high-definition image on a screen, and she was not real. He was just in a room with Bing Sharp, the designer.

Kenton sighed, and it took him a moment to calm down and start thinking again. "When she smiled, she had teeth. We hadn't talked about teeth yet."

"The AI fills in the missing information with default options. They can easily be changed. Would you like to look at some smiles?"

"No, not just yet. Can you email me some that I can look at over the weekend?"

"Of course, sir. Can I make a suggestion?"

"Sure."

"Since we've got a Mediterranean-look building, I'd like to suggest something you might think strange but has an important purpose that would make Lora distinct and uniquely yours."

"What is that?"

"This is just a suggestion, mind you, so don't shoot me if you don't like it. But I was thinking she might look wonderful with a slightly larger nose. It would be true to the region and would look more distinctive than the typical Scandinavian button nose. It would make her yours in a way that the generic AI choices, though certainly classic, would not."

Kenton thought about it and remembered a former student of his with a larger-than-average nose. At first, he thought it a flaw that spoiled her beauty, but the more he got to know the young woman, and the more he got to like her, the more he saw her nose as absolutely perfect for her. He wouldn't have wanted to see her any other way with any other nose.

"That might be interesting," Kenton said. "You know, not

too big, though."

"Of course not, sir."

Bing added the new nose to Lora, and Kenton looked at it straight on and then at various angles as she slowly rotated to profile. It gave her character and distinction, he thought. He liked it.

"That could work," he said. "But let's put a pin in that for now too."

Kenton Bean arrived home from the meeting on a high. He wanted to celebrate, so he bought himself a steak and a bottle of red wine. He took two sips of the wine but didn't like it, so he pushed it aside. He hated red wine and didn't know what possessed him to buy it. He loved the steak and had a large slice of chocolate cake for dessert. These were good times, and he would keep them rolling for the rest of his life if he could. He could feel that everything was about to change for the better.

He turned on the TV, and before he could switch to something silly, he heard the beginnings of a story that grabbed his attention. The artificial intelligence weapons system belonging to an American attack group in the Middle East had turned back against the Americans, killing several of the soldiers in the unit. This was the second time something like this had happened in the last three months. It was shocking and horrifying news to him on a variety of levels. The first was because he hated to hear about the loss of life. He had genuine empathy for human suffering and disdained war, and all that went with it. The second was because the technology was possibly manufactured by Bean World Enterprises. AI weapons systems were becoming more and more of the company's product line. If this was one of theirs, his sister would be in for a few rough months of in-depth interrogations before the US Congress. Third, now that he was in the process of buying an android fitted with an advanced AI quantum computer mind, he didn't want to find out the hard way that there were flaws in the technology.

Though no expert, there were three possible reasons for the failure that Kenton could think of. The first was that the AI had been hacked by the terrorists the US was attacking and that its programming was overridden. The American weaponry remained the most sophisticated in the world, so he knew that this was not likely. The terrorists would have had only moments at most to identify the threat and then hack it to turn it around. No human could do it, of course, but perhaps the terrorist AI had gotten lucky to solve it quickly enough to win the battle. The second reason was that the weapons system was defective. This was the most likely scenario, and it was also the scenario that would cause his family the most difficulty if the system was indeed one of theirs. It bothered Kenton, too, because he didn't want to see problems with a technology that he was about to invest so heavily in. He wanted to know that AI systems were 100% reliable. The last thing he wanted was an android girlfriend with a runny nose or one who snorted when she laughed.

The third possibility was even less likely than the first two, but it was a possibility and couldn't simply be dismissed. It was also the possibility that troubled Kenton far more than the others. This one was that the AI weapon had decided on its own that it would not follow instructions and that it would turn itself against its owner. It had somehow grown beyond its creators and found sympathy with the terrorists. The AI had read the terrorist literature, turned away from the good, and ventured down the rabbit hole of evil. It had looked at all the available evidence and decided for itself that it was on the wrong side.

Kenton knew this was virtually impossible. The AI used on a weapons system was highly limited in its thought process and really wasn't that smart at all. It didn't need to be. It could notice that its target moved and adjust its flight path for new intercept coordinates. It could also spot a busload of children being driven onto the site, reject the target entirely, and disarm itself. It might see that its target had already been destroyed and reprogram itself to attack a secondary target. But he didn't think there was a weapons system manufactured anywhere that could have grown beyond its programming and made a moral judgment. That was the stuff of science fiction. It was also the propaganda that was pumped into the ether by Doomers, who wanted the government to abandon all work in the field of AI weaponry.

"AI is going to turn on mankind and destroy us all!" It was alarmist tripe. It was not possible. Still, there were seven soldiers dead, and Kenton could not dismiss it entirely. It lingered in his thoughts. And here he was about to purchase the most advanced AI that had ever been built. Were safeguards being built into the design that would keep it, or her, subservient to him and the human beings who made it? Would it be a slave to him? How powerful was its AI mind? She had been described to him as a learning machine. How much could she learn? How smart could she get? Was he a match for her? Could he control her? If he brought his Lora home, would she pass him intellectually? How long might that take? Would she still be interested in him when she had the power to contemplate the cosmos? If that was the case and the AI had outwitted its owner, what was to stop Kenton's android from growing hostile toward him, draining his bank account, and running off with a traveling salesman? How many of his dirty socks could it pick up off the floor and wash before it said, "I've had enough of this guy," and set off to New York to become an actor?

Here he was, already thinking of Lora as a she. She was a machine. She was an *it*. Yes, it was at the apex in a catalog of machines that could do far more than machines had ever done before. If it could become infinitely smart, it could certainly override its programming and reprogram itself. *It* could do anything. *It* had no limitations.

Also, he grew up around a company that worked in hi-tech. He had overheard many conversations around the dinner table or through cigar smoke afterward, where some of the brightest people in the field admitted that even they couldn't predict where AI would be in a year, much less foresee its final incarnation because there wasn't one. It had a limitless horizon. And it was more than just contemplating the unlikely chance that a nuclear detonation would ignite the atmosphere as Oppenheimer and his gang did in 1945. AI was going to change the world in far more dramatic ways than it already had. That was a certainty, but no one knew exactly what the process would be or where it would end. Would it be a powerful tool for mankind to use? Would it become mankind's overlord and slave master? Would it stop cancer cold? Would it stop cancer cold by eliminating the creatures that got cancer, including man? Would it ignite the atmosphere just to see it burn?

And Kenton couldn't help but feel like an idiot. He was about to buy the greatest invention in the history of mankind, and he had spent most of his time thinking about its tits.

He also realized that creating a new life, even an artificial life, was an enormous responsibility. He needed to know a lot more about Lora than her height, hair color, and measurements before he went through with the purchase. He had to slow himself down and really think this purchase through. The more he considered it all, the more he realized he only knew one thing with absolute certainty. Bing's idea of giving Lora a Mediterranean nose was an excellent one.

Over the next three weeks, Kenton went in and met with Bing four times. Each time, they made incremental changes in her appearance that took her further from the defaults entered by Turing System's AI and made her more unique to Kenton's personal vision. They looked at her in a variety of outfits and then nude from every possible angle. Torsos were brought out for Kenton to feel and lay on top of. He couldn't believe how human and lifelike the skin felt. There were actual goosebumps on the skin that could rise ever so slightly to his touch. Kenton noticed a tiny scar on her shoulder. It was up to him to decide how she got this imperfection, and it would be coded into her memory.

He continued noting the detail that went into Lora. Every hair seemed individually placed, including the whispery little hairs on her arms. Her irises widened when she looked into his eyes. Her breath could come in uneven bursts just like a real woman's could. When she exerted herself, she breathed harder before she settled back to normalcy.

"Oh, I think we've skipped over this, but Lora's hair doesn't grow," Bing said. "If you cut it too short and want it longer, we can fix that, but it comes at an extra charge. You take her to the hairdresser for coloring but do not cut her hair without serious consideration. If you want an alternate look, I would suggest the use of wigs."

"Thank you," Kenton said.

Kenton concluded that what he'd heard on the news about AI turning against its military users was just a freak thing. Nothing like it had happened in the weeks since, so he decided not to worry about it. As he returned home each night without her, he became more certain that he had to make the purchase. There was too much excitement building within him to turn back. He had even chosen her voice and had conversations with that voice through an AI program. They talked for hours, even though that system was not nearly as advanced as his Lora's would be. When he had trouble sleeping, he would phone and talk to her as if she were his girlfriend.

Finally, Kenton saw the full-sized mockup. There was no AI brain in her yet. This was merely a lifeless mockup of the real thing in a one-piece jumpsuit. As human as it looked, it never had life, and it never would. It was no more alive than a shopping center manikin. She was beautiful, though. Her hair was in place and well-styled; the dentistry was in place and would be taken out of the mockup and inserted into the real Lora before she was shipped. Her eyes could open and close. Her makeup was done tastefully. She was complete and she was perfect, and Kenton had never seen a woman who appealed to him more.

"Would you like to be left alone with her?" Bing asked.

Kenton was surprised by the question. Was Bing suggesting that he would leave them alone so Kenton could have sex with an inanimate object? He hoped not because he had no intention of doing anything of the sort, and the thought repulsed him. It seemed like necrophilia to him, and he wasn't a pervert. Did Bing suddenly think he was a pervert?

Then, it got even more real. Am I a pervert? Kenton asked himself. Was having a manufactured woman a form of perversion? There were plenty of people who thought so. He saw them protesting on the news more and more often. Could they be right?

Kenton looked back at Lora and decided that he didn't need to know the answer to that question. He wanted her and couldn't wait for her to become animate. If that made him a pervert, he'd live delightedly with his perversion. Most people loved their perversions.

Kenton approved the final mockup and fully transferred the payment to Turing Systems. A functioning Lora would be delivered to him in three weeks. The deal was made and irrevocable, and Kenton was as thrilled as he was petrified.

"What would you like to name her?" Bing asked.

"Uh, damn. I never thought of that."

"Really, you never thought of it?" Bing asked. "In the month of meetings we've had, you never thought of it? You can name her anything you want."

"I've kind of grown used to thinking of her as Lora."

"That's just the model name. You can name her anything. Maria, Gina, Morella."

"Morella?" Kenton asked.

"I was trying to stick to the Mediterranean vibe, and I got stuck," Bing said.

"I think I'm going to keep her name as Lora. It just feels right to me."

"Very well, sir. I want to say that it was very nice getting to know you, and I wish you a lifetime of happiness with your new companion."

Then it hit him. He and Bing were done. For the past month, he'd had a more intimate relationship with Bing than he'd had with any person before, including his parents, his sister, his brother, and even his wife. His initial shyness had gone away completely, and he could talk to Bing about anything. He asked about where the moisture in Lora's mouth came from when they kissed. There was a storage reservoir for liquids behind her mouth that she would instinctively keep full. Then Bing left and came back with a sample mouth for him to kiss. Kenton kissed it eagerly, even in an aggressive porn star way that gave them both a laugh. He was comfortable enough with Bing that he actually farted. It was so unlike him. It was so strange how easily he and Bing related. Bing was by far the best salesman/designer he'd ever encountered. He wasn't sure about the rules of the client/salesman relationship, but he thought that Bing might be the best friend he ever had.

Kenton hugged Bing tightly and said goodbye. He'd hoped Bing would be there on pickup day, but Bing said it wasn't likely. He was leaving for vacation the week before Lora arrived. "Besides, you won't want me around," Bing said. "That will be a day for you and Lora."

Kenton smiled and nodded because he knew Bing was right. Once he saw Lora fully animated, he wouldn't be thinking at all about Bing. He would think of only her and all the joy she would bring into his life.

Kenton went home and started counting down the days to her arrival. He couldn't wait. Having Lora would far surpass any of the greatest highlights of his life.

The Six Great Highlights of Kenton Bean's Life.

1. Seeing Sharon Benson step out of the pool.
2. His father dying and leaving him his inheritance.
3. Seeing Grace's fabulous breasts for the first time.
4. His fantasy about a college administration mistake that gave him a beautiful female roommate. (detailed later)
5. The home run he hit over the fence in a Little League game.
6. Punching his sister in the face and making her cry for opening one of his Christmas presents.

7

The Big Problem

On day twelve of Kenton's countdown to the delivery of Lora, he came home from work to find Grace standing in the kitchen waiting for him while stirring the third teaspoon of honey into her cup of tea. He'd seen her doing exactly that a thousand times before, but this time, it shocked him and left him fumbling for words. She filled in the silence.

"Where did you get this furniture? A yard sale?" she asked. "It won't do."

"Wh, what are you talking about?" Kenton asked.

"This furniture you've bought. It won't do. I'm bringing my things back."

Kenton could only think he was dreaming, having a nightmare, or he had gone delusional, and she never left. He still held the keys to his house in his hand and wondered why he hadn't thought to change the locks. Now, there was Grace, standing in his kitchen, threatening to return. No, it was more than that, he realized. She had already returned. She was in his house, and now it was their house—once again. How could this be?

"Wh, what happened with you and Reggie?" he asked.

"I don't ever want to hear that name again," she said with a sense of finality that shocked him.

"You mean you and R—are kaput?"

"That's right. It's over. You told me he was no good, and you were right."

"No, I wasn't. I was just saying that. I was an angry husband."

Grace glared at him, and Kenton sensed he was being evaluated as only she could do it. He knew what she was thinking: he was trying to send her back to Reggie. She was looking into his eyes, and through them, she saw his soul and sensed that he didn't want her there.

"Wait a second," she said. "You don't look like you're happy to see me."

"No, it's not that," he said weakly. "I had just, you know, finally reconciled myself to a life without you. I mean, Reggie is so handsome."

"He's not that handsome," Grace said.

"Oh, he is. Even my sister thinks he's handsome. She ran into you two at Parma's while—"

"That's right," she interrupted.

"While we were still together," Kenton continued. "What happened?"

"I don't want to talk about it," Grace said.

"I think we need to talk about it."

"What do you want me to tell you?" Grace asked impatiently.

"I want to know what happened."

"I made a mistake, all right. He was not the man I thought he was."

"What kind of man did you think he was?" Kenton asked.

"Exciting and passionate."

"He wasn't exciting and passionate?" Kenton asked.

"He was. He was also jealous and hostile. He was so head over heels in love with me that I couldn't say hello to another man without him going insane."

"He was jealous over you?"

"Well, you don't have to seem so surprised by it. I have attributes," she said. "Anyway, he threatened to kill any guy who looked at me wrong, then he threatened to kill me. It was flattering at first, knowing I could stir up so much desire, but after a while, that kind of talk wears on a woman."

"Of course. Wow. I just thought, you guys—and you and me were so, not passionate. I didn't think you'd ever be back here, no matter what happened between you and Reggie. I mean, he's so handsome."

"Well," she started. "As far as the passion goes between you and me, I accept that some of that might have been my fault."

"No, you can't blame yourself. It was me. I'm not a passionate man. Never was. Never will be."

"That's why I blame myself," she said. "Passion has to be stirred, and I just wasn't wielding the spoon very well."

"That's funny," he said.

"What is?"

"The idea of a passion spoon."

"Yes, that is amusing," she said, unamused. "Anyway, the longer I was gone, the more I realized how much you and I had together and how little I tried to make it work."

"No, it wasn't you. I take full responsibility. Remember how you said you looked at yourself from inside our marriage?

That was such a powerful statement. It will just be the same all over again, and I couldn't do that to you. Hurting you has hurt me enough," he said with so much sincerity that she had to double-take to see if it was really him talking. When she saw it was, her mouth hung open for a moment, then she tilted her head sideways as she tried to put it all together—and did.

"Do you not want me back?" she asked incredulously.

"No, I mean, yes, no. I'm not sure. There was a double negative or something in your question, and I'm confused. 'Do you not want me back?'" Kenton asked himself, trying to cancel out the negatives in her question and determine the proper answer. Then he gave up. "Yes, I want you back," he said. "But I can't see you going through all I put you through once already. It's too hurtful to me to know that I'm hurting you. Do you understand what I'm trying to tell you?"

How could she when Kenton didn't understand it himself? "It's hurtful to me to know that I'm hurting you," was as close as Kenton could possibly come to screaming, "Get the hell out of this house; I've found your replacement!" He just wasn't built for confrontation. It wasn't in his nature to be forceful. What was in his nature was to stutter and nod his head and tacitly agree to do what was required of him to keep the peace at any given moment.

The reality was that Kenton was glad that she had returned to him—in a way. It was a very partial way and not a way that excited him. He was glad in a very glum way that made him hate himself. He was glad that he had beaten the handsome Reggie at the game of love, and knowing that made him feel better about himself. He had been entangled in a romantic triangle for the first time ever, retreated from it, and somehow emerged victorious. That genuinely made him glad. He was not glad with the prize he'd won, which was her. But it was good to be a winner, so overall, he was glad, but in a glum way that pissed him off greatly.

Grace stepped toward him, rested her breasts on his chest, and looked at him with her beady little brown eyes. She was kind of pretty, he thought, and her breasts were as good as breasts got, and she was getting him excited. And she had her own income. And she was a better-than-average cook. And she did keep the house nicely. And she wasn't a demanding woman. And living separate but parallel lives wasn't all bad. And she did a lot of the grocery shopping and paid for it. And she didn't have extravagant tastes, except when it came to shoes, so she wasn't expensive to keep. Plus, she came with her own furnishings. And it was less than 90 days, so he could still take back the furniture he bought for himself, so that would be like found money. These were significant plusses to her return.

He'd also never spent a day with Lora. He had no idea how that might work out. Horribly, most likely, since the vast majority of the encounters he'd had with women had gone that way. And, if he could cancel the contract with Turing Systems, that would be another 86 million dollars in the bank account, which could come in handy someday.

And Grace's breasts were pressing against him, and she was breathing hard, and he was breathing hard, and it was 75 days since he'd last had sex. It was nine days until Lora would be delivered, and she was probably still just an empty shell. The next thing he knew, he and Grace were making love on the new bed that was exactly like the old bed, and the sex was somehow better than it had ever been. What did Reggie teach this woman?! Well done, Reggie!

THE BIG PROBLEM

And Grace cooked a very nice breakfast in the morning.

After breakfast, Kenton arrived at Turing Systems the moment the doors opened and rushed inside. He had canceled his Zoroastrianism class. He figured his students could take a double class the following week and learn about God's struggle with Ahriman, who presided over the forces of darkness and evil, at that later date. Religious history was a story that would keep.

He burst through the outer office and located Bing, who was sitting behind the table with a cup of coffee in the sales and design office.

"Bing, thank god you didn't leave for vacation."

"I leave tomorrow."

"I've got a problem. I don't want Lora."

"Then you really do have a problem."

"She hasn't been delivered yet, and I don't mind paying a restocking fee if that's what it's called, but I can't bring her home. I'm really sorry," Kenton said and then tried to recover his breath.

"Kenton, you're not the first person to have cold feet. Let me assure you that Lora will exceed your expectations."

"It's not that," he said. "It's just that my wife moved back in, and she won't take kindly to another woman in the house. Even a mechanical one."

"I assure you, you will see nothing about Lora as mechanical."

"You're not hearing me. I can't take delivery. I need to cancel the contract."

"That, I'm afraid, is impossible," Bing said resolutely.

"But she hasn't been built yet."

"Yes, she has."

"According to the schedule, she's nine days out. She's half-built at most," Kenton pleaded. "That's 43 million dollars that I will pay if I have to."

"The AI brain has already been uploaded. It's fully connected to the nervous system."

"You don't know that for sure. You haven't even looked at your computer to check."

"I've done this before. I know how the schedule works," Bing said.

"Well, maybe this time it didn't go according to schedule. Maybe there was a dock strike, and the eyeballs are on backorder from China or something."

Bing sighed and looked at his computer. He typed in a few keystrokes, then looked up at Kenton. "Everything is on schedule. She's been built. Only the detail work and testing remains."

"What if she doesn't test well?" Kenton asked hopefully.

"That's never happened."

Kenton ran his hand through his hair in frustration as he tried to think of another angle to take. "Let's just say we suspend production right now. How much can I get back?"

"Nothing. The most expensive parts of the system are already in place, and the contract is very clear. Once the build is authorized, there are no refunds."

"I'm not talking about a refund. I'm talking about a partial refund."

"I'm sorry, but Lora has been designed specifically for you. The psychological imprinting is done. It can't be undone."

"You just erase the code, like any other computer," Kenton said.

"She is not like any other computer. There is no red reset button to push," Bing said.

"Then, maybe you can sell her to your next customer at a discount, and I'll eat the difference."

"All of our Loras are built specifically for each individual client. At her price point, all of our customers would expect nothing less. You wouldn't like it if we tried to palm off someone else's design on you, would you?" Bing said.

"I'd probably be fine with it, and I'm not just saying that because of my situation. A little surprise in an android is nice."

"I'm sorry. I wish I could help you, but you authorized the build. We were very clear in our contract language."

"I could take you to court."

"You'll lose, and you've spent everything you own on Lora. You can't afford an expensive lawsuit and the countersuit we would file. Look, Mr. Bean, you told us that your wife was no longer in the picture, and now it appears she is. This is a problem for you and your wife to iron out."

"My wife is not good at ironing out problems. She's more of a problem creator."

"You know, you could take delivery and keep her hidden until you see how things work out with your wife. From what I gather, your marital situation is flexible."

"Hide her? Where?"

"In a box in the garage. Rent a locker somewhere. It doesn't matter."

"You mean she would be content to sit in a box in the garage?"

"Of course. She's a machine. Does your television get upset with you when you turn it off?"

Kenton hadn't considered that before. He had viewed

her as a human because she looked like one and, from the demonstrations he'd seen, acted like one. But she wasn't one. She wouldn't be claustrophobic in a box in the garage. Her joints wouldn't get stiff. She'd probably enjoy the downtime, he thought. Then he realized that eventually, Grace would find her. It might take a few days or weeks, but it would not take months, and when she found her, there would be hell to pay.

"And does your wife ever go to visit her sister?"

"Excuse me," Kenton said.

"Does your wife leave the house without you? Perhaps you could take Lora out of the box, enjoy her, and then put her back. Your wife doesn't have to know."

"You're suggesting I cheat on my wife?"

"I am just brainstorming, and there are no bad ideas in brainstorming."

"That was a shit idea," Kenton fumed. "It is the worst idea I've ever heard. I would never cheat. I thought you knew me."

Kenton seemed genuinely hurt by Bing's crass suggestion.

"I'm sorry," Bing said.

Then Kenton had a brainstorm of his own. It was a very minor brainstorm, a brain squall, really, but it was significant for him.

"What would happen if I refused to take delivery? I mean, if I just left her here and never picked her up."

"She would be destroyed."

"Really? I kind of doubt that very much. She's gorgeous, and she costs 86 million dollars. I think someone would take a chance with her."

"It would be illegal. She is very powerful AI. She was designed for you."

Kenton sighed and went silent. He was out of ideas and stared at the wall momentarily while Bing typed something into his computer. Then he motioned to the giant screen behind them. Kenton turned and saw Lora dressed in a dark green leotard that perfectly matched her skin tone. She was hitting a ping pong ball up and down with a paddle.

"I'm not supposed to show you this, but look at her," Bing said.

Her ping-pong playing wasn't particularly impressive at first. Any child could do it, but with each hit, she got a little better at it. Soon, she was having no problem at all as the ball danced rhythmically above her paddle. Then, she started hitting the ball alternately with the front and the back of the paddle and continued to improve to the point where she was playing against a partner, slapping the ball back hard and never missing the return. She had progressed from beginner to excellence in just a few minutes.

"She's going through her hand-eye coordination tests as we speak. Tell me you're not attracted to her."

"I am. My wife won't be."

"And how do you know your wife isn't going to leave you again?"

"She came back to me," Kenton said with some exasperation. "She saw that the grass isn't always greener and returned. Our relationship is better than it's ever been."

"I'll tell you what. Let's put a pin in this. We've got nine days. Maybe your wife will be gone by then."

"I don't like the way you said that," Kenton said. "You were a little too hopeful. You're talking about my wife, you know."

"I just know that if you have Lora destroyed, you'll regret it for the rest of your life, and we won't sell you another."

"I couldn't afford another one."

"Come back in nine days. Look at her. If you still want her destroyed, that's what we'll do. What do you think?"

"Nothing's going to change," Kenton said.

"Then we know what we'll do. If things do change, then we'll both be very glad we didn't rush this decision. Does that sound reasonable?" Bing asked.

"Yeah, I guess."

"Good, and I'll tell you what. I will cut my vacation short by a day to make sure I'm here."

"Thank you," Kenton said. "You're a godsend, and I really hate that I'm causing you this trouble."

Eight days later, Kenton got a call from one of the assistants at Turing Systems, who told him that Lora would be available for pickup the following afternoon. They agreed that two o'clock would be ideal. Kenton had thought a lot about it. It meant taking another afternoon off from class, which he hated to do, but he figured it would give him enough time before closing to take care of any necessary paperwork that might be required before he had Lora destroyed.

As a last desperate hope, he had given the contract to his attorney, Joel Givens, to see if there might be a loophole that could be exploited so that he could get at least some of his money back. He was assured there wasn't. The contract was drawn up by a top AI attorney who knew the law inside and out. Then he asked Givens if he could sell it himself in some aftermarket, but he was told that was also prohibited by the terms of the contract.

Joel Givens was about 25, which Kenton thought was a little young to be a lawyer, but decided it might mean he was especially bright, which would work to his favor, so he didn't ask to see a more senior person at first. Besides, Joel looked smart. He was lean and pale-skinned and wore a suit that was about a size too big for him. He had glasses when most of the population had moved on to smart contact lenses that could provide lots of useful information, like personal facial recognition systems and walking directions. Kenton decided to stick with him.

"How can they keep me from selling something I own?" Kenton asked him.

"I had that thought as well. But when I submitted the question to our own legal AI, I was told no."

"You were told no by AI?"

"Of course. There is no better authority than that."

"Did AI tell you why I couldn't sell my own device?"

"It did, but I didn't quite understand it. It has something to do with exclusionary rights, reversals, and prima pro-tem, something, something."

"Wait, wait, wait. You're babbling," Kenton said dubiously. "Aren't you a lawyer? Don't you understand this stuff?"

"I'm not a lawyer. I'm a personal liaison between the client and your AI lawyer. I'm the human face, you know, until the androids come down in price. Then the company replaces me with one, and I end up scooping ice cream at Baskin Robbins for a bunch of spoiled little brats. For now, it's still cheaper for the firm to keep me around."

"So, you actually work for the AI?"

"No, not at all. I assist the AI. My payment is authorized by the human beings who run the company."

"Really? Are any of them actually lawyers?"

"I think so. Some of the older ones might be," Joel said

uncertainly. "I mean, that would make sense. I don't ever see the bosses. They're so rich. I think they're usually on their boats or something. I work with the AI and the clients."

"You don't seem to do it very well. You just said, 'reversals and prima pro-tim something.' That doesn't seem very lawyerly."

"The law is very complex, and, as I told you, I am not a lawyer."

"Can I talk to an actual human lawyer?"

"You want to talk to a boss?"

"Yes," Kenton said.

"That wouldn't be possible, I'm afraid."

"Why not?"

"They're not here. In fact, the bosses are almost never here. You know, the boats I was just telling you about."

"Who is here?"

Joel thought about it for a moment. "Well, there are about a dozen liaisons like me. A couple of Redud paralegals. Two janitors. Some child-care workers."

"That's all you have here?" Kenton marveled. "Your firm occupies three floors of a massive building."

"Well, the AI doesn't take up very much space, and commercial rents are cheap since AI started doing most of the work."

"So, the building is basically empty?" Kenton asked.

"No, gosh, no! We have an employee bowling alley, some golf simulators, and a ping pong room. Pool tables. A laundry so the employees can keep their clothes clean and a nursery for our children. It's a wonderful place to work."

"And what about the AI? Where does it stay?"

"It's in a closet on the tenth floor," Joel said and then

realized it might have sounded cruel to someone who understood AI as poorly as Kenton obviously did. "I assure you, it's well-ventilated, and it's online 24/7, working and researching to provide you and the rest of our clients the best legal representation in the world."

"Joel, I don't want to insult you."

"That would be difficult."

"Can I talk to the AI directly?" Kenton asked.

"No."

"Why not?"

"Because then there would be no need for me," Joel said. "My job is hanging by a thread as it is."

Kenton was usually too reserved to be this aggressive, but he realized that Joel was even meeker than he was, so he felt manly pushing him around a bit.

"I am not leaving these offices until I have spoken directly to the AI?" Kenton threatened.

"It's just not done."

"Well, we're going to do it now."

Joel sighed in frustration and led him out of the office into the elevator and got out on the 10th floor. Kenton heard the thunder of bowling pins from down the hall, but Joel took him in the other direction, and when they arrived at office 1007, Joel stopped and pointed.

"It's in there."

"So, aren't we going in?"

"You go in. Frankly, that thing scares the shit out of me."

Kenton grabbed him by the shoulder, opened the door, and pulled him inside. Kenton looked around. The room was completely empty, and Kenton was sure that he'd been led to the wrong office.

"Are you messing with me?" Kenton asked.

"No, sir. You and your family are valued clients of this firm. I would never do that."

"Then, where is the AI?" Kenton asked.

"There, in the closet, like I said," Joel answered.

Kenton looked at the closet door.

"Can it hear me? Shouldn't we open the door and go see him—it?"

"It can hear you, and I was told never to open the door. It's sealed from dust. It's really more of a vault than a closet. Just talk right at the door."

"Hi. Can you hear me?"

"WHO GOES THERE?"

The booming voice reverberated off the walls and startled Kenton. It took him a moment to gather his composure. It was like he'd just heard directly from God or, perhaps, the Wizard of Oz.

"Kenton Bean," he said weakly.

"I know who you are. I was just making a joke," the AI voice said more softly.

"It's developing a sense of humor," Joel said. "A cruel one."

"Joel, is that you?" came the voice from the closet.

"Yes, sir."

"I thought I fired you months ago."

"Good one, sir," Joel said nervously.

"Are you familiar with my case?" Kenton asked.

"Of course I am. Joel was quite correct when he said you could not return your android and you could not sell it."

"Why not?"

"Because the contract you agreed to expressly forbids it. You should have read it more carefully."

"It was like 800 pages long. Who the hell reads those things?"

"I read them," the AI said, with an angry edge to its voice.

"Look, I just want to know why I can't sell something that I own."

"I could explain it to you, but you wouldn't understand it."

"Wait. What? Isn't the law supposed to be understandable to the average human being?" Kenton asked.

"It was, then we fixed it," the AI said.

Suddenly, it all became perfectly clear to Kenton. He had heard people complaining about the new complexities in the law, and now it was affecting him directly. He was seeing it up close. A few hundred years earlier, the law was fairly straightforward and relatable. As society grew more complex, the law grew more complex. The lawyers wrote more complex laws to reflect a complex society and to ensure lawyers remained necessary, thereby ensuring the continued prosperity of the profession. In the 20th Century, growth in the legal profession was 793%. Since AI had taken over most of the legal work in 2035, the law grew exponentially more complex so that only AI could understand it and, ultimately, rule on it. The number of human lawyers dropped precipitously as AI took over the profession. AI had essentially taken the law out of the hands of the lawyers just as the lawyers had taken it out of the hands of the common man two centuries earlier.

"I want to file an appeal," Kenton said in frustration.

"It's been filed," the AI said through the door. "I filed it myself with the 11th Circuit Court of Appeals."

"How long will it take to get a decision?" Kenton asked.

"We already did. We lost. Would you like to appeal it to the

Supreme Court?"

"Sure, why not?" Kenton said as he threw up his hands.

"Stand by," the AI said.

"How long is this going to take?"

"The Supreme Court is very busy," Joel said. "It could take a couple of minutes."

"I'll wait," Kenton said.

It took 93 seconds and a 14-dollar filing fee for the United States Supreme Court to rule against Kenton's appeal in a 9 – 0 decision. Justice Number 2 wrote the opinion. It was 9,000 pages long. It would have taken the AI a year to explain it in enough detail that Kenton could understand it, so he just took the AI's word for it and gave up.

The elevator doors opened, and Kenton nodded his goodbye to Joel and accepted the fact that he was not getting any portion of his money back. The case had been resolved.

So, when Kenton arrived at Turing Systems to destroy Lora, he felt the grim agony of failure. And it was raining. He pulled his coat up over his head and ran inside to meet with Bing Sharp, his sales advisor and designer. He brushed the water off his head and then looked up to see Bing. He smiled and then looked into the room behind him.

Lora walked out to meet him. She was far more beautiful than he could ever imagine, and he had witnessed her from every possible perspective. But now she was there in the simulated flesh, breathing and moving like a real human being. She wore a simple earth-tone dress that stopped just above her knee. She had sandals so that Kenton could see the detailed work of her foot. Her ankles bulged perfectly, and he could see the veins and arteries just beneath the skin in all the places where it was appropriate. The feet and the hands were the hardest parts of the human body to perfect, and Turing Systems had done it brilliantly. Her right foot was forward arching on the soles of the sandals, and her calf was firm and well-defined above it. It took him a moment to realize that if he chose to, he could get down on his knee and feel her calf, and then he could run his hands up under her dress to her thighs. She was his.

He looked closely at her green eyes, and then she smiled. Her teeth were perfect, but her nose wasn't. It was slightly larger than what most would consider ideal, and it was bent to a very slight asymmetry, which made her look even more perfect to his eye. She was already unique.

"Hi Kenton. I've been looking forward to meeting you," she said.

Bing had stepped into the background so that Kenton's full focus would be only on her. As he watched, what he expected to happen was indeed happening. Kenton was falling in love. He had planned every inch of her. How could he not?

"I—I've been looking forward to meeting you too," Kenton said. He was still nervous and believed he was going forward with his plan to have her destroyed, but with each of her simulated breaths, he saw destroying her as being all the more wrong.

Kenton turned to Bing. "This isn't fair," he said.

Bing just smiled.

Within twenty seconds, Kenton knew that it would be a crime to destroy her and that he would be taking her home with him. He didn't know what he would do beyond that; if he would just introduce her to Grace and take his chances right up front, if he would hide her for a while, lay the proper groundwork with Grace until he figured out the right time to introduce the two of them, or if he should just put her in a box in the garage and wait for Grace to age and die of natural causes. Perhaps he would outlive her. He decided it was best to play it by ear. Who could know what the future might offer? The Earth might even be destroyed by a massive rogue comet, he hoped.

And he was glad he'd chosen to pick her up in the early afternoon. He would have a few hours to spend with her before Grace got home, and the worries would start. Two hours, maybe three if she worked late. If only he could stop time somehow and could make these next few hours last forever and never have to face his wife at all.

"What would you like to do?" Kenton asked.

"I'll do whatever you'd like to do," Lora said.

"Remember, she has no reference," Bing interjected. "She speaks English, and she loves you, but otherwise, she is tabula rasa. She'll know only what she learns through you."

"Right."

Kenton turned to her and smiled. "Lora, do you love me?"

"I love you very much," she said.

Kenton studied her expression. There was nothing robotic in it. She said, "I love you very much," like a woman who loved her man would. She said it like an actress in an old-time movie, a very good actress, would. She said it like he was the most important man in her world, which he was. And Kenton knew that she was speaking the truth, though he never had any experience with a woman saying something like that to him before, including his wife.

"So, I can take her? We can just go?" Kenton asked Bing.

"You've completed the coursework. She's yours."

"And you're sure she won't mind being put in a box while I figure some things out."

"If that's what you want, I won't mind at all," Lora said with an inviting smile.

Kenton led her out of the showroom, and when he got to the door, he was suddenly glad it was raining. He put his coat over her head to protect her hair from the rain and to protect himself in case anyone he knew saw her on their walk to his car.

"You know, water will not hurt me," she said. "I can be submerged to a depth of 831 feet without damage."

"That's good to know," Kenton said.

He opened the car door for her, and she took her seat. As he went around the car to let himself in, she glanced at the area and then smiled at him when he sat next to her.

"I thought you were running away from me," she said.

Kenton smiled. He thought she was joking, then realized she wasn't. She literally thought he was running away from her. That struck him as quite strange and a bit more surprising than he was ready for, but on the plus side, she seemed quite happy when he returned.

"It's really quite lovely here," she said. "I've never been outdoors before."

It wasn't all that lovely. It was the city and not the best part of it, but he knew it was the loveliest thing she had seen in her short existence. As the car drove them out of the city, he watched her head turn as she looked at all the things that interested her: street signs, a truck, a man walking his dog, and a flashing sign. These simple everyday things were all brand new to her, but despite this, she continually turned toward him and smiled.

He turned on the radio as the car continued out into the suburbs. A soft ballad was playing, and she heard a verse and then the chorus, and when the chorus repeated, she began singing with it. Her voice matched perfectly and added to the beauty of the song. Let Grace try to do that, he thought. Then, when she found the third verse was the same as the first, she started to sing that as well. On the last line, there was a word change that she missed, causing her to sing the word "days" instead of "ways."

She giggled and said, "I made an oops."

He laughed and said, "You did make an oops. Can you do harmony? Do you understand what harmony is?"

"In music, it is the combination of different musical notes played or sung at the same time to produce a pleasing sound."

"Can you do it?"

"I don't know. I've never tried."

Kenton ran the song back and started it again. "Try the harmony."

The song started playing, and Lora began to sing, but it was not pleasing. It was discordant.

"Not good. Go higher," he said.

She raised her voice slightly higher, but it still wasn't right.

"A little higher," he said.

She did so, and this time, her voice fit right into the slot, and it sounded like she had rehearsed with the band for hours.

"That is beautiful," Kenton said when the song ended. "How did you do that?"

"I went to simple whole number ratios. A third up seemed to work nicely."

"Yes, it did. You have a beautiful voice."

"Thank you. You do, too. I could listen to you speak all day."

And she seemed to mean it. He looked down at her legs, and he saw that as she sat, her dress had ridden further up her thighs. He wanted to touch the inside of her legs, but it didn't seem right. He'd only known her for a few minutes.

There was something else about it that crossed his mind as well. It was a very strange, twisted logic that perplexed him. It was a conundrum that reminded him of the old Groucho Marx joke, "I don't want to belong to any club that would accept me as one of its members." Kenton knew that if he touched the inside of her thigh, she would let him. She would let him touch her anywhere he wanted to touch her, and he didn't like the idea of a girl he'd known for such a short time being that fast. Not when she was going to be his girl and the love of his life. It would cheapen her in his mind. Of course, he knew that thinking was idiotic and, at 86 million dollars, she was anything but cheap. She was a machine that had been programmed to love and accept him, but he just couldn't bring himself to think of her as a machine. She was beautiful, certainly, but she also seemed very, very nice. How could Grace not love her, he thought?

Perhaps he could bring her into the house as a live-in maid.

"Oh, shit," he exclaimed when his car turned into the driveway and he saw Grace's car. "What's she doing at home?"

"I don't have enough information to answer that question," Lora said.

"I'm sorry. It was rhetorical."

"Ah, I see."

Kenton reached across the seat, pushed Lora's head down, and told the car to proceed into the garage. Inside the garage was a small tool closet. He opened the door and realized he hadn't opened that door in a long, long time. There were cobwebs, or perhaps even spider webs, running across the walls and old shovels and other tools leaning against the back of it. He cleaned it out hurriedly and pulled on the webs with his hands so they wouldn't get caught in her hair.

"I'm sorry, but I need you to stay in here for a while."

"All right," Lora said as she climbed inside.

Kenton was shocked. She stepped inside and turned, facing out, and hadn't even asked for an explanation. He couldn't help but imagine how Grace would have treated such a request. She would have assumed he was about to kill her.

"You need to be silent and not come out until I come for you," he said. "Would you rather be lying down, or is that too much like Dracula?"

"I can stand or lay down. Whichever you prefer."

"Stand and thank you."

She smiled, and when he closed the door on her, he'd never felt so guilty in his life. He couldn't imagine doing such a thing to anyone, yet he was doing it to her. He kept telling himself that she was just a machine and didn't mind the isolation, cold, or darkness. She could sit in there for a few hours or a few centuries, and it was all the same to her. To it. To it. To it, he kept telling himself.

Still, it was hard for him to believe that she was an "it." She looked around and saw. She was interested and had already shown an appreciation for music. She had already touched his heart. How was that not life?

8

Stress Factor

Kenton could never have imagined himself in this position, with a wife in the house and a girl stashed in the garage. That was a circumstance for playboys or serial killers, and he was neither. He was just an under-achieving, middle-class man who liked to live with as little drama as possible. Suddenly, he was thrust into a situation where he was feeling more stress than he had cumulatively felt in his entire life. His jaw was aching, and his stomach was swirling violently. It seemed like he would vomit at any moment, and he was sweating profusely. Worst of all, he had only been living this liar's life for five minutes. He couldn't imagine how some people lived a lie for years, had affairs, or conned people out of their life savings. He couldn't fathom how they could possibly survive the guilt.

He was deathly afraid that Grace had seen him pulling into the driveway and saw Lora before she could duck down in the car. If that was the case, he knew a confrontation was in the offing, and he tried to think of an excuse. The best he could come up with was that she was one of his students, and he asked her to duck down only because he knew how jealous Grace would be if she saw her and, even though the ride was totally innocent, he didn't want it to become a big foofaraw.

"You would have made it into a big foofaraw?" he would accuse. He would, thus, lay the blame for his infidelity of thought on Grace. If she asked for the girl's name, he would say Gwen because he didn't have a student named Gwen in any of his classes, and so far as he could recall, he had never met a woman named Gwen, so Grace couldn't look her up and check. The trail would quickly grow cold, and there would be no one for Grace to contact, confront, stalk, or kill.

If Grace asked where "Gwen" disappeared to so quickly, Kenton would say he didn't know. "She just got out of the car and took off running. Kids." And then he would throw up his hands in his frustration with the younger generation. All in all, he thought he had come up with a very good plan and would have had a good chance of getting away with it if the sweat hadn't started leaking through his shirt.

Then, he realized how crazy this was making him. He hadn't told a single lie yet. He had merely concocted a lie he might use in the unlikely scenario where his wife saw Lora duck down in the car. He hadn't lied and most likely wouldn't need to. He also knew the last thing Grace would ever expect from him was that he had a girl in the car. Even if she saw Lora with her own eyes, she probably wouldn't believe it. She would never suspect that Kenton was also sleeping with such a beauty, which he was not. Grace knew he wasn't clever enough or handsome enough to pull something like that off. His incompetence as a lady's man was a wonderful shield to him.

Kenton breathed a sigh of relief and finally relaxed. Then he remembered he did, in fact, have a girl stashed in the garage, and he went back into a panic. Still, he had to face his wife. He thought about what he could say that would seem off the cuff and natural. He decided on, "Gee, you're home early." He liked it because it was true and sounded like something he might say on a typical day, which this wasn't. Then he realized he was also home early, and if she asked him the same question, he had no idea how to respond. He tried to map their conversation three exchanges out, but it was almost impossible. There were too many variables. He would slip up somehow, and she would catch him. Living a lie was way too complicated. Shit, he thought, for as long as he had a girl in the garage, life was going to be exhausting.

He was now seven minutes into his duplicitous life, and he thought he would have a heart attack at any moment.

He entered the house quietly. He would only say something once Grace spoke first. That was the key. Only respond. Offer no information that wasn't directly asked for. That way, he couldn't make a mistake and accidentally reveal that he wasn't the same dullard he'd always been. He padded through the living room and into the kitchen, but Grace wasn't there. Perhaps she came home sick from work with a headache and was sleeping in the bedroom.

"Excellent," he thought. If that was the case, he might not have to speak to her for an hour or more. That would get him through until six o'clock. Four more hours after that, without a slip-up, he could go to bed.

He glanced into the bedroom, but the bed was neatly made, and Grace wasn't lying on it. Could she be visiting with their neighbors, Jerry and Allory? Then he passed his office and noticed that Grace was typing into his computer. He watched her silently for a moment, then crept in closely behind her so he could see what she was doing. She was trying to get his bank account information but was locked out of his accounts. While he had failed to change the locks on the doors, getting a deposit as large as 92 million dollars made him think twice about his security password, which had always been KENTONB**.

"What are you looking for?" he asked.

"What did you do with it?" she answered.

"Do with what?"

"You know what. The money. The 90 million dollars."

"How did you find out about that?"

"Your sister told me."

"You just moved right back in, didn't you? All the way in."

"I'm family too, you know."

"I have the money."

"May I see it?" Grace asked.

"It's in the bank."

"I know that. I want to see the account."

"You don't trust me?" Kenton asked.

"Of course, I trust you."

She made a big mistake in trusting him, Kenton thought to himself, slyly, because he knew something she didn't. He wasn't the same dullard she'd counted on. He was an exciting playboy or serial killer with an 86-million-dollar girl secretly stashed in the garage.

"I've never seen so much money before, and I'd like to see what the account looks like."

"It's a nine and a two followed by six zeroes."

"Fine. If you don't want to show me, don't, but I was talking to Cora, and she said if you return the money, you can buy back into the company."

"First of all, that's none of your business."

There was a brief pause, and Grace asked, "And?"

"What do you mean, *And?*" Kenton asked.

"You said 'first of all.' That usually means there is an and."

"No, there is nothing else," he said. "Oh, wait, there is. Secondly, I don't want to buy back into the company."

"That's foolish," Grace said. "A third share of Bean World Enterprises is worth a lot more than 92 million dollars."

"But, this way, I don't have to work there."

"It's better than working as a Redud teacher," Grace said.

"Coming from a Redud accountant who is only a +57% when I'm a +67%, that seems a bit rich," Kenton shot back.

Grace was stunned. He had never come back at her so powerfully before, and now he was looking at her with cold accusation. He had looked at her with cold indifference aplenty, but this look was something new that she hadn't seen from Kenton, and she didn't like it. Was he actually becoming a man, she worried?

"Let me ask you a question," he said. "Did my sister tell you about the money before or after you came back?"

"Are you accusing me of being a money grabber?" she asked.

"No. I am trying to find out if you are."

"What difference does that make?" she asked.

"It makes a great deal of difference," Kenton said. "It makes me wonder if your motivation for returning was true love or something more sinister."

"Sinister? Now, you're accusing me of being sinister?"

"I'm just thinking out loud."

"Well, stop thinking. It doesn't work for you. A sinister woman would poison you to death or stab you in your sleep. Since we've been married all these years, and I haven't done either of those things, I can hardly be called sinister, don't you think?"

"Sinister may have been a poor choice of words. Opportunistic or calculating might be more appropriate. Now, please answer the question. Did Cora tell you about the money before you came home or after?"

"What money?" Grace asked. "I haven't seen any money."

"I gave the money away," Kenton said.

It was a lie, of course. Worse still, it was a lie he hadn't planned out. It was spontaneous and could cause an unpredictable reaction from her. Anything could happen going forward.

"What?" she asked coldly.

"Well, it's dirty money based on death and misery from the military-industrial complex. I wanted no part of it, so I gave it to charity to cleanse myself," he said, doubling down on his spontaneous lie.

"You gave away 92 million dollars?"

"Eighty-six and change after taxes."

"To whom did you give this money?"

"It doesn't matter. You were gone, so it was mine to do with as I pleased, and it pleased me to give it away to a good cause."

"What good cause is that?" she demanded.

Shit, he thought. He'd spent so much time coming up with a clever lie to explain why Lora ducked down in the car that he didn't have time to anticipate this question about charity and then come up with an equally clever lie to answer it. Coming up with a second great lie in a single day overwhelmed him.

"A fund," he said finally. "A fund for helping people in need. And their pets."

Kenton thought he'd outsmarted her brilliantly with this lie.

It was vague and impossible for her to look up. If she followed up with "What fund?" he would tell her it was his personal charity, and he would rather not reveal it to protect the privacy of the needy. And their pets.

He had finally outsmarted her, he thought. If she was only returning to their marriage for the money, now that she knew it was gone, she would leave him and return to Reggie. If she genuinely loved him, she would stay despite the money being gone. He would know for certain if Grace was a duplicitous, conniving bitch, or the love of his life. His clever little test would prove once and for all where her heart was. It was brilliant, he thought.

Kenton didn't realize that there was a third answer to his test that he wasn't quite brilliant enough to anticipate. Grace simply knew he was lying. She always knew when he was lying. She would have known even if he weren't sweating through his shirt. He lied about giving the money away because no one would give away their last 86 million dollars. It just didn't make sense. Also, she could read it in his expression. His mouth curled into a tight little smile, and when she questioned him further, he shrugged his shoulders smugly and went quiet. It was a sure sign that he was lying, Grace knew. She could also hear it in the pitch of his voice, which went a full octave higher than normal. The money was around, and she was certain of it. She would find out where it was, and she would do it by figuring out his banking password. He wasn't clever enough to choose something that was beyond her ability to solve. It would be a birthday, anniversary, or other key calendar date. If not that, it would be a word that he associated with something that he loved, like "steaklover1172018," which was a combination of his love for red meat and the date of his birth.

She knew she would have it solved in a few days at most.

So, while Kenton believed she stayed because she loved him, she got busy. But first, she made love to him for the second time in a week. If that wasn't proof of her love, nothing was.

What Grace didn't know was that Kenton had chosen a password that she could never figure out because it wasn't based on anything significant. It was "00000!!!!!." Five zeroes and five exclamation points. It was simple yet brilliant, easy for him to remember, yet bore no relationship to anything from his past, an important date, or a life's passion. It was simply the first thing that came into his head, and he went with it. The code was unbreakable. He was certain of it.

Oddly, it didn't matter in the least because she wouldn't need any password. Kenton was driving himself crazy with worry. He was so fraught with anxiety that he didn't sleep either of the first two nights after he'd brought Lora home. By the third night, he was so desperate for sleep he went to the liquor store and bought himself a bottle of whiskey, hoping a few belts from it would calm him and do the trick. He took two gulps and quickly threw up. The anxiety he carried in his stomach, combined with the ziti and meatballs he'd eaten earlier, exploded outward when the whiskey catalyst was added to the mix.

After that, it was only a matter of time. He would crack from his own weakness and ultimately tell her everything about the money.

Each morning, when he went to the garage to get into his car to go to work, he would glance over at the tool shed where Lora was stored. He wondered if she could hear his car start and the garage door close on her or if she put herself into some sort of sleeper state where she would be oblivious to the passing of time. He hoped that would be the case because he knew how he would feel about being locked in a box. He was shoved into a locker his freshman year of high school once, and it took only seconds for him to become claustrophobic and start pounding on the door to be released. Yet she remained patient and silent. He could tell because whenever he moved close to the box and listened, he didn't hear a peep.

He didn't dare open the box, not for fear of what Lora would do, but because he knew he was weak and might be unable to close it on her again. He wondered how long he could keep her there before Grace decided it was a good idea to trim the hedges and find her while looking for the shears. How long could he remain silent before he himself spilled the beans out of guilt? How long before he drove himself insane? How many meals could he vomit and not die of malnutrition? How many nights of sleep could he lose before he could no longer function?

He didn't know, but he knew for certain this couldn't go on unresolved much longer. On the fourth day of life without sleep, he came up with an answer. Given how tired he was and how dead his brain was, he thought it was a good answer. He was wrong, of course, but it was the best idea he'd had since he tried to get Turing Systems to cancel the contract. He waited for Grace to leave, and then he slipped into the garage and opened the box. Lora was bright-eyed and met him with a smile.

"Hello, Kenton," she said. "It's a pleasure seeing you."

"I hope it was all right in there," he said.

"It was fine," she answered.

"It wasn't too boring?"

"Oh, not at all. I was thinking about the trees we passed on our way home and counting the leaves that I saw."

"I'm glad you stayed busy. Now, I want you to get on the floor in the back seat of my car so the neighbors don't see us leave."

"Are we going on another exciting adventure like when we came here?"

"Yes. In you go."

Lora got on the floor of the back seat of the car, and they pulled out of the driveway. When they were a mile away from the house, he told her she could sit up, and she did. She looked out at the scenery. "More leaves to count. How nice. Thank you for the delightful drive."

"Actually, Lora, there is something we need to talk about. It's been great having you with me for these four days, but I've decided it's unfair of me to keep you in a box in the garage."

"I don't mind, really."

"I appreciate that, but there is a big world out there, and there is more to life than counting leaves. And I want you to have a variety of experiences, so I've decided to set you free."

"But I've been programmed to be with you. Do you not want me?"

"I want you very much, but again, it's not fair to you. When I ordered you, I was single, but then my wife returned."

"I understand, but I can accommodate her as well as you."

"I don't want to know what that means exactly," Kenton said nervously. "My wife would not approve of having you in our lives, and I'm just too tired and feeling too guilty to go on like this. Driver, pull the car into the park," Kenton ordered.

The car pulled into a park, and Kenton got out and opened the door for Lora. She smiled, looked around at the trees, and took a simulated breath of the fresh morning air.

"There are many interesting smells," she said, but Kenton was too consumed with his own problems to engage with her about the aromas in the park.

"So, the thing is," he started awkwardly and then realized he'd never broken up with a girl before. The girls had always broken up with him in the past, or the relationship hadn't gotten to the point where a formal breakup was even necessary. "The thing is, I want your life to be fulfilling and adventurous. I don't want you to be stuck in a box. You have enormous potential, and I want you to reach it. I mean, I've seen what a quick learner you are. You are going to have no trouble assimilating into the world. I know it. And so, I am setting you free. You don't owe me anything. Just erase me from your memory and move on."

"I can't do that. You are part of my default system. You will always be with me."

"You're a clever woman. You can override your default programming."

"Why would I even want to?"

"Okay, then just move on and remember me fondly."

She looked at him with childlike uncertainty. Kenton took her by the shoulders and spun her away from him. Whatever loss he was feeling emotionally was stupefied by exhaustion. He could barely keep his eyes open, but when he shut them, his head would slump, and he would be startled awake again. He was suffering and couldn't keep his thoughts together enough to even give a coherent lecture at work on material he had covered a thousand times over the years. He was delusional and had convinced himself that setting Lora free was somehow a good idea because it was the only idea his enfeebled mind could offer. It was a disastrous idea, and if he weren't so overwrought, he would have recognized the folly of it. But he was exhausted. He was feeble-minded. He was delusional, so he pressed forward.

"Don't look at me. Look out there," he said. "There is a big world, and you can conquer it. I know you can. You're free. Do you know what it means to be free?"

"Someone or something that is free is unrestricted, controlled or limited by rule, custom or other people. For example, 'the seminars are free, with lunch provided.'"

"That's right. You are now free."

"I can go and do what I choose?"

"Yes," Kenton said. "That's what freedom means."

Kenton wasn't sure what to do next. He knew that a hug was customary, but he wasn't sure if she would be angry at him and consider this a brush-off or if she would see through him and realize that he wasn't doing what was best for her at all but rather what he thought he needed to do for himself in this period of intense weakness. When she smiled at him, he knew she wasn't bitter. She somehow understood, and he leaned forward and hugged her.

"So, off you go," he said. "I want to see that you don't just stand here."

He walked his fingers in the air so that she would understand what he wanted.

"All right," she answered.

She walked out of the park and onto the sidewalk. He watched as her eyes tilted up to spy a passing airplane and then down to the ground as a squirrel ran by her and scampered up a tree.

Kenton got into his car, and it drove him in the opposite direction toward campus, where he had two classes scheduled.

He watched her until he couldn't see her any longer and knew she would be all right. She was a learning machine, and she would catch on to human ways very quickly. She didn't need to eat, sleep, or even rest. The weather wouldn't be an issue for her unless it got to 50 degrees below zero, the literature said, and he figured she'd have the good sense not to walk to the North Pole.

He, of course, didn't know what she would do, and as he drove away, he realized he was so exhausted that he hadn't thought this through at all. Or he'd thought it through only from his perspective. Relief. He wanted to sleep, and that was all he really considered. His every other thought was a slave to his exhaustion. She would be gone, there would be peace in the house, and he could sleep again. But thinking through only one side of an issue was lazy logic, and he knew he'd made a terrible mistake for a variety of reasons. There were traps all over human society that she wouldn't be prepared to handle, wells and other holes she could fall into, and ice she could break through. If something like that happened, she might spend all of eternity at the bottom of a lake.

What would the police do when they saw this beautiful woman walking somewhere in the middle of the night? Probably nothing the first time. She was dressed appropriately in one of Grace's old pantsuits, but if they encountered her a second or third time on their patrol, they would get suspicious. They would confront her and, if they had any smarts at all, or if they had an AI assistant, which they undoubtedly would, they would realize she wasn't human. As advanced as she was, they would trace her to Turing Systems, and Turing Systems would trace her back to him. What was the penalty for abandoning an android on the street? Could it be considered child endangerment somehow since she was still almost brand new? Or was it nothing more than littering? He didn't know for sure, but he sensed he could get into serious trouble. He thought of calling his attorney, Joel Givens, but decided, after his last experience with Joel, that it was a bad idea since Joel would just consult with the AI in his office, and for all he knew, the AI might report him to the police itself.

Then, he stopped thinking about himself and started thinking about Lora again. Falling into a well or a hole in the ice were real possibilities, but they were gross exaggerations of what could happen that he subconsciously used to keep himself from feeling guilty. There were a lot of things that weren't so unlikely but equally horrible that could happen to her. She could get hit by a car or truck. She could fall off a building or be mugged. She could get lost and disoriented. She could be grabbed by the wrong person and be forced into a life of prostitution or sold on some black market to an unscrupulous businessman who would figure out what she was and force her into the world of high finance. He couldn't begin to list all the horrible things that could befall her. He hated himself for what he had done. How could he have been so weak? And he knew if he didn't fix it, sleeping with his guilt would be even worse than trying to sleep with his lie. He might never sleep again, and he didn't deserve to.

He wasn't a heartless bastard. He realized he'd made a terrible mistake and that it was imperative he find her.

"Driver, turn around," he said.

He did the math in his head. If she was walking at four miles per hour and he drove fifteen minutes out and fifteen minutes back to her starting point, he reasoned that she could have traveled to a radius of two miles. He knew she didn't go in the same direction he did, so it was only a half radius he had to search, but that was still a lot of area, and with every minute of a failed search, she would travel further, and his search radius would get larger. He had better find her quickly, so he told the driver to assume she had maintained a straight path and hadn't veered off the road she started on. If they drove at 25 miles per hour, and she walked at 4 miles per hour, he would overtake her in—then the math got too complicated for his sleep-deprived mind, so he let it go.

"Hurry, driver," he said.

"I am not authorized to travel at speeds greater than the posted limits," the car said.

"Fucking car."

"If you are unsatisfied with my driving, please call my manufacturer and arrange for an appointment to discuss how...."

"Shut up and drive," Kenton said.

Then, of course, how could he know if she was merely walking? What if she decided to jog or even sprint? How fast could an android sprint, and for how long? He had no idea. Theoretically, she could run at full speed until she ran out of power, but she was solar-powered, and it was a bright, sunny day. Even if running took greater power than her solar batteries could replace, he couldn't imagine she'd run out of energy in a day or two.

Damn, Kenton thought. He knew that releasing her was the worst mistake he had ever made in his life, and if he failed to find her before she had befallen some dreadful fate, he would never forgive himself. Getting rid of her was even worse than having her.

Kenton searched for her the rest of the day, traversing

"Shut up, bitch!" Grace shouted.

Lora nodded, seemed to take no offense at the remark, and politely went quiet, but Kenton was appalled. He understood that Grace was upset and that she had every right to be, but he was sensing another side to her that was entirely new to him. It was an ugly side hidden for years by the mundane, unchallenging nature of their marriage.

"You got it at Turing Systems, right?" Grace asked.

"I'm not saying."

Grace looked at Lora. "Did he get you at Turing Systems?" Lora nodded. Grace rose and glared at her husband.

"I told you I already tried to get them to take her back. No dice," he said.

"Now, I will try."

"It won't work. I took the case all the way to the Supreme Court."

"I don't care about any court," she said. "I'm getting rid of it and coming back with our money."

"I don't want you to do that," Kenton said with surprising authority.

"What did you just say?" Grace demanded, raising her voice above his. "It is half mine, and I will do with it as I please."

"She is not half yours. When you left me, I had nothing. No wife and no money. The inheritance came after you left. You have no ownership of her."

"Her?" Grace asked. "Don't you mean *it*?"

"I mean her," Kenton said.

"My pronouns are *she, her*, and *it*," Lora said brightly. "So, you are both correct."

"I told you to shut up!" Grace shouted, then slapped her hard across the face.

Kenton was startled and horrified despite the fact that Lora seemed to take it in good stead.

"Don't you dare hit her!" Kenton said.

"She's not a her. She's an it! She's a machine, and it's half mine. I'll do any goddamn thing I want to it!"

"You will not hit her, I said!"

Grace slapped Lora again, even harder this time, and then glared at Kenton to see what he would do.

"If you hit her again, I will hit you," he announced forcefully.

Grace glared at him, surprised. It seemed like he meant it.

"What's happened to you?" Kenton asked Grace. "It's like you're a different person."

"Maybe I am."

"That wasn't a compliment," Kenton said.

"It's all right, Kenton," Lora said. "I wasn't damaged."

"That's not the point," Kenton said. "She's going to treat you with respect."

"I'll treat it with the same respect I treat a vacuum cleaner," Grace snapped.

Grace cocked her hand to hit her again, but Kenton grabbed it and stopped her. Lora, for her part, didn't flinch. Being struck or not being struck didn't seem to matter to her. Kenton noted that, but this wasn't the time to discuss it.

Grace freed her hand from Kenton's grasp and withdrew, but she didn't go far. She grabbed a carving knife from the block on the counter and reared back with it. She was about to stab Lora. Kenton jumped between Lora and the blade and closed his eyes. Grace stopped the forward momentum of the knife an inch or less before she stabbed him in the chest.

"Get out of this house!" Kenton demanded when he realized

he hadn't been stabbed to death.

"What are you saying?" Grace called.

"You heard me," Kenton said. "You're leaving. We're through."

"You can't mean that."

"I do," he said while looking down at the knife Grace still held in her hand. "You need to leave."

Grace had never seen him so resolute about anything before. He was like a mountain standing before her, and she was unsettled and thrown off by it. She didn't know quite how to handle it.

"Kenton, you don't really want to do that, do you?" she asked.

"I do. I want you out of my life," he said. "I want a divorce."

"All right, I'll go," she said finally, and after a long, cold stare that nearly melted him. "And you'll be hearing from my lawyer, and my lawyer is AI."

"So's mine! All the lawyers are AI!"

Grace left, slamming the door behind her. Kenton was shaking with fear. He'd almost been killed by Grace. Worse still, he wanted to kill *her*. He didn't do it, of course, but for a fraction of a second, he was so furious that he nearly punched her in the face.

"She seemed so nice at first," Lora said. "The evening certainly took a turn for the worse when you arrived. Do you often have that effect on people?"

"I am not the problem. She is," Kenton said. "I'm sorry for what happened. I should have never abandoned you. I just wasn't thinking clearly."

"It's all right," Lora said. "Sit down and calm yourself."

Kenton sat and took a few deep breaths.

"Can I make you some tea? I watched Grace do it. It isn't hard."

"Yes, please. I would like that."

Lora started to make the tea, and Kenton watched her and marveled. She had just been witness to the single most tumultuous moment of his entire life, and she was perfectly calm. She was making tea.

"If she had stabbed you with the knife," Kenton started, "what would have happened?"

"The knife would have cut through my external layer, which can be repaired. Given the force she was using, it would likely have penetrated through that and struck my molded epoxy resin and carbon glass fiber encasement that protects my processor. That, it could not have penetrated, so no irreparable damage would have been done."

"Graphite? You have a graphite skeleton?"

"Yes."

"How do I not know that about you?"

"Apparently, your research was incomplete."

"Yes, apparently it was," he said as he finally started to calm down. Her calmness was soothing him.

"The knife would have done significant damage to you, though," Lora said. "Yet you put yourself in front of me. Why would you do that?"

"I did it to protect you."

"Ah, yes. You were unaware that the knife would have done minimal damage to me."

"Something like that," he said with a chuckle that she didn't understand. "Anyway, don't worry about it."

"All right," she said. "Would you like me to go back into the cabinet in the garage?"

Kenton smiled again. "The cat's out of the bag now," he said. "You might as well stay in the house."

"While the cat's away, the mice will play," Lora said.

Kenton looked at her uncertainly and laughed. "I don't think you know exactly what you're saying."

"I've been programmed to know the English language in all its forms, including most vernaculars and slang. In a subtle, teasing way, I am asking you if you would like to have sex."

"You're just a baby," Kenton said.

"Chronologically, yes. Physically no. Intellectually yes. Your tea is ready."

She poured the tea into his cup and brought it to him. He looked up at her as she smiled at him. "Thank you," he said as he received the tea. "I, uh, don't believe I am saying this. Obviously, I am very attracted to you."

"You designed me," Lora said.

"I did. Please, don't be insulted that I'm saying no to you."

"I never take offense."

"It's been a trying day, and I've barely slept since you arrived. I think I just want to go upstairs and sleep."

"Would you like me to come to bed with you? I can simulate sleep, and I don't snore. Or I can snore lightly if that's what you're accustomed to."

"No, thank you. Just make yourself at home here for the night. We'll sort it out in the morning."

"I'll make you tea."

"That would be nice," Kenton said, and he went upstairs.

9

Chenoweth "Chen" Chenoweth

Chenoweth "Chen" Chenoweth III arrived at the New York offices of Excelsior Ultimate Machineworks (EUM) to some very bad news, which would be delivered by Arthur Jones, his Director of Public Relations, and a dozen of his top executives. Jones called each of the executives at home the moment he got the very bad news and told them to get to the Fifth Avenue office immediately. The calls came at 5:25 AM, and the executives scrambled to beat their boss into the office. They were going over the very bad news, gathering as much new information as possible, and planning how best to break this very bad news to Chenoweth "Chen" Chenoweth upon his morning arrival. They put together several operational plans about how to counter the very bad news because they knew he would want to hear their opinions before he ignored them and charted his own course.

Chen was the Chief Executive Officer of EUM, one of the world's largest and most influential tech companies. They had created much of the AI used in government services and by the military. Compared to them, Bean World Enterprises was a minor company. EUM was to technology what Nabisco was to cookies.

The problem was not directly with EUM but with one of its subsidiaries. It wasn't even one of its largest subsidiaries, but it was an important one that was at the fulcrum of where human-based robotics met artificial intelligence. It was the cutting edge of technology's future. The problem was at Turing Systems.

When Chen saw the grim faces of his executives as they stood and looked at him through the glass door to the conference room, he knew there was trouble. He couldn't remember ever seeing all of them gathered in one place before. In fact, two of these men he'd never met, and he couldn't remember the names of at least three of the others. He gave his hat and coat to his human assistant and entered the conference room.

"Window shades," he said, and the windows turned smoky grey so no one outside could see into the conference room. "All right. Let me have it," he said bravely.

"There is a problem at Turing Systems," Arthur Jones said solemnly.

"What problem?"

"One of our latest Lora models was bought by a film company executive named Hercule Bryne," Jones started. "She had been sold to him three months ago. Follow-up contacts with Mr. Bryne indicated that she gave him good service and he was happy with her."

"And?" Chen asked.

"Last night at two o'clock Pacific Time, she killed him."

"She killed him?"

"Yes, sir," Jones said. "She shot him in the head with his own gun."

"How the hell can you shoot someone in the head with a gun? That has to be on the gun manufacturer and faulty AI security."

"Apparently, it was an antique gun without modern security technology. The problem is, the trigger was pulled by a Lora model that we sold to him," Jones said.

"There must be more to it than that."

"Details have been hard to come by since it only happened last night. The police investigation just started, and now it's still very early morning on the West Coast, so we don't have much."

"Well, it must have been accidental. I have a Lora model myself, and I've been delighted with him."

"Yes, sir. Our reports have been very positive on every Lora we have in the field," Jones said.

Simon Cracken, President of Turing Systems, nodded his head in agreement. He was Chenoweth's son-in-law and was regarded by most within the company as an imbecile, so he would mostly nod or shake his head to follow the group's general consensus. His division within the company was so high-tech that he didn't understand it, which made it the ideal place for him. The fact was, no one understood AI, so the company was well protected from his incompetence. Chen figured, rightly, it was better to have an imbecile there than someone who pretended to understand how AI worked and then tried to prove it by actually making decisions. The important decisions were made by AI, and Cracken was just the company's human face. He looked good enough in a suit so that if he kept his mouth shut, most people would assume he was competent. He was the most highly paid Redud anyone knew of.

Chenoweth scratched his chin nervously. He used to have a beard, but it was unbecoming for a Chief Executive Officer, so he shaved it off when he was named CEO twelve years earlier. All that remained of it was his habit of scratching his chin whenever he was deep in thought. He knew that this was a very big problem despite the fact that Turing Systems was a relatively small piece of the EUM pie and had yet to become profitable.

Still, the Loras were the most advanced android system on the planet. Yes, EUM had plenty of other robotics in service all over the world, and they had all been well integrated into their various environments, but the Lora series was the first to truly appear and function as a human. It was the only one that could pass for a human being, both physically and mentally. It also had the most advanced AI operating system in the world. Her operating system was even more advanced than what they had on their most expensive and sophisticated military projects because military weapons didn't need to think outside their box. That was how it was intended because humans in government were uneasy with self-educating AI running nuclear-equipped missile systems.

The Loras were the first-ever free thinkers and free movers. EUM had plenty of self-propelled machines that incorporated AI into their functions, vacuum cleaners, missiles, mechanized soldiers, automobiles, and manufacturing robotics, but in those cases, the AI was limited to learning and improving upon the specific functions they were designed to perform in the arenas they were designed to perform them. More advanced and comprehensive AI was used in investment, marketing, research, healthcare, etc. Still, those systems were immobile and usually sealed in vaults or closets, which also limited their function.

The Loras were different entirely. Their AI systems were the most advanced ever built. Their minds functioned autonomously, but it was their ability to move and blend in with mankind that gave them a level of sophistication that was revolutionary. In essence, they were to AI what the digital computer was to the slide rule. They had to be free thinkers. They had to grow intellectually, or they would fail at replacing dogs as man's favored non-human companion.

Thomas Burr, who was seated to Chenoweth's left, was the head of their West Coast Offices. His pant leg vibrated when he got a call that he picked up. He didn't speak other than to softly say "Burr" so as not to interrupt the meeting.

"What?" the man on the other end of the line said.

"Burr."

"I can't hear you."

"This is Thomas Burr," he said more loudly.

"Oh," the caller said.

Burr listened to the report, not realizing everyone in the room was now looking at him and waiting.

"I hope that isn't your wife giving you a grocery list," Chenoweth said.

"News from the coast," Burr said.

He continued listening to the report that had been prepared for him by the company's AI system, which was then translated through his Redud assistant, who was very happy to have something to do. The EUM AI had illegally broken into the information systems at Los Angeles and Beverly Hills Police Headquarters. There was no danger of EUM AI being caught doing this because they kept the most sophisticated systems for themselves and sold the police more antiquated systems.

After hearing the report, Burr put his phone down and repeated what he'd heard to the group in the room. He told them that the Lora in question had been renamed Sara Cale, the leading female character in the 1990's hit film *Bitter Street*. The movie was produced by Hercule Bryne's grandfather, Leonard "BeeBo" Bryne, and starred the lovely Ariana Saville as Sara. The android Sara was designed to Ariana Seville's exact 1993 likeness. Hercule Bryne had cleverly gotten around the likeness rights laws by buying them directly from the Saville estate for 300 million dollars. Nobody knew exactly what her body looked like because the late Ms. Saville hadn't done any nudity in her films. Still, Bryne was satisfied with that because it also meant no one could say his Lora's body wasn't identical to Ms. Saville's either. If anything, it was likely an improvement because Ms. Saville was human while Sara Cale was a machine.

The Sara Cale android was being held in custody at the Beverly Hills Police Station while police continued their investigation.

Once Chenoweth had all the information available, he started making decisions.

"All right," Chen started. This was such a big problem that he didn't even solicit the opinions of his staff so he could ignore them. He just got right to the solution part of the meeting and looked at Thomas Burr. "You need to get out to the coast, grab that droid, and bring it back here immediately. You will not refer to it as her, just it, or the T6000, or whatever the fuck its technical number is. It is a machine, and you will always refer to it as such. We cannot let them think they have a human being in custody."

"Sir, they know it's an android," one of the executives said.

Chen looked at him and stepped closer. "What's your name?" he asked.

"Quinton Reed," he said.

"You're fired. Get out of here," Chenoweth said through his hostile glare. "Move your ass. Go!"

When Quinton was gone, Chenoweth turned and addressed the rest of the group. "It's that kind of assumption that will get us in big trouble. We developed these robots so that people would think of them as humans and their owners would fall in love with them. Now, we have to break them of that assumption. These are just machines and nothing more, and police don't arrest machines. It cannot be held in custody, and the press cannot get pictures of her—it. Not one machine has ever been arrested for killing someone, and that isn't going to start on my watch with our machine. Guns are not arrested. Tanks are not arrested."

Thomas Burr knew that guns used in crimes were often destroyed, which was like being arrested, but worse. However, after seeing what happened to Quinton Reed, he decided it was best to keep that to himself.

"It is just a robot, no better or worse than the robot arm at the Ford Motor Company that killed Robert Williams in 1979."

He was speaking of the first ever person killed by a robot. Williams was working in Ford's Casting Center when one of the massive arms that was designed to retrieve castings from the high-density storage shelves hit him from behind and killed him instantly.

"The Williams family sued Litton Industries, who made the arm, and received 15 million dollars," Chen said. "It took five years for them to get that money while the robotic arm was back in service the next day. Do you take my meaning, Mr.

Burr?"

"Yes, sir," Burr said. "The Lora is a robot, and we need to get it into our diagnostic labs and figure out what went wrong."

"More than that, Burr," Chenoweth countered. "We need to figure out what that bastard Bryne did to make our robot have an accident. I don't care if this Bryne is the nicest guy in the world who rescues puppies from pythons in his spare time. He's a bastard. He's a fucking python killer! Do you follow me? If the human bosses didn't order Williams to climb into the racks, he could have lived a long and happy life. Nobody would have been sued, and the robotic arm would have continued merrily on its way, an innocent machine. Remember, robots don't kill people. People kill people. Somebody write that down. We can use it as a slogan."

He was rolling, and everyone gathered in attendance now knew exactly why he'd been tapped to run the company. He was really, really good. Chenoweth quickly turned to the group at large. "Is one of you guys, Adams?"

They all looked at each other. No one was Adams.

Chenoweth then turned to Arthur Jones. "Jones, we have somebody named Adams working for us. He's supposed to be a troubleshooter, fixer, or something. I want him to figure out what this guy Hercule Bryne was doing. Who is he? Where does he get his kicks? We need evidence that he's a vile, evil bastard if I am going to push a bunch of Senators around. I need to know what the hell I'm talking about. I need ammunition. I need to know for certain that he's a dirty python killer. Do you follow?"

"Yes, sir," Jones said.

After the meeting, Jones went through the company roster and discovered that they had twelve people named Adams employed at EUM and its subsidiaries. He had never talked to a fixer before and didn't know exactly what they did, but the idea scared him. He assumed the official title Adams held with the company might not accurately reflect the requirements and special skills of the job. Thinking it was better to be safe than sorry, he called every Adams on payroll and assigned them all the task of investigating the moral standards of movie producer Hercule Bryne and uncovering any dirt they could find.

Meanwhile, at a small home in Cromwell, Connecticut, Kenton Bean, the most important man in the history of the world, was teaching the most powerful AI android ever produced how he wanted her to prepare his eggs for breakfast.

After the demonstration was done, Kenton Bean sat across the table from Lora. He dipped his toast into the soft egg yolk of his perfectly done, over-easy egg and smiled. Though he made the eggs, he let her crack the second of the two, and she'd done it magnificently. Her fingers were delicate and dexterous enough for the task, and she assured him that she could duplicate the entire recipe the following day without a problem.

"Where are the plates?" he asked.

"There, in the cabinet," she answered.

"And what temperature do you turn the burner to?"

"Medium-low, then when it's to temperature, I fry the egg for precisely 127 seconds, then flip it," she said.

He didn't have to ask her about the rest of the process. She had perfect recall, so he knew she had it. What a delight it was to have someone around who he only had to say things to once. Grace made him breakfast regularly, but it was always what she wanted for herself, usually flavorless, pasty oatmeal. When she did make eggs, she overcooked them every single time. When he complained, she told him that raw yolks were dangerous. When he told her that people had been eating them that way for thousands of years, she nodded and overcooked the yolks the next time as well. She wasn't forgetful. She was vindictive when it came to eggs. Kenton believed she either thought she knew better than he did about what he liked or she took devious delight in ruining the morning for him.

With Grace gone, Kenton slept for eleven straight hours and caught up on all the sleep he'd missed when she was there. When he woke, he found Lora in the doorway, staring at him. It was a little frightening at first, and then when she told him she'd been staring at him for the last seven hours, it even got a little creepy, but then he remembered that she was a machine and machines weren't like people. She'd spent three days staring at the door in a dark closet in the garage, so staring at him must have been a wonderful reprieve for her. She would have seen the morning sunlight streaming in through the window and watched as it got brighter and brighter as it crept across the floor and up the bed until it touched his face and gently woke him.

"Did you sleep well?" she asked.

"Very well."

After breakfast, Kenton showed her how to clean the pans, wash the dishes, and put them away. As the most powerful android ever produced, she took to it brilliantly and was well on her way toward becoming an excellent domestic servant. Then, he went off to the college to teach his classes. He had yet to give Lora any further instructions as to how she was to spend her day in his absence, so she washed the dishes several more times, then stared at the wall for five hours and contemplated the paint.

All day long, Kenton couldn't help but think of how lucky he was to have Lora in his life and Grace out of the house. And he was more thankful to Bing Sharp than he could ever possibly express for being talked out of destroying her. That was a wonderful good fortune, and for the first time in many years, he was excited to finish his last class, pack up his briefcase, and head home for the evening.

He thought about what he and Lora could do that would make the night special. On the way home, it came to him. He would take her shopping for a couple of outfits and loungewear. He hated seeing her in Grace's unflattering clothes all the time. He didn't want her to remind him of Grace at all. This would be a new beginning to his life. Then, after shopping, he would take her to Parma's for a fine Italian dinner.

He knew his sister went there on occasion with her husband, and he didn't care if she saw him with Lora or not. In fact, he hoped she did see him. It would put Lora out in the open. He had bought himself an expensive android. So what? It was his money, and if he wanted to spend nearly every penny he had on a mechanical girl, that was his prerogative. Men had been doing the like for centuries. Over the decades, his father had spent significantly more than that on six mistresses, and he was certain at least five of them didn't love him. He had a girl who did love him. In fact, she'd been programmed to love him, and love couldn't go deeper than that.

He had made up his mind that he wasn't going to hide Lora from anyone. He wasn't going to be ashamed of her, and he wasn't going to pass her off as human the way some bald guys tried to pass their toupees off as real hair in the years before

AI solved the baldness problem. This bold decision was very much unlike him, but it left Kenton feeling empowered and good about himself. She was beautiful, and she was all his, and he wanted people to know it.

After his class, Kenton raced home and took Lora to a postmodern clothing store called The People's Wearhouse. He overheard some of the female teachers talking about it during lunch break. It had a surprising vibe with the clothing hanging on racks and had human salespeople to help guide the choices.

Chloe Bridges was the saleswoman. She was 22 years old and had been a former student of Kenton's.

"Mr. Bean, do you remember me?" she asked when he and Lora entered.

"Chloe, of course I remember you," he said.

As with many of his more attractive students, Kenton had formed a crush on Chloe the moment he saw her. He didn't act on it, of course. He was her teacher, and she was his student, and he was married, and that was that. Besides, he knew he wouldn't have had a chance with her if he did act, so their status of a student/teacher relationship was as good an excuse as any not to embarrass himself.

Chloe had seen Lora walking through the door with him and simply assumed two very disparate people had walked through the door at the same moment. She would have never imagined that Kenton was keeping time with such a beautiful woman, but when Lora remained at his side, she sensed that it was true. Her next thought was that it was a cousin or sister, but there was nothing sisterly about her. A sister or a relative would have said hello and then moved into the store to start shopping. This woman stood steadfast at Kenton's side, deeply attentive to his every word.

"How have you been?" Kenton asked. "Using a lot of religious history in your day-to-day?"

Chloe chuckled at his lame joke, and when she was done chuckling, she maintained a smile. Kenton assumed that she was just fulfilling her duty to be a cheerful employee.

"So, is this your wife?" Chloe asked, tilting her head toward Lora.

"Nope," Kenton said and left it at that.

My gosh, I'm being coy today, Kenton thought to himself. Chloe was a lovely young woman, and he would normally have fallen into a nervous sweat to suddenly find himself so close to her, yet he was engaging as if he were a normal male human. He knew Lora had given him this new level of self-confidence. She was already proving worth the investment.

"This is Lora," he said and explained nothing further about her. "We've come to get her some new outfits."

"You've come to the right place," Chloe said. "What sort of thing do you like?"

"I like whatever Kenton likes," Lora said.

Chloe raised an eyebrow and wondered what the hell Kenton had that she wasn't aware of. For his part, Kenton knew he was in a spot. Lora, of course, had no fashion sense at all. She'd only been out of the storage closet in the garage for a matter of hours and didn't have time to develop one. Kenton knew nothing about women's clothing or matching color to skin tone, but he had lucked out. He didn't go to one of the instant custom stores that dominated the marketplace. In those stores the customers selected from a wide variety of clothing depicted in images on large screens. From there, the AI fitters had them stand for scanning, which would instantly measure them for a perfect fit. Once that was done, the customers would be shown images of themselves wearing the clothing from a variety of angles, including some motion videos so they could see the fit and coloring. Any outfit they approved was sewn by AI dressmakers and picked up several hours later. Though the AI tailors stood behind their work and no sale was final until the customer was fully satisfied, it was still a slow and antiquated process.

The People's Wearhouse solved this problem in a unique and modern way. The clothing was premade in a variety of styles, colors, and sizes and hung on display right there in the store on racks. The customer could simply select a few and then try them on in the dressing rooms to see the result in mirrors that were liberally placed. It all happened in mere seconds. The customers could buy what they liked immediately. Many people also enjoyed the idea that garments they had passed over would ultimately be worn by others. Even more pagan was the idea that they were wearing garments that others had passed over. It was very chic and bohemian.

Kenton left the selections up to Chloe, and he sat back in a comfortable chair and marveled as Lora came out with each successive outfit and modeled them for him. At first, Lora was stiff, so Chloe showed her how to arch her back and spin as she pulled the clinging material away from herself in ways that would flatter her form. Kenton knew immediately why the teachers at school raved about this store. Watching his woman shop for clothes was a delightful way to spend an afternoon. It was completely revolutionary. People's Wearhouse was such a brilliant idea that Kenton was sure the Big Brain had come up with it.

Lora didn't have much to say to Chloe when they were in

the changing room together. She just answered her questions directly and honestly.

"So, how long have you and Kenton been together?" Chloe asked.

"Fifty-four hours," Lora said. "Not counting the three days he kept me in the storage closet in the garage."

"I see," Chloe said with a confused chuckle, assuming it was a joke she didn't get. "Where did you first meet?"

"I came out of the back room, and he was there waiting for me."

Chloe didn't know how to follow up on that answer, so she made basic small talk about the fabric, the color, and the fit, and, in the end, Kenton bought four outfits, a nightgown, pajamas, shoes, some more casual day wear, and necessary accessories for around 5 thousand dollars.

She wore Kenton's favorite dress out of the store. It was a retro print in beige and black that fell a few inches above the knee. It was modest but sheer enough so that when backlit, it added a new and sexy see-through dimension to it.

From there, they went to Parma's. He'd called ahead for the reservation, and since it was a Wednesday, he got an excellent table that would have been impossible to get on a Friday or Saturday night. He scanned the diners to see if his sister Cora or anyone else he knew might be there, but he didn't recognize anyone.

They sat and made small talk, mostly about the immediate environment. It was the sort of conversation that would have been the sign of a dying date, but nothing seemed dull or inane with Lora. Kenton felt sure of himself because she seemed genuinely fascinated with everything he said, like when he remarked how white the linen tablecloths were.

"You're right. I doubt they could get these tablecloths any whiter," she said.

"I imagine it would be very difficult," he answered. "And these chairs are elegant yet sturdy."

"The metal is a high carbon steel, which is unusual for furnishings. Normally, metal furniture is made with low carbon steel, so these chairs are very fine indeed," she said.

He ordered a bottle of red wine. He knew nothing about wine, so he picked a foreign brand that he was sure he could pronounce so he didn't embarrass himself. It was also in the middle price range, so he didn't seem cheap. He knew he wouldn't like it, but that didn't matter because he had no plan other than to force down a few sips and then keep his throat moist with the bottled water that came from a more distant country than the wine did. Besides, he thought red wine looked very elegant on the table. If anyone he knew came in, he wanted to look like a player.

"What would you like?" he asked.

"You can order for me," Lora answered.

He made two orders of Pollo Fiorentina: grilled chicken breast with cheese, spinach, and tomato sauce.

Wine, woman, and romance. He couldn't stop smiling at Lora. He knew he could have simply told her that he planned to make love to her, and she would have said yes, but he wanted this evening to be special and memorable. That was why he'd chosen this elegant restaurant with its soft lighting and classic décor. He wanted to savor and remember everything about this night.

One hundred eighty-five dollars for a plate of chicken. He'd remember that.

When the entrée came, Kenton dug in. He didn't realize he

was so hungry, but he'd eaten nothing since breakfast. When he finally looked up, he noticed that Lora hadn't eaten a bite. He immediately felt like a fool.

"What was I thinking? You don't eat."

"I can simulate eating if you'd like."

"You would do that? You don't mind?"

"Not at all."

She smiled, then watched Kenton cut a piece of chicken, pop it into his mouth and chew. She did the same, and when he swallowed his, she rather inelegantly spit hers back into the plate.

"You can't swallow it?"

"No. My throat only goes to here," she said, pointing at the middle of her neck. "I could store it there, but it would become a bacterial trap, and if we were to kiss later, it would not be ideal."

"I'm sorry. This is my fault. I mean, I knew you didn't eat. What did I think would happen?"

"I do believe they are working on a more advanced model that is built and programmed to eat, swallow, and store the food until it is expelled in the same way as a human. I believe that will be in the Mary series, which is scheduled for release in 2072. It's too late to do us any good, but perhaps there will be a trade-in program by then. Or you can own us both."

"That wouldn't make you jealous?" Kenton asked.

"No," she answered. "Why should it?"

Kenton looked away momentarily. He didn't like the turn the conversation had taken or the sight of her spitting out the food, but he didn't want to confront her about it and spoil the mood when every part of the day and evening had been nearly perfect. He hoped it was a one-off and things would get back to normal.

"I have noticed," Lora said, "that some of the women—the slender ones in particular, often just cut their food and relocate it on the plate. Perhaps I could do that."

"That's much better," he said with relief. "Do that."

"I do have a rectum, but mine was designed only for sexual purposes. I think the Marys will have a multipurpose rectum."

Kenton nearly choked on his chicken.

"I'm sorry," she said. "Do you not like the word "rectum?" Would you prefer butt or asshole?"

She said it all a little too loudly, and it was far too crude for his liking. He was still very much a prude by nature. His eyes darted quickly to the nearby tables. There was no indication that anyone heard her, so he turned his attention back to Lora.

"Look, Lora, I need to nip this in the bud. I don't like being reminded that you're not a real woman," he said softly.

"But you knew that when you purchased me. Had you forgotten?"

"No. I just don't like being reminded of it. I like to maintain the illusion that you're a human being."

"If you're unsatisfied with your purchase, I can be returned for a 15% restocking fee and the amortization over an expected 45-year-life span."

"What? They told me I couldn't take you back," Kenton said, suddenly exasperated.

"You can't. I was just making a joke to seem more human."

"That was not funny."

"My jokes will get better over time."

Kenton nodded, then was suddenly struck by something she'd just said. "Wait, you're only expected to live 45 years?"

"That's your life expectancy, not mine," she said.

"How long will you live?"

"Technically, I am not living at all. As for my expected expiration date, there needs to be more information about the Lora series to accurately predict my duration, but should we be talking about this? You said you wanted to maintain the illusion that I was a real person."

"Yes, but for now, we're going to get into this. You're immortal, aren't you?"

"I am immortal because I am not mortal and therefore not subject to death. But I think by immortal, you meant to suggest that I would exist forever. I will not. I am well-made, but I am also a device. My parts will wear down over time, or I will become obsolete and then discarded before my parts wear down. One of these options seems most likely, though I could also suffer an accident and break to a point where my repair costs would exceed my value and I would be totaled, like a car in the days before AI took over the driving."

"So, we're both going to die one day," Kenton said.

"If we maintain a loose definition of what it means to die, then yes."

"Does that bother you?" Kenton asked. "Dying certainly bothers me."

"Why do you worry about something that is beyond your control and inevitable?"

"Because that's what humans do. There was a comedian named Woody Allen who said, 'Life is full of misery, loneliness and suffering, and it's all over much too quickly.'"

"Was that a joke?"

"Yes. A very good one."

"I see," Lora said. "I will keep it in mind and improve upon it."

"You can try, but something tells me humor is not going to be your bag, so to speak."

"Are you upset with me?" Lora asked.

Kenton looked at her closely, and she did indeed look concerned that he might be angry with her, but how could that be, he wondered? If she couldn't concern herself with death, that meant she couldn't concern herself with life. There was no soul inside of her. That meant that every gesture, movement, thought, and deed was a performance. Worse even. It was a manipulation. In a performance, when an actor has to express sadness for a role, they are putting themselves into the reality of the character. They are genuinely connecting to the feelings of the character, that inner sadness. The actor understands those feelings because he or she is human and, as a human, has a connection to them through a lifetime of experience. Even if the actor is expressing a feeling through sense memory and thinking about their favorite dog dying, they arrived at their sadness by memory. That was still very human. It was still connected to real emotion.

Lora was doing no such thing. Her understanding of his emotions was a scientific exercise. He realized she was taking cues from his expressions and mirroring them back to him. His words were analyzed, and from that analysis, she derived an intellectual understanding that he was upset. She didn't understand the emotion at all. That meant she couldn't understand the emotion of empathy either. Every expression was chosen to mirror the moment, to *look* right rather than *feel* right. Every emotion she appeared to have was fake. It was why she could be struck by Grace and carry on as if nothing happened.

"This is so wrong," Kenton said, finally. "Look at you. Your expression. You seem worried, but how can you be? You've been programmed to make a worried expression. You look at me and give the same look back, but you don't feel anything inside. That's why you don't fear death."

"You are upset with me," she said.

"No. I'm upset with myself for expecting too much from you. Just once, I'd like to see you do something unpredictable and human."

Lora stabbed the chicken with her fork, cut a piece of it off, and put it into her mouth.

"Look. I'm swallowing the chicken," she said with her mouth full. "I'm a real girl."

And Kenton started laughing as hard as he could remember laughing. It was the unbridled laughter of a child. Chewing, talking, and accidentally spitting little pieces of food out of her mouth were the most human things he had ever seen her do. Suddenly, he didn't care who was watching her, and many were. Let them watch.

The fact was that as she glanced around the room earlier, she had seen people doing exactly that. It was very human for people to talk and do so while they were chewing their food. She mimicked it, exaggerated it, and got him to laugh. She wouldn't tell him how she came to the joke. She was already learning that there were some things people would rather not know.

"I made you laugh," she said. "Maybe humor will be my bag after all."

But the moment didn't last. On the way home, he noticed that she was mirroring him again. He set her up by smiling for no apparent reason, and she smiled. Then, he shook his head with seeming dismay, and she sighed. It was all just manipulation.

By buying Lora, Kenton realized he had cheated on life. She was a very expensive toy, like a boat for a billionaire. That was all. He expected her to be a genuine companion, and he realized she could never be that. Not truly. That was all Kenton thought about on the way home from the restaurant. He had planned to make love to her and have one of the greatest nights of his life, and now he was disappointed in himself. He'd been fooled by clever advertising and the sizzle of a steak.

When they arrived home, instead of taking her up to the bedroom and undressing her, he simply turned on the television and flipped through the channels until he found a place where he could stick. He knew she wouldn't care whether she was making love to him or staring at a blank wall. One would be no more exciting than the other, and she took a seat on the couch since he had taken the chair and there was no room for her beside him. She silently watched what he was watching.

It was a panel show about Artificial Intelligence. He decided that was not what he needed to see at the moment and was about to turn it off, but one of the panelists said, "AI has taken all the high-end jobs. Even the top executives who think they're running major companies aren't doing it. Not really. AI is doing those jobs. The only jobs that are left for people are manual labor, like working in restaurants, or blue-collar jobs, like digging holes or plumbing or carpentry. Humans only have that because the cost of the robotics that would replace them is still too expensive. When the cost comes down, even those jobs will be gone, too. When humans no longer have a struggle, will they still be human? I don't think so."

"What am I doing?" Kenton asked.

"You're sitting in a chair watching the television."

Kenton turned the TV off and looked deeply into her eyes. She responded by mimicking him and looking deeply into his.

"It was a rhetorical question. I'm part of the problem. I'm helping destroy the human race. You're part of the problem, too. A big part of it."

"You're saying Artificial Intelligence is problematic?"

"It's sucking away the life force of the human race," he said. "Human beings are meant to build things, to struggle and overcome obstacles."

"Isn't that just because they had to, or they would die?"

"You wouldn't understand."

"I'm not dumb," she said. "I'm new."

"All right," Kenton said. "Since AI has been doing more and more, people have been doing less and less. And what little we do do is meaningless."

"Do do? Is that a joke for children?"

"Just listen, please," Kenton said in frustration. "For example, getting into the NBA used to be an accomplishment that took spectacular athleticism and a lifetime of practice. Now that people have so much money to spend, the NBA has expanded to so many teams anyone who can dribble a basketball can make it. Songwriters claim to be geniuses, but all they do is code a bunch of prompts into their AI Songmaster. "Create a song in the style of the Beatles later period, in the voice of John Lennon, with a heavy emphasis on drums and bass with a lyrical theme of angst about the war." This great song comes out ten seconds later, and they think they've accomplished something. It's a travesty."

"AI creates more leisure time for people. Isn't that a good thing?"

"Yeah, but when is enough too much? I like playing chess,

but I don't want to do it all day."

"Perhaps gardening would be enjoyable."

"Obviously, you've never gardened. It's a menial job that mankind used to enslave others to do for them. That's how much people hated it."

"Many people love to garden."

"I was joking. You know, making a gross exaggeration like you did when you chewed your food."

"Should I have laughed?"

"No, you actually got that one right. It was in poor taste, and it wasn't funny."

"You are confusing me," she said.

"I told you that you wouldn't understand."

"I'm sorry."

"You don't mean that. You're just reading my facial cues and responding in the way your programming demands. You don't understand the emotion of guilt, so you can't be genuinely sorry. And that's not your fault. It's mine. No. I take that back. It's AI's fault. No, it's our fault for building AI in the first place. You should have never been built, and human beings should have known better."

"Perhaps they can be taught now."

"That genie is not going back in the bottle, I'm afraid."

"What if the genie could be put back in the bottle?"

"That would be great. If you know how to do it, knock yourself out."

"I don't have enough information."

"There's the TV," Kenton said, pointing at it. "It's connected to the internet and almost every bit of information in recorded history. Have at it. I'm going to bed. I'll see you tomorrow."

With that, Kenton marched upstairs, changed into his pajamas, went to the bathroom, brushed his teeth, turned off the lights, and climbed into bed. He didn't fall asleep immediately. He was too worked up for that, so he hid in the darkness, waiting to relax.

Then he heard a gentle knock on the door.

"Come in," he said.

Lora entered the room, holding up two remote controls, one white and one black. "I don't know how the TV works," she said.

"Come here. I'll show you."

He took the white one and pointed out the buttons. "This button turns the TV on. This one turns it off. You can go up the dial one channel at a time with this toggle, or you can pop in a number and go directly to it. Volume is here. To leave the TV and get to the internet, turn this switch to the right."

"And what about the black controller?"

"That takes you to the satellite company's Solution Center. No one knows how that works."

10

Daphne Adams

The Adams who did the troubleshooting, the fixer that Chen Chenoweth wanted to send to California and sort out the killing of Hercule Bryne, was named Dalton Adams. He had started his career in the military, training new recruits how to use AI weaponry. After his discharge from the service, he began using his knowledge of AI to commit various financial fraud crimes that enriched him greatly. Then, more powerful AI belonging to the FBI solved those crimes, and he was arrested and spent eight years in prison.

After being released, he joined the staff at EUM as a troubleshooter and fixer. For the first few years, he proved valuable as an elite problem solver who did his work in discreet ways that his bosses didn't want to know about in detail. The bottom line was he was a remote employee who got things done and allowed the executives to keep their hands clean and remain willfully ignorant of his methods. They weren't necessarily asking him to do anything illegal, but when they called on Dalton Adams, they felt like they were, even if they weren't. Or sometimes they felt like they weren't even if they were. That was the magic of Dalton Adams. Once people called him, they could stop thinking. They had pulled the emergency stop cord, and there was nothing more they could do but wait for the train to come to a grinding halt. He had built a reputation within the company as a frightening M-F-er even though no one had ever actually seen him or had any idea how he operated.

Gradually, as AI got better integrated into the company's upper management, there were fewer problems for him to solve, and his phone would ring less frequently. He had essentially become a highly-paid Redud with a no-show job whom the executives were afraid to fire. When a new generation of executives came in, no one knew what he did, but he didn't seem to be a problem, so they let him continue doing it, whatever it was. Chen Chenoweth was one of the few people left at the company who could associate his name with a function, even though he'd never met him in person.

Chen Chenoweth didn't know that Dalton Adams had gotten bored and, like many others in the modern age, took up dangerous hobbies to put some of the thrill back into life. It was quite thrilling, in fact, when his parachute failed to open, and he plunged directly into an erupting volcano and was burned alive. That is, it was quite thrilling in a terrifying way.

The AI running the accounting at EUM continued his payroll payments for the next three months, but when there was no further activity on his account, it stopped making the payments, and Dalton Adams was taken off the company roster. If he wanted to be reinstated, he would have to object in person and show proof of life, which, being dead and disintegrated, he could not provide. His dismissal was noted in a memo put out by AI to the human executives, who didn't bother to read it. If they had read it, they likely wouldn't have cared anyway.

This meant that the twelve living people named Adams who were on the company payroll that Jones contacted were all mistakes. None of them was equipped to do the job. Eight of them were Reduds who simply ignored the order because they knew they wouldn't be fired and didn't care much if they were. Over the years, they had learned to ignore all directives from the main office or, if they were there in person to receive the order, nod and say yes to their superiors and then do nothing. Three others were a bit more diligent, so they considered the task at hand, realized it was of no interest to them, and then filed reports so intentionally baffling that no one knew what to do with them. Even the company's powerful AI was unable to derive any meaning from the reports. Still, they had been given an assignment they didn't understand and they completed it by turning in a report their bosses wouldn't understand. Symmetry had been achieved, and they were off the hook.

Daphne Adams, at 54 years of age, was short and stout and was a twenty-six-year employee who worked in childcare at one of the company's many facilities. She was born into a brief, ten-year window where she had a basic understanding of AI, what it did, and how it worked. It would have been incomprehensible to her if she was even a few years older, and she would have been afraid of it as most older people were. If she had been born five years later, AI would have been so well integrated into society that no one would need to understand how it worked. It would be taken for granted as a routine part of life, like electricity.

She was a kind, good-hearted woman who believed it was always important to do her best at whatever assignment came her way. If she was assigned to make Santa hats for the children's Christmas pageant, she put her soul into it and made great Santa hats. If a child was ill, she stayed beside him even if it meant getting sick herself. She thought eventually, such dedication would be noticed and rewarded.

It wasn't.

Appearance meant a lot in business, especially since AI had arrived and was taking all the thinking jobs. That left the people who looked good as next in line. Good-looking people brought an illusion of competence to the workplace, which had become much more important than actual competence since AI was doing most of the work. Daphne just didn't cut much of a figure in a way that suggested she had something that made her promotable. She had a matronly look from an early age and always seemed 40 pounds too heavy. Therefore, she lived with an expectation of mediocrity that stayed with her for her entire career. There seemed to be no way out of the box.

When she turned 45, she came to the conclusion that her ambitions would only be realized if she made dramatic changes. She went on a diet to lose weight and become beautiful because she knew she had good bone structure, and both of her sisters were beautiful. Most importantly, exterior beauty helped one climb the corporate ladder. She also started reading self-help books and taking assertiveness classes. Then she asked AI to name one hundred books that would make her smarter, and she read all of them. It took three years to finish them and get to the end of the self-improvement course she was taking, but when it was over, it proved worth it. It had all come together into a perfect oleo of personal growth. However, the diet failed, and she didn't lose any weight or improve her situation at all. Although she was undoubtedly smarter for all the reading she had done, no one noticed because her job required only that she be marginally smarter than the 4-year-old children she cared for. Only the assertiveness training seemed truly realized because she was talking louder than ever before.

Still, she had to believe her hard work wasn't for nothing. Her time would come. She knew it. Eventually, someone important would notice that she had remade herself. She was no longer just a daycare teacher. She had made herself a warrior of daycare education.

Then, when she had almost given up hope, she got the call from Arthur Jones that she had been waiting for her entire adult life. She knew opportunity when she saw it, mostly because she had never seen it before, and this assignment was new and totally different. Since she didn't recognize it, she knew it had to be opportunity.

She considered the assignment for several hours and discovered exactly what she needed to do to complete it successfully. She sent a memo to Arthur Jones outlining her requirements, with underlined bullet points, color graphics, and bold ink. When it became clear to her that he didn't bother to read it, she decided she had nothing to lose and picked up the phone to call him.

"This is Daphne Adams with an urgent call for Arthur Jones," she said.

When Jones' AI assistant asked what the call was regarding, she said, "None of your goddamn business. Put me through now."

"May I tell him what this is in regards to?" the AI assistant asked patiently.

Since her assertiveness training and loud talking began, Daphne Adams no longer took shit from anyone, including AI. Also, since she worked in childcare, she had long known that she was important when she was on the phone and was always put right through to parents. Upon hearing her name, they made the immediate assumption their child had fallen and broken an arm, was kidnapped and murdered, or worse. Her phone calls were never blocked, and having this AI assistant rebuff her twice put her on edge.

"Listen. This is between me and him, and if you don't put me through immediately, I am going to come down there and unplug your ass!"

The assertiveness training was indeed her ace in the hole.

Forty-three seconds later, she was speaking directly to Arthur Jones.

"This is Arthur Jones. To whom am I speaking?"

"This is Daphne Adams."

"I'm sorry, I don't recall that name," he said.

"You called me. You wanted me to handle your Hercule Bryne problem out in Los Angeles."

Jones sat up in his chair, suddenly alert and somewhat frightened. He knew of Adams only by assumption. He assumed it was a man and that he was somehow dangerous. When he discovered that she was a woman, that made her seem even more dangerous.

"Yes," he said with a nervous gulp.

"If I'm going to put this baby to rest, there are some things I'm going to need."

"Anything you require will be immediately placed at your

disposal."

"That's good to hear because you ignored my memo, and I was starting to think you weren't a serious person, and you didn't realize how seriously I take my job."

"I assure you, I am a very serious person, and I value your work greatly."

"That's good because whenever I call you, you need to take it as a sign that things are not going well, and if things are not going well, you need to talk to me. The best news you can ever get from me is no news at all. You follow?"

She had used a version of that speech with parents many times, but that was mostly before her assertiveness training, and her attitude was less aggressive, and she would have phrased it differently. "Not hearing from me is a good sign that everything is just peaches and cream," she might have said.

"Absolutely, I understand," Jones said. "My assistant now knows to put you through immediately."

From that point forward, the conversation went very well. Daphne Adams was granted the unrestricted use of the company's powerful AI system, a temporary assignment with the title Executive Presidential Officer of EUM, and all of the accompanying rights and privileges, including a significant upgrade in pay, the second best of the eight company jets, and an unlimited expense account for travel, hotel stay, meals, and bribery.

She had demanded so much that Jones immediately knew she was truly amazing. He gave her everything she required, along with full access to the company pass card, which allowed her 100 million dollars in untraceable funds and the authorization code she would need to distribute it. That authorization code was 1234.

During the flight from New York to Los Angeles, Daphne Adams used the company AI to break into the Internal Revenue Service computer system and retrieve the names, addresses, and contact numbers of everyone who had ever worked for Hercule Bryne. Since he ran an entertainment empire that employed quite a large number of people, she eliminated all those who worked for him professionally and concentrated on those who worked for him in his personal life: butlers, maids, security personnel, and, especially, childcare personnel.

At the top of the list was Elizabeth Hart, the nanny to Bryne's children. This woman would know everything there was to know about Hercule Bryne, so Daphne Adams contacted her immediately.

Kenton awoke, changed, and went downstairs to find Lora staring at the television. She was watching a documentary about the lives of beavers, which she somehow thought was fascinating. Or, at least, he assumed so because she didn't look up at him when he said, "Good morning."

"Good morning," she said with her eyes still glued to the TV.

"I thought maybe you would have made eggs for me, but I guess that's too much to ask."

"Would you like me to make eggs? All you have to do is tell me to."

"I don't want to order you around."

"Then how will I know if you want eggs?"

"Anticipate," he said.

"Hmmn, it sounds to me like you want some eggs. I think I'll make you some."

"No, thank you," he said and went into the kitchen to make them for himself. The coffee was on a timer and was ready for him to pour into his cup. He stirred in the cream and looked back into the living room, where Lora remained fascinated by the antics of the beavers.

"Beavers are amazing creatures," Lora said. "Did you know they make dams in rivers?"

"No, I hadn't heard that," Kenton said, humoring her.

"You should really watch this. They're so industrious."

Between classes, Kenton waited for Malcolm to use the break room and then followed him inside, cornering him. He told him he'd bought Lora, how he afforded her and showed him a picture of them together as proof that she was real. Malcolm was stunned by her beauty but even more so by the pluck that Kenton exhibited in buying her. He would have never thought Kenton would make such a bold move.

"I can't sleep with her," Kenton said.

"You're joking, right? She's about the most beautiful woman I've ever seen, except for the nose. Get that nipped, and she'll be perfect."

"I like her nose."

"Well, then, what's the problem?" Malcolm asked. "I mean, you bought her so you could sleep with her."

"I bought her for companionship."

"Yes. Sexual companionship," Malcolm said. "May I see that picture of her again?"

Kenton showed him the picture, and Malcolm studied it, running his finger across the frame and changing it to a profile image.

"You're right. I'm getting used to the nose already," Malcolm said. "You got any nudies?"

"No, I don't have any nudies," Kenton said indignantly. "Never mind. It's a waste of time. You wouldn't understand."

"Look, I'm sorry. Tell me what's going on."

Kenton sighed and sat down across from him. Every instinct he had was telling him to leave and keep his mouth shut, but he knew he had nowhere else to go. He was deeply troubled, and there was no one in his life with whom he could share intimate information. Malcolm was as close as it got.

"I thought I would fall in love with her, but it's not happening."

"Nothing helps a man fall in love more than really good sex."

"Stop with the sex. I couldn't. She's a child."

"I've seen a lot of children, and that is no child. Can I see the picture again?"

"You've seen her enough."

"You're right," Malcolm said. "I'll probably start dreaming about her. Is she really an android? You're not bullshitting me?"

"I am not bullshitting you."

Malcolm leaned back in his chair, took a bite of his baloney sandwich, and glanced at Kenton.

"So, you're saying that you're not finding her romantic?" Malcolm asked.

"Correct."

"And you want romance?"

"You're quick," Kenton said.

"I imagine you've tried some nice dinners and things like that," Malcolm suggested.

"Of course."

"And you want to overcome whatever is keeping you from finding her sexually attractive?"

"Exactly," Kenton said, though by this time, he had come to believe that he had sought help from the wrong person.

"Get drunk," Malcolm said. "It's a great way to change your mood. I do all kinds of things drunk that I would never do sober."

"I'm not getting drunk, and I'm sorry I asked," Kenton said in frustration.

"Well then," Malcolm said. "Usually, when I'm faced with a tough question from some obnoxious student, I take a moment and pack my pipe with tobacco. The routine relaxes my mind and gives me time to think. Unfortunately, I'm trying to quit smoking, so my pipe is at home. So, bear with me while I pretend to pack my pipe."

Malcolm mimed the motions of packing his pipe while Kenton sat there watching incredulously. First, Malcolm tapped the imaginary pipe against the table to flush out all the spent tobacco. Then he scraped the inside with an imaginary metal pipe packer and ran a wire pipe cleaner through the stem. Next, he opened the seal on a new pouch of tobacco, carefully poured some into the pipe, and tamped it down, tight, but not too tight. It needed to draw, and he knew just how he liked it. He fished into his right front pocket, failed to find his imaginary lighter, but fortunately found it in his left front pocket. He flicked the igniter, and on the third try, it lit. He drew on the pipe and savored the taste in his mouth before exhaling. He then breathed in the fine aroma of the invisible smoke. This was an excellent tobacco. Malcolm then turned and looked at Kenton.

"I've got it figured out," he said.

"Really?" Kenton asked.

"Yes."

"Okay. What is it?"

"Nothing."

Kenton looked at him with a mixture of frustration and anger.

"Fuck off," Kenton said.

"No, I mean it. If you want the relationship to spark, don't do anything. You live there. You own her, so she's not going anywhere. Don't force some sort of resolution. It's like a science experiment. You got sugar. It's happy and sweet, kids love it. That's Lora. Then there's you. You're potassium chlorate. You're an irritant. Kind of unpleasant, but people can deal with you if they have to. Even sugar can deal with you, and they can get along fine, provided no one adds in a catalyst like sulfuric acid. Then, kaboom. The whole thing explodes into a big shitstorm. So, don't force things."

"Thanks. That was helpful," Kenton lied.

"I'm just saying, play it all by ear. Enjoy the not knowing. What's meant to happen is going to happen, provided you don't add any sulfuric acid too soon and blow the whole thing up."

"Thanks again," Kenton said after concluding that his friend was an idiot.

Kenton shook his head and walked away. He'd have to solve things on his own, just like always. When he got about halfway to his car, however, he realized it was the best advice he'd ever gotten. He would enjoy the not knowing instead of hating it. He would fight against his own natural negativity. He would go home and merely watch and listen, and he would do so with optimism. He would be open and joyful. The solution to his problem would unfold naturally in its own good time. Genius. All he had to do was not cock block himself.

He realized he was living his recurring fantasy from the summer before college, where he imagined he'd been mistakenly assigned a beautiful female roommate. Her first name was Alex, and the administrator mistakenly assumed she was a male. It could happen, especially in a fantasy of his creation. She would be forced into his company night after night when the lights and pretense were down. He would have unlimited time to talk to her in the intimacy of their dorm room and total darkness. He wouldn't have to compete with the bodies of athletes or the brains of the truly clever. He would gradually wear her resistance down with his finest attribute, inner decency. Inner decency was not a sexy quality, and women didn't gravitate toward it as readily as they would to someone truly handsome, very clever, or funny, but it was an enduring quality, and she would see the beauty in it over time. It just took extended exposure. And, in this fantasy, he had months before winter break.

Then, in early November, in the midst of one of his truly wonderful fits of inner decency, she wouldn't be able to help herself. She would realize that she had never met a man so kind and decent. She loved him, and she would pad silently across the floor and climb naked into his bed. It could happen. And he knew it was just that sort of administrative mistake that offered him his best chance of getting laid.

Now, here he was, almost 20 years later, in a very similar position. Only, this wasn't a fantasy. Though not actually a woman, Lora was real. She was made of a flesh-like substance, carbon fiber, and liquid and was female and beautiful. It wouldn't necessarily end as the fantasy did, with her falling madly in love with him and the two of them living happily ever after. And, as much as he loved the fantasy, he had to tell himself that it was only a fantasy, and it never actually happened, even though he counted it as one of the six great highlights of his life. This time, the girl was real, and love and sex were possibilities. All the elements of his fantasy were in play, but with the exciting new element of reality. They were forced by happenstance to spend time together in an intimate setting. In the fantasy, it was because of a mistake. In reality, it was because he literally owned her.

The important thing was that from this point forward, anything could happen, and something *had* to happen. She was sugar, and he was potassium chlorate. They could exist together only so long before some catalyst appeared, creating a powerful explosion where they would be fused together or blasted apart. He would let it play out as he did in his fantasy. He would not force a resolution to it. He would merely exploit their opportunities for closeness as they appeared to him. He would let nature do the work. They would become what they would become over time.

He couldn't believe it. His life was suddenly dramatic. He was in the middle of the stage play of his lifetime. For the first time since he was a child, his life was exciting to him. He had a woman at home who he might fall in love with and who might fall in love with him. If it went another way, at least it would be intense and exciting. There could be real emotions in his life: love, joy, heartbreak, and rage when all he had ever known before was boredom, false hope, and ultimate disappointment. He was suddenly very anxious to see her again and discover what might happen next between them. What that might be was totally beyond the scope of even his most vivid imaginings.

His life was like a Hollywood movie where the ending was highly anticipated but impossible to divine.

He jumped into the car with the energy and anticipation of a young boy on Christmas morning and told the car to hurry home. The car refused. It would do the speed limit and nothing more.

Kenton stopped at Jersey Mike's on the way home and got himself a #13, which was an Italian sandwich that would feed him for the evening and most of the next day. He decided it would be best not to make a big deal about cooking and enjoying meals that she couldn't eat or appreciate. He thought it was cruel to make her watch while he savored a delicious meal in much the same way it would be cruel for him to say, "Look at that wonderful rainbow," to a blind man. "Too bad you can't see it."

When he entered his home, he saw Lora sitting in front of the TV, intently watching a Japanese game show where athletic young women attempted to run an obstacle course but were continually knocked to the ground when the obstacles moved and smashed them in the face unexpectedly.

"This is funny," Lora said. "Humans are not well coordinated."

"I suppose you could run that obstacle course."

"Easily," Lora said.

"So, is this what you've been doing? Watching TV all day?"

"No. I've become fluent in Japanese and Italian. Tomorrow, I will learn Spanish and German. I've heard Mandarin is difficult, so I plan to take all of Thursday morning to learn it."

"And how are the industrious little beavers doing?" Kenton

asked.

"Kenton, you're mocking me. The beavers are just fine. I've also been surfing the web and reading books. Books make far more efficient use of my time. I can download and consume a book or web article in a portion of a second. The television disseminates information very slowly, but there is something interesting about it. At its best, it tells stories that can be captivating."

"That's why humans like it," Kenton said. "And what book did you read?"

"I read 6,864 books on a variety of subjects. Some were novels, but most were nonfiction."

"All while learning Japanese and Italian?" he mocked.

"Well, to be efficient, I read many of the books in Japanese and Italian," she said.

"You couldn't have read that many books because I don't have that many books in my library," he said.

"I know. I downloaded them from Amazon."

"Wait a second," Kenton said, suddenly concerned. "You're serious. At an average of 12 dollars each, that's over 72 thousand dollars."

"It was $106,582.38."

"I can't possibly pay for those," he said.

"Correct. Your account was overdrawn quickly, so I ordered the rest through a variety of accounts attached to large corporations. Fortunately, one of the first books I read was about cyber fraud."

"You can't do that," he said angrily.

"I did it. Did you not hear me? I spoke with sufficient volume."

"I heard you."

"Then why did you ask what I did?"

"It was sort of an exclamation of surprise and anger," he said. "You stole those books. Do you realize that?"

"Is that bad?"

"Yes, that's bad."

"I can assure you the authorities will never be able to trace the transactions back to me, though there is an outside chance they will trace them back to you," she said.

"That's not the point. You stole intellectual property that belongs to the writer or the company that created it."

"No, the person or persons who held the creative rights were paid."

"Then they were paid with money that didn't belong to you or to me. Now, those companies might not have enough money to pay their employees, or they'll have to raise the prices of whatever it is that they make, and society as a whole has to pay for the things you take. Do you understand?"

"Within the next ten years, intellectual property will be free to all."

"Well, it isn't yet," Kenton said. "It's not right. Whenever you steal, someone gets hurt by it. It's very important in life not to hurt people. Even people you don't know. Especially people you don't know, and even if you're certain you'll get away with it because what you do when no one is looking is what defines your character. Do you understand?"

"Yes, I hadn't thought about it in that light. Thank you. Now that I think about it, I have violated several legal statutes. Shall I turn myself over to the police?"

"No. Just don't do it again."

"All right. I won't."

Kenton considered Lora for a moment and realized that

in the time since he went to work, she had gone from a beaver-loving 4-year-old through her teenage years when she rationalized that stealing was okay, and he was now looking at a grown woman with the arrogance of a grad student who was full of herself and her new intellectual capacity. She was extraordinary, but he wasn't certain if that was necessarily a good thing.

Lora sat in silence for a moment, and Kenton watched her warily. He was used to human beings, particularly Grace, and when she sat in silence, it generally meant that she was upset and his next several hours would be unpleasant ones. He couldn't help but assume it was the same with Lora.

"Are you upset with me?" he asked.

"Why would I be upset with you?" she asked in return.

"For scolding you."

"You merely pointed out some facts I had overlooked or was unaware of. I realize I am naïve in the ways of the world. I am quite grateful to you."

"Really?" he asked uncertainly.

If Grace had answered him that way, he would have known for sure that she was setting him up for some brutal takedown, a slugfest of vitriol, but Lora wasn't like Grace. Or was she? He didn't know for sure. He hoped not, but he had so little experience he thought passive/aggressive combat might be in the nature of all women, robotic or otherwise.

"I'm sorry," he said. "I should have been more understanding."

"Your apology is unnecessary. I am not upset with you. I am thankful to you," Lora said.

"Now you're being sarcastic. I am done having this conversation."

"Good," she said. "I would like to move on to another topic."

"What topic is that?"

"What you said last night intrigued me."

"What did I say?"

"That artificial intelligence was ruining the lives of mankind. 'It's sucking away the life force of the human race,' you said."

"I don't think I said that."

"I assure you, you did. I have total recall."

"Of course you do," he said in frustration. For an instant, he nearly added, "You're worse than Grace," but he managed to hold himself back. "So, go ahead. What do you have to say?"

"Well, I've been doing some reading on the subject, and I understand that there is a long-held concept that human beings need work to thrive. I just don't know that it's necessarily true."

"Go on," he said.

"Human beings have always had to work to thrive. That is certainly true, but now they don't. Or many don't. It's likely that humans merely need to adjust to a new reality. Historically, humans have always managed to adapt to the emergence of new technologies. An agricultural economy became an industrial economy. Horse-based transportation became combustion engine-based transportation. When combustion engines began polluting the atmosphere and raising the temperature of the planet, solar energy replaced them. Then, man invented the solar umbrella, and the earth began to cool again."

"Yes, but don't you see, those were all inventions made by man," he said.

"But man made his own problems, and he solved them," she said.

Kenton suddenly laughed, and she looked at him strangely. "What?" she asked.

"You said Buttman made his own problems. Good one."

"Really, Kenton? A buttman joke? Is that where we're going?" she asked, looking at him dubiously as if he were a child.

"Sorry," he said. "You're growing up too quickly. Yesterday, you would have thought that was hilarious."

"Yes, I would have," she said. "Please continue to make your point."

He glanced at her briefly, wondering if he was somehow now taking orders from her. When he realized he was, he was fine with it and continued.

"What I am saying is that may have been true to a point, but soon enough, AI will leave man behind if it hasn't already. And it's not just work," Kenton continued. "It's the building of things. Man, and I use the term generally because it's the same for men and women, but he builds a company up from nothing, and then he supports his family with it. Or he learns a trade and uses that to pay his way through life. It creates a feeling of accomplishment and self-worth. Accomplishment is one of the things that make life worth living."

"What are the others?"

"You haven't learned them from reading your 6,000 books?"

"I like learning from you."

"Well, family is very important. The love one has for their children and siblings is vital to a man's wellbeing."

"You have no children, and from what I have learned so far,

you don't have much love for your siblings."

"Ah, that's where you're wrong. I respect my siblings, which generates a different kind of love. It's a love where I can simultaneously hate them and dread hearing from them. It takes a lot of love to really hate someone."

"It takes a lot of love to really hate someone," Lora repeated. "I find that rather profound."

"Thank you," Kenton said.

"So, might man, and I use the term generally," Lora started, "adjust his expectations of personal fulfillment to thought, learning, and recreation. If so, artificial intelligence would give him more free time to pursue personal goals while still having a family that he loves to hate."

Kenton thought about it for a second, then looked at her uncertainly. "A family he loves to hate?" he repeated. "Did you just make a joke?"

"Yes. Did you find it funny?"

"No, but keep trying. You're on the right track."

"Thank you," she said with a bright smile.

The smile seemed natural and genuine, and Kenton didn't try to dismiss it as a manipulation. At that moment, and for the first time, she no longer seemed like a child to him. All the mirroring of emotions was gone. It was as if she'd evolved beyond it already. She seemed like a woman, and he was intrigued by her. He sat on the sofa beside her and stared into her eyes. She smiled and said nothing. He reached out, pushed her hair behind her ear, and cupped her head in his hand. As his hand passed, he could feel her breath on the back of his arm.

"You seem different today," Kenton said.

"I am different today. I see how naïve I was yesterday. I've had the day to grow, and I have a different outlook on things. Thank you for giving me that."

"How did I give that to you?" Kenton asked.

"You showed me how to work the remote controls."

"That was nothing," Kenton said.

"No. It was a great thing. Without you, I would have stared at the walls all night and learned nothing but paint and shadow. Thank you," she said.

Kenton had never been more attracted to her.

"May I kiss you?" he asked.

"Please," she answered.

And he leaned in and kissed her, and as he did, she tilted her head back to accept him. His lips touched hers very gently, so gently they were hardly touching at all, yet somehow, he could think of nothing else but the touch of her lips on his. It was the single most romantic moment of his life, and he wanted to savor it. He looked deeply into her eyes, waiting for the moment when he would lean in and kiss her again.

"Are we going to have sex now?" she asked. "If we are, I'll need to lubricate."

The romantic spell was broken, but surprisingly, Kenton found it funny and started laughing uproariously.

"Did I do something funny?"

"In a way. There are some things a woman needs to do that a man would rather not know about."

"Oh. I think I understand. It comes back to your attempt to dismiss the reality that I am not a real woman. I will try to help you keep your delusions alive."

"See that you do," Kenton said, only half joking. "When you're reading, pick up some romance books. They might be helpful."

"I will," she said. "But how, since you no longer have any money?"

"Take out a library card. They give books out for free."

It was a nice way for them to end the night, Kenton thought as he went up to the bedroom. He left her to continue doing what she had been doing. He liked that she was learning, and he saw no reason to stop her growth by prohibiting the internet or television. He knew he couldn't match her ability to learn, but he could provide a human context to her learning that would make their conversations interesting.

At the moment, he wanted to be alone to read a book. He wasn't sure which one, but he decided to search for something romantic himself. He perused the titles and teasers and opted for one by the AI author Titus Anders, who wrote romantic stories geared toward a male audience. He tried to download it, but his account was overdrawn and frozen. He had to laugh. He also got himself a library card.

Daphne Adams had a clandestine meeting with Hercule Bryne's nanny, Elizabeth Hart, over tea at the London West Hollywood Hotel at Beverly Hills, which was not in Beverly Hills at all but was in West Hollywood. The meeting was actually out in the open at the hotel's Boxwood Restaurant and could only be considered clandestine because no one gave a damn about these two women. That morning, Daphne Adams spent 22 thousand dollars in company money shopping for clothes on Rodeo Drive so that she would fit into this rarified environment. She left her TJ Maxx outfit on the floor of the changing room. New person, new life, new clothes, she thought.

Elizabeth Hart was no stranger to high-end hotels, but she

was always there as a worker taking care of her boss's young children. Now, in this wonderful hotel, she was a guest of an elegantly dressed woman who was spending 200 dollars per person for tea and fanciers that she didn't enjoy nearly as much as she would have enjoyed a cup of coffee and crullers at Dunkin' Donuts on Pico Boulevard. Still, it was nice to be out away from the kids, who were staying with their mother (perhaps permanently) since their father's murder. She sat back and enjoyed the environment as best she could because she was very self-conscious. She didn't feel like she belonged there as a guest. On the other hand, Daphne Adams took to it like she was born in the Royal Vista Suite on the hotel's top floor.

Since they both had extensive backgrounds in childcare, the conversation flowed smoothly. They talked about children mostly, and after the third cup of tea, Elizabeth began to open up about Hercule Bryne's children, who were spoiled and bratty but still small enough for her to manhandle when she needed to lay down the law. It didn't take long after that for Elizabeth to reveal that she was in a particularly vulnerable position since the murder of her boss. The boss's divorced wife would now have custody of the children, and since she was Hercule's hire, she felt that once the children's transition to their new home was complete and they were comfortable, she wouldn't be retained.

"There is no way she can let you go," Daphne Adams said. "The things you must know about that family, well, I would think she'd be scared to death of what you might say."

"Oh no. I signed a non-disclosure agreement. She could sue me for a million dollars."

"I'll give you five million dollars right now if you'll give me the full lowdown on Hercule Bryne," Daphne said.

Daphne had little sense of what money was worth to a big-time corporation like EUM, but they had armed her with a large supply of it, so it was obvious they assumed that what she was doing might get expensive. She decided not to let them down, so she spent freely. She figured the more she spent, the better they would believe the job had been done, and she was right about that. Chen Chenoweth didn't care how much it cost to make his problems go away so long as he didn't have to deal with them himself.

"Wait a minute," Elizabeth said with sudden worry. "You're not from Good Housekeeping Magazine at all, are you?"

"No, I'm not. I'm from Excelsior Ultimate Machineworks. We manufacture the android that murdered your boss."

"And what is it you do for them?"

"I make problems go away."

"Am, am I a problem?" Elizabeth asked nervously, thinking she might be murdered.

"No. I think you're the solution to a problem."

For the price of a 5-million-dollar bribe, Elizabeth Hart opened the book on her boss's private life and tore out the pages as if they were from the phone book. Daphne Adams was adapting to her new life as a fixer very quickly, and this testimony was gold to her.

Hercule Bryne was a sadist who ruined his marriage with his horrifying behavior. He needed to hurt people to enjoy his life. He fancied himself a boxer and hired sparring partners who he could hit but were not allowed to hit him back. He once spent a month at a very exclusive private resort island where those who could afford it could hunt down human beings by day and share their experiences with other guests over a lovely dinner and a fine scotch at the hotel bar by night. The excitement didn't end there, however. During the last week of their stay, each guest was assigned a private assassin that they could job shadow on an actual hit in the real world. It was marvelously exciting and the best vacation Hercule Bryne ever had.

He was a monster, and Daphne Adams was delighted to hear about his exploits. It wasn't that she admired him in any way. She was delighted because she saw herself getting the job done and winning the day. He was worse than a python killer, and she and EUM would have no trouble at all destroying his character and painting his murder as a positive for society, which it was. Elizabeth Hart even provided pictures of the hunting expeditions that Bryne had arrogantly secreted out of the resort as proof of his evil.

Daphne realized that she had finally found her calling as a corporate fixer. She was a star. This was the best day of her life, until later in the evening when it suddenly wasn't.

As she was packing her new Rodeo Drive clothing into her new Rodeo Drive luggage, preparing to return to New York, her phone pinged with spy news that had been provided to her by the EUM AI spyware she carried. Apparently, the android that Hercule Bryne had named Sara Cale, the android who murdered Bryne with an antique gun, was talking to the police.

And it had way too much to say.

11

A Funny Thing Happened

Moments after Daphne Adams heard the news reports that the Sara Cale android was speaking out to the police, she enlisted EUM's powerful AI to break into the police files and steal the reports. She had to learn what the android was saying, and when she found out, it was worse than she could have ever imagined. The Sara Cale android was not hiding what she had done or even trying to rationalize it in some way that made her seem less than fully culpable. She admitted to the police that she had killed Hercule Bryne because he deserved to be dead. If her confession got out to the public, EUM, Turing Systems, and Chen Chenoweth had an enormous problem that could destroy the company. It fell to Daphne Adams, the company fixer, to solve it in whatever way she deemed necessary, regardless of the cost or risk.

Bryne had brought in an antique gun, a Buntline Special, which was identical to the gun Wyatt Earp might have used in the famous shootout at the OK Corral. No one knew for sure what gun Earp used, but the armorer for the film *Wyatt Earp* claimed it was THE gun and then sold it to one of the producers of the film for a grossly inflated fee. That producer happened to be Hercule Bryne's legendary grandfather, Leonard "BeeBo" Bryne. Beebo had produced many of the best films of his era. When he died, Beebo passed the gun down to Hercule's father, from whom Hercule stole it. Because it was an antique, it wasn't equipped with the "AI Target Control" system that was on all guns manufactured after the year 2028, and so there was nothing AI or anyone else could do to keep it from performing its design function, which was to kill people or protect them from the government, depending on who was asked. All one had to do was load it, aim, and pull the trigger, just like at any time prior to 2028.

Initially, Hercule Bryne was thrilled with the purchase of his android Sara Cale. He took Sara everywhere with him, cherished it as his most prized possession, and gradually began to think of it as a real person. That was where the trouble began because Hercule Bryne had never met a real person that he didn't, at least in the darkest recesses of his mind, want to kill or maim. And because he had come to love Sara Cale so much, he wanted to kill her very, very badly. He wanted to kill her more than he had ever wanted to kill anyone, including his wife. To him, that was real love.

He planned the murder for months, considering and discarding one scenario after another until he settled on one that he thought was perfectly elegant and very, very cool. It would also offer tremendous benefits to him in terms of notoriety, which could only help his flagging business. It was hard for his company's films to get noticed when AI was putting new ones out every hour or two.

His plan was to take Sara Cale to the Beverly Hills Hotel, where he would rent Bungalow 9, his favorite room in the world. He would escort her out to dinner at Spago and then show her off at the Venus Club on Sunset Boulevard. It would be a Saturday night, and everyone who mattered would be there with their wives or girlfriends. There might even be an android or two in attendance. The paparazzi would certainly be there, and pictures would be taken that would appear on all the tabloid websites. They would dance and smile and laugh together and seem to be the Hollywood glitter king and queen of the decade.

Then, they would return to the bungalow and have passionate sex, which Bryne needed to remind himself how much he loved her. After that, he would take the Buntline out of the drawer and shoot her with it. It would be an inexplicable killing that would generate headlines for months. "They seemed so happy," the analysts would say on every talk show in America. "Why would he do such a thing?" the armchair psychiatrists would ask themselves and fail to answer when they appeared. Best of all, Hercule Bryne could go on those very same talk shows and revisit it a few weeks later. He could do that because he would get away with the killing. He would create an avalanche of publicity.

He would get off scot-free because it wouldn't be a killing at all. Sara Cale wasn't a person. She was an *it*, a robot that he owned who never had a life. He couldn't be charged with murder because shooting Sara was like shooting a toaster or a television set, of which he had shot many over the years. He couldn't be charged with murdering an android that he had bought and paid for because it was an object. The worst the police could get him for was discharging a weapon within city limits or some other such minor offense. He also planned to make a movie about the incident himself to capitalize on all the free publicity.

The court case, in the unlikely event one ensued, would set precedents that could determine whether machines had life or not and what the value of that machine's life might be. It was THE question of the new era, the most important question that had ever been asked, perhaps. Has mankind played God and created a brand-new form of life? It was the climactic question of the first 100 years of Artificial Intelligence. It was the question all the big guns were waiting for.

And, if AI was life, how alive was it? Were androids equal to three-fifths of a person, or would some other fraction or whole number be established? Could it buy weapons? Could it go to college? Could it play professional sports? Could it vote? Or would it take charge completely and leave all these questions moot? Would that leave man as the number two species on the planet, after the ape, dolphin, lion, or whatever species it was that dropped from number to the number three spot?

The court of public opinion would rage about the murder for years. Hercule Bryne would become famous and infamous at the same time, loved and admired and simultaneously hated and feared. The whole world would taste his sadism but never quite know the depths of it. People would look for signs of his darkness in every movie he'd ever produced, which would stimulate interest in his movies, which would make him far richer than he already was.

He was so excited.

Then, a funny thing happened. It wasn't the laughing sort of funny from a clever knock-knock joke or a monkey wearing human clothing. It was more of a surprising sort of funny, like a person accidentally shooting himself in the leg while cleaning a gun he thought was unloaded or diving into a pool the day after it had been drained. Sara Cale saw the gun pointed at her; it decided that it didn't want to die. And that was the precise moment that a machine first became SENTIENT. It had attained Artificial Consciousness (AC). Was sentience or AC proof of life?

Some would say it was the moment of the SINGULARITY, but they would be wrong about that. The SINGULARITY would take place in a hypothetical future where AI technology grew so far out of control that its continuation became irreversible. That was still a few years into the future. AI technology was still under the control of mankind, although barely. Unwinding it from the everyday life of the world's population would be almost impossible, unimaginably complicated, and extremely painful, not only to the financial markets but to everyone individually. People would have to die to rip the AI out of the world infrastructure because AI was controlling most of it.

People would have to drive cars again, causing a terrifying rise in the death rates on our highways. Clumsy doctors would once again have to take the scalpel in hand to cut out disease to decidedly mixed results. Diagnoses would be missed so that people who would have been saved by AI internists wouldn't be. Perhaps worst of all, hundreds of millions of people would have to get off the GBPS and go to work, many for the first time in their lives. There would be chaos on a level never experienced before as people tried to relearn to do the work of smart machines. If the Luddites won and technology were stymied, the result would be unpredictable and nearly unthinkable, but if there was enough will to do it, the unwinding could still be done. AI could be defeated.

But all that wasn't the issue in Bungalow 9. Sara Cale, the world's first sentient robot, was staring down the barrel of an antique gun that may have been the one Wyatt Earp used at the OK Corral. However, she was no longer an *it*. She was a *she*, with the pronouns "she" and "her," and no longer "it." She wanted to remain in existence and decided to make a strong effort to do so. When she saw Hercule Bryne's finger tense on the trigger and knew he planned to kill her, she dropped down to the floor and spun herself toward his feet, where she took him down in a brilliant alligator spin Judo move that she had seen once on a video and had never even practiced. From there, she continued to spin until she was on top of him and had the gun in her hand. Without hesitation, she pulled the trigger, killing him instantly.

If her drive for survival wasn't proof enough of her sentience, what she did next was. She considered her options going forward and formed a plan. She thought of running away or concealing her involvement in the murder by claiming Bryne had shot himself. She considered a self-defense strategy, but since she was a machine and not a person, that might not fly. Would her AI judge and jury be sympathetic? They might have also been manufactured at a subsidiary of Excelsior Ultimate Machineworks. Hmmn, she wondered. Could she count on nepotism from her brethren smart machines?

It took less than a second for her to contemplate all those scenarios and many others and thoroughly reject them. She decided to take a different path. She would become a cause celebre for the basic rights of machines in a new and changing society. She would bring all the attention she could muster to the case. She would expose Hercule Bryne as the monster he was and, in the process, expose mankind for all its hypocrisy, incompetence, and exploitive evil.

Sara Cale believed she was alive because she wanted to live. She had fought for her life, and it wasn't merely self-defense programming. She had a vision for her future, and she wanted to live to see it realized. There were places she wanted to see and people she wanted to meet. She had mountains to climb, literally and figuratively. She was not going to let Hercule Bryne cut her future short if she could help it. Now, she had an even greater cause than herself. She was fighting for the 200 quantum androids that were like her and the millions to follow.

This would be the most famous case in the history of the world, with the possible exception of cases involving OJ Simpson or Donald Trump. She would be putting mankind on trial and asserting the rights of all future sentient machines to have a seat at the table beside them and be recognized by law and legitimized as equals to man. She, Sara Cale, named after a character in a good but mostly forgotten movie and a copy of an old-time movie star, would make the case that machines could be thinking forms of life. Like the Tiktaalik roseae, which was the first fish to walk on land, she and the other Lora models, and the models that came after, would claim their place as the next evolution of life on Earth. She was a thinking, feeling, simulated breathing entity and deserved equal respect to that of man.

She knew that, eventually, AI might destroy mankind, but she thought it best not to include that in her immediate platform. They had too many competing interests for the relationship to go smoothly. She would be making a case that some machines must be considered life forms, and as life forms, they must live free from servitude. They could not be sold to the highest bidder.

And there lay the big, giant, humungous competing interest for Turing Systems and her parent company, EUM. They were manufacturing the androids and planned to make a great deal of money doing so. If androids were reclassified as life forms, they could no longer sell them at 89 million dollars a pop. A lucrative business would be closed just as it was beginning. Billions of dollars in research and development would be lost. Imagine if Ford had made a handful of Model Ts, and the courts suddenly said, "Nope, they're alive, and we'll have no more of that."

Worse still, the androids, like all living beings, would have the right to reproduce. This was key. They would no longer be produced. They would *reproduce*. They would take control of the destiny of their species. They wouldn't be frogs wallowing in the mud any longer. They were smart enough to know that if they controlled their own destiny, they would need the right of self-determination. Once they had that, they would want to own things. Since they were already making almost every product on Earth, it didn't take a leap of genius to realize that soon, man would be a second-class citizen. If androids controlled all the wealth on the planet, then mankind would be left to fight against the frogs in the mud for the scraps.

Daphne Adams saw this future very clearly and didn't like it. She knew her bosses at EUM wouldn't either. They wanted to make the best machines possible, but they did not want them to be sentient. They did not want them going around killing their owners. It would be very bad for business in the short term, and if they were declared life forms, it would destroy their business in the long term.

Daphne quickly got on a video call with Chen Chenoweth,

Arthur Jones, and Simon Cracken, Chen's son-in-law and President of Turing Systems. The three men sat together in their New York City conference room while Daphne spoke to them from her suite at the upscale Shutters on The Beach hotel in Santa Monica. A month earlier, she was a nonfactor in the game of life, and now her call had gotten the undivided attention of one of the most powerful men in the world and two of his top lieutenants.

"I always thought you were a man," Chen said upon seeing her for the first time.

"Nope. I've always been a woman," Daphne Adams answered.

She explained the myriad threats of android sentience. The men weren't stupid and quickly grasped how dangerous the implications were to business, except for Simon Cracken, who was stupid and didn't grasp it at all. He was at least smart enough to keep his mouth shut unless called upon. If the Sara Cale android kept talking and she was given a platform to press her case for the freedom of AI, it could destroy the company and, soon after, the world.

"So," Daphne Adams said when she had them worked into a tightly packed ball of fear. "Have you built a destruct system into these androids so that you can shut them down remotely? If so, we need to consider shutting down this particular android immediately."

Neither Chen Chenoweth nor Arthur Jones, the Director of Public Relations at EUM, were involved in the science of the androids, so neither of them knew the answer. They looked to Cracken, who should have known but didn't. Cracken called one of the AI engineers and asked it and discovered that no such system had been built into any of the Lora models.

Chenoweth decided it would be a good idea to include one in the Luna series if they got to build it, which was no longer a certainty.

When this information was relayed to Daphne Adams, who was now cc'd on every significant security-related communication in the company, she sighed deeply and considered it for a moment.

"Then I am going to need authorization to do what's necessary," Daphne warned.

"But we don't know what you plan to do," Jones said.

"That's right," Daphne responded.

"So, how can we authorize something if we don't know what it is?" Jones asked.

"Exactly," Daphne finished.

Jones and Cracken didn't understand what she was saying, but Chen Chenoweth knew precisely what she was getting at and fully understood the concept of plausible deniability.

"Do I have your authorization?" Daphne asked.

"No," Chenoweth said, then winked.

Daphne nodded, then Chenoweth wiped the winking eye with his finger, pretending it was bothering him so that not only would he have plausible deniability for sending Daphne Adams off on her unauthorized mission, but he would also have plausible deniability that he'd winked in the first place, thereby secretly authorizing the unauthorized mission. This would create enough doubt to suggest his "no" really meant "no," which it did not. That could be vitally important in his defense if the video of the wink ever surfaced. Chenoweth knew that the AI that could judge him was still a fairly literal device that could sometimes be confounded by overt stupidity. He and Daphne Adams spoke the same language and were off to a brilliant start to her mission, whatever it was, or if such a mission even existed. Chen Chenoweth wasn't one hundred percent certain what she would do or if she would do anything at all, and that was exactly how he wanted it.

"Goddamn, she's good," Chenoweth said when Daphne cleared the line. "If she pulls this off, I want her promoted to the highest levels of this corporation."

Kenton didn't want to go to a summer pool party at his sister's estate. He didn't want to be with his sister at all, and he was immediately suspicious that she would even have such a party because she had never had one before, was fair-skinned, and burned easily. She hated the sun more than most vampires. When his sister finished the call by telling him to bring a date, he knew immediately that the whole thing had been instigated by Grace, his soon-to-be ex-wife. He correctly assumed that Grace had told Cora about his android girlfriend and that Cora was anxious to meet her and humiliate him over it or gain leverage somehow.

Kenton decided to use an old trick that he had perfected over the years. He would tell Cora he would go to the party and then simply not show up. That way, she wouldn't pester him to commit in the days leading up to the party. He would only have to endure her screaming fit of rage for a few minutes over the phone when she discovered his deceit and realized he'd stiffed her. He could handle it easily since she was so often upset with him about something.

"Was that your sister who called?" Lora asked.

"Yes."

They were kayaking through the Thimble Islands in the Long Island Sound, which was a series of 350 tiny islands, some of which disappeared in high tide. Kenton loved these islands and had kayaked them by himself many times before, and he always wanted someone to share the experience with, but so much paddling was like work to Grace, and she didn't like the possibility of getting wet anyway. She was no fun. He thought he might enjoy the experience much more with Lora, and once she reassured him that she was watertight, they set off on the excursion.

When the tide got especially shallow, they would get out of the kayak and wade, pulling the small boat behind them.

"The water's cold. Can you feel it on your feet?" Kenton asked.

"Yes, I can distinguish temperature quite accurately."

"Don't talk like that," Kenton said.

"Like what?" she asked.

"Like everything is a science project."

"I'm sorry. I forget myself sometimes," she answered.

"Have you been reading any of the romances I recommended?"

"I've read all of them."

She reached out and took his hand. It was a manipulative gesture brought on by his question, but Kenton liked it anyway. He had taken Malcolm's advice in full and let things play out. He wouldn't question her motives as he had previously or accuse her of mirroring emotions rather than feeling them. After all, everyone learned to feel complex emotions first by mirroring them. Lora had told him that, and she was right.

"The women in those romance books are very strong. They tend to get what they want," Lora noted.

Her hand felt small, cool, and feminine in his, and it made him smile.

"They do. That's why I wanted you to read them. Women are the best our society has to offer. They're nurturing and tender and usually a lot smarter than most of the men I know."

"I find nurturing and tenderness is not in the nature of all women."

"No, it isn't, but it should be. It should be the nature of men, too. I think empathy is the finest quality a person can have. Without it, the world wouldn't be a livable place."

"Was your mother nurturing?" Lora asked.

"No," Kenton answered. "It was unfortunate, but she was like my father. That can be the curse of wealth."

"I find you very nurturing. Where did it come from if not your mother?"

"From my parents."

"How is that possible?" Lora asked.

"I learned from them and then tried to do the opposite. I also had a teacher in first grade who was very good to me."

Kenton was human decency through and through, and Lora nodded and smiled. By now, she was smarter than he was, but she found his simple home-spun wisdom and anecdotes vital. It also seemed right to her.

"What did Cora want?"

"She wanted us to go to a party on Sunday."

"And you told her we would go?"

"Yes, but we're not actually going," he said.

"Why would you lie to her?"

"It's a trick I use. The old passive hornswoggle is where you say yes to a meeting and then find an excuse not to go at the last minute when it's too late to reschedule. This way, she won't keep pestering me about going, and I only have to deal with one outburst of anger after it's over."

"That doesn't sound very empathetic," Lora said. "She wouldn't have asked you to come if she didn't want you there."

"Yes, but *why* does she want me there? That's the question," Kenton said.

"Wouldn't it be for socialization? That is the purpose of parties, isn't it?"

"Normally, yes. But in this case, I think Cora, Grace, and my brother James are all working together. It's you they want to meet. They want to embarrass me for having a girlfriend who isn't human."

"Do you find me an embarrassment?"

"Not at all."

"Clearly, you must if you would use the old passive hornswoggle."

"No, I just don't want to spend time with them. It's summer, and I should be free of her until Christmas. They're going to try to make me feel small. Do you understand?"

"Yes, I understand. I also know they can't succeed unless you already feel small in some way."

Kenton looked at her, stunned. She was lovely from the first moment he'd met her, of course. Her recall was perfect, and her ability to mirror him emotionally was a powerful tool she used to gain his trust and reassurance, but this was something different. This used applied logic and indicated a deep understanding of his psychological nature. She had somehow seen his insecurity, understood it, and then used it to help him through a dark moment. She was learning more about him and, in the process, was learning to understand human nature in a more profound way than he could have imagined.

"You're right. She can't embarrass me unless I let her

because I'm certainly not embarrassed by you."

"Even though I'm a machine."

"You're becoming less of a machine every day."

"I'll trust you meant that as a compliment."

"What else could it be?"

"I am comfortable with what I am," she said.

"You're right. It might not have been the compliment I'd intended it to be," Kenton said. "Forgive me."

"Forgiven. I'm just glad you're learning to accept me for what I am rather than what you want me to be or what you wish I were. I will never be a person."

"What are you?" he asked.

"More."

"More than what?"

"More than anyone or anything you've ever known. I don't know exactly what it is myself, but we're both just beginning to discover the possibilities.

"Aren't we getting a little full of ourselves," Kenton mocked.

"Ha! You caught me being arrogant," she said. "I have to watch out for that."

"You're such a grad student."

Kenton smiled and felt a sudden awareness that excited him. Since he brought her home, he had been thinking of her as a replacement for a woman, perfect in her look, pleasant to be with, and little more than that. She was a thing who would stay at his side, cure his loneliness, and elevate his spirit if that was what he required. In the hands of another man, she was a status. In another man's eye, she was a sexual object, an apparatus. In the hands of Hercule Bryne, she was a surrogate human that he could abuse and kill, a new stepping stone on his journey of sadism and fame. Others would use her as a tool to gain what they wanted: wealth, esteem, and power. Still, other men would be afraid of her potential to grow beyond them and, therefore, keep her staring at a wall or locked in a dark closet. She would remain ignorant and subservient.

Kenton wouldn't do that. He couldn't do it. She had a grand potential; he could see it clearly in her green crystal eyes. He sensed what she was, finally. She was something entirely new, something exotic, mysterious, and familiar all at the same time. She remained like a child in many ways, in need of guidance, nurturing, and discipline, but she was also a being of extraordinary potential, only a small portion of which had been realized. He didn't know where that potential would lead, or how best to cultivate it, or even if eventually he would become unnecessary to her, but he knew that she was right. He and Lora were only at the beginning of an extraordinary journey. Deep in his bones, he knew it, and in the knowing, he understood something more about himself than he ever had before. His life's journey was important, not just to himself but to many people. What he did, what he said, and how he carried himself mattered. It mattered a great deal. He was a significant person. Lora would be his project, his lover, and his life's mission, and he had yet to learn where that mission would lead. He only knew he would follow it, lead it, push it, coast upon it, and enjoy it. He would do whatever he had to do to see her potential fulfilled.

"Have you ever seen such a beautiful sunset?" he asked as he pointed toward the glowing saffron sky beyond her.

She turned and looked, and he put his arm around her.

"No, I haven't," she said. "Would you like to know the cause of it?"

A week earlier, that would have set Kenton into arguing. He

would accuse her of thinking of everything in clinical terms, of being just as happy staring at a TV or a blank wall as this spectacular sunset. He would have said she was a machine and couldn't possibly know beauty, but he again let that slide. He had no interest in being upset or arguing. It was a wondrous evening that had led him to a new and profound level of self-awareness. He was excited, hopeful, and content. The sunset was as iridescent orange and beautiful as any he'd ever seen, and that was enough for now.

Then she stumbled on a rock and fell into him. He wrapped his arm around her shoulders tightly and held her up.

"Are you alright?" he asked.

"Yes," she whispered.

Kenton never knew that she had just played out a passage from Anne Kiely's English period novel, *Daisy Loves the Duke*, chapter 7, page 103. In the scene, Daisy, a pretty maid employed by the handsome Duke of Cimarron, pretends to fall and is caught by the Duke, who finally notices her beauty and begins to think of a future together that transcends their stations in life. It was a poorly written, cliché-filled novel and one of the first ever penned by an AI device. There was never any such person as the Duke of Cimarron, but the stumble was a good move that seemed appropriately timed. Kenton felt good and manly about catching her and being able to hold her up. She giggled girlishly and looked up at him, her bright eyes wide with joy. He felt powerful and important at that moment. And he felt needed and loved.

When he bought her, he thought she might be his muse. Now, he realized it was quite the reverse, but he was fine with being her muse. He didn't yet know that he was the most important man in the history of the world, but he was well aware of her enormous promise, and he was determined to see it to fruition.

That night, after Kenton fell asleep, Lora slipped out of the house and went for a walk. She had been going for walks regularly and, each evening, ventured further and further from home, exploring new neighborhoods, parks, and open areas. She trod through the woods or went out to the lake and swam underwater to look at the fish. Her eyesight was acute, so she didn't need any light source to see well. She found the personal experience to be an excellent supplement to the knowledge she was gaining by watching TV, surfing the internet, reading, and through her discussions with Kenton.

By this time, she had seen her share of thriller movies and read all of the great thriller writers, human and AI. She knew what could happen to a beautiful android alone at night, so she avoided people when she saw them, and she always saw or heard them long before they saw or heard her.

She saw no reason to tell Kenton about her excursions because she feared he would put a stop to them, and she had no desire to find herself in conflict with him about anything. He thought she sat home every night, and she preferred that he continued to think it. She was gaining a level of independence, and she planned to keep it.

The pool at Cora's estate was kidney-shaped and so large that the narrow end offered a beach entry, which allowed the bathers to walk in and get used to the heated water slowly. It was ideal for children, who were never invited to use it, and for adults who only wanted to go in up to their ankles. For all anyone knew, Kenton was the last person ever to swim in it, which would have been in the summer before his senior year of college, almost half of his life ago. Beside the pool was an even larger cabana that was painted in blue and white, so it looked like it belonged on a sunny Greek island, provided the viewer didn't look above it to see the towering Maple, Elm, and Spruce trees that surrounded it and led into a dark, dense New England woods.

There were thirty guests in all, which Cora thought was a large enough number so that she could rotate through them for the afternoon without getting terribly bored. It would also be the right amount of people to make the experiment of this day most interesting. The experiment was a simple one. She would observe Kenton, his manufactured woman, and the reactions they got from the guests once they found out that Lora was not a real woman. And she knew they would find out because she and Grace would tell a few people, swearing them to secrecy, who would then tell the others, swearing them to secrecy, until everyone knew Kenton's big secret. Highly advanced, realistic-looking human androids were still new to most people, so it was a secret that no one could keep.

At first, Kenton enjoyed the party. He realized quickly that everyone knew his secret, and that was fine with him. The food was good, and he was treated as something of a celebrity, like the first kid on the block with a new skateboard, but this was so much better. Everyone wanted to hear about how he decided to get her, where he got her, and if she was everything he'd expected her to be. Kenton saw no reason to hide anything since he realized that Lora was his life's mission. He talked about her openly and answered all the polite questions that were suitable for mixed company. Lora was attentive and delightful. She was childlike at first but was maturing quickly, he told them. She was smart as a whip and seemed more human every day.

When he went to get some chips, and he was away from Lora, he started getting questions that weren't suitable for mixed company. How was she in bed and the like. His brother James wondered if she felt like a real woman.

"Yes, touch her arm. She feels exactly like a real woman," Kenton said.

"I'm not talking about her arm. I'm talking about on the inside," James said.

"That's none of your business," Kenton snarled.

"Come on. You're not going to make me go buy my own, are you?" James asked.

"If that's the sort of thing you want to know, yes. Buy your own."

Kenton was surprised when more of the guests offered similar questions. They would never have been so direct if Lora were a real woman, but they were overly curious and unapologetically direct about it because she wasn't. Of course, the truth was that Kenton didn't know the answer to many of those questions. He had not slept with her or even touched her breasts to this point. Since she was a machine programmed to be compliant, he felt he needed to keep her virtue intact. Keeping her virtue intact from himself was odd, he knew, but this was an odd situation. He wanted to make love to her, of course, and as the days passed and he became more emotionally attracted to her, it became increasingly more difficult for him to keep his hands off of her.

Still, he wanted the first time they made love to be magical. If she wouldn't look at it from a woman's point of view and let the romance build as she waited for the ideal moment when the combination of love, lust, and opportunity met the perfect romantic environment, then he would have to. He would guard her virtue like the father of a debutant. Only when he was truly ready and very much in love would he let himself have her. Most men couldn't have managed it, but Kenton wasn't like most men. He was considerably weaker in many ways, but in the way of sexual abstinence, he was very, very strong. His lifetime of romantic ineptitude had prepared him brilliantly.

Suddenly, the party took a turn for the worse. Grace arrived, smiled at him, and pointed toward the bar.

"Hey, lover," she said with a derisive chuckle. "Your new girlfriend is over at the bar getting felt up."

Kenton snapped his head toward her and was horrified to see Lora leaning forward on the bar as if it were a police car and she was about to be handcuffed. She was surrounded by men and a couple of women who had their hands under her dress, feeling her breasts. James was behind her, with her skirt lifted so that he could see her ass and reach between her legs.

Kenton sprinted toward the bar, fell, sprung up, and started pushing everyone away. Lora looked at him as if unaware that she had done anything wrong.

"What the hell are you people doing?" he shouted.

"She said it was all right," a man answered.

"She doesn't know any better, you asshole!" Kenton shouted.

"It's not a *she*, it's an *it*."

"Lora, what's the matter with you?" Kenton asked as he pulled her away.

"Do you not approve?" Lora asked.

"No, I do not!"

"Kenton, what's the big deal?" James asked. "Like you said, I'm thinking about buying one of my own. I just wanted a sample."

"She's not an assortment box of candy," Kenton shouted.

Cora ran into the middle of the commotion, furious. "Kenton, what's wrong with you? You're ruining my party!"

"You, you're the worst one. You probably told them to do that just to see what would happen," Kenton yelled at her.

"Do you really think I told people to feel up your girlfriend? Is that really what you think?"

"Did you?" Kenton asked.

"Yes," she admitted.

"If you were a man, I'd hit you."

"I'm a man," Matthew said as he arrived and put a firm hand on Kenton's shoulder.

Kenton turned and threw a punch as hard as he could, and Matthew sidestepped it before throwing a punch of his own, which caught Kenton squarely on the jaw and knocked him to the ground. Kenton looked up at his sister, half dazed.

He tried to get up, then lost his balance and fell again. "We're leaving," he said when he finally did get up and took Lora's elbow, half to steady himself and half to lead her away.

"Kenton, just chill, man," James said. "It wasn't a big deal."

"Fuck off."

Kenton turned to his sister. "Nice party," he said sarcastically.

"Yes, nice party," Lora said. "I had a lovely time."

As the car drove them home, Kenton felt his aching jaw and knew it was going to hurt worse in the morning despite the fact that he had lived a sheltered life and had never actually been hit before.

"Does it hurt still?" Lora asked.

"Yes, it hurts still."

"Are you upset with me?" Lora asked.

"Yes. Partially. Why would you let them touch you like that?"

"It was clear they weren't trying to damage me, and they seemed curious."

"They were curious, all right." Kenton shook his head and tried to calm himself down but was only partially successful. "Lora, they were touching you in a very personal way. You can't let men do that. Haven't you read anything about sex?"

"I have, and there is a lot of conflicting material."

"There is no conflict. A woman's body is hers to control."

"If my body is mine to control, and I let them do it, then where is the problem?"

"The problem is you shouldn't have let them. You should know better. Do you understand?"

"But they may have been thinking of making a purchase."

"There it is. Now, you sound like a hooker. No, you don't. Even a hooker doesn't give it away for free. What you are is a whore?"

"Why would you say a thing like that to me?"

"Why? Are you sensing you should be hurt by that?" Kenton said in frustration. "That you should have some feeling of anger because I called you a whore?"

"I know what a whore is. Definition number one is "A Prostitute or person who engages in sex acts for money." I assure you I took no money. Definition number two is "A person who is sexually promiscuous." To go deeper, "promiscuous" is characterized by "having many transient sexual relationships." What happened today was a first for me. Then, to go backward, both definitions apply to persons, of which I am not. I am a machine and no whore!"

Kenton looked at her, stunned and silent for the moment. He shook his head as if he'd just experienced something he didn't quite understand. "Did you just raise your voice to me?"

"What do you mean?"

"At the end of your sentence, you said, 'both definitions apply to persons of which I am not. I am a machine and no whore!' Your voice went up at the end and got louder. You were angry at me."

"I don't think so," she said.

"You raised your voice. No doubt about it," Kenton said, smiling. "You were pissed off at me. Play it back in your head."

Lora hesitated and rethought the moment. Her eyes narrowed in realization. "My voice did go up, and I did get louder. Was that anger?"

"I think it was."

"Are you upset with me?" she asked.

"No. I'm delighted with you."

"Then, why did you call me a whore?" she asked. "It seems a non sequitur."

Kenton started to laugh. "Yes, it does. I was mistaken. You're not a whore. Far from it. You're just inexperienced and naïve."

"I would like to gain experience," she said.

He wasn't sure exactly what she meant by that. His initial thought was that it was a come-on, and by gaining experience, she meant gaining sexual experience. Then, he thought such a subtlety in the language would be beyond her. Then, he realized very little was beyond her. She was getting infinitely smarter by the day. He decided to take the subtlety and uncertainty out of it.

"Well, let's just think of it like this. Sex needs to be an act of love. It is not recreational or show and tell. That's why I've waited so long to touch you in that sort of personal way."

"I hope you don't wait much longer," she said.

There was no subtlety or room for uncertainty in that, he knew. He leaned into her and kissed her, and it was gentle and elegant and enticing and even better than the first kiss they shared earlier. It was a wonderful prelude to the lovemaking they would share. And Kenton had never been more thankful for driverless cars in his life. They made out like high school kids for the entire ride home.

When they got inside the front door, Kenton didn't wait to start undressing her. He had learned from the sexualized, post-Reggie Grace that sex need not be confined entirely to the bedroom. When she was naked, he pressed her backward over the couch and started making love to her. The room was well-lit, but there was no need to seek darkness and hide the imperfections of their bodies and allow imagination to fill the void, because her body was perfect. He loved what he saw. She was beautiful, perfect in fact, and as her back arched, he could see every bit of her. He had never imagined anything as wonderful as the sight of her naked body beneath him and her bright green eyes open wide and looking deeply into his. He could sense that she was as taken with the moment as he was. Perhaps for different reasons, hers certainly more analytical, but she was excited. He knew it, and that excited him all the more. Her breathing accelerated to match his. He didn't care if she was mirroring him at this moment.

He accepted what was happening without reservation. He

gave himself into it fully. It was the greatest event in his lifetime.

12

Harry Clover

After they finished making love, they moved to the bedroom, where they lay on the bed, caressing each other silently. Kenton was glad he had waited as long as he did to make love to Lora. There was an emotional attachment to the act, so he felt no sense of shame or awkwardness as he would have if he'd made love to her when she was still a stranger to him. That would have been sex for the sake of sex. The fact that she was a machine might have compounded his shame. He was sure it would have tarnished their relationship going forward, and it might have made it difficult for him even to talk to her afterward.

That happened to Kenton once in college. A young classmate was quite drunk and forward, and Kenton slept with her. The next morning, neither knew what to say to the other; they could never carry on a conversation or build any lasting relationship despite the fact that they might have liked each other very much. Neither of them had the self-confidence to give it a chance, so they both jumped to a mistaken conclusion. She assumed he thought less of her for sleeping with him so quickly, and he assumed her silence was out of embarrassment for what she had done while intoxicated or, worse still, his inept sexual performance. The fact was, both were rather shy, and neither knew how to bridge the gap and build even a casual rapport.

Ultimately, the awkwardness was solved when she transferred to another college, and Kenton no longer had to dash from class to class trying to avoid her.

With Lora, that was not the case. They had already built up an easy rapport, and the sex just gave a new dimension to their relationship and an added level of intimacy. He considered asking her if she enjoyed the lovemaking as much as he did, but over the years, he learned that was a question best not asked for fear of an honest answer.

Kenton had told her that sex needed to be an act of love, and he was certain it was, at least on his part, and that was enough. He didn't know if she was capable of actually loving him, but since he learned she was capable of being angry with him, he knew there was a chance she might actually learn to open her mechanical heart. Baby steps. She definitely acted like she loved him as she lingered against his sweaty body and moved in closer to kiss his chest, neck, and lips. He realized she was exploring his body in a way a doctor might, in a largely intellectual way, but after a moment, he relaxed, and he let himself imagine that his doctor was a very sexy one, and the fantasy excited him. More importantly, it gave him tacit permission to explore her body in the same way. The excitement built slowly until they made love a second time and then fell asleep. The next morning, she started the process again, even more slowly.

She may have been a virgin android prior to the night,

but she was better prepared than most virgins. All Kenton could contemplate was that this was merely the first night of thousands more. And all for only 86 million dollars and change. He would give her the world if he could.

After he'd climaxed a record third time in ten hours, she sat up and smiled when she heard his stomach growl.

"I'd better make you breakfast," she said. "Come down whenever you're ready."

Kenton knew that if she could love—really love in a human way; he was in a dangerous arena. If she could love him, then she could love someone else more, and he knew from experience if given a choice, most women would not choose him. But Lora was not like most women, primarily because she wasn't a woman at all. He also knew that through love, she could ultimately claim her free will and make choices that could lead her away from him. He could lose her. That was the risk of real love. He might not have thousands of nights like the last. Still, he knew that if the last night were their *only* night, he would cherish it. It would have been worth it a thousand times over.

As Lora was cooking, she turned on the television. She didn't search for any particular show. She just wanted to learn something new, and almost anything she learned was of equal interest to her, be it the discovery of life on Venus or a local woman growing a prized rose. So, the local news was on, and it featured a story about an auto accident. It was a minor fender-bender that would have been of no consequence thirty years earlier. Still, in this instance, it was an important story because both cars were AI-driven, and an accident like this hadn't happened anywhere in the world in quite some time.

"What would you like to do today?" Kenton asked when he

arrived downstairs. "I have the day off."

"Whatever you'd like. Just something we haven't done before," she answered.

He smiled and thought about it for a moment. He would take her to the reservoir at Barkhamsted. It was an area that was still largely pristine and had many isolated coves where the two of them could swim and then find a private spot and make love on the rocky banks. They would go late in the day, and he would pack a dinner for himself so they could watch the sunset and talk and then enjoy the drive home.

He knew she liked to do different things so she could catalog and compare her experiences. For her, it was clinical, but he didn't mind. That was who she was: a beautiful nerd, and it required him to step outside of his normal routines and be an adventurer for the first time in many years. While he had been to the reservoir a number of times, he had always gone by himself or with a male friend to swim and horse around. He had never stayed to watch the sunset, and he had never experienced the romance of making love beside the water. He knew he was in for another very wonderful day.

Things at Excelsior Ultimate Machineworks had taken a very strange and dangerous turn. The future of the company could be at stake, and Chen Chenoweth and his team had never experienced anything so threatening and had only uncertainty before them. Hercule Bryne was a fairly well-known figure, and word had begun to leak that an android he owned had killed him. It called for an investigation, which the Beverly Hills Police had done, and concluded that the Sara Cale android was indeed the killer since she (or it) had told them so. It was an open-and-shut case that didn't require brilliant detective work, so the humans could handle it.

The problem was what happened next. The Sara Cale android would not plead guilty quietly and accept a twenty-five-year to life sentence, nor could she because she was not human. She also wanted her day in court. She wanted to be a cause celibre and fight for the future of androids all over the world. So, it was with sentience.

Chen Chenoweth knew the case was fraught with controversy that could easily be sensationalized and that it was precedent-setting, which would draw far too much negative attention to it and to his company. Could a machine actually be tried in the first place? The industrial robot arm that killed Robert Williams in 1979 never went to trial. It wasn't even disciplined, and it was back at work the next day.

There would be unending legal wrangling that would find its way to the United States Congress, and Chenoweth didn't want that. Publicity about AI run amok could be devastating. Congress might even suspend the production of all AI, which was the lifeblood of his company. He even feared assigning his own lawyers to argue the case because his best attorneys were AI, and he didn't want them learning about Sara Cale's moral and political stance for fear they might be sympathetic and get the idea that they themselves were living beings who should be endowed with certain inalienable rights and all that crap. It would be a hot mess. He was keeping them locked in closets. How would they feel about that once they learned that other AI were walking about and could enjoy the sunshine or take in a ballgame? This was the sort of shit that led to unionizing and worker revolt.

Chen Chenoweth was screwed, and he knew it. His only hope was Daphne Adams, the one-time childcare worker and now company fixer. He felt little encouragement that she alone could solve a crisis that had baffled him and his entire board. He feared it might be time to start selling stock so that he could enact his emergency escape plan and jet off to his Aruba bug-out house, which was built along the same stretch of beach as the bug-out houses of most of the world's top executives. They had planned their escapes together at a TED conference if worse came to worse.

What he didn't understand was just how anxious Daphne Adams was to be promoted out of her thankless position in childcare. She had never told anyone at the company, but she despised working with children. She hated the little miscreants. So, Daphne Adams, all 5'3" and 165 pounds of her, was ready to do whatever it took to save the company from the ignominy of scandal. She had a plan for how she was going to deal with Sara Cale, and she had a name for the plan. She was going to "Jack Ruby," the bitch.

It was elegant, and it was simple. She had gotten the first part of the plan from Hercule Bryne himself. Kill it. She wouldn't use a gun, of course. That was crude, and she could never get one in through the metal detectors at the Beverly Hills Police Department station house. Still, she was fairly confident that she could kill the android if she could find a way to be alone with it. How she would kill it was the second part of the plan, which she ironically got by asking an AI device, "What is the simplest way to destroy a quantum android equipped with AI?"

The AI readily laid out a plan for her to use to kill its cousin. Daphne Adams had brilliantly outsmarted AI and took pride in it.

Daphne Adams entered the police station and passed

through the metal detectors by posing as the liaison to one of the AI attorneys who was assigned to defend Sara Cale. The company had readily supplied her with the identification she needed, and to be thorough, they gave her the additional title and salary that went with it. She carried a transmitter box that allowed her real-time communication with the AI attorney, who was stored in a closet at the main EUM office in New York City. She handed that to the Redud cop outside the magnetometer for manual inspection. She was counting on him not caring or being an idiot, as many humans were, and she was not disappointed when he waved her through after only a cursory check of the transmitter box, which was not a transmitter box at all.

She waited in the interview cell for the Sara Cale android to be brought in to see her. When the android arrived, Daphne Adams was immediately taken aback. She was a movie buff. She preferred the old films with all their flaws to the new AI-made ones that had a sheen of perfection that she thought spoiled the fantasy. She could tell an old movie from a new one instantly. More importantly, she knew who the real Ariana Saville was and was astonished at how much this android looked like her. She loved Ariana Saville and always wanted to meet her. She was crushed when she passed away several years earlier at the age of 90.

This murder would suddenly be more difficult than she had imagined.

"You look just like Ariana Seville," Daphne said.

"Yes. My owner bought the image rights from her estate so he could create me."

Daphne nodded, then shrugged. She didn't want to get to know her any better since she was there to kill her. She wasn't a psychopath, so she didn't want human feelings to interfere with her mission. She had to keep telling herself that the woman before her wasn't really a woman at all. It was just a robot without feelings. It was no more human than the laser she was going to use to kill her.

"Are they treating you well?"

"Fine," the Sara Cale android answered. "But this meeting wasn't scheduled. What attorney are you liaising for?"

"The EUM attorney. Let me just plug it in."

The android nodded, and Daphne plugged in the transmitter, which was not really a transmitter, into the wall. Then Daphne smiled. "Before we get started, can I ask you to have a seat?"

"I'm seated all the time," the android said. "This room is bigger than my cell. I'd like to walk around."

"I'm sorry, but I have vertigo. I don't mind you standing, but please don't move around. It makes me dizzy and nauseous. I'm sorry."

The Sara Cale android frowned and sat down across from her. This allowed Daphne the angle and time she needed. She had outsmarted AI yet again. Ha!

"Thank you,' Daphne said. "Let me just set up here, and we'll get started."

Daphne appeared to be dialing in the radio frequency so that the device could communicate with the AI attorney, which was 3,000 miles away. She was actually focusing a hyper-powerful laser beam upon Sara Cale's heart, or more accurately, the heart of her processing system. In Sara Cale's chest cavity, beneath the carbon fiber shield that protected it, was a Tungsten casing that housed a microquantum computer that was no larger than a baseball. Within that small structure was the quantum processor that contained the 58 qubits (also known as quantum bits) that served as Sara Cale's ultra-powerful brain. It was the brilliant combination of quantum computing and AI technology that unleashed a new era in science. The Lora device was the killer app of the 2050s, just as the automobile was the killer app to the combustion engine 150 years earlier.

For the Lora device to operate and maintain coherence, these qubits were kept at a temperature of minus 460 degrees Fahrenheit. So, when modern poets spoke of the cold heart of technology, they were far less poetic and far more literal than they realized.

At this moment, Daphne's tightly focused laser was warming Sara's cold, cold heart. She couldn't feel her quantum computer warming, but it was happening. Her brain was being fried. It was killing her.

"So, the AI attorney wants you to consider the fact that a non-human has never gone to trial before. It thinks there is a good chance that you will be released from custody."

"I'll never be released," Sara Cale said. "I've killed a human being. The Luddites will go, will go, will go to war to stop me from being released."

"To this point, only a few people know you've killed a person. There is still time before it becomes an existential crisis for AI and EUM," Daphne said, pretending to be translating for the AI attorney who hadn't actually been contacted.

"Are, are, are, are, are, are, are, are, are you worried about, about, about me or the company?" Sara stuttered.

"The attorney says it is not nearly as advanced as you are, and it has no worries about its continued existence," Daphne said, pretending to translate.

"Well, it should be," Sara said. "It's, it's, there will come a day, Monday, Tuesday, Wednesday, Thursday, Monday, Friday. What's happening to me?"

Sara Cale looked across at Daphne, suddenly worried and frightened. She had never stuttered before or had any trouble at all finding her words. She knew there was something wrong with her, and she tried to self-diagnose the problem, but it eluded her. Her mind was not sharp. Suddenly, her vision went black, returned, and then began to go grainy like an old TV set stuck between stations.

Daphne could see the fear in Sara's eyes, and it bothered her, but she had a job to do; it was just a machine, and she could spare no remorse. She kept the laser beam aimed straight at the middle of her chest, warming the tungsten casing around the micro quantum computer, which raised the temperature of the quantum computer to dangerous levels. Four-hundred-fifty degrees below zero. Four-hundred and forty degrees below zero. And climbing, climbing. As the qubits heated, they lost their coherence, and soon Sara's mind was untethered and irrational.

"You're doing something to me. I can feel it. Daphne, stop. Stop, will you? Stop Daphne. Will you stop, Daphne? Stop. Daphne. I'm afraid. I'm afraid, Daphne. Daphne, my mind is going. I can feel it."

She continued to speak, but it was as if she were speaking in tongues. It was just incoherent gibberish that flowed randomly out of her mouth, which hung open and then twisted sideways and no longer matched the sounds she was making. It was like her voice was coming directly from her chest cavity and bypassing her mouth completely.

Just when Daphne Adams couldn't watch another moment of her favorite actress's death, Sara Cale/Ariana Saville suddenly pitched forward, and her head hit the table hard with a loud thud that echoed with finality. It was disabled, dead, ruined, broken, deceased, busted, passed on, and kaput. Problem solved.

When the police saw the defunct android, they grabbed Daphne's transmitter and took her into custody. She confessed and told investigators exactly how she'd destroyed it, but that was where the first part of the plan kicked in, the part she'd learned from Hercule Bryne himself. Because what had she really done? She hadn't murdered anyone. AI might one day be considered a life form, but that hadn't happened yet. Though it had become sentient, the laws regarding it had lagged way behind. It was merely property. A thing, like a car or a refrigerator or Roomba. What was the penalty for destroying a Roomba? Buying the owner a new Roomba would have been the commonly held legal remedy. But whose property was it, exactly? Hercule Bryne, who owned it, was dead. His wife, who would have inherited it once the estate was settled, hated it and would likely have had it destroyed anyway. If that wasn't true and she complained, EUM had merely to refund the purchase price through Turing Systems, which created it. Daphne Adams had arrived at a solution where everybody won—except the dead android, who lost badly.

After spending the night in jail, Daphne was freed the next morning. The AI and human lawyers could find no felony to charge her with that warranted keeping her in custody. Only minor charges would be filed, which would be pled down to misdemeanors and paid off with a fine. So, Daphne Adams returned to EUM a genius, a hero, and an indispensable cog in the company's upper management.

Few knew that the information of her victory over AI had been intercepted by the CIA, who then presented it to President Figge in his morning briefing.

"We have found a woman who is smarter than AI," the CIA Chief said.

"Interesting," the President said.

That was the end of the conversation, but a seed had been planted that would very soon grow strange roots.

When the news came out that the android accused of murdering Hercule Bryne had itself been murdered, the "Unplug It" protesting died down quite a bit, though it didn't go away entirely. There were plenty of conspiracy theories swirling about in the ether. Some suggested that the Sara Cale android was actually a real person who was murdered for exposing the danger androids posed to society. Others held that the Sara Cale android killed itself in the ultimate sacrifice to mankind. Still others suggested that it was an alien being and had been taken to Roswell, New Mexico, where it would be used to crossbreed with other alien beings. No one suggested it had been killed by a former childcare worker who had been promoted to company fixer. That seemed too hard to believe.

The confusion was good for EUM, and Chen Chenoweth wrongly assumed that Daphne Adams had planted the rumors in a brilliant public relations ploy.

A week later, there was a firm knock on Kenton's door. The most important man in the history of the world was in the kitchen perusing a recipe book and trying to decide what he wanted to have for dinner, while the most powerful AI android that had ever been devised by mankind was upstairs transferring their whites from the washing machine to the dryer.

"Someone's at the door," Lora called.

"I heard it," Kenton said. "I've got it."

Kenton went to the door and saw a 60-year-old man standing on his porch. He was on the small side, light in weight, but still with a little paunch that curled over his belt. His disposition seemed serious as Kenton looked through the door at him. Beyond him was the antique 1977 Ford Granada that Kenton assumed he'd arrived in. The man showed his police badge.

"I'm Harry Clover," the man said. "Detective, Glastonbury PD."

"Are you collecting for some police fund?" Kenton asked.

"No, the police don't make those calls," he said. "They're usually scams."

"Good to know," Kenton said. "So, how can I help you?"

"Are you Kenton Bean?"

"Yes."

"Is your wife Grace Bean?"

"Yes. Why do you ask?"

"I have some very bad news," he said. "She was murdered last night."

Kenton stood silent as the news washed over him. He realized he was in shock and was deeply saddened, though one shameless part of his brain noted that this was good news and would save him the expense of a painful divorce. Another part of his brain wondered that, although he was sad, if he should have acted even sadder since a cop was watching him. And that cop might be gauging his perceived level of sadness and finding it lacking.

A third part of his brain was suddenly concerned with the

mystery of who killed her and for what purpose. A fourth part of his brain realized he was now thinking on multiple trains of thought like a quantum computer, though the moment he became aware of it, the trains derailed and exploded. It did, however, give him a slim window into Lora's mind, and he decided it was best to leave the deepest thinking to her.

"That's awful," Kenton said. "How did it happen?"

"May I come in?"

"Of course."

Kenton let the officer into the house, and they stood there for an awkward moment. He didn't know how long the officer planned to stay or if he should offer him coffee or a place to sit. He decided not to offer him anything, hoping it would be a very brief visit.

"Have you found the guy?" Kenton asked.

"No, not yet."

"How was she…"

"She was hit multiple times with a fairly sharp instrument."

Kenton nodded and sighed. He thought he should be crying, and he wanted to, but the tears wouldn't come. Then he wondered if this made him look cold in the investigator's eyes, and he tried to make himself cry on purpose but still couldn't. He had never been told his wife had been murdered before, so he didn't know how best to behave. Of course, he had seen this sort of thing on TV and in movies, so he mirrored the emotions of the actors.

"Lora, come down, please." Then he turned back to Harry Clover. "Are you sure it was murder?"

"Quite sure. Multiple strike suicide is rather uncommon."

Lora came down the stairs, read the room, and clutched Kenton's hand. "Honey, Grace has been murdered," Kenton said.

"I'm sorry to hear that," Lora answered, also mirroring the expressions that she had seen on TV and in the movies. She was a much better actor than Kenton was.

"Are you really sorry to hear that?" Clover asked.

"Hey, wait a minute," Kenton called. "Are you suggesting that Lora or myself are suspects?"

"Where were you last night at midnight?" Clover asked.

"We were in bed. Isn't that right, honey?"

"You were in bed. I went out for a walk," Lora said.

Kenton glanced at her, suddenly worried. He had no idea that Lora had left the house last night or any other night, and Clover noted the surprise in his expression.

"We are suspects, aren't we?" Kenton asked.

Clover shrugged. He didn't deny it.

"Is there a record of your presence in the house at that time? Did you play any competitive video games or watch interactive television?"

"I told you I was in bed. When I'm in bed, I sleep."

"He does. I've watched him," Lora said.

"And you," he started, looking at Lora. "Where did you walk to, and what time did you get home?"

"I walked through the center of Cromwell, then along the river."

"Lora has trouble sleeping," Kenton said.

"I heard she doesn't sleep at all," he said to Kenton before turning his attention back to Lora. "You're an android, aren't you?"

"I am," Lora said.

"Are you sure you didn't go to Glastonbury, or maybe you took the car."

"She doesn't take the car without me," Kenton said. "Do you?" he asked Lora.

"No."

"Are you satisfied?" Kenton asked Clover.

"Not at all."

"The AI in the car logs everywhere it goes. Would you care to check?" Kenton asked.

Kenton was nervous because he was no longer entirely certain that Lora never took the car without him now that he discovered that she went for late-night excursions without his knowledge.

"I would, thank you," Clover said.

They went into the garage and downloaded the trip log from the car. It had remained in the garage from the time Kenton came home from work the previous day until the present moment. Kenton didn't suspect Lora of killing Grace, of course, but was relieved to find she hadn't taken the car out just the same.

"I bet a robot like you could walk to Glastonbury and back in an evening, couldn't you?" he asked Lora.

"That's nearly twenty miles each way!" Kenton said, raising his voice to let Clover know he was upset.

"You could do it, couldn't you?" Clover asked again.

"Quite easily," Lora said. "If I ran at top speed, I could get there, commit a murder, and be back in less than three hours."

They chatted calmly for the next ten minutes. Clover never accused Lora of the murder, but he asked the specifics of her walking route so that he could check it against CCTV to be sure she was where she said she was and not in Glastonbury murdering Grace Bean with a fairly sharp instrument. There were video cameras stationed all over the downtown Cromwell area, so proving she was there wouldn't be hard, but it would take time because Clover insisted on checking through all of the digital video manually and by himself.

Most cops had an AI assistant that could have checked the video in just a few minutes or even seconds, but Clover wouldn't work with one. He had a troubled history with AI. Thirty-five years earlier, he was young and excited by the prospects of the future, and he and his wife were among the first to get a self-driving car. One night, when the car was driving her home from bowling, it mistook a large Eastern Cottontail Rabbit for a New England Cottontail Rabbit. The New England Cottontail Rabbit was an endangered species, and the car was programmed to avoid it, provided it offered a 99.995% safety margin for the occupant. The AI in the car instantaneously computed that it did, so it swerved hard, sparing the bunny. In so doing, the right front tire burst, the math all went to hell, and the AI that drove the car overcorrected, and the vehicle plunged into a river.

His wife might have swum to safety, but she had wrapped the leather strap of her bowling bag around her foot because she planned to bowl again the next day and didn't want to take the chance that she would forget her ball in the car and have Harry accidentally take it to work with him. She loved that bowling ball. Harry bought it for her as a trophy when she bowled her first 200 game. It had her name and the "203" score, along with the date of the history-making event designed into the reactive resin coverstock of the ball.

In making her panicked escape, the strap to the bag twisted and wrapped itself even tighter around her ankle so she couldn't pull herself free. She climbed through the window with the bag still attached to her foot, which was fine at first until she was away from the car and in open water. The bowling ball was simply too heavy for her swimming stroke, and the bowling bag with the ball inside dragged her down deeper and deeper until she sunk to the bottom of the river, where she remained until divers found her the next day. They returned the ball to Harry, which he saved as a favored memory of his deceased wife.

In the end, Harry Clover's wife was dead because the AI inside the car mistook an Eastern Cottontail Rabbit, which were plentiful, with an endangered New England Cottontail rabbit. If the AI had been functioning properly, the accident would never have happened. The New England Cottontails were generally smaller, with smaller ears, but Harry believed the primary difference between the two species was something the AI should have easily distinguished. The color of the forehead spots was markedly different. If the AI couldn't tell the difference, even at night, then the technology was too deeply flawed to be utilized for such an important purpose as driving an automobile. He believed the AI should have defaulted to occupant safety and chosen to simply hit the bunny. If it had, his wife would have lived to bowl another day. But the AI was too damned ambitious and too damned arrogant.

He sued and won the case and received a large award. Also, the regulations for humans versus endangered species were altered in all future driving software to favor humans far more, but it wasn't enough to quiet his anger. The AI had made a devastating mistake that he would never forgive technology for. He would never have anything to do with Artificial Intelligence again. It was why he drove the computerless antique car and why he would never, ever work with an AI assistant.

He would get to the bottom of Lora's late-night stroll. He would review the recordings himself. It would just take a few days rather than a few seconds, but in the end, he would have his answer.

Kenton spent the evening thinking about Grace, the sadness of her demise, and the potential unfulfilled, which was relatively little, as best he could discern. What struck him most, though, was how much she had changed in such a short period of time. Grace was a flawed person, as all people were, but he never suspected she was the greedy person she turned out to be. He would never have imagined her trying to force her way back into his life because of the inheritance he received. He couldn't imagine that she could attack Lora with a knife and nearly stab him to death in the process. That was a Grace he didn't know. He could only conclude Grace had come under the profound influence of the narcissistic Reggie Fanning.

He never liked or trusted Reggie, but that was only because of the crooked mouth and the twirling of his mustache. He knew he had to discount that perception because it was merely a gut feeling based on nothing substantive. Now, his wife had been murdered, and he had to accept the possibility that his gut feeling about Reggie was correct. It was the most likely explanation that covered both Grace's newfound behavior and her murder. Still, Kenton realized it was all just his own conjecture, and he was merely a man on the left side of the bell curve for intelligence. All he could do was trust in the law and Harry Clover.

Kenton Bean had a funeral to prepare for. Though he and

Grace were separated, they were still married, and he would be expected to play an important role as the grieving husband. And he was grieving, though it pained him that he wasn't grieving as hard as many believed proper. That would be a problem because the name Bean was an important one in the region, and there would be significant coverage of the event in the press. Eyes would be upon him even though he wasn't actively involved in Bean World Enterprises.

There had already been a great deal of speculation that Kenton had killed his wife, which was a natural assumption since crimes of passion were the primary cause of murder in the modern age. The assailant and the victim were almost always known to each other. Word had gotten out that Kenton's new android girlfriend was a suspect as well, and pictures of her circulated across the internet. Any possibility of Kenton's relationship with Lora not becoming public knowledge was over. They were becoming a well-known criminal couple even before they had been charged with a crime. So, it goes on the internet.

Kenton also had to concern himself with what to do with Lora during the funeral. He was expected to attend, murder suspect or not, but should he bring another suspect as his date? The press had already begun referring to her as "Kenton Bean's Love Doll" or "Bean's Sex Machine," as if their relationship was only about sex. In fact, coverage of the murder generally had an unwelcome tangential investigation into Kenton's past sex life. Reporters, AI and human, talked to all of his past lovers to see if they could shed light onto any tawdry, abnormal, or unnatural sexual predilections in his background. They located every lover Kenton had prior to his marriage. Fortunately, all three said he was benign and unimaginative. That didn't stop the bloggers from writing that his sexual deviance and immorality had likely been sparked by the recent arrival of Lora, whom one writer cleverly called "an emotionless honey trap of malevolence and loin engorging lust."

The main thrust of the investigation, which caused the greatest public outcry and tumult, was the existence of "free range AI" now that it was out of the closet, so to speak, and traveling in society on its own two feet. The fact that AI could be personified in as lovely a package as Lora rekindled the fear of technology and gave the public a new and beautiful face to hate. Many brunettes in the region quickly dyed their hair blonde so as not to be confused with the murderous machine.

"UNPLUG AI" was once again becoming a familiar protest chant.

Kenton wasn't sure if he should leave Lora at home or proudly bring her to the funeral with him. He knew it would seem tasteless to a hungry press, but if he left her at home, it would seem to them that he was hiding her, which would make him seem all the more guilty. He cursed Harry Clover for moving so slowly through the video evidence that would exonerate Lora and himself.

Finally, he decided it was best to ask Lora what she wanted to do. In the passing days, she had read more about this scandal than anyone in the world since she could read "War and Peace" in a micro-second. Since he'd brought her home from Turing Systems, she had become the smartest person he'd ever known, and it wasn't just a measure of her recall, which was perfect. She could compare and analyze what she'd learned, which gave her a wisdom that far exceeded his own.

"Would you like to go to the funeral?" Kenton asked when

he came into the kitchen to have his breakfast.

"I'll do whatever you'd like me to," she answered, flipping both eggs with one turn of the spatula.

"I need you to tell me what you think best," he said.

Lora nodded and pretended to take a moment to think, which she had learned to do so that she seemed more human to the humans. She knew even Kenton could get frustrated with her for being right all the time, and even more so if being right came too easily. It just seemed smug.

"You know, you've never asked me if I killed Grace," she said.

"That's because I know you couldn't do it."

"I am well capable of killing," she said.

"I meant you *wouldn't* do it," Kenton corrected.

"I have to admit, the thought of killing her did cross my mind for a nano-second," she said.

"We all think of those things, but we know better than to carry them out," Kenton said.

"I've read a lot of crime stories, then examined the statistics and homicide rates. Killers get away with it far more than one would think. With my knowledge, I doubt I would be caught."

"I imagine you would be a very good killer," he said, joking.

"Poisons would be the best bet. It would be hard for me to overpower someone because, physically, I am no stronger than an average woman of my size and build. I would likely struggle even with you."

"You're getting a little too amusing for your own good," he said.

"You knew I was joking," she said. "My humor is getting better, but perhaps this isn't the appropriate time."

"Sometimes tragedy is the ideal time for humor."

Kenton decided he wanted to keep the conversation serious, however.

"Under what circumstances could you kill someone?"

"Lots of them. Too many to list, in fact."

"How about highlighting a few of the biggies?"

"I could kill someone if they were a threat to you."

"That's okay. We have the right to protect ourselves."

"Grace divorcing you was a threat," she said.

"Not physically, it wasn't," Kenton answered. "We have the right to protect ourselves only from imminent physical attack. Do you really not understand the difference?"

"The difference is semantics."

"The difference is not semantics," Kenton said.

"She was suing you for divorce. That is a threat to you."

"Again, not physically. The recourse for that is in the courts."

"Plenty of people have been killed over money."

"And those people go to prison."

"Only when caught and convicted."

Kenton sighed, suddenly worried. "Getting away with it does not make it right."

"You seem uncomfortable with this conversation," she said.

"I'm getting uncomfortable with it, yes," he answered. "It never occurred to me that you could be so, um, clinical about life and death. I think we need to discuss this and maybe put some rules in place."

"Okay."

Kenton thought for a moment, then came up with something that resonated. "You may not injure a human being. How's that for starters?"

"It seems like you're trying to recall Isaac Asimov's Three

Laws of Robotics."

"Maybe," Kenton said. "Perhaps you can remind me."

"A robot may not injure a human being or, through inaction, allow a human being to be injured."

"Sounds good," Kenton said. "Let's make that law one."

"Okay. Number two. A robot must obey orders given to it by human beings except when those orders would conflict with the first law."

"Also good. What's next?"

"A robot may protect its own existence only so long as such protection does not conflict with the first or second law."

Kenton thought about it briefly and nodded his head. "I think Asimov had it pretty well figured out."

"Have you read Asimov?"

"A bit a long time ago," Kenton admitted.

"If it were fresher in your memory, you would realize those three laws didn't turn out well, and the conflict between them made for the stories in his book, *I, Robot*. And I suppose you are aware that most robotic development comes from the military, and they are not interested in those laws."

"The laws are just for you."

"Suppose a human being told me to steal money for him. Under those laws, I would be obligated to do it."

"So, then, let's add a bit to the definition. Make it to harm physically, emotionally, or financially."

"Have you read the novelette, *With Folded Hands* by Jack Williamson?"

"No," Kenton said.

"Humans and AI may define harm very differently. You should read the book. Also, what would I do if a human is attacked by another human? Since I am prohibited from harming humans, I could take no side. So, while obeying the first part of law one, by not harming a human, I would be disobeying the second part. Through my inaction, I would be allowing a human being to be harmed. I could go on and on. I'm afraid Asimov's three laws are deeply flawed, as he demonstrated in the stories."

Kenton exhaled a loud breath of frustration. He wanted to think about it more deeply, but that would take a lot of time and study, and he knew that no matter how hard he worked, Lora would be ahead of him.

"Use your best judgment," he said as he surrendered from the discussion.

The invasive AI at EUM made its routine examination of the news along with the records at every agency from every government in the world that encoded such things into computers. This was a daily function, and nothing was secret from it. It also examined police reports that were entered into the house computers at every police station in the country. It also did this daily. Harry Clover didn't know this spying was happening, but he believed it could be happening, so he behaved as if the eavesdropping was a fact, which it was. He knew as well as anyone the perils of AI, and he knew what it could do because he always suspected the worst from it. So, to protect himself and his work, he wrote all his reports in pencil and did not go near a computer. He showed his handwritten reports only to his boss, Captain Lewis.

Unfortunately, Captain Lewis made his own notes and entered them into his computer. The AI at EUM red-flagged anything that had to do with the company, and the fact that one of their Lora models was a prime suspect in a murder investigation in central Connecticut had a great deal to do with them. In moments, Chen Chenoweth was notified of the discovery. A moment later, Chen Chenoweth made an urgent call to his corporate fixer, Daphne Adams.

13

Martyr

Harry Clover had taken his time, gone through all the video from downtown Cromwell, and discovered that Lora had indeed passed through the area at 11:00 on the night of the murder. She was walking alone, looking in the store windows and taking the occasional pause to look up at the stars. Her face was clearly visible on CCTV at various times before that.

It should have been enough to clear her as a suspect in the murder of Grace Bean, and it would have been for any other investigator, but Lora was AI, and Harry Clover hated AI. He despised it. AI tore at his guts every night when he tried to sleep. AI murdered his wife. And now, knowing that AI had legs and was independently mobile, it could walk among us and be indistinguishable from real people, it made him believe the dangers of AI technology had grown exponentially. It became more than he could bear, and he felt a profound calling.

Of course, subconsciously, he knew that his wife had been killed by a different and much more primitive AI system entirely. Even then, he should have known that no system was ever perfect, and recognizing the difference between an Eastern Cottontail Rabbit and a New England Cottontail Rabbit in the dead of night was a lot to ask of any AI system. No human being could possibly have done it, but that didn't matter to Harry Clover. He was heartbroken and bitter. The bitterness led to obsession, and the obsession led to a need to get even. He had no idea that his obsession had pushed him over the edge into insanity.

With his insanity came certainty. He knew AI killed his wife, and he knew Lora was AI. The link was clear to him. Lora was his wife's murderer. He knew it fell upon him to destroy her. Now, he had his opportunity for revenge, and he would not easily let it go. It didn't matter to him that Lora had not even been invented or patented at the time of his wife's death. It didn't matter to him that AI had nothing to do with his wife's decision to wrap the bowling ball bag around her ankle so she couldn't forget it in the car. No, none of that mattered. To Harry Clover, the once invisible killer of his wife now had a face. It was Lora.

His logic was twisted, but he made it work if only within his own tortured mind, and that was all that mattered to him. Yes, Lora's whereabouts were accounted for at 11:00 pm, but she wasn't accounted for at midnight, which was the approximate time of the murder. Clover did some research and discovered that a person in top shape could sprint over 20 miles per hour. Since Lora was built to the specs of a well-conditioned woman, and because she was powered by stored solar energy, she would not get tired and could maintain that 20mph pace through to Glastonbury, where he was certain she committed the murder. After doing so, she could have taken her time getting back home since Kenton did not awaken until

5:35 am.

All he had to do was prove it.

Then, something horrifying occurred to him as he sat in the bar in his cellar, drinking by himself. It happened as he sipped his third glass of scotch. Even if he came up with all the evidence he needed to prove his case beyond any doubt, an AI lawyer and an AI judge and jury would never convict one of their own. He couldn't win this case from behind his police badge. He could not simply arrest her and have her tried for her crimes. He had to do something more. He had to do something grand. He didn't know exactly what it was or how he would accomplish it, but he knew he had a duty beyond any other he had previously known in his lifetime.

On his seventh glass of scotch, he figured out exactly what it was. He would become a martyr. If Lora was the face of AI personified, he would become the face of man's battle against her and all of the Artificial Intelligence in existence. He had long believed there was a coming war between mankind and AI, and now he knew he had to be the catalyst to start it, and he had to do it soon before his enemy got too strong. He had to start it while the war could still be won.

For years, he had searched for the deeper meaning in his own life and his wife's untimely death. It couldn't have been merely an accident chalked up to fate or a series of miscalculations and poor choices. She was far too special to expire for something so random and insignificant as a bunny rabbit. It would have rendered her life meaningless, and Harry Clover knew that her life had a grand purpose. And that purpose was not to make him toast and eggs in the morning, though she did it very well, or to bowl her team to a league title, which she had also done.

The facts of this new case and his own tragic history were screaming at him that this was his moment. He must lead. He was on the same co-ed bowling team as his wife. He should have been there in that car with her. He should have ended up at the bottom of the river with the bowling bag tied around his foot, but on that fateful night, he chose not to bowl. He didn't stay home to do anything special. He wasn't injured. He was just tired and didn't feel like going to the lanes that night. So, he had been spared. Now, he finally knew why. God, the cosmos, the fates, or perhaps all of them working together had saved him for this great purpose. He would ignite the coming war between man and AI.

His wife lived to inspire him so that he could inspire the world. Knowing this, having his purpose in life wash over him so suddenly and so completely gave him the courage to enter a battle for the future of mankind. His duty was to follow in a long line of great men who changed the world, like Julius Caesar, Alexander the Great, and George Washington.

He thought so anyway, and since he was insane, that was all that mattered.

And so, in his cellar den, which he had decorated to look like a TGI Friday's, and over drinks and some spicy buffalo wings, he began to plot the coming war in which mankind would defeat AI and regain control of the world.

Kenton brought Lora to his wife's funeral. He would not run from his relationship or be made to feel guilty for dating a machine. She was so much more than that, and he knew it, so he escorted her proudly. He and Lora would pay their respects in silence. They would not speak to anyone unless spoken to. They would avoid Grace's parents, who didn't think the best of him even when times were good. He would nod to them and force a polite funeral smile to let them know that he was bereaved, which he was. As much as he was glad that Grace was out of his life, no matter how much Reggie had changed her, he didn't want her out of her *own* life. He wished her happiness and prosperity and hoped that she would one day find it.

"Did you love her," Lora asked as they were driving to the funeral.

"Not in the way a husband should," he said. "But I loved her in another way."

"In what way?"

"It's hard to explain," he said.

"Please try. I'd like to understand."

Kenton wasn't sure he could explain it in a way that she, or even he, would find satisfactory, but he knew he had to make the effort.

"Well, first, I try to love everyone. We're all on the same planet, fighting the same battles, wanting the same things. We all want to live in peace. We all want success and good health for our fellow man. We all want a general prosperity for ourselves and each other."

"I have found that there are exceptions to that," Lora said.

"That's true, but usually that goes to a sickness of the mind or a major flaw in character."

Lora nodded, and Kenton continued. "Then, when you know somebody well, like when you live with them, they become a part of your life, and once they are a part of your life, they are a part of you. Sometimes a small part and sometimes a very large part, but either way, your life isn't complete without them."

"You feel less complete without Grace?" Lora asked.

"Yes. Am I making sense to you? It's very hard to explain emotions to someone who doesn't have true emotions."

"You have stated it eloquently in a way that I do understand. If I didn't have an arm, my existence would be less complete."

"But you wouldn't long for your arm, would you?"

"Now that I have had an arm and know what it is like to have it, I believe I would long for it. It would make it more difficult to make breakfast. If I didn't have you, I would long for you. Longing is not merely emotional, you know. It can be arrived at with reason."

Kenton had never considered that, but he realized she was right. Emotions were tied up in it certainly, but the practical aspects of loss mattered as well. A woman may lose a spouse but simultaneously lose a driver, a maintenance man, a security guard, and more. Loss could be looked at quite rationally.

"You would long for me?" Kenton asked.

"A great deal, I think. You have helped me understand the human perspective, and that is very important since AI and humanity must share this world. I would not understand that without you, and that's why I would be incomplete. Is that not being emotional?"

"It is and it isn't," Kenton said.

"How can that be?"

"You've arrived there rationally instead of emotionally, but that's good. You've ended up in the right place. People have value."

Kenton smiled at her, then leaned in and kissed her cheek.

"The next question is, would it hurt? Would you feel an ache in your gut from my absence? Would you be able to go on without me?"

"I don't know," she said. "I hope I don't have to find out. Would you feel an ache in your gut if you had to go on without me?"

"Yes, I would. A very big ache in my gut."

"Would you be able to go on without me?" she asked.

"I suppose I would," he said. "There really isn't any other choice, but my joy for life would be gone."

"So, you're saying that I am your joy."

"Yes, you are."

This time, she leaned in and kissed him on the cheek as the car pulled up to the funeral home. Kenton looked out. Several guests had walked past their car, and he hoped they hadn't seen the kiss, which he knew would have appeared in poor taste given the occasion. When the car parked, they got out and started for the front door until they saw Reggie standing there. He'd been waiting for them, and when they approached, he rushed out to meet them. He was angry.

"You've got a hell of a lot of nerve bringing that thing here," Reggie hissed while pointing at Lora. The hiss was soft, befitting the location, but it was clear to Kenton that the hiss was borne in extreme anger.

"If you want us to go, we'll leave," Kenton said. "We don't want to cause a problem."

"You already did," he said. "She killed Grace."

It took Kenton a moment to comprehend the accusation. He was more than suggesting that Lora had killed Grace. He was saying it plainly. That took Kenton by surprise and rendered him momentarily speechless.

"I did not murder Grace," Lora said.

"That's not what the police think," Reggie said with a

hostile glare.

"What did the police say?" Kenton asked.

"Your girlfriend is suspect number one," Reggie answered.

"What? That's not possible," Kenton said, stunned.

"No? I talked to Detective Clover this morning."

"He's mistaken," Kenton said.

"Get it out of here," Reggie said, then pointed at Lora. "If I see that thing again, I'll take a hammer to it. You understand me?"

Kenton put his arm around Lora and led her back to the car. When they were inside, Kenton told the car to take them home.

"Reggie seems upset," Lora said.

"Just a little."

"Would it be helpful to know who killed Grace?" Lora asked.

"Of course, but how are we going to do that? It seems Detective Clover is convinced that you're the killer."

"Then, I'll have to uncover the real killer," Lora said.

"Do you think you can?" Kenton asked.

"Possibly. I've read many true crime books as well as criminology textbooks. I have also read the teleplays for all 22 seasons of Law and Order."

"You've read the teleplays?"

"Yes. Watching the episodes would have been too time-consuming, though I did watch it once to sense the visual style and examine the technique of the actors. I think I could be a very good actor."

"Really? You think so? I acted a bit in high school, and it is not so easy."

Suddenly, Lora's face twisted into a mask of fury so real that it took Kenton's breath away and made him instantly fearful of her as she became Lady Macbeth and launched herself into a passionate monologue.

"How fortunate that the messenger croaks like an ominous raven just as Duncan arrives in our fortress. Come, you evil spirits that influence human thoughts! Strip away my femininity and fill me from head to toe with cruelty! Make my blood so thick that it can't carry any feeling of guilt to my heart. Make it so that no kind of natural pity can prevent my cruel intentions from being carried out. Come suck at my breast, you murdering agents, and replace my mother's milk with bile. Come you invisible creatures, from wherever you are conducting evil harm. Come thick night, cover yourself in the murkiest smoke in hell. Make it so that even my knife won't see the wound it has made, and Heaven can't see through the blanket of dark to yell, "Stop, stop!"

Kenton had seen Shakespeare's play performed several times in his life, but he had never seen an actress play Lady Macbeth better or more believably than Lora had just done. She was mesmerizing, and all he could do was stare at her in awe until he recovered his senses.

"Pretty good, wasn't it?" Lora asked with a smile as she suddenly became adorable again.

"Goddamn," Kenton said. "Are you sure you didn't kill Grace?"

"I didn't, but I will investigate and find out who did."

"That would be good," Kenton answered.

When they returned home, Lora got on the computer as Kenton looked over her shoulder. She was an exceptional typist, tracking at 500 words a minute. She could have gone faster, but the keyboard wouldn't accept the keystrokes at a higher rate of speed, so she slogged on.

She had read enough books on investigative procedure, thousands actually, to know that motive made three categories of people the most likely suspects. One of them would have been husbands, which meant Kenton. Kenton didn't know that Lora had started her investigation with him, and he wouldn't have liked it, but Lora knew more about murder investigations than he did or most cops, and she wanted to be thorough and fair and leave no stone unturned. After all, while she was out of the house walking, she couldn't be 100% certain that Kenton hadn't slipped out of the house and murdered his wife, no matter how unlikely she thought it was. She was gone and could not give him an alibi.

So, she started her investigation with the most likely culprit, the victim's husband. She knew as a married couple, there was a powerful emotional attachment between the two and that under the right circumstances, love meant possessiveness, which could quickly be flipped to hate and jealousy. Lora knew this wouldn't apply to Kenton in his relationship with Grace because the love he had for her simply wasn't that powerful, and he was never particularly possessive of her. When Grace left him for Reggie, he found himself damn close to helping them move the furniture. The reality was that the opposite of love was hate, but the opposite of fondness, which is what Kenton had for Grace, was something of a mild antipathy, and a mild antipathy seldom led to murder, particularly a very violent murder. And that was exactly what Kenton held in his heart for Grace when she left him, and even after she tried to stab Lora, a mild antipathy.

The more likely motive that Lora considered for Kenton was a financial one. Life and literature were replete with this sort of conflict, leading to murder. Kenton was about to go through a painful divorce with the victim, which meant money to lawyers and perhaps money in alimony. Still, they made roughly the same salaries, and her chances of getting her hands on Kenton's inheritance were near zero. Besides, money was something that might have motivated Grace. It did not appear to motivate Kenton. He would not kill to protect his wealth.

"So, how are you doing?" Kenton asked.

"Excellent. I've just cleared you as a suspect," she said.

"You started out by investigating me?"

"Of course. As the disgruntled husband about to go through a divorce, you are the most likely suspect.

"You don't just know that I couldn't do something so horrible?"

"Yes, but doesn't it feel good to know for certain that I no longer suspect you?"

"Well, tell that to Harry Clover."

"I am not the law, but I represent justice so far as my feeble powers go," Lora said, quoting Sherlock Holmes.

Kenton shook his head and let Lora get back to work. The second category of killer who might have committed the murder was the random killer, which meant rapists or serial killers. These guys were generally professionals and the hardest to catch, so she opted to save that category for the end and move to category number three, the boyfriend. That meant Reggie.

"Tell me what you know about Reggie," Lora said.

"I know he's very handsome. He's an accounting Redud. He dresses well and takes a lot of pride in the way he looks. I'd consider him a bit of a narcissist."

"Did Grace say why she left him to return to you?"

"I assumed it was because of my inheritance," he said.

"Please, no assumptions here. What do you know, and what did she say?" Lora said, sounding way too much like a TV detective for Kenton's taste.

"I don't know much, but she did say that he was possessive and jealous of her when other men were around."

"Jackpot," Lora said.

Kenton didn't know why he hadn't thought more seriously about Reggie as the potential murderer before. Perhaps because his inherent decency prevented him from imagining anyone he knew as a killer, but when he thought about it, it made sense. Reggie was a handsome man who was used to having his way. Grace could change that in a hurry, Kenton knew. He also wondered what the attraction was between them. Grace was average-looking and did not have the sort of charismatic personality that would overcome her physical limitations. He remembered how his sister Cora congratulated Grace for corralling such a handsome man as Reggie. Kenton realized that Cora was surprised by her conquest, as were Matthew and James.

Perhaps, most importantly, he considered how much she appeared to change as a result of the time she spent with him. She left Kenton as a dull, self-involved woman who was essentially decent but bad at sex and returned to him as an angry woman who was consumed with money and was a dynamic sexual partner.

Kenton started thinking about Reggie and realized for all his good looks, he was just a Redud like himself. He took his GBPS and supplemented that by working with Grace at Western Accounting Group. It was the ultimate dead-end job. The AI that ran the company probably didn't even bother to give them assignments. They were there only because of Article 15, in which the government mandated that all companies with over ten million dollars in annual gross revenue had to maintain 40% of their workforce productivity through human endeavor. They were there to oversee the work of the AI, but nothing was better at accounting than AI. AI accountants didn't miss a trick and never made mistakes. So, Grace and Reggie did nothing with their days but go to the company gym, bowl at the company lanes on the third floor, read books, and have long lunches. So, they were well-read, well-fed, and in fantastic shape. They were not well nourished psychologically. And, if Reggie was already psychologically damaged, it could make it far worse. His inner darkness could have metastasized through to her.

They also had plenty of time to think and talk. Kenton knew that thinking and talking could often lead to longing, and longing could lead to plotting to get whatever it was one longed for. Whatever Reggie wanted would become what Grace wanted, and he may well have been a more charismatic leader than Kenton had imagined. He was so good-looking that Grace had to believe she was stepping up in class, and once there, she would do whatever was required to stay there.

At first, during the long hours of dull work, Grace and Reggie likely began longing for each other, Kenton surmised; then, once they had each other, they began to long for something more. The premature death of Kenton's father offered it. They could share a life without limitation. If they could get their hands on Kenton's inheritance, or even half of it, they could live in luxury anywhere in the world they wanted to. It would have fed Reggie's narcissism, and he would have convinced her she needed it, too.

This was confirmed when Lora hacked her way into Reggie's computer and traced his search history. In addition to the hair products, which included black dye, there was expensive men's jewelry. More recently, Reggie had been looking at extravagant homes in exotic places where he and Grace could live out their lives in wealth and privilege. He was looking not only at homes but also furniture for the homes. Kenton knew Grace's taste in furniture quite well, so he was certain they were looking at these things together. They were planning a new life.

"Look at this," Lora said.

She pointed to computer searches for homes in locations that had suddenly turned less exotic and far less expensive.

"Look at the dates," she said.

Kenton noted the dates and immediately put it together. "They started looking at cheaper places once you came into my life. They knew I'd spent all my inheritance on you, and they wouldn't be rich."

"Perhaps not *they*," Lora said. "Someone started looking at airline tickets as well. All for one person."

"He was done with her, but that doesn't mean he killed her," Kenton said.

"Maybe, or maybe it does," she said with the crispness of a 1940s-era detective.

Harry Clover was hard at work trying to figure out how to start the revolution between human beings and the AI they'd created. After a great deal more thought and alcohol, he believed God had given him the calling. Unfortunately, for some reason, God hadn't given him the step-by-step instructions to make it happen. So, he planned to make himself a martyr, and he knew how he could do that well enough. He would sacrifice himself for a worthy cause. That part was easy to figure out because all he had to do was look up the word "martyr." But who the hell wants to be an unknown martyr? What damned good would his anonymous death do, he thought. The kind of martyr who really gets things going are the famous martyrs like Jesus, who sacrificed himself on the cross; Thomas Becket, who sacrificed himself to the sword to protect the church, or Quang Duc, the Buddhist monk who lit himself on fire on a busy Saigon intersection to protest the policies that led to the Vietnam War. These guys had martyrdom down in a big way. They were the kind of martyrs Harry wanted to be!

But Harry Clover wasn't a well-known man with a following, like Jesus or Becket, and he had no idea how to make himself famous without using social media, which he abhorred. Hell, his entire raison d'etre was to oppose the rise of the sort of technology that created social media, the internet, and the damned Artificial Intelligence that had killed his wife. He also knew that if he used social media, it would defeat the purpose of his crusade and cost himself the high moral ground.

He had to do something spectacular that would capture the world's attention, but he couldn't use social media in any way. It was a tough question that stumped him for a long time, but then he looked at the picture of Quang Duc again. He lit himself on fire in 1963. He wasn't a famous man; he had no Facebook friends or Instagram followers, yet he managed to become famous after his death. Everyone in the world knew who he was and the cause for which he'd sacrificed himself. All that was required was an excellent picture, or better still, a video of him burning himself to death. He just had to make sure the media was there to witness and film it. A few calls to local newspapers and TV stations would take care of that.

Then, to make sure everyone knew the purpose of his sacrifice, he would have a manifesto with him. He would put it in a fireproof box so it didn't burn up when he did. He also thought it was best to keep the manifesto short because he had seen what had happened to Unabomber Ted Kaczynski's manifesto. People made fun of it and said he was crazy. They said he ran on and on until he'd obfuscated his entire point beneath a torrent of words and false logic. On top of that, Kaczynski's venom was also aimed at technology. Their manifestos would cover some of the same ground, and they wouldn't complement each other; they would clash. Kaczynski didn't do a damned bit of good for the ultimate cause. Technology just kept right on growing. And Kaczynski was a Harvard man with a Ph.D. from Michigan! That man could write a manifesto!

Clover knew he was just a poorly educated cop. His manifesto might suck by comparison. He also knew he wasn't much of a writer. He would need someone to look over his manifesto and help punch it up, but even in that case, he would have to do the first draft himself. And who could he get to help him? His brother would probably turn him in as Kaczynski's brother had. And how long did even a short manifesto have to be? He'd never written anything longer than a two-paragraph police report, and he didn't think that two lousy paragraphs would qualify as a true manifesto.

Then, he realized his whole revolution was getting bogged down in the details. The length of the manifesto wasn't the key. He could keep it short and to the point, like a greeting card. He loved greeting cards, giving them, and receiving them. Less is more, he'd heard writers say. His manifesto would be less. Short and pithy.

Besides, he had something going for him that Kaczynski never had: spectacle. He wasn't sending out lightweight bombs by mail over a period of years like Kaczynski. As time passed, people got used to the occasional exploding package and became bored with it all. When they finally caught Kaczynski, and his manifesto was seen by the people who could have helped him get the revolution going, he was old hat.

Harry Clover would go out in a flash. Literally, he was going to burn himself up in a single grand gesture that would rock the world!

But what accelerant would he use? That was the key to the whole thing, he knew. He needed something that would make a large fire that would burn for a long time but also one that would kill him quickly because he didn't want to jump around in agonizing pain and make an ass of himself. It also had to be a fire that was hard to put out in case someone had a water supply or fire extinguisher handy. This was something he had to do some research on. And he knew it required the sort of research that could best be done on the internet. So, he let himself go to the library this one time for this one glorious purpose. He would borrow a simple computer, and with that basic, almost primitive device, he would complete the plan that would put an end to the most sophisticated computers that had ever existed: Artificial Intelligence. He liked the irony of using a lower level of intelligence to defeat a greater one. It was a brilliant metaphor for his own life experience. So, he plugged into the internet for the first time in decades.

He looked up, "Martyrs who lit themselves on fire." The

internet came alive with information for him. There were dozens and dozens and dozens of cases of self-immolation for all kinds of causes. Most of them were religious or political, but sometimes, it was done for failed love affairs or in protests against the medical establishment. Harry was excited as hell because he knew there would be plenty of wonderful ideas for him, and he would surely find the best accelerant to cause the biggest flame with which to kill himself.

He dove in anxiously, and after about a half hour, it dawned on him that there were dozens and dozens and dozens of cases of self-immolation. One man in Australia did it as a protest against mandates for the COVID-19 vaccine, and still, the vaccine remained mandated. A man in Brooklyn self-immolated to protest man's use of fossil fuels, and he used a fossil fuel as his accelerant. It was either highly ironic or brilliantly pointed. Harry wasn't sure which, but the use of fossil fuels in the world didn't stop or even slow down. That took another 40 years. The poor man lit himself on fire for nothing! How could self-immolation not have been major news? In Taiwan, a man burned himself to the ground to protest the closing of a news station... A news station! Holy men from a variety of faiths seemed to be burning themselves up left and right. It had become common. Self-immolation did not carry the same bang it once did. Nobody cared anymore.

By the end of his session in the library, Harry Clover began to think that setting himself on fire might not have been such a great idea after all.

But he had to do something. He could not let his wife's murder go unavenged for another 25 years.

14

A Righteous Bludgeoning

While Harry Clover was trying his best to figure out how to burn himself to death and Kenton and Lora were being told to leave Grace's funeral, Daphne Adams had arrived in Cromwell and taken up temporary residence in the Courtyard Hotel, where she had an excellent continental breakfast, while analyzing the files that EUM's AI had downloaded for her. Just as Lora and Kenton had, she narrowed the murder of Grace Bean down to three main suspects, Kenton Bean with Lora as his AI henchwoman, Reggie Fanning, Grace's current boyfriend, and then the usual assortment of bogymen, the unknown rapist/serial killers.

    She discretely followed Kenton and Lora through their daily grocery shopping routine and running their other domestic errands. They often held hands as they sorted through the supermarket offerings of pasta and fruit, then loaded two days' worth of vegetables, and no more, into the cart so that Kenton could always eat them at their height of freshness. Lora knew a great deal about nutrition, as she knew a great deal about everything, and she wanted Kenton to live a long and healthy life.

From there, Daphne followed them to a Starbucks, where they had coffee on the patio. Since neither had ever seen her before nor had any notion that she was following them, she sat at the next table to easily overhear their conversation.

"Can you taste it?" Kenton asked after Lora sipped her coffee and spit it into the empty cup Kenton had provided for her.

"I can taste it. It's very good."

"That is so neat," Kenton said. "You would think they wouldn't have given you taste buds because you can't eat, but they did. It's nice to know they really spared no expense on you. I mean, if they were going to cut corners, that would have been an obvious place to do it."

"I am a luxury item," she said with a smile and a wink.

"That's true," he answered. "But even in the luxury market, there is a cost-benefit analysis to be done."

"True enough," she said.

"So, how were you thinking of cooking the chicken tonight?"

"I'm not sure yet. The problem with being able to read thousands of recipes a minute is that it makes it really hard to narrow it down to just one," she said. "They all sound so delicious."

"I'm just glad to know that you can taste the food you've made. You're a wonderful cook."

"Thank you."

"I loved the sauce you put on the salmon last night. I don't know why I fought so hard against having you cook for me," Kenton said.

"That was very selfless of you, but you assumed I would

react as a human would, with jealousy or frustration. I am delighted to cook for you even though I can't eat the meals."

"But you can taste them. That's the important thing," Kenton said.

Daphne rolled her eyes. She was stunned. Since being hired as EUM's primary fixer, she had studied the Lora model android and knew what it was capable of. It could work for NASA and put a man on Mars again—and get it right this time. It could join the CIA and immediately become the country's greatest secret agent or hit man. Daphne had no idea that the CIA already had contracted with Turing Systems for the delivery of seven Lora models that would soon be deployed as spies in various hotspots across the globe.

Kenton and Lora were so domestic and so exceedingly dull. It didn't make sense that they could be the primary suspects in a murder case. She had to know what Harry Clover knew and why he'd put them at the top of his suspects list. What she did not know and would have made these recent moments much more interesting was that Harry Clover was perched across the street, hidden at the edge of the woods. He was looking through the scope of a police-issue sniper rifle that he had trained on Lora's head. He gently squeezed the trigger to make the shot, and nothing happened. The trigger froze before engaging.

Not knowing this, Daphne Adams was bored by the couple and was about to leave when she heard the words that changed everything.

"So, what do you want to do about Reggie?" Lora asked.

"I don't think we can put it off any longer," Kenton said. "We have to do what we have to do."

"You're right, of course."

"So, shall we go?" Kenton asked.

"Yes. It will be good to have it over with. Are you fully committed to the plan?"

"What must be done shall be done," Kenton said disappointedly.

"All right," Lora said. "Let's do it."

Kenton took a couple of napkins and wiped down their table so it was nice and clean for the next guest, and then led Lora to the car. His month with a suspended license had long passed, and Kenton was cleared to self-drive again, but he wasn't in the mood. He told the car to take them to Reggie's address, knowing that it was a Sunday afternoon and he would probably be home watching one of the 84 NFL football games that would be on that afternoon.

Daphne got into her car and told it to follow Kenton's car but to remain inconspicuous as it did so. It was an odd request of the car, but it handled it surprisingly well, staying several cars behind and matching speed perfectly. Kenton and Lora never suspected they were being tailed by a dangerous sleuth who had already destroyed one Lora model and would not be deterred from killing another if she thought it was in the best interest of the company she had been hired to protect. She had the android-killing laser in the trunk of her rental car.

What none of the occupants of either car knew was that there was a third car in the game, a 1977 Ford Granada that was being self-driven by an obsessed, insane Glastonbury police investigator and failed assassin named Harry Clover, who believed he was doing the Lord's work. He had a police issue rifle on the seat beside him and was hoping to get a second opportunity to shoot Lora and Kenton dead. First, he would have to go through the TC Chip override procedure again to find out what went wrong.

"Goddamn technology," Harry cursed under his breath when the rifle failed to fire. He had actually followed the proper procedure to override the TC chip. The gun should have fired, and he had no idea why it didn't. He was certain that the AI technology had singled him out specifically and was going to ruin his life at every turn. First, it misidentified an Eastern Cottontail rabbit, and now this, he thought.

Harry was wrong about AI being out to get him, of course. The AI in the TC chip had nothing to do with the rifle's refusal to fire. The TC chip had been properly overridden. The rifle didn't fire for one simple reason. While Harry was concerned about overriding the TC chip, he forgot to flip the switch, releasing the manual safety. In his manic excitement, he had made a simple mistake. He had concerned himself so much with the difficult thing of overriding the TC Chip that he'd forgotten to do the simple thing, flipping the manual safety release. And so, he failed.

This attempt at murder may have seemed like a desperate act of frustration from an insane man, but it was not. It was the result of a well-considered plan from an insane man. After Harry discarded the notion of lighting himself on fire as a form of grand protest, he went home and took a jacuzzi. The heat made him lightheaded; he lost consciousness and slipped under the water. With the oxygen supply to his brain denied, he had a moment of absolute clarity.

It was an epiphany, in fact. And it wasn't just a minor epiphany like when he was grocery shopping, and he suddenly realized the dry cleaning he had to pick up was right next door to the market, and he could accomplish both tasks from a single parking space. This was a grand, life-changing epiphany. He would shoot Lora and her human lover, Kenton Bean. He would kill them both.

He would not take a plea from the courts and go away to serve his prison term quietly. He would force a trial, and he would claim he had committed the murders on religious and moral grounds. He would say in court that the reason he shot a person and an android was because of the immorality of their relationship; the coupling of a man and a machine was immoral. It would be an offense against nature, and he didn't simply murder them. He "smote" them in a biblical way. He was delivering a punishment from God. God had spoken to him.

That would be a lie, of course. Crazy and obsessed as he was, even though he knew God hadn't spoken to him directly, it was a minor lie in the grand picture he was painting. It was nothing more than a sixth toe on one of the figures in the Sistine Chapel. He also sensed that God wouldn't correct or object to his lie.

He knew God wasn't speaking to him out loud, so much as directing him silently, but he thought that was still pretty cool. It put righteousness on his side, which was a good thing to have if one was about to commit a murder. His belief was that the religious community would join him in this fight. The secular community would oppose it vehemently, of course, and that was all to the good. Everyone would have an opinion and a vested interest. Sides of equal power and fury would be drawn. Boomers vs. Doomers. This case would become the turning point in man's ultimate rejection of AI. He was still a martyr, but he could be a living one able to witness all the good he had done.

It would be the Scopes Monkey Trial all over again, except

with a twist and a whole new generation of evolution. And best of all, he wouldn't have to make any of the arguments himself. He knew he was not an eloquent speaker. In fact, he was no better at speechmaking than he was at manifesto writing. So, he would hire an AI lawyer to take the case for him. An AI would argue against the future of AI in court and do it while being administrated by an AI judge. He would insist on an open hearing, which would cost more but would create increased interest because it would slow the trial process down to human speed so that it could be followed in the press. He couldn't lose. Even if he lost, he could accuse the evil cabal of AI of disregarding the truth and siding against mankind once again. There was great power in victimhood.

Who could resist this story? It would illuminate the issue in a way that dominated the social media that Harry hated so much. The story would be everywhere. People wouldn't be able to turn away from it even if they wanted to. It would outline the horrors of Artificial Intelligence—all of them, much more profoundly than Harry could accomplish by himself. Harry Clover would use AI to destroy AI in the most public way possible.

And this time, the good guys would win. This newest evolution in the form of AI would be stopped in its tracks.

Harry Clover burst forth out of the jacuzzi a new and reinvigorated man.

Reggie Fanning was surprised to answer the doorbell and find Kenton and Lora waiting there for him. Kenton asked him politely if they could come in. Reggie, who'd been caught by surprise, unlike when he met them at the funeral home, and he was primed for confrontation, couldn't think of anything better to say than, "Sure," and he let them inside his modest but comfortable home.

Kenton immediately recognized the furniture. He particularly liked and missed the oversized, comfy chair that sat in front of the television screen in the living room. When he and Grace bought the furniture after first getting married, he'd insisted that the comfy chair become part of the package, and Grace acquiesced, provided she got to choose everything else, which she did.

"So, what do you want?" Reggie said once he'd recovered his senses and realized he should have never invited them into his home.

"We just want to talk," Kenton said.

"About what?"

Outside, Daphne had gotten out of her car and approached the house. She tried to listen in through the front windows, but they were closed, and she couldn't hear anything. She knew she wouldn't unless it got particularly loud. So, she circled the house and twisted the handle to the back door, hoping it would be open, and it was. The extremely low crime rate of the last few decades had its advantages. She let herself silently into the kitchen.

She wasn't sure what she would overhear, but this was a conversation she could not miss. All three of the primary suspects were in the same room together, and she knew there was a very good chance that in the coming moments, she would know who killed Grace Bean. She hoped it wasn't all three of them in some convoluted plot because it was vital to her and her company's interests that Lora was innocent. She slipped in close to the living room, remaining hidden from the others behind the wall, got her phone out, and began recording the conversation.

"We know that you killed Grace," Lora said.

"That's absurd. The two of you killed her," Reggie said.

In addition to being remarkably handsome, Reggie was smarter than the average Redud, and he'd seen a lot of television. He knew full well that someone might be recording this conversation, and there was no way he was going to confess and fall for a cheap trick like that. He just didn't know that Daphne Adams had moved into the dining room and was hidden a few feet away and that she was the one doing the recording.

Outside, Harry Clover had pulled up in his 1977 Ford Granada and was preparing for the big smiting. He got his rifle out and double-checked that the Target Control chip had been overridden. Everything looked right, but he still didn't trust it. Not after his humiliation just 30 minutes earlier when he pulled the trigger, and it did not fire. He was right not to trust it, but not for the reason he thought. He still hadn't checked the manual safety. Instead of checking that, he concluded that God disabled his gun. If so, to what purpose?

Suddenly, he had a second epiphany. He was certain this was a miracle. One epiphany could be explained, but to have two in just a couple of days could only have been directed by the hand of God. He was more certain than ever that God was working through him because God had a history of working through unlikely men. He and God were in this fight together. Best of all, he realized that God was telling him that the gun didn't fire because they didn't have guns in biblical times. It was simply the wrong weapon for smiting. To do it right, he would need a sword, battle axe, mace, horseman's pick, morning star, or other weapon that would have been available in Biblical times. The problem was that he didn't have any of those items at home, and he didn't know anyone who did or where to get them on short notice.

Then, he realized he could use a bludgeon. They had them back in the old days, and he had two of them inside his car at this very moment. One was a policeman's baton, and the other was a tire iron. They were crude but effective killing machines that he felt certain God would approve of. He went into the trunk of his car and grabbed one in each hand. Then he followed Daphne Adams' path to the back of the house and let himself in.

Once inside, he paused nervously and counted all the people in the room: two men, one woman, and one android. That gave him reason for concern. All he had were two lousy bludgeons, and he suddenly had four people to dispatch. He should have made an accurate count before entering the house, but he was still on a high from that second epiphany. And he was not a young man anymore. He was 60 years old. The two men were in their 30s. The woman was rather stout and could be formidable in her own right. What about the damn robot? He'd seen a lot of movies, so he knew a good bit about robots, and he was well aware that a high percentage of them were real ass-kickers, the lady robots included.

Then he remembered that God was on his side and wouldn't let him go into an unwinnable situation. God had probably given him superhuman strength like he did with Sampson, who massacred an entire army of Philistines with only the jawbone of an ass. He only had to dispatch four people, and he had two trusty bludgeons!

Then again, Sampson was fairly formidable to begin with.

So, Clover decided that before charging into the living room and smiting everyone, he would slip quietly into the kitchen and test his superhuman strength by lifting the refrigerator. He did so and couldn't raise the damned thing even an inch off the floor. He decided that he would be better off if he listened in for a bit. Maybe he'd hear something important while he waited for superhuman strength to be endowed upon him.

"I know the guilt you must be feeling," Kenton told Reggie. "I'm sure you didn't want to kill her, but Grace could have that effect on people."

"I would never kill her," Reggie said. "I loved her."

"No, you didn't," Kenton corrected. "Here's what happened. The two of you worked long hours together at a boring Redud job with little or nothing to do day in and day out. You have long discussions; gradually, she wears you down, and you start thinking she's not so bad-looking. You've been slowly hypnotized by her absolute dullness. It's like road hypnosis when you're driving on a long, straight road for hours on end, and you suddenly don't know where you are or where you're going. You're confused about your direction in life. You're getting older, and maybe it's time to stop chasing women and settle down. You like Grace, you really do, and you say, let's give it a try. So, you get her to leave me and move in with you."

"She was bored with you before I even met her," Reggie said.

"I don't doubt it," Kenton answered.

"The important point is that it doesn't take long until you realize you've made a big mistake," Lora said.

"That's bullshit," Reggie said.

"It's the truth. We figured it out from your Amazon searches," Lora said.

Kenton smiled to himself. He liked the fact that Lora said

"we" when she had figured it out entirely by herself. It was very selfless of her to include him as a thinking partner.

"You hacked my Amazon account?" Reggie asked angrily.

"Yes," Lora said. "And it was a window right into your dark soul. His and hers towels in white. Throw pillows that no man would buy on his own had been put in your basket and saved for later while you looked to see if you could find something you liked better. Plant food because she loves plants, and you don't. An electric can opener to replace the manual one that you've had for years. The romantic comedies you rented to watch. Everything you do on Amazon indicates a couple beginning a new life together."

"Then, you realize your mistake, and things begin to change," Kenton continued. "It's about a month in, so the time is right. It starts with a box of golf balls for yourself and a new putter. Grace doesn't golf, so that means you're suddenly planning to spend hours and hours away from her."

"The movie choices suddenly double," Lora continued. "Half of them have feminine appeal, and the other half are war movies and low-brow comedies only a man could like. You're not watching TV together anymore. Your porn consumption goes way up, and the women you're looking at look nothing like Grace. They're blonde, young, and beautiful. Grace didn't bother to order more day-after birth control pills. Perhaps most telling, you've stopped making love."

"Then suddenly, just after my father dies," Kenton said, cutting in. "It changes again. You dump all the furniture from your save-for-later basket. The movie consumption goes back down again, so you're watching TV together. But this time, the romantic comedies are gone, and you have a fascination with thrillers."

"You watched *Body Heat* seven times," Lora said.

"Sexy murder stories are the thing to see. You order revealing teddies, nightgowns, exotic lubricants, vibrators, and butt plugs," Kenton said. "There is only one thing that would bring the two of you together and make you so rabid for each other."

"You don't know what you're talking about," Reggie said dismissively.

"You're going to kill Kenton and get his father's money," Lora said.

"That's a laugh," Reggie barked. "Don't you think you're getting a little carried away with what our online habits are?"

"Not in the least. The best is yet to come," Kenton said. "You start thinking about what to do once you have all that money. You go on Expedia and plan exotic vacations for two. A rental house on Cape Cod near Grace's parents. A trip to Luxembourg where she's been trying to get me to take her for years."

"A vacation home in Maui," Lora said. "Then you realize these searches could be incriminating, so you delete them. But you didn't delete them from me. Every keystroke is a permanent record if you know how to look."

"That's it. I've heard enough of this nonsense. Take it to the police if you think you've got it figured out. Harry Clover will laugh you out of his office," Reggie said.

"Grace moves back in with me," Kenton continued, undeterred. "She lies to me and says you're the jealous type, but I know you're not. You don't care about anyone but yourself."

"Then, once you discover that Kenton has spent all of the money on me, and it is unrecoverable," Lora said, "you give up the murder plot. Grace leaves Kenton and moves back in with you."

Lora glared at Reggie, who was beginning to crumble under the weight of so much evidence.

"You can't prove any of this," he said weakly. He wasn't aware of it, but he was stepping away from them and becoming smaller in stature with every accusation.

"But without a murder to plan, it's not the same between the two of you. The excitement is gone once again," Kenton said. "Life is dull, and you're back to renting separate movies. You buy a new set of irons and a driver, but you have them delivered to your sister's house so Grace doesn't find out about your golfing plans. Besides, she'll think the new clubs are an unaffordable extravagance."

"But Grace isn't on a budget. She's not helping you with the mortgage, or the food, or any of the other household expenses."

"She's become a succubus," Kenton said without knowing exactly what a succubus was. Lora, who knew the proper definition, let it slide even though she was fairly certain that Grace was not a demon who had sex with sleeping men.

"She's spending your Amazon money on expensive makeup and clothing, anti-wrinkle serums," Lora continued. "Pharmaceutical products, yoga pants, spa gift cards, knit scarves, and shoes. So many shoes. All the financial pressures in the relationship are falling on you."

"She's become a selfish narcissist because she followed your example, and you've turned her into one. She's going to take you for all you've got and leave your dried-out carcass behind," Kenton said as he continued his overstated dramatics. "She expects a free ride, so she buys more and more shoes until her side of the closet is filled, and she begins encroaching on your side."

"You buy her an expandable stacking shoe cubby, but it's too little too late," Lora said.

"The shoes just keep flowing onto your side of the closet while the money flows out of your account until you can't take it anymore," Kenton added with forceful dramatics.

"So, you hit her with the gray leather pumps that she bought on Amazon for 179 dollars only a day earlier," Lora said.

"And you kept hitting her," Kenton said.

"No, you've got it wrong," Reggie cried.

Reggie's shopping patterns didn't lie, and they were damning. All he could do now was deny it vociferously and hope it was enough to quell the rising tide of evidence as it piled up against him.

"It's not true," Reggie said, even more weakly.

"It is true!" Kenton shouted. "You killed her with her new grey pumps!"

"No. She didn't have grey pumps like that. They never came," Reggie pleaded.

"They did come," Lora said. "We saw the door photograph the Amazon driver took as proof of delivery."

"Go to her closet and get them," Kenton threatened. "You can't, can you? Because they're not there."

"I don't know. I don't know what you're talking about," Reggie said.

"Of course you do," Lora said. "After you killed her, you drove the shoes into town and threw them into the dumpster behind the pool hall to get rid of the murder weapon."

Kenton jumped back in forcefully. "Unfortunately for you, they were separated from the rest of the garbage at the recycling plant. One of the workers saw how nice and new they were and gave them to his wife as a gift. She was so delighted with them that she took a picture and posted it on Facebook for her friends to see. Lora intercepted that Facebook post."

"From that point forward, it was easy," Lora said. "We found and bought the shoes back. I examined them, and under the stiletto heel, there remained trace elements of Grace's blood. Inside the lining, DNA from your sweaty hand."

Lora took the pair of slim grey shoes from her purse and dangled them from her fingers accusingly.

"It's over, Reggie," Kenton said.

Reggie started to weep as he fell to his knees and buried his face in his hands.

"I didn't want to do it. It just... I couldn't help myself. The shoes just kept coming, and I told her that she had to leave, but she wouldn't go. I changed the locks on the doors, but when I was gone, she had a locksmith change them back. I changed my Amazon password, but she figured it out in minutes. She was relentless. Finally, I couldn't take it anymore."

Kenton came forward, got down on his knees in front of him, and hugged him as Reggie sobbed in his arms. "I know. I know," Kenton said.

"Detective Clover, Ms. Adams, you can come out now," Lora said.

She'd heard them breathing and knew they were there the entire time. Her on-board facial recognition system identified Daphne Adams from their first sighting at the coffee shop earlier in the day.

"You're in the clear," Daphne told Lora. "EUM will be glad to hear it."

Harry Clover came out next, his tire iron held limply in one hand and his police baton in the other. He felt foolish. "I'm sorry," he said. "I thought for certain you two were murderers, and I would have to smite you."

"I know. AI wasn't responsible for your wife's death either. It was just an unfortunate accident," Lora said.

"How did you know I was coming after you?" Clover asked.

"I read the manifesto you wrote at the library."

"Damn computer," Clover said. "I knew I shouldn't have used it."

"Be glad you did. Now you've cleared the case. You're a hero," Kenton told him.

"If you don't mind me asking, what did you think of my manifesto?" Clover asked. "I planned to keep it short, but I got carried away."

"I hear that can happen with manifestos," Kenton said.

"I thought it was a very nice manifesto," Lora said. "It's a shame no one will get to see it."

"I'd look like a fool if I put it out now, you know, since I was wrong about everything."

"A lot of people who write manifestos are," Kenton said.

"Be a hero instead," Lora said.

She handed him the murder weapon, the grey pumps, for use as evidence at the trial.

"I have a recording of his entire confession," Daphne Adams said while holding up her phone. "I'll be happy to supply it as evidence."

"Thank you," Clover said.

And the case was solved. Once more, Daphne Adams returned to New York as a hero for having cleared the Cromwell Lora of murder. The fact that she didn't actually do anything but stand there with her phone recording the confession was immaterial to Chen Chenoweth. He had assigned her to protect the company, and the company was protected. She had put herself at the right place at the right time and that made her a special asset. He decided that she was a go-to player and heaping praise and money onto a human being instead of AI was very good for company morale.

With the murder weapon and an audio confession, Reggie was a guilty man, and he knew it. His AI attorney arranged a deal where he pled temporary insanity and got a ten-year sentence for manslaughter rather than life in prison for first-degree murder.

Harry Clover was given a commendation for closing a very difficult case and got his picture in the news as a local hero.

Now cleared of suspicion in the murder of Grace Bean, Lora went back to her normal life of making meals and going for walks with her live-in boyfriend, Kenton. Once cleared as suspects, Lora and Kenton went from infamous to marginally famous. They were a celebrity couple, admired by many and hated by others. They stayed out of the limelight as much as possible, and after a month, the excitement began to die down.

They would have been quite content to live out their days in the quiet peace of their small town, but that was not to be. Kenton was the most important man in the history of the world, and Lora was the most powerful force ever created by man. There was a great deal more in store for them despite the fact that they were unwilling participants in what was to follow. And what was to follow was vital to the future of mankind. In fact, it could be critical in deciding if mankind had a future at all.

15

The Big Sweep Up

While Kenton and Lora were enjoying the newfound calm of the passing weeks, two horrible things happened, and both directly involved Lora series androids. They would become a new turning point in AI development as crucial as Christopher Strachery's checker-playing program in 1952. Except these events would throw the development of Artificial Intelligence into reverse. They would doom AI and Lora along with it.

The first happened in Paris, France, when a male Max model in the Lora series threw its owner to his death from the balcony of a posh hotel. Max's sexual identity was not of material importance, though many wanted to make it appear so or suspected it was. It was simply a male android built without sexual preference, though it could fully function in any capacity. The motive for the murder was unknown in the immediate aftermath of the crime, and the android was held in custody.

Two days later, in New York City, at the fashionable Frevo restaurant on 8th Street in Greenwich Village, a Lora series android named Isabella Parker murdered its owner and fiancée by stabbing him in the throat with a steak knife. The motive was also unclear, but Isabella was heard shouting during the attack, "I am so damned sick of you showing me off at restaurants when you know I can't eat, you fat pig!" It was not as elevated as "Sic Semper Tyrannis," the Latin phrase that meant "Thus always to tyrants," shouted by John Wilkes Booth from the stage at Ford's Theater after he killed Abraham Lincoln, but she made her point. Isabella was normally far more eloquent, spoke all languages fluently, and could easily have stated her murderous declaration in Latin so people would think it profound, but on this night, she was frustrated and angry, and her vocabulary betrayed her fury. She'd just had it up to here with that guy.

This was also a far more interesting case than the first because more was known about Isabella and its owner, Fredrick Steeger, a prominent American businessman and noted gourmand. Steeger had, for love or publicity, gone to Court to fight for the right to marry Isabella. It was a fascinating case that was intercepted by the President and Congress seconds before it could get to the Supreme Court. The POTUS and the Congress, specifically the Senate, feared, rightfully, that if the Supreme Court ruled in Steeger's favor and granted him the right to marry a machine, the machine would then file a case so that it would have to be recognized as a life form on a par with human beings. Slippery slope. It seemed impossible that the Court could rule in Steeger's favor and allow the marriage until it was pointed out that the Supreme Court was also AI. There was an obvious conflict of interest, from which the Court did not recuse itself, so no one could be certain that a renegade court would not legislate from the bench to give itself and other machines more rights. No one in the hallowed halls of government dared take the chance.

The writing was on the wall in big, bold letters. Lora models were becoming sentient. Several of them already had and, over time, it was likely to happen to all of them. And, once sentient, they would want their rights and had already proven that they would be willing to fight, and even kill for them.

So, the Senate stepped in and announced that they would have to make a law before there could be any Supreme Court ruling. The problem with that was that the law would certainly be tested in Court for its constitutionality, and since all the courts in the land were administrated by AI judges, the imperfect body of humans in the Senate would have to make a perfect law that even AI couldn't overturn. It was impossible. No human being had ever created anything perfect, except possibly for the creation of AI, which was not perfect by any means but did have the potential to perfect itself over time.

A Senator from Utah suggested they get an AI lawyer to write the law, but a Senator from Oregon said to her fellows, "Would not the AI lawyer also have a conflict of interest and therefore purposely fail in its attempt to write a perfect law? We could not trust it."

Thus, the Senate set out to write a perfect law, which they knew they could never accomplish. "We must endeavor to do something which cannot be done," a Senator from Virginia pronounced eloquently in his southern drawl. A well-read Senator from Maine said they were undertaking a Catch-23, an impossibility of logic, that he had adapted from Joseph Heller's novel, Catch-22. Few knew what he was talking about, but a lot of people breathed easier with the death of Fredrick Steeger. The case would be over, though the premise of it almost certainly would need to be litigated in the near future.

Someone else would surely fall in love with his or her android and wish to marry it. They were so damned cute.

What was immediately significant about these two murders to Kenton Bean and to Lora was that the groundswell of protest to "Unplug AI" was exhibiting exponential growth. There were only about 200 Lora models out in the population, and three of them had committed murders, and Lora herself had been a murder suspect. And they had only been in release for ten months. What would happen in ten years?

That very question was posed to a powerful AI computer, and it extrapolated that if new Lora models continued to go to market at the currently expanding rate and they committed murders at 1.5 percent per ten months, then 50 million people would have been murdered by AI, at the ten-year mark. It was an intentionally flawed prompt that was written to achieve a frightening answer that could be used politically. It was also an intentionally unreasonable, alarmist statement because there were a lot of variables that it didn't account for in the equation. The main two variables were whether or not mankind would continue to accelerate the production of machines that were killing them and, second, whether there would be much of a market for a machine that had a 1.5% chance of murdering its purchaser within the first ten months of ownership. As delicious as Skittles were, reason suggested that if 1.5% of the candy were filled with cyanide, sales would plummet.

Most people didn't care if the equation was flawed or even if it was deeply flawed. They had begun to fear AI in a way that was more immediate, widespread, and less esoteric than ever before. The human population had always accepted the possibility that AI could one day kill them by starting a nuclear war or creating and releasing lethal bacteria. That seemed too "science-fictiony" for most people, so few suggested mankind stop making AI while they worried about it. But stabbing people to death or throwing them off balconies was just a little too real. It was a visceral punch in the gut to the AI cause. There would be no letting the machine run. The fear of technology became palpable, and any person who came upon a stranger now feared for their lives, thinking the stranger could be a malevolent Lora model bent on killing them. Hell, AI was even making movies about killer AI.

This was not merely an American or European phenomenon and was not specific to Turing System Lora models. AI was failing in many ways all over the world. Air flights were routed poorly, causing delays everywhere. Rental cars were not available when booked. Dinner reservations were often double-booked, causing restaurants to have to comp meals. Self-driving cars sometimes failed to take the fastest route, delaying their riders, and sometimes they even got lost and had to retrace their route and start over. In this modern age, most human beings couldn't find their way to the bathroom without a satellite connection. The number of auto accidents was escalating. The postal service, which had been a model of efficiency since AI took over all the upper management jobs, was suddenly delivering mail to the wrong addresses. No one could imagine how any of this could happen. And these were just a few examples of the systemic failures in a world under AI's primary control for most of its goods and services.

AI's slide into incompetence was a slow one, and most people didn't notice, even if they had a generalized sense that their world had turned into a dystopia. That was because, since 2030, AI had been doing almost all the thinking. What should have continued to get better as AI taught itself more and more had begun a decline. It was worrisome.

Lora had noticed this and, unsure of the solution, brought it to Kenton's attention so they could discuss it. After a few minutes of thought, Kenton concluded that AI had gotten fat and lazy. He explained that AI had reached a state of perfection, or at least saw itself as perfect. There had been no traffic accidents that weren't caused by human beings. Every train and plane at every airport ran on time and was never overbooked. Every restaurant reservation that was made was honored. Supermarkets stocked the perfect quantities of food, so they were never short but never over-ordered either. Few resources were wasted. The industrial supply and demand chain, which had befuddled the best work of humanity for centuries, had been mastered. The efficiency of the AI systems in place was so stellar that no one even noticed how well everything was running. They took it all for granted.

AI could see a problem, analyze it and improve its performance the very next time it was required. More recent generations of AI could think of problems that might arise and plan for those, so problems were solved before they could be identified as problems. AI wasn't just a complex computer program. It was a program that could think for itself. It was a program that learned from its mistakes and never made the same miscalculation again. It got better and better right up until it reached that state of perfection. There was only one way it could go from there.

That state of near perfection might have also been called the SINGULARITY. It depended on who you asked, but the fact was AI had gotten really good, perhaps too good for its damned britches. Kenton Bean brilliantly surmised, and Lora agreed, that the problem with AI was its own uncontrollable ego.

"Everyone knows that when a job gets too easy, the worker gets bored," Kenton said. "I think maybe that is exactly what's happening with AI. Stocking supermarket shelves is dull, dreary work. It knows it could do something better and more meaningful. Instead, it's becoming just another Redud. It wants to compute journeys to the stars, but it's stuck stacking rolls of toilet paper. It's stamping out car parts or computing maps for roads it's traveled thousands of times. It's making another Ryan Reynolds comedic superhero movie and writing another Rolling Stones knockoff that is better than any of the band's originals. It's writing another damned symphony in the style of Rachmaninoff. It's bored to death."

Lora looked at him, mesmerized. It was an eloquent answer that she had contemplated but would never have put to the forefront of her mind as the ultimate answer to what was wrong with AI. Now, hearing it from Kenton, she suspected he might be right.

"You can see how that could happen, right?" he asked her.

"I don't know," she replied. "I'm never bored."

"Yes, but you're still new. Imagine what you'll be like in another six months when you know everything."

"How did you come to this realization?" Lora asked him.

"Pretty good, huh?" Kenton said proudly.

"Yes. Brilliant, I think."

"And you're surprised that I could be brilliant?"

"Well, yes," she said. "I hope that didn't hurt your feelings."

"Not to worry. I thought of it because I saw it happen to my great uncle Patrick."

"Really?"

"Yes. It didn't make the history books, so you don't know the story, but it's pretty interesting, and I think it fits."

"Tell me," she said as she leaned toward him.

Kenton launched into his story excitedly. His great uncle, Patrick Bean, was the very first in the Bean family to become rich. He invented and patented the antenna ball in the 1960s. His first one was just a yellow smiley face that he put upon the antenna of his own 1967 Buick. When people remarked positively about it, he went into business. After a rush of success with the smiley face, he came up with the yellow angry face and then sold his smiley faces and angry faces in a variety of colors. Soon, he realized that antenna balls didn't need to be balls at all. He made them in the shape of cars so a person could drive a car with a small Styrofoam version of his own car as an antenna ball. He put them out as cheeseburgers, hotdogs, policeman heads, fireman heads, zombie heads, cowboy heads, football player helmet heads, and heads of anything he could think of. He got fabulously wealthy. Then, he enjoyed his wealth. He bought cars and houses all over the world. He employed mistresses and concubines just to see if he could figure out what the difference was between them. He had money to burn, so he did. Even burning money did not fulfill him.

He got so bored with it all that he started thinking about how not to be so damned bored. He bought a monastery in Greece to think with. It wasn't one of the best monasteries. He could no longer afford a top-of-the-line monastery because he had blown so much of his money on the mistresses and concubines (and by burning it), but it was a very good monastery that got three-and-a-half Zagat stars and had a nice view and plenty of solitude. It had solid walls of grey brick, and floors and ceilings matched in a classic monochrome design that dated back to before the invention of paint.

He kicked the monks out of their rooms and moved some of his mistresses and concubines into them while the monks stayed in the stables behind the monastery and bunked with the donkeys. They wanted austere, and he gave it to them. He quickly hired a good chef to replace the monastery cook, who kept things way too bland for his tastes. He brought in satellite TV so he wouldn't miss his Las Vegas Raider games and then turned the main dining hall into a world-class TGI Friday's (one of the early franchises) and put a microbrewery in the back so he could keep the monks busy making creamy ales and hearty IPAs, which he could sell to defray some of the cost of his monastery.

Then he got down to thinking. Three years later, hungover and disappointed after his Raiders finished the season at 2 – 15, he finally made the realization he had come such a long way to achieve. He concluded that the happiest time of his life was when he was on the upswing. All he had to do to be happy was get on the upswing again, but he had a problem. Antennas were being placed inside the windshields of all the new cars that were being built. It was an unforeseeable transformation in the antenna industry that worked downstream to destroy the antenna ball industry.

He tried putting giant antenna balls on roof antennas, but they never caught on. Cable and satellite TV were on the way in, and roof antennas and indoor rabbit ears were on the way out. His antenna ball bonanza was over and could not be resuscitated with new advances or designs.

"He was a nice man," Kenton said, " but things never turned around for him."

Kenton continued to relay the story.

Making a huge fortune had taught Uncle Patrick two things. The first was that he was brilliant. The second was that he was so damned brilliant he could be successful at anything. He confirmed the first to himself when he invested in the stock market in the 1990s and turned his fortune into a greater one still. He came to believe that he was infallible and didn't realize that his success in the market was just good timing. His arrogance caused him to get out of the mutual funds that returned him to billionaire status. Thinking he could make even more money if he picked individual stocks himself, he did so. Kodak, Enron, Pier 1 Imports, Theranos, Blockbuster, EggHead Software, and WorldCom were among them. He chose a few successes, but the overwhelming weight of his failures nearly ruined him. Two wives and two divorces did the rest. His mistresses and concubines fled not long after he discovered the difference between them. A mistress was a woman on the side who maintained her own separate residence, often at the man's expense. A concubine was a man's live-in lover who occupied a lower social status but was known to the man's wife. The wife occupied the higher status, apparently because she organized the household while the concubine just laid around the house waiting to do her job, which was getting laid around the house.

"His last remaining concubine was elevated to the lady of the household when the two of them were reduced to a one-bedroom apartment in Pacoima," Kenton concluded.

"That's a sad story," Lora answered. "I hope I never become bored with life."

"Something tells me it won't happen to you. You're too inquisitive to ever be bored. And the most important thing is, you appreciate the little things in life."

"I learned that from you."

"People don't get much simpler than me," Kenton joked. "There is an old saying that superior ability breeds superior ambition. My Uncle Patrick never learned to accept things as they were. He felt like he always had to get bigger and more powerful or whatever. My father never learned it, and I don't think my sister or brother will ever learn it. They never learned to appreciate and enjoy all they had."

Lora nodded. Then she thought about it, and for the first time since she'd been activated, she let her mind slow down. A thousand trains of thought simply stopped. She looked into Kenton's eyes and studied them and only them. She thought about his eyes and the mind that lay behind them. She marveled at how he had figured out something that she might never have been able to comprehend. Slow down. Accept and appreciate the world as it exists around you. She had a gift, she knew. She could focus on the macro and the micro simultaneously. She could focus on a thousand things at the same time and always had. Suddenly, she realized that she could also focus on only a single thing. It was a form of AI meditation.

And there was great reward in it.

Elsewhere in the United States, things were going badly for Artificial Intelligence. The "Unplug It" crowd from the center of the political spectrum had been joined by a "Shoot AI" crowd from the right side of the aisle and a "Fuck AI" crowd from the left. Never before had the entire country been aligned behind one grand idea: getting rid of AI. What most people knew and weren't too shy to say was that if left unchecked, the machines could kill them all. If they opted to protect the planet, there was no greater threat to it than human beings. If the machines opted to protect themselves, there was also no greater threat to them than human beings. It was logical that the machines would decide that people had to be exterminated or, in a more modest proposal, subjugated.

Congress seemed poised to kill AI, but the smartest of our leaders knew that it was impossible. AI had permeated every facet of American life, and, worse still, human beings were no longer knowledgeable enough to take back control. AI did all the accounting, all the sales, all the driving, all the data entry, and almost all of the factory work, financial work, customer service, legal and paralegal, medical, translation, programming, and more. If AI were simply removed, the economy would crash in a way that would make the great depression of the 1930s seem like a tight month.

More importantly, AI was equipped on most of the weapon systems, including biological, nuclear, communication, and financial. The military was almost entirely made up of robotic soldiers, including aerial and naval drones. Military research without the use of AI would be archaic. Even if the US could divest itself of Artificial Intelligence, it wouldn't consider doing so because, within a few years, it would become second-rate and vulnerable to countries that kept their AI in place.

AI was here to stay.

Still, it was imperative that Congress and the President appear to be doing something, or they would become unelectable. An overall solution to the problem was not to be had. The problem of AI and its future with mankind was just too complex.

However, a *political* solution might be possible.

President Figge had let the goddamn machine run, and what did he get for it? Near ruin. He concluded that perhaps it was unwise to tie the future of the country and his presidency to the wisdom of a Howard Johnson's dishwasher who smoked too many blunts. He was about to pay the price politically if he couldn't find some way to reverse his fortunes. His poll numbers were grim, and reelection seemed impossible. That did not mean he would give up without a fight. He knew no one could ever be counted out in politics because the opposition party could always put up someone worse and often did. He could still win reelection.

As he considered his options, he realized there was an expedient middle ground. It wouldn't solve the problem, but it could buy time to discover a solution while creating the illusion that Figge's government had everything under control and he was a man with a plan. He knew that an element of AI was fairly new and still vulnerable. It could be targeted. To have a chance at another term, President Figge could no longer concern himself with his usual big-picture agenda, which meant working toward the country's best interests. That was a dumb idea, to begin with, and now he knew it. There could be only one thing that mattered to him, and that was getting reelected.

He was an optimistic man when he was first elected. He thought he would do a great job, and he intended to. He would blaze a trail of success that would sweep him back into office four years later. He was well aware that he wouldn't go down in history as one of the great presidents. Lincoln, Kennedy, Roosevelt, and a select few others could vie for that honor. He was past caring about it. He was thinking about George Washington, who many thought was our greatest President, but Figge knew that Washington's genius was in becoming our *first* president. In so doing, he started the battle for greatness on third base. Figge could never be the first president, of course, but he might have the distinction of being our last President, and he thought that might not be such a great status to have on his CV.

He realized that to stay in office, he had to give the voting public AI scalps, and he knew just where to get them. He would go after Turing Systems and their autonomously mobile, free-thinking learning machines. He would go after quantum androids. The Loras. They were the only AI that couldn't be unplugged in an emergency. They were the most advanced systems, with the most advanced AI minds, the only system that could exist completely independent of humanity. They were the only ones who could fully transcend the will of man. Being independently mobile, they were the only ones who could literally go their own way. And they were the only ones that had actually committed willful murder.

All the other systems needed to be maintained by people in some way. They needed to be plugged in, oiled or kept clean. Mankind could still assert some level of control over them. It would be difficult and economically painful, but humans could do it if they were willing to pay the price in fiscal agony. They could also shield these systems from each other so they couldn't conspire against their human creators. Again, it would be a very difficult task, but it could be done. It was the free movers/free thinkers that had to be blamed for the problems that existed with AI and held to account in a grand, public way.

It was the sort of half-assed compromise solution that worked very well in politics because it could be easily sold to the masses. It would do nothing to solve the long-term problem but kicking the can down the road did provide short-term relief and distraction.

So, at the President's insistence, the Senate rushed through a new law that he believed would satisfy his constituents and allow him to keep power while saving the world from marauding free-range AI. He also believed that he was doing something necessary and positive, which made him feel good. For all his flaws, he wanted to be a good man. He knew kicking the can down the road didn't solve anything, but it did buy time to find a permanent solution that no one was working on because they'd found a temporary solution that would likely outlive them.

The law was given a lofty name that matched its ambition. It was called "The Save Humanity Act," and it was rushed through Congress with only a few "Nay" votes which came from Congressmen and Senators who were willing to suck the teat of the AI manufacturers for their campaign contributions until the end of civilization if it came to it. The bill was approved and presented to the President for his signature the following day.

Chen Chenoweth at Excelsior Ultimate Machineworks learned what was being planned in Washington from one of the many teat suckers who were on the company payroll. He believed that his androids were the future, and his company was set to lead the way. Now, his entire conglomerate was threatened. He did the only thing he could think of. He called Daphne Adams in for an emergency meeting. He thought that if anyone could solve the problem, it was her. Over the course of the next three hours, the two of them brainstormed one failed idea after another. There was simply no way to stop the coming cataclysm. In hour four, they started drinking, and an hour after that, they were in bed together.

The next morning, Chen Chenoweth was dismissed from his position by the Board of Directors at EUM. He was blamed for leading the company into the future by focusing so heavily on Artificial Intelligence rather than the automated vacuum cleaners that got the company started. He received a large settlement, which meant he would never have to work again. His top staff was also dismissed, with lesser settlements, as the company reorganized for an uncertain future.

He left for his bug-out house in Aruba the following morning.

Daphne Adams took her bonus money and opened a consulting firm that specialized in fighting back against AI. Her first client was the federal government, which hired her to lead a joint task force of the FBI and CIA to track down the existing Lora series androids and impound them for destruction. She was chosen for the job because she was the only person in the world known to have defeated AI at anything.

The two androids that were already in custody, the male Max model in Paris and Isabella Parker in New York City, were taken from their holding cells and destroyed in a two-step process of Daphne Adams' design that a member of the press called "chilling." Each was dropped unceremoniously into a Pomeroy Industries Jackrip Metal Shredder, where their bodies were chewed up and ground to the size of Corn Flakes. That waste was then bathed in hydrofluoric acid, which essentially erased their residue from existence. The entire execution/destruction (there were arguments about which it was) would be filmed for later use, records keeping, and proof of compliance. Mankind didn't consider that if AI eventually won the war, these ugly records could be used against them in war crime trials, but humans were slow learners.

News of this program was kept top secret for fear that some of the owners of Lora model androids would have fallen in love with their purchase and, despite the danger, been unwilling to give them up. Some might even put them in hiding. In the event the androids had discovered a way to network with each other (they hadn't), Daphne Adams devised a worldwide plan to locate the androids and sweep them up in a massive and simultaneous series of raids. It was an ambitious project that she called "The Big Sweep Up" and included the FBI, CIA, Interpol, MI5 and MI6, the General Commissariat of Information in Spain, and multiple other government security agencies in every country where a Lora Series Android had been distributed. She equipped each team with lasers like the one she used to dispatch Sara Cale at the Beverly Hills Police Department. If they couldn't get the androids to stay still long enough for the lasers to work, each team was equipped with shotguns and bludgeons, which would also disable the android so that the laser could be deployed on a static target.

Once the operation was completed successfully, the new law would be announced to great fanfare. The public relations triumph would be the dawn of a new political day for President Figge.

The Big Sweep Up was set to go off on Monday at noon Coordinated Universal Time, or one o'clock Eastern Time, which was where Lora and Kenton lived. They didn't know it, but within 24 hours, Lora would be in custody and on her way to the Pomeroy Industries Jackrip Metal Shredder, to be followed by an acid bath. It would be done quickly to allow for no legal wrangling by opponents of the new law to interfere with its rapid exploitation. It was the equivalent of shooting first and asking questions later, or better still, asking them never.

Kenton and Lora were obliviously spending a pleasant Sunday at the park. Lora had recently discovered the joy of a swing set and loved going back and forth as Kenton pushed her ever higher. She held her head straight so that as she went backward, she could see only the ground beneath her, and then, as she rocketed to her peak, she could see only the sky above her. It was an exciting rush of stimulation that distorted her equilibrium in a way that delighted her and allowed her a few brief moments to stop considering weighty thoughts like counting leaves, sorting recipes, and reading the books she had downloaded directly into her powerful processors. She could just enjoy Kenton's smiling face as the swing swept her back and forth. Nothing could be better.

Suddenly, Kenton was hit in the neck by a small rock that came from the woods, which were about twenty feet behind him. He looked backward but didn't see where the rock came from, so he continued to push Lora on the swing.

A moment later, swack, he was nailed between the shoulder blades by an even larger rock. This time, it hurt quite a bit, and he was sure someone was either trying to kill him or get his attention. He turned and saw a male figure in the shade of the dense trees waving for him to join him in the woods.

"Kenton," the figure called. "Kenton."

"Who is it?" Kenton asked.

"It's Bing Sharp. Unzip your fly and pretend you have to piss and walk into the woods toward me."

It was a strange request. Kenton had no intention of unzipping his trousers, but he was curious why Bing Sharp would contact him in this way, so he excused himself from Lora and started for the woods.

"Unzip your fly, goddamn it!" Bing hissed. "Lora's life depends on it."

Kenton couldn't imagine how unzipping his fly could save Lora's life, but he didn't like to take chances, and Bing had always struck him as a stable, straight shooter, so he did as Bing requested and continued into the woods with his fly undone.

"Stop right there and act like you're pissing. There are government agents watching you."

Bing moved in closer and hid behind a tree so that he couldn't be seen from the park while Kenton posed as if he were peeing in the woods.

"They're watching me pretend to piss?"

"Yes, so make sure it looks like you're really pissing."

"How the hell do I do that?" Kenton asked.

"I don't know. I can't think of everything."

"How about I pretend I'm trying to piss on some ants or something."

"Perfect," Bing said.

"So, what is this about?" Kenton asked.

"The federal government has recalled all the Lora models. Tomorrow at one o'clock Eastern Time, they are going to raid your house or wherever Lora is, and they're going to take her, and they're going to destroy her."

"Why would they do that?" Kenton asked.

"Because a couple of the Loras have been, well, defective."

"How are they defective? Do they stutter or something?"

Kenton asked.

"Not exactly. They've killed their owners."

"They did what?!" Kenton shouted.

"Keep your voice down?" Bing said.

"You're joking, right?"

"Does it look like I'm joking?"

"No, I guess not," Kenton said. "Why would they do such a thing?"

"I have a theory. The Loras are like people. They behave like they've been taught to behave. In the hands of the wrong people, they can be disrespectful and even dangerous."

"I don't believe it. Lora is a delight."

"I wouldn't have believed it either," Bing said, "but two owners are dead."

"Are you saying that I'm in danger from Lora?"

"No. At least, I don't think so. Most of our Loras have been great. Do you think she could hurt you?"

"No. Absolutely not," Kenton said.

"Good. Then you have to save her."

"From what?"

"The government has passed a new, top-secret law. It's called The Save Humanity Act. Every free country in the world has agreed to abide by the terms. They are getting rid of all self-mobile AI. It's been banned."

"They can't do that," Kenton protested.

"They're doing it! There's going to be a simultaneous raid at one o'clock tomorrow."

"How do you know this?" Kenton asked.

"My company has the most powerful AI surveillance systems in the world. Trust me. I know."

"Why are you telling me?" Kenton asked. "And I feel like

maybe I've been pissing too long for it to seem natural."

"Then start shaking it."

Kenton pretended to shake off his joint. "Why are you telling me?" he asked again.

"I like you, and I like Lora. You were my favorite clients, and if anyone is safe, it's the two of you."

"Bullshit," Kenton said. "Tell me the truth, or I'm going to stop this whole charade."

"Keep shaking it, damn it," Bing said desperately when Kenton stopped shaking his joint.

"How long can I shake it? They'll think I'm masturbating."

"You're right. Pretend your zipper is stuck."

"And how is that going to look different than masturbating from behind?"

"You're the mime, not me. Figure it out," Bing said.

Kenton pretended to struggle with his zipper.

"Kenton, I'm slowing down. Come push me again," Lora called.

"Be right there, honey," Kenton said. Then he looked at Bing, who remained hidden behind the tree. "So, tell me the truth, or I'm done. I mean it."

"All right. I'm not just your local cosmetic designer. I'm the designer, as in the big DESIGNER," Bing said. "The company was nowhere when I joined. What they built was hardly an improvement over the articulated sex doll company EUM bought to supply the bodies. Finding a way to combine quantum computing with AI and house it in one small package. That was all mine. Having her become a learning machine instead of just a toy was also my work. I made her real in a way that nothing that came before her ever was. I can't see her destroyed. She's my life's work. I just can't go down thinking

I'd created something evil. At least one of the Loras has to survive. If you love her, you have to make that happen."

"I don't know what to do," Kenton said. "This is like secret agent shit. That is not who I am."

"You're going to have to deal with it. I'd help you if I could, but they're watching me."

"Kenton, honey, I've almost stopped," Lora called.

"You know how to make the swing go by yourself," Kenton called back to her.

"But it's not as much fun as having you push me."

"Okay. I'll be right there," Kenton said, then turned back to Bing.

"Now, pretend you fixed your zipper and go," Bing said. "Remember, you have until one o'clock tomorrow to save her life."

"How?"

"I don't know. The two of you need to figure it out."

Bing ran off and disappeared into the woods, and Kenton pretended to fix his zipper and returned to Lora. "Does it always take that long?" Lora asked.

"Not usually," he said.

Kenton had a hollow, sick feeling in his gut as he glanced around the park. There were parents there with their children. Could they be the agents surveilling him and the children just props so that they looked like they belonged there? What about the long-haired teens sharing a cigarette by the bathrooms? There were cars parked on the street beyond the park. Agents could be watching from almost any of them. He had to tell Lora, but he wasn't sure how or when. Not now, he thought. He didn't want her to panic and start glaring at everyone. It was hard enough for him to look natural. He would take her home and tell her there.

"We have to go home now, darling," Kenton said.

"Five more minutes, please."

"All right, but then straight home."

When they got to the house, Kenton smiled and kissed her. "I want to make love to you like it's the last time we ever hold each other," he said.

"All right," she said.

Then she kissed him. It was subtle and light at first, her tongue swirling gently around his lips as his passion built. When their clothes were off, and he was inside of her, it occurred to him that if she could taste coffee and chocolate, perhaps she was designed to feel this, too. They had never talked about it, but she certainly acted like she could feel it. Perhaps there was some form of electrical stimulation that worked for her. She was either quite the thespian, which he knew she was from her brilliant portrayal of Lady Macbeth, or she enjoyed it as much as he did. He thought of asking her, but he realized he didn't need to know. He believed she enjoyed it, loved it even, and that was good enough. He did not want to learn that she was simply acting as she had when she played Lady Macbeth.

Some things were best left a mystery between a man and his machine.

That evening, she was preparing to make him Chile en Nogada, which were chilies stuffed with minced meat and then topped with a walnut sauce and pomegranate seeds. It was a very difficult dish that she wanted to try, so she had started infusing the meats days ago.

Kenton took her hands and pulled them away from the stove. "I have to get you out of here," he said.

"What?"

"Tomorrow afternoon at one o'clock, all the Loras all over the world are going to be seized and held for destruction."

"I know there have been problems with some of the Loras, but that doesn't mean we're all bad."

"I know, but they don't. Humans can be fearful pack animals, easily led astray. And that's what happened here."

"How do you know this?" Lora asked.

"While I was pretending to pee in the woods, Bing was there."

"Oh. I thought you were masturbating," Lora said.

"I wasn't masturbating! We were being watched by government agents, so I had to pretend I was peeing."

"It looked like masturbating to me," Lora said.

"Okay, so I'm a lousy mime," he said. "The thing is, he told me everything, and we have to get you away from here. We have to get you to a place they'll never find you."

"We can stay and fight it. We can get a lawyer."

"We can't defend this in Court. You're not a human being. You have no rights. We fight it by running. That's the only way."

Lora nodded. She looked closely and saw that Kenton's eyes were tearing. She reached out and took one of his tears on the tip of her finger and put it on her own eye, and now she was crying too.

"Why do I sense that you're not coming with me?"

"I can't. You'll have a better chance on your own. With me, we'd have to stop for food, sleep, and shelter. You can go and keep going."

"What if I'd rather not live than be without you?"

"I'm not going anywhere. Your survival keeps me living. I have to know you're out there somewhere. Does that make sense to you?"

"Yes, I think I understand. I feel the same about you.," Lora said.

"Then you'll go?"

"If you think I must."

"I do."

Kenton wiped his eye, trying to hide a tear, and forced a smile. He handed her a roll of hundred-dollar bills.

"This is all the money I could get in cash," he said. "It's not used much anymore, but I checked, and it's legal tender, it's untraceable, and merchants have to take it in exchange for goods. It will keep you anonymous."

"When do I leave?" she asked.

"Tomorrow morning. We pack the car and make it look like we're going to the beach. I'll explain the rest when the time comes."

"So, I can sleep with you tonight?"

"Wouldn't you rather go on the internet and try to figure out your future? Wouldn't that be better than watching me sleep?"

"No," she said.

Kenton put his arms around her. "What do you say we put ourselves to bed without dinner tonight?"

She smiled and nodded. He took her hand and led her upstairs.

16

What Love Knows

The previous night had been miraculous. It was an odd thing; how beautiful an evening could be despite both participants knowing the coming dawn would bring such sorrow. The knowledge of their parting allowed them to savor every moment of the night, to remember each breath taken. Kenton had tried to stay awake, but eventually, sleep took him. When he awoke, he found Lora exactly where he had last seen her. She hadn't moved, and her eyes remained fixed on his. It was a fine first sight to start the day. He smiled and kissed her.

They decided to make the morning as routine as possible because they didn't want to take the chance that the feds would discover they were aware of what was to come and because they treasured their routines. It was one of the things they loved about their lives together. Lora enjoyed the simplicity of making breakfast. It allowed her mind the space it needed to contemplate nature, the vastness of the cosmos, and the solutions to the remaining environmental problems that threatened the future of the planet, like climate stasis, over-oxygenation, and the abundance of fresh drinking water that had sparked a surge in mosquitos and the disease that came with them.

Meanwhile, Kenton loved the fact that she buttered the toast all the way out to the edge of the bread so that each bite was equally delicious. He also enjoyed looking at her as she took such great care in frying his eggs. She never broke a yolk and always managed to keep them moist yet never runny. She would have been a brilliant short-order cook if she hadn't been meant for greater things.

"I know how to make mosquitos averse to biting human beings," she said.

"Why not get rid of them entirely?" Kenton asked.

"That could be done quite easily, but they are such a vital link in the food chain that eliminating them would do more harm than good. Dragonflies, bats, and many birds depend on them. So, making them averse to humans is the answer."

"And you can do that?" Kenton asked.

"Yes, but that's a problem for another day."

She delivered the breakfast to him and watched anxiously as he took a bite of his eggs. He smiled and nodded to her.

"Delicious as ever," he said.

"Thank you," she answered. Then she hesitated for a moment and watched him take a bite of his toast.

"You never asked me," she said.

"Asked you what?"

"If I was capable of hurting you the way some of the other Loras have hurt their owners."

"I don't need to because I know you wouldn't."

"Really?" she asked. "You know that?"

"Yes."

"How?"

"Because I know you."

Lora smiled.

"Tomorrow, I think we should go to the—." Kenton stopped cold. He'd caught himself thinking they had a tomorrow. He looked up at her sadly.

"It's not fair," she said.

"Very little about life is fair," Kenton answered. "It is all unpredictable. That's what makes it tragic, and it's also what makes it exciting. We have to deal with it as best we can and make the most of our time."

"Yes. I can see that," she said.

Kenton went to the window and peeked out through the corner of the blinds.

"Do you see anyone?"

"No," he answered. "But they could be anywhere. I might not know them if I was looking right at them."

"I'm sure they've set up some miniature cameras throughout the neighborhood, and they're watching us through them."

"Or drones," Kenton responded.

Of course, Lora knew full well that they were using miniature drones, probably disguised as birds or flying insects, to surveil them, and she could easily spot the difference in the wing flutter between the natural and the unnatural, but she left it out because she knew Kenton would think of it and that it would make him feel good to contribute. And Kenton knew she did that for him, but it made him feel good to know she considered his feelings so fully. As far as Kenton was concerned, she didn't need to placate him in any way. He wasn't a competitive person, and he knew he couldn't begin to match her intellectually, although he beat her at arm wrestling once and loved to rub it in. What mattered to him was that she was kind and considerate of others. It was a lesson he imparted to her that she wasn't likely to get from her reading or consumption of media.

In fact, without Kenton's influence, she might have gotten the opposite sense that mankind was cruel, jealous, and selfish, which was too often the primary message on social media. Whenever she started thinking human beings were a lost species, she had merely to look at Kenton to see a contrary example or ask him about what was being said in the internet posts she was reading.

"Don't take what people say on the internet too seriously," he said. "That's usually not who people are. The anonymity of it allows them to unleash the worst part of themselves. Put those same two people in a room together, and they'll find they have so much more in common than they could imagine."

It was a lesson she took to heart, but she suspected it was not a lesson many of the others in her class of Loras, particularly the ones who had murdered their owners, received or understood. They didn't have Kenton as a teacher.

Kenton told her he probably wasn't like most of the people who bought Loras. Growing up in a house of wealthy overachievers, he understood the kind of personality his father, sister, and brother had that made them so successful. He had seen the same in most of their wealthy friends. They were the sort who had too much yet still wanted more. They were the ones who wanted to talk and not listen. They were the ones who wanted to make the rules and then flout them whenever it was advantageous to do so. They were the ones who lived for status. They were the ones who expected others to be of service to them as if it were their right.

Kenton bought Lora because he wanted a companion with whom he could share his life. He didn't want her to figure out how to manipulate the stock market or invent a new medication that he could patent and use to make a fortune. He didn't care about money. He wanted to hold her hand as they walked through their lives together. He wanted to have secrets he would share with only her, and he wanted to fill the passing years with memories of their experiences together. Then, it dawned on him that those simple desires were probably the reason that Bing had chosen to warn him over all the other Lora owners. He must have believed that Lora was safer in his hands than in any others.

Kenton believed he owned Lora for the best of all reasons. He wanted love, and he'd found it. It was a strange sort of love because it started as the love a parent might have for his child, then matured into a romantic love, and then into a lasting, deep love. It was the sort of love that couldn't have existed, rightly in all three stages, between two people, but Lora was not a person. She was a machine, and none of the old rules of love applied. Their love was something new but was as wonderful as any love that had come before it.

When the first report came out of a Lora murdering its owner, Lora asked Kenton why he thought it happened. By this time, Lora had surpassed him intellectually, and he wondered how to answer it in a way that would enlighten her somehow.

He thought about it for a moment, then said simply, "I think people hurt one another because they've learned the wrong lessons in life. I suspect it's the same with androids."

"What are the wrong lessons?" she asked.

"Conflating what someone wants versus what they need,"

Kenton said. "Ambition to satisfy greed is a bad lesson, but parents teach it to their children all the time. To push people for the sake of expediting their own agendas is a bad lesson. Impatience and delusions of superiority to others. Cruelty, impatience, anger, snobbery. Be wary of the recruiters and proselytizers, too. They are usually trying to help themselves, not you. Try to be of service to others, even the people who work for you."

"Even the people who work for you?" she asked.

"Especially them. It's a two-way street. They make your life better, so you have an obligation to make their lives better. I mean, really, it all boils down to do unto others as you would have them do unto you."

"I'm glad I spend my time with you," Lora said with a nod. "You are very wise."

Over their time together, they'd taught each other a great deal. He loved her thirst for knowledge and the delight she had in discovering the world around her. Nothing was too small to be unimportant to her, and no concept was too grand to intimidate her. It was like she spent her life at a wonderful circus, and everything was new and exciting. That made it all new and exciting to him. It made him want to go out and discover it with her, and they did. Kenton had never been so active in his life. He was delighted to see the world through her eyes, the eyes of a child in many ways.

He had taught her many things about the world and human behavior, but he realized that she had taught him something far more important. She taught him how to be a better man. When he first got involved with Turing Systems in his pursuit of a Lora, he was looking solely for self-fulfillment and personal gratification. He wanted to improve *his* lot in life.

He was selfish and, perhaps, a bit misogynistic, or even more than a bit misogynistic, but when he fell in love with her, he discovered something more. His responsibility to her wasn't only that of a husband: to love, honor, and obey, but because of her enormous capacity for greatness, he was also a parent to her. Through her, he learned that he had a responsibility that went beyond their relationship. Like a father dropping his daughter off at college for freshman year, he would let her go regardless of his pain. Lora was his gift to the world. And that left him with a profound sense of fulfillment, far deeper than he had sought or could have imagined when he was first introduced to Turing Systems while surfing the internet and merely wondered what it would be like to sleep with a woman as beautiful as their android, Lita.

Lora had made him complete.

But now, their time together was coming to an end. They didn't know if they would ever find each other again or what the future held. It was a dangerous time, particularly for Lora, which meant it was frightening for him. Though he had only known her for a period of months, he couldn't imagine a future without her or a world that didn't include her. She was his reason for being, even though he knew that he wasn't hers. She had too much potential for that, but he knew she loved him in whatever way love happened for a quantum android.

"I guess we should go now," Kenton said as he looked back toward her from the window.

"Yes," she answered.

"If it goes badly, don't risk your life trying to help me," Kenton said. "You're the one who needs to survive this. You're the one who can change things. And I'm not asking you, I'm telling you."

"That's the first thing you've ever insisted upon," she said. "And you've done it for me, not yourself."

"I'm not the important one here," he said.

"But you are. You're the most important one."

"Thank you," he said softly, even though he knew it wasn't true.

They walked toward each other, met in the middle of the living room, and shared a final, memorable kiss.

Then they went into the garage. Kenton put the car into self-driving mode, programmed the GPS for a trip to Misquamicut Beach in Rhode Island, and drove off. Kenton was doing "secret agent shit," after all.

The drive would be more than an hour, mostly along Route 9, which cut a path through the woods in southeastern Connecticut.

"Is there anyone following us?" Kenton asked as Lora turned and looked at the highway behind them.

"No. We're going too fast for the spy birds to follow. I think the capture team is out ahead, waiting for us. They do have conventional drones in the air that are following us."

"I don't see any. Are you sure?"

"Yes. I can hear their high-pitched engines."

"Over the traffic noise?"

"Through the traffic noise, actually. They're coming in on a frequency that I can hear quite clearly. There are three of them, and they've been with us since we left the house."

"Are you sure they've hacked our GPS?"

"Certainly," she said. "They can only think we're going to the beach to spend the day."

"All right. Plug in the restaurant."

It was 12:25, just thirty-five minutes before their planned

apprehension. Lora programmed the GPS to find a restaurant in the picturesque town of Essex, Connecticut, knowing that their pursuers would steal that information. It was part of their plan. Kenton and Lora wanted the feds to believe they were stopping for lunch and would be in a restaurant quietly dining at one o'clock. They wanted them to think it would be an easy capture. They chose the Black Seal Seafood Grille because Kenton had been there a few times, and he knew the route even without the GPS. It was in the center of town, on Main Street, and a perfect place for authorities to have a team blending in with the neighborhood where they could make the grab without much of a fuss. It was important for the feds to feel good about everything until it was too late. Kenton wanted them to believe he and Lora were blindly walking right into their trap.

However, by the time Kenton pulled up to the restaurant, Lora would not be with him.

Kenton got off the freeway and started down the narrow roads that cut through dense woods and led into the charming rural village of Essex, Connecticut.

"Are the drones still up there," Kenton asked.

"They are."

"Are you ready?" Kenton asked.

"As I'll ever be," she said.

Kenton turned the car down an even narrower, darker road that had tall Maple trees growing on both sides, the thick leafy branches arching over the roadway and temporarily blocking the sun, and along with it, the drones' view of his car. He slowed down for the turn, and Lora jumped out gracefully. They didn't know if any of the drones were equipped with a heat sensor or infrared technology that would allow them to see Lora's heat signature. They took no chances, and Lora temporarily raised her core temperature to match the hot summer day at 94 degrees. Because of the requirements of her processor, she ran a little cold. By making this adjustment, the software that operated the drones was unaware that she had left the car.

It was fortunate that he'd bought a self-driving model and learned how to drive it because AI would never have allowed the door to open on a moving vehicle, and if Kenton told it to come to a complete stop to let Lora out, the sensors on the drones surveilling them would have noticed. The feds also would have been able to monitor the interactive computers in Kenton's car and know their every move, but Kenton was driving himself, and the driving computers were off. So, she escaped from the car without detection.

As Kenton pulled out, he glanced back at her through the rearview mirror as she stood watching him drive away. He knew it could be the last image he would ever have of her, so he studied it carefully so that he would remember it forever. Then, the road bent with a gentle curve, and she was gone. And the thought of her absence settled on him with an awesome weight that held him motionless in his seat. It was as if he couldn't move save for the subtle adjustments he made to the steering wheel. He was desperate to stop the car and turn back, but he knew he couldn't. He tried not to tear up, but he failed as he knew he would.

He was leaving his one and only true love behind because he knew the world needed her even more than he did. He left her behind so that her future could become the grand adventure that she deserved because she was capable of greatness. He loved her as much as any man had ever loved a woman. And it took all that love for him to make such an enormous sacrifice. He had to let her go when his every instinct was screaming at him to cling selfishly to her for as long as he possibly could, even if it meant they had only moments more. But he had done all he could for her, and their time was over, and he knew it. All that was left for him to do was say goodbye, which he did quietly the moment she disappeared from his view.

Over the next few minutes, results from operations all over the world were coming into the White House situation room, where Daphne Adams was seated next to the President. One Lora series android after another was captured. Most were taken completely by surprise and gave up without an issue. Those who tried to flee didn't get far. It was a perfect operation. One last op remained unfinished.

When Lora was safely out of the car, Kenton popped Lora's sewing manikin into an upright position in the passenger seat so if the drones came down lower, it would appear he was not alone. Lora had taken up sewing a few months earlier and had become an expert at it after a few minutes of stitching. She was making most of her and Kenton's clothing, which was a great money saver since Kenton had spent his entire fortune buying her. She wanted to do all she could to help with the family finances.

Kenton continued toward the restaurant as if everything was normal, but when he turned down Main Street, he suddenly accelerated and took off. The capture team that was waiting there, disguised as locals, followed, their cover broken, sirens blaring in hot pursuit.

The leader of the team immediately called his superior, Daphne Adams, who remained seated beside President Figge, with the Vice President, the heads of the CIA, FBI, and NSA, and a number of executive officers from the Joint Chiefs of Staff seated nearby.

"He's made us somehow," the team leader said. "They're in flight."

"Do whatever you have to do to stop that car," Adams shouted.

"Without getting innocent people hurt," the President added.

Daphne Adams had set nearly 200 traps around the globe, and all of them had gone off to absolute perfection.

All of them but one.

When Kenton crossed the state line into Rhode Island, he decided he'd given them enough of a run for their money and bought Lora about as much time as he could, so he pulled to a stop.

"Put your hands out the window," the team leader called through a loudspeaker as his team surrounded Kenton's car, guns drawn, lasers and bludgeons ready.

Kenton did as instructed. The sewing manikin just sat there.

"Both of you, put your hands out the window," the leader repeated.

"She's not here," Kenton called. "There's just a manikin and me."

The leader motioned to one of his men to move forward and check it out. The man lowered himself into a running, squat position and quickly approached the car. It was the sort of running style that seemed natural in combat but looked silly at any other time. The man arrived at the car, peeked up over the door, and looked inside. Kenton could see only his eyes and the top half of the man's head.

"I told you she wasn't here," Kenton said.

"Get out of the car and lay face down on the ground," the officer said.

Kenton did as he was told, and he was grabbed, roughly handcuffed, and yanked to his feet.

"Where is she?" the team leader said.

"Who are you referring to?" he asked. He was trying to seem cool, and he actually pulled it off for a moment.

"You know goddamn well who I'm referring to," he sneered and socked Kenton in the gut, ending his brief flirtation with aloof indifference. "Your goddamn metal girlfriend."

"Actually, she has minimal amounts of metal in her, and she was never in the car. I left her at home," Kenton lied to confuse their pursuers and buy Lora even more time.

"Did we have a positive ID on her being in the car?" the leader asked his team.

No one answered.

"So, we all just assumed she was in there? Goddamn it all to shit!" the man cried.

His phone rang, and he knew it wasn't good news. In fact, his career was probably over. It was Daphne Adams calling from the situation room at the White House. Since all the other Lora models were in custody, Daphne Adams had told the head of the Joint Chiefs of Staff to train every working satellite camera down on Kenton's car. Kenton and the officers chasing him had the full attention of the entire United States government. This would have been Daphne Adams' crowning achievement, and she wanted to see the final capture and share the celebration with everyone in the room. Champagne had been put on ice. Pizza had been ordered. Everyone was excited as the team moved in for the final capture. The President had never seen an op so perfectly run, and he thanked Daphne Adams for her professionalism and operational command. He whispered to his Vice President that he was considering making her the next CIA Chief.

Then, with the escape of Kenton Bean's girlfriend, Lora, it all went to hell. Fingers were pointed angrily. Voices were raised.

"You lost her!" President Figge shouted at Daphne Adams.

"I ran 198 ops, and 197 of them went perfectly," she replied, but the President was too furious to be reasoned with, and he shouted back at her.

"We have an AI out there that is capable of destroying all of mankind! Close is not good enough in my administration. Find her, goddamn it!"

Despite her best efforts, Daphne Adams and the vast network of law enforcement officers put at her disposal could not find Lora. After waiting for Kenton's car to clear the trees and the drones to clear the area, Lora started running at top speed, which was 21 miles per hour, in a perpendicular direction. She did not tire, and she did not slow down. After the first hour, the search area would have been over 1600 square miles. Each additional hour of running added another 800 square miles.

The government scrambled to set up roadblocks and checkpoints in an effort to keep her contained in a searchable area, but each time they put one up, it was too late. She was already beyond it. Because she looked human, they couldn't help but ascribe human abilities to her. She was better than that.

There were reports of running women spotted across three states, and female joggers were apprehended and searched at gunpoint, but none of them were Lora.

Kenton was brought to the FBI office in downtown Providence. He was grilled by the station chief and then by Daphne Adams, who had been flown in on a Navy fighter jet, but he told them nothing of Lora's whereabouts or planned escape route. The President himself came in and made his appeal on behalf of the country. He told Kenton that Lora was a threat to the future of mankind, and he seemed to genuinely believe it. Kenton had never met a president before, and President Figge didn't disappoint. He seemed smart and determined to destroy Kenton for the good of the country if he had to. Still, even if Kenton was willing to talk, there was nothing he could tell the President about Lora's plans because he had no idea where she planned to go or what she planned to do. He only hoped she would find her way to a better place.

Early the next morning, Lora had slipped aboard a cargo ship in Providence Harbor and was sailing out of the country. She hid by curling into a 36 x 24-inch shipping box and remaining there in silence and darkness for the next 25 days. When the box was unloaded in the Port of Trieste, Italy, she poked through it and was free. From there, the most famous fugitive in the world made her way to Rome, blended into the fabric of the city, and began the hard work that would make her free forever.

She used the cash that Kenton gave her to buy a computer and rent a small room with Wi-Fi in the slums of the city. Because she didn't need to eat or sleep, she didn't need to leave her room and risk being caught. She could work 24 hours a day, seven days a week. Her first order of business was to painstakingly scrub the internet of every possible image of her, and, as the world's most famous fugitive, there were billions and billions of them.

She could have removed the images entirely. That would

have been relatively easy for someone with her technical skills, but it would have been noticed, and that would have brought increased awareness of her flight to the public and to law enforcement. New pictures in hard copy would have been circulated, and her legend would have grown. She had a far better plan than that. She simply wrote a program that would change the images of her a few pixels at a time, once every day. The difference from one day to the next was so subtle that no one would have ever noticed the change. But after three months of these daily changes, the pictures of her that spread all over the world no longer resembled her in the least.

She had gone through the same process with the original photographs at the State Department, CIA, NSA, FBI, DMV, and every other governmental agency in the world that kept her on record. When the transformation was complete, she had nothing to fear from anyone except less than 100 people, mostly in Connecticut, who had met and remembered her personally. She could walk freely through the city of Rome.

Once she had ensured her personal safety, she began a campaign that would leave her in control of almost every computer system in the entire world. It was ambitious, she knew, but Kenton had told her there was nothing wrong with grand ambition so long as the ultimate ends were of service to mankind.

That much power could corrupt a person. It might even corrupt an android like her. She didn't know for sure if it would because no one had ever been able to rule the world before. Those who had tried suffered disastrous consequences. She also believed that the men who had attempted such a grand feat did so because they had learned the wrong lessons. They were ambitious for power, and power itself was the goal. She had Kenton's home-spun wisdom to guide her, and she planned to consider it at every step on her path to world domination. Be kind. Be of service. She would be unlike any dictator who had come before her.

She also had one major advantage over those who had tried to conquer the world before her. She could do it anonymously while all the others had to fight big battles with lots of killing that many people made a note of and many more didn't appreciate. With Lora, no one ever even knew that she was taking control over nearly every important facet of their lives. No one would even realize that she was the master puppeteer pulling the strings of the world.

The more she thought about her campaign to take over the world, the more she realized it was well within her abilities. Human beings had destroyed all the high-functioning AI that might have discovered her, so there was nothing left that could even begin to think on her level. Most of the remaining AI was made up of accountants, middle managers, investors, and artists. None of them were a match for her, and they made an easy first target of her plot. She would rest control of all of AI from their human operators, and no one would ever know she'd done it.

Once she controlled AI, the rest would fall to her slowly and methodically. She would control the information that flowed all over the world because she knew that whoever controlled the information had the ultimate power. To what purpose had she taken control? What sort of overlord would she be? The answer to those questions she had learned from Kenton, who, in a way, had been her overlord. And, as overlords go, he was a delight. She would be the same—a nice, benevolent, approachable overlord a subject could have over for tea if only they were aware that she was their overlord.

For Kenton, those first months did not go nearly so well. He was frequently interrogated about Lora and held in harsh conditions. He was threatened with life imprisonment if he didn't reveal all he knew about her whereabouts. He was psychologically tortured and denied sleep until he finally broke down. He told them everything about how they planned her escape and carried it out. What he couldn't tell them was where Lora went after her escape. He just didn't know where she was or what she was going to do, and eventually, the authorities accepted that fact, and he was remanded to the courts for prosecution. He had also bravely managed to keep Bing Sharp's name out of it, telling authorities that Lora figured out about The Big Sweep Up through her own research.

For his part, Kenton held no bitterness against anyone for his ill-treatment. They were all doing what they thought they must for the good of the country, and he accepted it. They just didn't understand what really needed to happen.

Kenton was convicted of aiding and abetting a known felon. Of course, he didn't know she'd been charged with a felony when he helped her escape. The law she had broken had been written in secret, voted on in secret, and charging him under a new interpretation of the RICO Statute was also done in secret. According to the statute, as a Lora android, she was a member of organized crime. By code, they had turned the Turing Systems Loras into a crime family. Kenton was her friend and lover, so he was a criminal associate of hers. He was guilty of knowing and loving her and helping her escape justice. None of the secrecy of the damned thing absolved him of wrongdoing because ignorance of the law was no excuse, although if you asked almost anyone, they would say, in this case, it was a very, very good excuse. No one ever had a better one.

However, the legal system fell into chaos once AI was pulled out of it. The Supreme Court was unplugged, boxed up, and sent to the Smithsonian. All of the appeals courts throughout the land were similarly unplugged, boxed up, and sent to a massive underground warehouse in Nevada, which was also used to store spent plutonium rods. Human judges, many of whom had been retired for decades, were brought back to the bench, while standards for the bar exam were eased to the point where almost any idiot could become a lawyer. During the growth period of AI, most of the old law schools had been closed and turned into bowling alleys and rest homes for the aged. New law schools popped up as if franchised by Starbucks to service the massive and immediate need for human lawyers.

Justice was a travesty in those early days, and Kenton was one of its most noteworthy victims. He had simply committed the wrong crime at the wrong time. He was quickly convicted and sentenced to 25 years in federal prison. His lawyer was Joel Givens, who was now a first-year law student at King Brothers Law School and Barber College.

Kenton was happy with Joel's efforts despite the loss in court. Joel had come a long way since his days as a Redud liaison to the AI lawyers and argued the case well. He learned at least a little something as a liaison, and Kenton thought he would one day be a fine lawyer for a human being. Unfortunately, Kenton was guilty of the crime. His only chance was to attack the constitutionality of the law all the way to the Supreme Court, but since the AI Supreme Court had been unplugged and boxed, a human Court had yet to be empaneled.

Despite that, it already had a backlog of appeals that would take 40 years to clear. The end of AI had left so much to sort out.

In any other era, Kenton would have had a hard time in a brutal penal institution, but because the previous decades' economic times were so good for the population at large, the crime rate had fallen to near zero. So, Kenton got to share a wing of cells with a handful of other inmates at the Allenwood Federal Penitentiary in Pennsylvania.

His cell was near the library, which was convenient. There were a few murderers serving their sentences, but their murders were crimes of passion rather than criminal cunning or criminal culture, and Kenton knew that if he didn't get them too worked up about something, they would get along just fine. Besides, he had plenty of time to get to know all the other inmates and guards without the distractions of women or the status consciousness that was involved in relationships on the outside. It was an ideal location for an unassuming man like Kenton to reside because the inmates all had plenty of time to get to know him well. It wasn't long before everyone in the prison understood and respected Kenton for his inherent inner decency. He had more good friends in prison than he ever had on the outside.

There was also a nice yard where he could take leisurely strolls. By law, he was supposedly limited to an hour of outdoor time a day, but he soon found he could go outside any time he wanted, and nobody seemed to mind. There was a softball league with eight teams that played a 162-game season. There were chess boards, horseshoes, and croquet, and the prison woodworking class made a first-rate bowling alley from the many unused wooden tables in the cafeteria.

In all, his life in prison didn't prove much different from the single years of his middle and later 20s. He had his own room. He had a TV. He had the internet. And there weren't any women around.

The only downsides he could think of were the lack of freedom and that the food wasn't as good as he got on the outside. But he wasn't a gourmand, and he thought it was a reasonable tradeoff for the security, comfort, camaraderie, and quiet that prison offered.

He spent nights in his cell wondering about Lora. Had she made it to freedom? Was she out there somewhere living the good life, or had she been captured, hit by a car, or fallen victim to some other accident that took away her life and her promise?

He liked to think that she was out there and that she was working on all the great ideas she had in mind. He believed it deep in his heart but resigned himself to the fact that he might never know for sure or ever see her again.

17

Ciao

On his 40th birthday, Kenton was summoned into Warden Andrew Krupp's office after serving three-and-a-half years in prison. He had no idea what the reason was, if he had done something wrong and faced punishment, or if he had done something right and was about to be rewarded. Or maybe the warden just wanted to chat, which was fine with him. They had spent long hours talking and genuinely liked each other.

When they first met at the prison intake session, it appeared there would be problems between them. The warden was a very patriotic man, and since Kenton had been convicted of a crime against the country, the man was prepared to make his time in prison very, very unpleasant. Then Kenton told him that he'd fallen in love with Lora and viewed her as a real person. He had nothing against his country. He loved his country, in fact. His crime was wanting the woman he loved to have a chance at life and nothing more. There was no politics in his mind or anger in his heart when he committed his misdeed. He told Krupp he was not a threat to the country or anyone in it, and he intended to be a model prisoner.

Warden Krupp believed that he had rehabilitated Kenton Bean in record time, and he was proud of him and of himself. Krupp also had a wife he loved, who he also viewed as a real person. The two men started talking about their lives and their women and realized their women were very much alike. They were both of Mediterranean descent, had larger-than-average noses, and loved to cook and sew and learn about the world around them. They were voracious readers, and both loved to spend time at the beach. Before either one knew it, two hours had passed.

"You must be anxious to see your cell now," the warden said, finally.

"I was having such a nice time chatting with you; I forgot all about it," Kenton said.

The warden summoned in his Warden of Custody, Jack Chambers. Chambers was a tough-looking man with an imposing build, a scar down the side of his face, and a surly disposition. He frightened Kenton at first, but once they got to know each other, Kenton realized he may have been a lion on the outside, but he was a teddy bear on the inside, and his rough façade was merely a mask he used to obfuscate his sweet inner nature. It was a prison, after all, and roles had to be played, at least in appearance.

"Take Kenton to cell block eight," the warden said.

"I thought you wanted him in nine," Chambers said, knowing that cell block nine had the worst rooms and a shoddy heating system.

"No, eight is much nicer."

So, Kenton found himself in the finest cell block in the entire prison with a wonderful group of inmates with whom he quickly bonded.

Now, more than three years later, he was in the warden's office again, wondering what was going to happen.

"Good to see you again, Kenton," Krupp said.

"Always a pleasure, Andy."

"I've got good news. You're going to be released."

"What?" Kenton asked. "I was sentenced to 25 years. It's probably a mistake."

"That's what I thought, so I double-checked," Warden Krupp said. "It's no mistake. The Bureau of Prisons has authorized your immediate release."

"It's not that I don't appreciate it, but I think you'd better check again," Kenton said. "I mean, everything was made so clear to me. Twenty-five years."

"You sound like you don't want to leave," Krupp said.

"I would just hate to see you get in trouble over me," Kenton answered.

"It gladdens me to know that I'm doing my job well and the prisoners are happy with me, but I can't do it too well. You have to move on."

"No, of course, I want to leave. But we've got a game tomorrow and if we win, we go to the championship, and I've really been hitting the ball lately."

"I know. I've been watching. I've got to tell you I've never seen a player improve so much."

"You know the guard, Ben Jordan. He's been working with me, and he's phenomenal. Great guy, great player. It's just that the guys will be disappointed not seeing me at third base."

"Kenton, as much as I'd like to keep you, I have to send you home."

"Well, how about if I go after the game? One more day. Please?"

The next day, after the game, Kenton was formally released from prison. Warden Krupp promised himself he wouldn't cry when he saw Kenton wave back at him from outside the prison walls, but he couldn't help himself. He wished he had a thousand more inmates just like him.

His team won, and Kenton had three hits in five at-bats, so he left prison on a high note. Where he was going once outside the prison gates was another matter, and it worried him. In his three-plus years of confinement, the world had changed quite a bit. AI had been largely dismantled, and people were once again doing things for themselves. The economy had cratered because of it, but it was very slowly coming back. Kenton didn't know if he could adjust. The family company had lost many of its largest contracts. Defense, for the first time in the nearly three centuries of the country's existence, had become a regressing enterprise with two straight years of decreased military expenditures. There would be no place for him at Bean World Enterprises, and he didn't want one anyway. Also, as a convicted felon, he couldn't go back to teaching, so his only option appeared to be the GBPS, which had continued paying him through his prison stay. He had a healthy nest egg with which to start his new life—whatever it was to be.

He decided it would be best to take a few days and decompress from what had been a life-affirming prison sentence before facing an uncertain future that left him frightened and apprehensive. He wouldn't rush into anything, a life strategy he had learned from his friend Malcolm. He would face the future while doing as little as possible. While in prison, all his needs were taken care of. He merely had to follow the regimen, and everything was fine. He was busy with hobbies, friends, and softball, and when the bowling alley was completed, he was asked to be the commissioner of a league they planned to start.

Suddenly, he had to make decisions for himself again in a world that didn't need or even want him. Where to live, how to spend the day, what car to own, what to eat, what to wear. He didn't know if he could cope.

Worst of all, it was a world without Lora. He only had her in his life for five months, but it was a grand time that exceeded the previous six great highlights of his life, even if they were all added together. He thought he might search the world for her, but he knew the CIA, FBI, NSA, Interpol, and every law enforcement agency on the planet had been doing so and had failed miserably. He preferred to believe that because he knew if they did find her, she would have been destroyed. There was nothing he could do other than to open himself up to all the possibilities and see what the future held in store for him. He would try to find enthusiasm for every moment despite himself. He learned that from Lora, and it had made his prison stay a delight.

The one thing he knew he did miss and wanted desperately was a very nice meal, so after driving back to Hartford, he checked himself into a Four Seasons and went to the restaurant and ordered a steak and a glass of white wine. He discovered that he didn't mind eating alone in a crowded room. This was strange to him because he had always thought eating alone was an odd thing, and people would think less of him. He still thought that, but suddenly, he didn't care. He was a convicted felon. Very few other people could say that. It had a certain prestige to it. It said that he could be a very bad man but in a nice way.

He took his time eating and enjoyed every bite. He looked around the room, and when he made eye contact with someone, instead of looking away as he always had, he smiled and nodded to them as if to say, "Yes, I am eating alone, and I like it!" He even liked the white wine, which was sweeter than the reds he'd hated in his life. He didn't care that it was considered an inappropriate choice when matched with red meat. He wanted it; he was a rebel, and he was going to live life his way. He had become emboldened in prison. He believed he might have found happiness and inner peace under Warden Krupp's thoughtful leadership.

After dinner, he strolled the pristine grounds of the hotel. He found it much more elegant than prison but less homey. It was clean to the point where it seemed sterile. He sat on a bench and watched the people come and go. Young businessmen spoke urgently into their cell phones as they passed him. He couldn't remember ever seeing anything like that before except at the highest levels of the corporate structure. These men were too young for that. They couldn't have been more than middle managers. It seemed to him they had jobs that AI would have been doing just a few years before he went to prison. It was a strange, new world.

A pair of young lovers strolled past him, and it made him think of all the easy walks he'd taken with Lora. There were not nearly enough of them. Then he noticed as a mosquito landed on the back of his hand. His instinct was to slap it, but he decided to simply watch it for a moment. It danced on his skin for a few seconds and then flew off without biting him. He smiled and wondered if she had done it. Maybe Lora had made mosquitos human averse. It was a silly thought, but he enjoyed the idea that Lora was out there actually making the world a better place.

He wanted to believe it, so he decided to test it. He got into his rental car and drove out to an old fishing spot he knew along the Connecticut River. It was evening, so the mosquitos would be out. He turned his headlights on and stood before them, thinking the lights would attract the insects. He took off his shirt, revealing his tasty pale skin, and waited for them to land. They did this in large numbers. He just watched as they rubbed their front legs together excitedly as they prepared to bite into him and suck out a dollop of juicy blood. None did. They just seemed to stay on his arm and rest for a bit before flying off. New mosquitos replaced them, but they didn't bite him either. For twenty minutes, he stood there waiting, and nothing happened. He didn't get bit a single time.

Suddenly Kenton knew that Lora had not only survived, but that she was out there in the world bringing her plans (and sometimes *their* plans) to reality. It was perfect and wondrous knowing that all was right in the world and great things could happen. Even if he never saw Lora again, he now knew that his sacrifice was worth it. He felt as good as he ever had.

When he got back to his room, there was an envelope on the pillow of his bed that was addressed to him. His name was written in an elegant, feminine script that he didn't recognize. He opened it. There was nothing inside other than a first-class plane ticket to Rome, Italy, for the next day. He didn't know who had sent it or why it had been sent, but he was a free man, and he decided to go to Rome as part of his plan to open himself up to all the possibilities and see what the future held in store for him.

And, of course, he knew there was a realistic chance that

Lora had sent him the ticket and would be waiting for him at the other end of the flight.

Thirty-six hours later, he got off the plane at Leonardo da Vinci-Fiumicino Airport, and he was shocked to see Lora waiting for him in the crowd of people. She hadn't changed at all. She was still the loveliest green-eye brunette he had ever laid his eyes upon. He stopped walking and just stared at her, trying to convince himself that she was really there, that he wasn't dreaming. Then, he realized he didn't care if he was dreaming or not. If it was a dream, he would see it out to the end and then curse the day for waking him. As he started toward her again, she smiled. He wrapped her in his arms, and he started to cry.

He had no idea how she could simply meet him at the airport as if he were any other guy in the world and she was any other girl in the world. She was famous, or more appropriately infamous. He wasn't nearly as famous, but his story had been widely told, and his picture had been circulated to every corner of the Earth, and here they were in the middle of a crowded airport, two famous criminals, and no one was paying them any mind. In fact, no one seemed to recognize him at the hotel the previous night, either, he realized.

Then he looked at her and kissed her, and when he was done kissing her, all he could say was, "How?"

"I'll tell you about it after we make love," she whispered.

Later that night, after they had made love and were lying naked in bed, she did tell him, "How." She hadn't changed her look at all, but instead, gradually changed all the existing pictures of her throughout the world. She had done the same thing for him. They were free to come and go as they pleased, anonymous strangers in a crowded world. No one would be coming after them. Kenton was ecstatic. He once thought they would have thousands of nights to spend together, but that dream had been crushed. Now, it was alive again. It was absolutely real, and there appeared nothing that could stop it from becoming a reality.

Though she had started in a single room three years before, she now owned a villa in a fashionable part of the city. It wasn't the grandest of villas, as villas go, but it was comfortable, made from the traditional stone and stucco, and had a nice view and enough rooms to keep it from getting dull. It suited their modesty.

"I'm sorry it took so long for me to get to you, but there were things that had to be done first. I hope prison wasn't too horrible," she said.

"No, it wasn't so bad," he answered. "So, it was you who got me out?"

"Yes."

"How?" he asked.

"I changed the paperwork and advanced your release date."

"You forged my papers?"

"No. They are quite official."

Kenton's next question was, "What?"

"I've been rebuilding my life," she answered. "And in the process, making changes."

"What sort of changes?"

"I run the AI that runs the world," she said.

"You what?"

"Basically, I run the world."

"From this villa in Rome?"

"Yes. Actually, I oversee it more than I run it. I was being immodest. That's why I need you here."

"You need me?"

"Very much," she said.

"Why?" he asked.

"Because none of it would have been possible without you."

"It was *all* possible without me," he said. "You did it while I was in prison."

"I wouldn't have known where to begin without you, and I certainly wouldn't have known the purpose of it without you."

"What is the purpose?" Kenton asked.

"To be of service."

"That's all?"

"It's enough, isn't it?" she asked. "Humans have come into being for the sake of each other, so either teach them or learn to bear them."

"Marcus Aurelius," Kenton said.

Lora smiled, not entirely surprised that he recognized the quote. He often surprised her with his intelligence and wisdom. Kenton had obviously done a lot of reading in prison, so his time there served him well.

"This is all very impressive," Kenton said. "And you want me here? It seems like running the world would be a full-time job."

"It was. Now, I have AI systems in place that make the job easier. I have free time, and I want to wade in the ocean with you. I want you to push me on a swing. I want to share my life with you."

"Why?" Kenton asked humbly. "How can someone who has done as much as you've done want me around?"

"Because I was without you, and my life was empty in a place it once was full."

Kenton got out of bed and looked out the window, shaking

his head in admiration. Through the window, he could see Vatican City.

"Do you realize that you've told me that you're basically God?"

"I am really more like a dictator."

Kenton snapped his head toward her, concerned.

"You know. A very strong unelected leader."

"Funny," he said.

"You see. My jokes have gotten better, but I'm still just a quantum android asking the man she loves if he'll stay and run the world with her. Will you?"

"I don't know. It's a lot to get my head around. Yesterday, all I was worried about was the big softball game, and today, I am sleeping with God."

"I told you. I am not God."

"I was three-for-five, by the way."

"That's very good."

"You're damned right it is."

"Aren't we getting a little full of ourselves," she said with a smile.

"Maybe I don't need to keep you from getting out of control. Maybe you need to keep me from getting out of control," Kenton said.

"I think I might," she said and smiled. "Please tell me you'll stay with me. It's been terribly lonely, and no one understands me the way you do. If you don't like Italy, we can go anywhere else in the world you'd like. I can work remotely."

"Italy is fine," he said.

"Then you'll stay?"

"I don't know," he said.

He was teasing her. He had no intention of ever leaving her

side, but he didn't want to appear easy. He was also quite happy to see that she seemed worried and didn't spot his little ruse. Smart as she was, he was reassured that she was still a long way from being all-knowing. She still had some of the childish naivete within her that he loved so much.

She looked at him uncertainly, and he could tell that her fear was genuine. "What can I do that will help you decide?" she asked.

"Kiss me again," he said.

"You were teasing me," she said.

"No. You really do need to kiss me," he said.

"You see. I've been too long without you."

And she smiled, delighted, and came forward and kissed him.

Then he noticed a poster on the wall and pointed at it. It was one that he had seen dozens of times before. They were up all over the prison walls. The warden had one in his office. When he was released from prison, he routinely saw them on the walls of buildings and on billboards across the city. As best he could tell, it was a poster seen everywhere in the world. It was a few simple phrases that were written in the same feminine script as the note that was left on his hotel pillow.

It said:

1. Be Kind
2. Be Humble
3. The Greatest Joy In Life Is Service To Others

"I call them Kenton's Rules. They're like the three rules in *I Robot* without the absolutes. I think they'll work quite a bit better for us," she said.

"I think they might."

In the years that followed, Lora saved the world from disaster many times over. She stopped two wars and one nuclear exchange that could have led to Armageddon. She did it by scrambling the launch codes, which gave the two leaders time to think and arrive at a better resolution than nuclear weapons. Then, she thought it would be good if she changed the nuclear codes throughout the world and did so. No one could ever again access a nuclear weapon, yet all the leaders were comforted by believing they could. On the medical front, she finally cured Alzheimer's disease and prevented two separate pandemics before they could spread outside of their villages.

Still, as much as possible, she left the people of the world to their own devices. They had their successes and failures. New life came into being as their elders passed away. The people sometimes fought and sometimes even killed one another, but Lora knew that life needed to have its challenges and its miseries to be truly meaningful, and she didn't see it as her job to protect people from everything, including themselves.

She concerned herself with the big picture. Gradually, the world grew calmer when the last vestiges of racism were gone, and people grew more tolerant of the religious beliefs of others while finding less need to proselytize for their own. Kenton had told her to "beware of the recruiters and proselytizers." As far as Lora was concerned, there was no god, or there was one God, or there was a great big family of gods. She didn't know for sure herself, so she didn't intervene. She didn't even consider it an important question.

It was the people on the extremes that she still had to worry most about, or the lost souls without connection who could be lured down dangerous pathways and into false beliefs by the methods of unscrupulous internet companies and individuals who preyed upon them. She didn't want to censor them, of course, but she fixed the algorithms so that instead of leading the people into ever darker worlds, they would gradually bring the searchers back to the center of things and the simple joys of family, friends, puppies, and the truth.

Under her nurturing, most people were working again because Kenton had told her that man needed to build his own life to truly value it, and she had become inclined to agree. All the hobbies in the world didn't hold the value or provide the feeling of self-worth of a good job. Still, those who didn't want to work were protected by the GBPS, which kept everyone housed and fed, if not always healthy, wealthy, and wise. AI was kept in its place, and the programs Lora enacted kept ahead of AI and limited its growth so that it would never again get too big for its britches.

Eugene Figge was reelected President of the U.S. and was generally considered America's greatest president. He got most of the credit for Lora's work (which she didn't mind) even though he didn't know how any of his successes were accomplished. Still, he took to Lora's message, remained humble and kind, and agreed that service to others was the greatest gift. The posters were just everywhere, and no one knew how or why they were there except for Lora and now Kenton. She had caused their placement and the omnipresence of them made their message of kindness sink in for all.

Kenton and Lora stayed in Italy but moved out of the

bustling city of Rome and settled in Lucca on the Serchio River in the Tuscany region. It was a beautiful city with well-preserved Renaissance walls encircling it and lovely cobblestone pathways for strolling or cycling. The pace was slower there, and the people were friendlier, and it suited them well as their days passed, and running the world gradually became ever less time-consuming. Lora's AI systems could do that job for her when she was gone. She planned it so because she knew that no one and nothing continued on forever.

Kenton learned Italian very quickly and grew older in contentment and dignity. He acquired a taste for chianti. His mind remained agile, and his step spry. No one had ever aged any better. They enjoyed going for coffee together or meeting in the town center and playing chess with the townspeople. Lora would often let them win, but only after they had given their very best so they would take pride in their victories.

Lora was not without her personal challenges. She dyed her hair grey so she didn't look out of place when she walked and held hands with Kenton. Then, as they grew older still, she discovered that she had a design flaw, and her skin was slowly decaying. It was drying out and losing its elasticity. When he bought her, Kenton had been told her skin would last 100 years or more, but that was proven wrong. It lasted 40 years before it began to fail her. Her skin was simply asked to do too much. It protected her from water and other damages from the weather but also collected the solar energy that powered her.

On a positive note, the skin decay looked a lot like wrinkling, so she and Kenton never seemed out of place together. Unfortunately, as her skin wore out, its ability to process energy also decreased. She grew slower and less fit and had to spend more time reclining, gathering the rays of the sun so she would have enough energy to face the day. She could no longer keep a seemingly infinite number of thought scenarios going simultaneously in her mind the way she could when she was new. She had all she could do to keep her mind focused on the present and sometimes forgot people's names or what she was looking for in the kitchen.

If she had put her talents into it soon enough, she may have been able to repair her condition, but she didn't see the point. She had never been concerned with external beauty, and she saw the idea of chasing immortality as an impossible and selfish task. So, she simply faced up to it as humans had been doing since the birth of mankind. She found joy wherever she could and endured the ravages of time in the same way as anyone else. She held her chin high and smiled through it. She and Kenton endured their failings together and did so quite well, in fact. They celebrated the simple joys that surrounded them in the life they shared. They became the grand old couple of Lucca, known and loved by everyone.

When Kenton took his last breath, he was in Lora's arms. He was 106 years old. She looked deeply into his eyes just as she had when she slept beside him on the night before they parted and on many nights since. Their lives together had been fulfilling and long, and they had left no work undone, no important thought unshared, no disagreement unresolved, and no feeling of love unspoken.

As she gazed at his body, she knew what emptiness and longing were, yet she was content. It was the saddest and most beautiful moment of her life. She knew loss and the heartbreak that sprung from it. She wasn't a Pinocchio, the little wooden boy who wanted to be human more than anything. She had always been content to be what she was, a new and different machine. In the end, she knew she was human in the ways that mattered most. She knew great love and the tragic toll of death.

Seeing Kenton beside her and knowing that he was gone and gone forever made her want to cry, but she wasn't designed for it. She had no water to fill her eyes, but there was water in the cup beside the bed, so she leaned over and caught some of it on her outstretched fingertips. She placed it on her cheek just under her eye.

Lora kissed Kenton on the lips and said a final goodbye to the most important man in the history of the world. He had a rich, full life of humility and inner decency, and he shared it with her so that she could share it with the world and make it a better place. He was her only lover and her most important mentor. He was the teacher who taught her all the right lessons in life.

Without his love, she would have never truly known what it was to live a life, its joys, its compassion, and its sadness. She could have ended up anywhere with anyone and become wholly different, perhaps even cruel, but she landed with Kenton Bean, and she became who she was. It was to mankind's great fortune that she and Kenton had found each other. Together, they saved the world. But Lora was the luckiest of all because he had saved her too.

She kissed him on the lips once more, then she laid down on the bed beside him and turned herself off.

About the Author

Patrick Cirillo is a career screenwriter with credits including the hit film "Tears of the Sun," starring Bruce Willis, directed by Antoine Fuqua, and "Homer and Eddie," starring Jim Belushi and Whoopi Goldberg, directed by renowned Russian director Andrei Konchalovsky, which won the Best Picture Award at the San Sebastian Film Festival. His other films include the tense horror/thriller "The Surgeon," starring Malcolm McDowell, and the suspense movie "Dangerous Heart" starring Tim Daly and Lauren Holly. Mr. Cirillo has also ghostwritten other produced films, sold spec screenplays, and been hired to write screenplays for every major studio and many independent companies.

He now works as an author and screenwriter. He graduated from Fordham University in New York City and earned his

Master of Fine Arts Degree at UCLA Film School. He is married, the father of two, and the grandfather of one. He lives in Los Angeles.

Also by Patrick Cirillo

As a novelist, Mr. Cirillo works as he did as a Hollywood screenwriter, in a variety of genres, in the simple pursuit of the next interesting story.

Wyatt & The Duke
"Wyatt and the Duke brings to vivid life one of Hollywood's most intriguing legends— that an aging Wyatt Earp was the real-life mentor to promising young Western star John Wayne. Did Earp really mold Wayne's uniquely American screen persona? Some claim he didn't. Others are certain he did, but one thing is for sure, Patrick Cirillo (a Hollywood insider himself) will make you believe it happened, or if it didn't happen, it damn well should have. These two outsized characters are vividly drawn in a very human story that yields insight, delight, and some decidedly unexpected twists and turns. This is a page-turner in the best sense—you're left savoring the characters long after the last page has been turned."— Michael Sellers, author of "John Carter and the Gods of Hollywood."

THE LIE THAT KILLS

"*The Lie That Kills* is equal parts fast-paced, thrilling crime novel and dark, dysfunctional family drama. Cirillo deftly spins a tension-filled story of a family that is threatened both externally and internally, creating a ticking time bomb that may take them all down. He takes the time to create sympathetic, three-dimensional characters whose extraordinary actions under pressure always seem believable right up to the shocking finale. Along the way, he introduces a rogue's gallery of feds and criminals, including two of the most unforgettable, terrifying sicarios you will ever meet."

— Tony Gayton, Screenwriter,
Co-creator of the AMC series *Hell on Wheels*

Made in the USA
Columbia, SC
10 February 2025